Robert Pollok

Tales of the Covenanters

With Biographical Sketch of the Author

Robert Pollok

Tales of the Covenanters
With Biographical Sketch of the Author

ISBN/EAN: 9783337120689

Printed in Europe, USA, Canada, Australia, Japan

Cover: Foto ©Andreas Hilbeck / pixelio.de

More available books at **www.hansebooks.com**

Tales

of

The Covenanters

BY ROBERT POLLOK, M.A.

AUTHOR OF "THE COURSE OF TIME"

WITH BIOGRAPHICAL SKETCH
OF THE AUTHOR

BY THE

REV. ANDREW THOMSON, D.D.

AND ILLUSTRATIONS

BY

H. M. BROCK

PUBLISHED BY

OLIPHANT ANDERSON AND FERRIER

EDINBURGH AND LONDON

1895

Preface to the New Edition

THE *Tales of the Covenanters*, written by Robert Pollok when a student of divinity, upwards of seventy years ago, were at once received with a popular favour, which they have retained up to the present time. To the Publishers it is a special pleasure to issue this new Edition. The Illustrations are from original sketches by Mr. H. M. Brock, and the value of the book is enhanced by a chapter giving a general view of the Characters, Literature, Aims, and Attained Objects of the Covenanter, which, through the kindness of Messrs. Gall & Inglis, they have been permitted to reprint from the Rev. George Gilfillan's *Martyrs and Heroes of the Scottish Covenant.*

Contents

※

Tales of the Covenanters

Sketch of the Life and Character of

Robert Pollok

THE pen of an affectionate brother has already given to the world an elaborate memoir of Robert Pollok. We should consider it alike indecent and presumptuous to lay rude hands on that interesting tribute of fraternal regard, or to attempt clothing in other language, those touching reminiscences of a brother's excellencies in which the author has unconsciously disclosed his own. The task assigned us may be far more briefly done. While not inattentive to the order of time, our main endeavour shall be, to select from the history of his too rapid course, those events which appear to us to have exerted the most powerful influence in the formation of his character and development of his genius.

Robert Pollok was born on Friday the 19th day of October 1798, at North Moorhouse, in the parish of Eaglesham, Renfrewshire. His father belonged to that respectable class of small farmers, among whom we so often trace the simple manners and rigid morality that have grown, for ages, from that noble theology which was restored to Scotland at the Reformation. His forefathers appear for centuries before to have been tenants of the soil in this district ; and it is interesting to notice, that his ancestors, on the maternal side, were honoured to suffer in those persecutions which desolated this part of Scotland between 1660 and 1688 ; one having suffered banishment ; another having not only been driven into exile, but reduced to slavery, and a third apprehended by a troop of dragoons and shot. This was a noble pedigree, not without a manifest influence on Pollok's dispositions and tastes.

His childhood, spent amid the simplicity and solitude of these rural scenes, gave frequent indications of that indomitable resoluteness and energy which, at a later period, formed so prominent a feature of his character. But two circumstances in his early youth deserve especial notice, as exerting a permanent and salutary influence in training the intellect and affections of the future poet.

One of these was the instructions of a mother, who, amid the cares of a numerous household, and the toils imposed by circumstances which called for industry as well as frugality, found time to imbue the minds of her children with heavenly truth. "By her he was taught to read the Bible, and made to commit to memory the Shorter Catechism, with part of the Psalms of David." The testimony of many of the excellent of the earth, from the days of Timothy in the first century to those of Richard Cecil in the nineteenth, might well vindicate us from any suspicion of attaching too much importance to the home education which Pollok enjoyed from this woman of "unfeigned piety"; but we have his own grateful testimony recorded long afterwards, when his *Course of Time* had been given to the world, and his ear had begun to drink in the voice of fame. Speaking of the theology of his poem, he remarked to his brother, "It has my mother's divinity, the divinity that she taught me when I was a boy. I may have amplified it from what I learned afterwards ; but in writing the poem, I always found that hers formed the groundwork, the point from which I set out. I always drew on hers first, and I was never at a loss. This shows," he added, with devout gratitude, " what kind of a divine she was."

Nor in tracing the development of a mind of high poetical susceptibility like Pollok's should we attach small importance to the scenery around Mid-Moorhouse, to which he removed with his parents in his seventh year. The daily communion which he there held with nature formed a large part of his education as a thinker and a poet ; and few spots could have been better fitted for a poet's sanctuary. It was his practice, from a very early age, to ascend to the summit of Balagich, the highest mountain in the neighbourhood, and there, seated on the Crow Stone, which marked its loftiest point, he would gaze for hours upon the scene of mingled beauty and wild magnificence that spread itself before him. On the one side there stretched a long range of moorland, with here and there an ancient battlefield or martyr's grave, the view terminated in the east by the far-off Tinto, and on the south by Wardlaw and Cairntable, Cairnsmore of Carsphairn, and Buchan of Galloway,—classic hills along whose sides the lonely Covenanter had often glided, and in whose caves and masses a suffering remnant of the faithful had often sung their midnight psalm. On another side appeared " the green hills of Carrick," " the grassy plains of Kyle and Cunningham " sloping towards the Clyde, and, far beyond, the sublime ridge of Goatfell, the solitary rock of Ailsa, and the blue peaks of Jura rising in dim and misty grandeur to the clouds. And then, turning in another direction, the eye drank in the glories of another scene, the rich pasture lands of Lanark and Renfrew embosoming vast cities, and strewed with scattered villages ; and, rising now gradually and now abruptly in the farther distance, the hoary and rugged summits of the Grampian range, that from creation's dawn till now, had stood the grim and giant sentinels of the world beyond,—Ben Lomond, Ben Cruachan, Ben Voirlich, Ben Ledi, Ben Venue.

From the age of seven to that of seventeen, Pollok spent some of his happiest hours in the contemplation of scenes like these, deriving from them impressions of grandeur and images of beauty; cherishing in his bosom the instincts of freedom, and fanning a devotion which was yet to find meet utterance in words that men would not willingly let die. Foster has devoted one of those fine essays of meditative philosophy, by which he has at once enriched the English literature and instructed the English mind, to illustrate the influence of scenery upon thought and character. The poetry of Alfred Tennyson might be adduced to confirm his principles. And Pollok long afterwards, owned the same influence in the following characteristic lines descriptive of his communion with nature and with himself—

> Nor is the hour of lonely walk forgot,
> In the wide desert, where the view was large.
> Pleasant were many scenes, but most to me
> The solitude of vast extent, untouched
> By hand of art, where Nature sowed herself,
> And reaped her crops; whose garments were the clouds;
> Whose minstrels, brooks; whose lamps, the moon and stars;
> Whose organ-choir, the voice of many waters;
> Whose banquets, morning dews; whose heroes, storms;
> Whose warriors, mighty winds; whose lovers, flowers;
> Whose orators, the thunderbolts of God;
> Whose palaces, the everlasting hills;
> Whose ceiling, heaven's unfathomable blue;
> And from whose rocky turrets, battled high,
> Prospect immense spread out on all sides round,
> Lost now between the welkin and the main,
> Now walled with hills that slept above the storm.
>
> Most fit was such a place for musing men,
> Happiest, sometimes, when musing without aim.
> It was, indeed, a wondrous sort of bliss
> The lonely bard enjoyed, when forth he walked,
> Unpurposed; stood, and knew not why; sat down,
> And knew not where; arose, and knew not when;
> Had eyes, and saw not; ears, and nothing heard;
> And sought—sought neither heaven nor earth—sought nought,
> Nor meant to think; but ran, meantime, through vast
> Of visionary things, fairer than aught

That was ; and saw the distant tops of thoughts,
Which men of common stature never saw,
Greater than aught the largest words could hold,
Or give idea of, to those who read.

While the elements of poetry were thus gathering
within him, a little incident occurred, which, however
unimportant it might seem in the lives of most men, must
be regarded as marking an important era in the mental
history of Robert Pollok, which it is the chief design
of these remarks to trace. While residing in the house
of an intelligent relative, two books fell into his hands,
which introduced him to his first acquaintance with
British poets. One of these was Pope's *Essay on Man*,
which charmed him with the exquisite harmony of its
versification, and led him to make some attempts in
rhyme. It could not be said of him, however, as of Pope,
that he " lisped in numbers, for the numbers came " ;
and it soon became evident that rhyme was not destined
to be the vehicle of his thoughts. But, soon after,
another book fell into his hands, which exerted a far
mightier influence over his character, not merely informing him in regard to the structure of poetry but unveil-
ing to him its essence, and haunting him with thoughts
which at length stirred within him, if not an equal, at
least a kindred flame. This was Milton's *Paradise
Lost*.

" He found a copy of it one day," says his brother,
" among some old books on the upper shelf of a wall-
press in the kitchen, where it had lain neglected for
years. Though he had never seen *Paradise Lost* before,
he had often heard of it, and he began to read it immediately. He was captivated with it at the very first ; and,
after that, as long as he stayed at Horsehill, he took it
up whenever he had the least opportunity, and read with
great eagerness. When he was leaving the place, his
uncle seeing him so fond of the book, gave it to him in a
present, and from that time Milton became his favourite
author, and, I may say, next to the Bible, his chief

companion. Henceforward he read more or less of him almost every day, and used often to repeat aloud, in bed, immediately before rising in the morning, what was his favourite passage in *Paradise Lost*—the apostrophe to Light in the beginning of the Third Book." From this hour Pollok became the subject of a new impulse. The vow of self-consecration to poetry was taken not the less solemnly, that as yet it was unbreathed to mortal ear. The strains of the bard of Paradise found congenial echoes in his inmost soul, and in the spirit of that young Themistocles who could not sleep in sight of the field of Marathon and the trophies of Miltiades, he began to "measure his soul severely" with bards of honourable name, and "search for theme deserving of immortal verse."

At the age of nineteen we find Pollok entering as a student at the University of Glasgow. Some years before, he had solemnly dedicated himself to the work of the Christian ministry, in connection with the United Secession Church. That Church has, from the commencement, wisely required of all aspirants to the pastoral office in her communion, a lengthened preparatory course of attendance at one of our Scottish universities, before entering on the systematic study of sacred literature and divinity in her theological halls. And to pass from the disturbed and undisciplined studies of Moorhouse to the University was, on the part of Pollok, not merely to discharge a duty but to gratify a passion. To be an ambassador of grace to guilty men was an office which he had been taught to regard as casting dignity on the noblest human powers; and now he had taken the first formal step in that path of sacred ambition. But more than this, his love of knowledge and of mental excellence had become intense, and, from the first, he evidently set himself in good earnest to the mastering of those various branches of literature and philosophy which each session of his curriculum opened before him. The rapid progress of his mind at this period is visible in the numerous specimens of thought

and composition which his brother's affection has preserved. It would be wrong, however, to imagine that
the range of his thought was limited to the beaten path
of academic study—his intellect was omnivorous—it
" glanced from heaven to earth, from earth to heaven " ;
there was not only variety but eccentricity in its course ;
and we trace him now consciously, and oftener unconsciously, gathering around him the materials and images
for that work which he had already vowed, in his inmost
bosom, to attempt and to achieve.

At the close of the session of 1822, Pollok finished his
course of study at the University of Glasgow, and left
behind him that venerable seminary, bearing with him a
degree in Master of Arts, and other more decided marks
of distinction.

In the autumn of the same year we find him entering
on the study of theology in the Hall of the Secession
Church, under the tuition of Dr. Dick, a professor whose
finely balanced powers fitted him not merely to occupy
but to adorn his office ; combining, as he did, in most
rare conjunction, independence of judgment, without
the silly affectation of originality or novelty ; solid learning, without pedantic display ; dignity, without reserve ;
and in whose academic instructions theology was beheld,
not in the ungainly dress of the schools but in the
beautiful and seemly garments of an elegant literature,—

> " Not harsh and crabbed as dull fools suppose,
> But musical as is Apollo's lute."

It was in the earlier part of Pollok's career as a
student of theology that the *Tales of the Covenanters*
were produced. The immediate circumstance that
prompted their publication must not be unnoticed in a
sketch of his character. He was in straitened circumstances ; and yet, at the age he had now reached, he
could no longer brook the thought of being dependent on
a parent who had laboured up to his ability, yea and
beyond his ability, to secure for him and his brother the

privileges of a college life. What was to be done? He
would write a tale—a series of tales. And where could
a fitter theme than the days of the Covenant be found for
one whose earliest associations were interwoven with
stories of martyr and moss-trooper? whose enthusiasm
had led him, in his earlier days, to institute an annual
pilgrimage of all the youth of the district to Lochgoin,
where John Howie penned the *Scots Worthies*, and
where a flag, a drum, and a pair of drumsticks, with
Captain Paton's sword and Bible,—strange associates,
but all the fitter emblems of the times,—are still preserved as venerable relics of the days when the Church
registered her second martyrology, and a second time
won her birthright.

The Tales were published, and realised a sum sufficient
to relieve the immediate wants of Pollok. It has been
said that they are hasty productions. No doubt they
are ; but it has been well answered, that they are the
hasty productions of a man of genius ; and, especially
in their descriptive parts, we can trace the germs of
some of the finest passages in *The Course of Time*.
For our own part we acknowledge, that, in their pre-
vading piety, in their fine moral tendency, in the
generous sympathy with suffering and love of liberty
which they express and excite, they go to enhance our
estimate of Pollok. And dark will be the day for
Scotland when the page that records the days of the
Covenant is turned from by its people with affected
grimace. Never is that page truly understood until it is
seen as recording, not merely the struggle of parties but
of principles, principles for the successful vindication of
which the best blood of Scotland was not too dearly
shed. The real contest of that hour was not between
opposing forms of religion, but between the mere form
and the life. And how shameless the injustice and
ingratitude of those who laugh at men goaded ¹most
to madness by persecution, because they did not sti
all the proprieties of language, or display all the eleg⸗

and etiquette of courts ! And how narrow and intolerant
the spirit which would blame the martyrs and confessors
of the seventeenth century, because they did not possess
all the light and liberality of the nineteenth !

But we now reach the most important era in the life
of Pollok, when with a mind braced by studious nights
and laborious days, girded by vows not rashly taken,
and by the study of ancient bards of honourable name,
with a heart sublimed and purified by the faith of the
truth, and no stranger to the hard lessons of adversity,
he set himself to that work which was to enrich the
English literature, to give at once expression and impulse
to the deep-toned piety of his native country, and to
earn for himself an early immortality. There are not
wanting indications that he had, more than once, been
in some danger of being seduced to those frivolous themes
which were the fashion of the hour, and of wandering
from that holy mount on which Milton and the ancient
prophets sat. But these temptations, like the ill-omened
birds that crossed the path of the seer, rather passed
before his mind than rested on it, and, when at length
he did consecrate his genius to a worthy theme, it was
with no lingering look to those more crowded regions
where poetry submits to be shorn of its strength,
and to make sport before the Philistines, when it
might have roused slumbering nations to life, and
sounded a note that would have been heard through
all time.

The mental struggle, terminating in entire devotedness, has been described by himself in a passage of
uncommon moral interest, as well as poetic merit, and
which has been justly regarded as not merely describing
his struggle with temptation, and his victory over it,
but tracing the outlines of that inward moral revolution,
without which a man cannot enter into the kingdom of
^r. It will remind the reader of some of those
te passages of autobiography which abound in
ges of Cowper.

2

One of this mood I do remember well :
We name him not, what now are earthly names ?
In humble dwelling born, retired, remote ;
In rural quietude, 'mong hills and streams,
And melancholy deserts, where the Sun
Saw, as he pass'd, a shepherd only, here
And there, watching his little flock, or heard
The ploughman talking to his steers ; his hopes,
His morning hopes, awoke before him, smiling,
Among the dews and holy mountain airs ;
And fancy coloured them with every hue
Of heavenly loveliness. But soon his dreams
Of childhood fled away—those rainbow dreams
So innocent and fair that withered Age,
Even at the grave cleared up his dusty eye,
And passing all between, looked fondly back
To see them once again, ere he departed :
These fled away, and anxious thought, that wished
To go, yet whither knew not well to go,
Possessed his soul, and held it still awhile.
He listened, and heard from far the voice of fame,
Heard and was charmed : and deep and sudden vow
Of resolution made to be renowned ;
And deeper vowed again to keep his vow.
His parents saw, his parents whom God made
Of kindest heart, saw, and indulged his hope.
The   ancient   page,   he   turned,   read   much,   thought
     much,
And with old bards of honourable name
Measured his soul severely ; and looked up
To fame, ambitious of no second place.
Hope grew from inward faith, and promised fair,
And out before him opened many a path
Ascending, where the laurel highest waved
Her branch of endless green. He stood admiring ;
But stood, admired, not long. The harp he seized,
The harp he loved, loved better than his life,
The harp which uttered deepest notes, and held
The ear of thought a captive to its song.
He searched and meditated much, and whiles,
With rapturous hand, in secret touched the lyre,
Aiming at glorious strains ; and searched again
For theme deserving of immortal verse ;
Chose now, and now refused, unsatisfied ;
Pleased, then displeased, and hesitating still.

Thus stood his mind, when round him came a cloud,
Slowly and heavily it came, a cloud
Of ills we mention not ; enough to say,
'Twas cold, and dead, impenetrable gloom.
He saw its dark approach, and saw his hopes,
One after one, put out, as nearer still
It drew his soul ; but fainted not at first,
Fainted not soon. He knew the lot of man
Was trouble, and prepared to bear the worst ;
Endure whate'er should come, without a sigh
Endure, and drink, even to the very dregs,
The bitterest cup, that time could measure out :
And, having done, look up, and ask for more.

He called philosophy, and with his heart
Reasoned. He called religion, too, but called
Reluctantly, and therefore was not heard.
Ashamed to be o'ermatched by earthly woes,
He sought, and sought with eye that dimmed apace,
To find some avenue to light, some place
On which to rest a hope ; but sought in vain.
Darker and darker still the darkness grew.
At length he sank, and Disappointment stood
His only comforter, and mournfully
Told all was past. His interest in life,
In being, ceased : and now he seemed to feel,
And shuddered as he felt, his powers of mind
Decaying in the spring-time of his day.
The vigorous, weak became ; the clear, obscure ;
Memory gave up her charge ; Decision reeled,
And from her flight, Fancy returned, returned
Because she found no nourishment abroad.
The blue heavens withered ; and the moon, and sun,
And all the stars, and the green earth, and morn
And evening, withered, and the eyes, and smiles,
And faces of all men and women, withered,
Withered to him ; and all the universe,
Like something which had been, appeared, but now
Was dead and mouldering fast away. He tried
No more to hope, wished to forget his vow,
Wished to forget his harp ; then ceased to wish !
That was his last ; enjoyment now was done.
He had no hope, no wish, and scarce a fear,
Of being sensible, and sensible
Of loss, he as some atom seemed, which God
Had made superfluously, and needed not

To build creation with; but back again
To nothing threw, and left it in the void,
With everlasting sense that once it was.

Oh! who can tell what days, what nights he spent,
Of tideless, waveless, sailless, shoreless wo!
And who can tell how many, glorious once,
To others and themselves of promise full,
Conducted to this pass of human thought,
This wilderness of intellectual death,
Wasted and pined, and vanished from the earth,
Leaving no vestige of memorial there!

It was not so with him. When thus he lay,
Forlorn of heart, withered and desolate,
As leaf of Autumn, which the wolfish winds,
Selecting from its falling sisters, chase,
Far from its native grove, to lifeless wastes,
And leave it there alone, to be forgotten
Eternally, God passed in mercy by—
His praise be ever new!—and on him breathed,
And bade him live, and put into his hands
A holy harp, into his lips a song,
That rolled its numbers down the tide of Time.
Ambitious now but little to be praised
Of men alone; ambitious most to be
Approved of God, the Judge of all; and have
His name recorded in the Book of Life.

It was in this spirit of devout self-consecration that
Pollok entered on the composition of *The Course of
Time*, in the beginning of December 1824, and at the
age of twenty-seven. The first hint of his poem, we
learn from some interesting reminiscences by his brother,
was suggested by Byron's lines to Darkness, which he
took up one evening in a moment of great mental desolation. While perusing those lines, he was led to think of
the Resurrection as a theme on which something new
might be written. He proceeded, and on the same
night finished a thousand verses, intending that the
subject of the poem should be the Resurrection. Meanwhile, thoughts and images crowded upon his mind,
which it would have been unnatural to introduce under

such a theme ; when all at once the whole plan of his work rose before him, with the completeness and the vividness of a prophet's vision. " One night," says his brother, "when he was sitting alone in Moorhouse' old room, letting his mind wander back and forward over things at large, in a moment, as if by an immediate inspiration, the idea of the poem struck him, and the plan of it, as it now stands, stretched out before him ; so that at one glance he saw through it from end to end, like an avenue, with the Resurrection as only part of the scene. He never felt, he said, as he did then ; and he shook from head to foot, overpowered with feeling ; knowing that to pursue the subject was to have no middle way between great success and great failure. From this time, in selecting and arranging materials, he saw through the plan so well that he knew to what book, as he expressed it, the thoughts belonged whenever they set up their heads."

From this time till the finishing of his poem, his whole soul was on fire with his subject. In the old room at Moorhouse, on the sublime path between Moorhouse and Eaglesham, when hastening to join the worshippers on the "hallowed morn," on the lofty summits of Balagich, and, oftenest of all, when he communed with his own heart upon his bed and was silent, he was struggling with his great argument, and seeking to give to the images of truth that moved before his spirit, "immortal shape and form." Thoughts rushed upon his mind as if, like the widow's cruse, it had been supplied by miracle, and only the weariness and faintings of his body seemed to clog the movements of a spirit that, at this period, spurned repose.

In some poets, such as Pope, we trace the progress of the composition, from the first rude and inharmonious sketch, to the perfect verse ; but in Pollok some of his finest passages were thrown off at once ; they were not laboriously beaten into shape, but, coming forth fused and molten, in a moment took their appropriate and permanent form.

There is one fact connected with this composition which we have peculiar pleasure in recording. His brother informs us that "he kept the Bible constantly beside him, and read in different places of it, according to the nature of what he was composing; so that his mind, it may be said, was all along regulated by the Bible. Finally, he prayed to God daily, morning and evening, for direction and assistance in the work." *The Course of Time* is thus literally the fruit of prayer; the inspiration that dictated it was implored on bended knees; and those beautiful lines of his invocation are not a mere compliance with the fashion of poets, but the genuine "cardiphonia,"—the deep utterance of the heart.

> Hold my right hand, Almighty! and me teach
> To strike the lyre, but seldom struck, to notes
> Harmonious with the morning stars, and pure
> As those by sainted bards and angels sung,
> Which wake the echoes of Eternity ;
> That fools may hear and tremble, and the wise,
> Instructed, listen of ages yet to come.

In the beginning of July 1826, Pollok brought the writing of his great poem to a close. Nineteen months had thus elapsed from the time of his commencing the composition ; but enfeebled health and other influences had created considerable pauses ; and we have his own authority for believing, that the time in which he was actually engaged in versification did not exceed eight months.

The intense and protracted mental exertion imposed by the composition of such a work, in so short a space of time—an exertion, compared with which he found the study of the most difficult Greek and Roman classics to be an amusement, and which, night after night, brought him to the borders of fever—may well be imagined to have told unfavourably on a constitution which had already been shaken by disease. The chariot-wheels had indeed caught fire through the rapidity of their own motion, the consequence of which was, that, by the time the poem was concluded, he appeared emaciated and pale, and distressing fears were awakened, that in writing *The Course of Time* he had been intwining a splendid wreath to be laid upon an early grave. The labours and anxieties connected with obtaining a publisher and carrying his poem through the press, served to give the disease a deeper seat in his constitution, and to bring out more unfavourable symptoms.

The consequence was, that when, in the spring of 1827, having been admitted a licentiate of the Secession Church, he delivered his first public discourse in one of the chapels of his own denomination in Edinburgh, the practised eye of Dr. Belfrage of Slateford, a minister and physician of the same religious body, detected in his feeble appearance, and countenance alternately flushed and wan, the inroads of pulmonary disease. This was followed, on the part of the kind physician, by an invitation to Slateford Manse, a lovely retreat, situated a few miles from Edinburgh, at the base of the Pentland Hills, where Pollok, in addition to the luxury of retirement, could enjoy the double advantage of Dr Belfrage's Christian friendship and medical skill. The invitation was gratefully accepted, and from this sweet spot we find Pollok soon after writing to his venerable father at Moorhouse, in terms of high satisfaction both with his host and with the scene. " I am still at Slateford," says he ; "my health is improving ; but Dr. Belfrage insists that two or three weeks more of medical treatment are necessary, and he refuses to let me leave him. I am therefore a prisoner, but it is in a paradise ; for everything here looks as if our world had never fallen."

The growing voice of fame now began to reach him from all quarters of the kingdom. Reviews of highest authority sounded the praise of the young poet, who, all at once, unpatronised and unprophesied, had ascended to mid-heaven. From the very throne of criticism, laurels were flung upon his path, and men of high authority, whose praise was fame, sought out the young poet in his retreat to cheer him in his onward course. Among these attentions, none gratified him so much as the visits of the venerable Henry Mackenzie, author of *The Man of Feeling*, then in his eighty-fourth year. "I felt his attention," says he, in a letter to his father, "to be as if some literary patriarch had risen from the grave to bless me and do me honour."

Still the insidious malady was secretly advancing, and its progress was at once increased and betrayed by an alarming illness which seized him in the month of June, and greatly diminished his strength. It now became evident to Dr. Belfrage, and other medical advisers of first eminence, that removal to a foreign climate was indispensable, and even this was tremblingly recommended, as affording but faint hope that his sun would not go down at noonday.

Italy was proposed, and especially the salubrious air of Pisa, in the Grand Duchy of Tuscany. In this proposal Pollok cheerfully acquiesced: and it is with a kind of sad interest that we behold the dying poet, under the influence of that false hope with which consumption dazzles her victims, indulging day-dreams of returning health, to be devoted to yet higher achievements in literature, when he returned laden with the classic stores, and refreshed by the bright remembrances of Italy.

Generous friends now hastened to provide a fund sufficient for the respectable maintenance of the poet in a foreign clime. Among these, honourable mention must be made of Sir John Sinclair, Dr. John Brown, Dr. Belfrage, and Sir John Pirie, afterwards Lord Mayor of London, whose prompt and thoughtful regard, not exhausted in a few distant and splendid acts, displayed all the tender earnestness of parental solicitude.

A short experimental voyage to Aberdeen and a sad farewell to Moorhouse, in which, under the influence of dark forebodings scarcely owned and yet impossible to be repressed, every eye but his own was suffused with tears, and every voice but his own faltered with emotion, was followed by a speedy departure for London, whence it was intended that he should now sail, with all dispatch, for Italy. Arrived in London, places were taken, in a ship bound for Leghorn, for himself and a kind sister, who was chosen to be the companion of his voyage.

But it was destined that he should never see the Italian shores. The ship not sailing on the appointed day, he was visited by a distinguished physician in the interval, who, perceiving that all hope of recovery was now gone, soothingly but firmly discouraged his leaving his native country. A residence in the south-west of England was recommended, and the neighbourhood of Southampton ultimately fixed upon. There, after a journey of two days, most fatiguing to his fevered and emaciated frame, we find him arriving on Saturday, 1st September ; in a few weeks more to " shake hands with death, and smile that he was free."

He took up his abode in a neat cottage at Shirley Common, about a mile from Southampton. The mild air of that rich and lovely region helped to soothe his chafed spirit. In a spacious garden adjoining the cottage, where the air was so calm that " you could hear the apples falling from the trees one after another," he delighted to walk with his sister, and feel at times the gentle breezes borne to him from the neighbouring sea, and laden with autumnal incense ; and then sitting down, at intervals, on a cushion which he had brought with him from London, he would hear his sister read to him from the Bible, which had now become his only book.

But his weakness rapidly increasing, he was soon compelled to abandon this congenial exercise, and to confine himself entirely to bed. His faithful sister, whose deep affection had so long made her "hope against hope," now found it necessary to apprise him of the solemn prospect that "the earthly house of his tabernacle was soon to be dissolved." This was done with all the tender skill of a woman and a sister, and was received by him in a manner worthy of the author of *The Course of Time*. His mind was solemnised, but not saddened ; and if, in the thought of soon entering on eternity, he knew no raptures, neither did he know any fears. Once, and only for a moment, did a shade of doubt obscure his hopes, but it passed away, leaving him gazing upon the unclouded truth. There have been men of genius who have rushed into the arms of death mortified by the world's ingratitude or neglect ; but Pollok, with the voice of the world's praise swelling and deepening around him, willingly heard the summons which called him up to a nobler immortality.

Writing to his father, of whom he had frequently spoken during his illness with great veneration, he thus expressed himself: "My sister is often much distressed, but we pray for one another, and take comfort in the gracious promises of God. I hope I am prepared for the issue of this trouble, whether life or death."

His growing weakness brought on frequent seasons of drowsiness, the intervals between which were employed by his sister, at his own request, in reading to him from the Scriptures, especially from the Book of Psalms and the Gospel of John, which he greatly relished. In this manner several of his last days and nights were spent, when at length, on the morning of Tuesday, September 18, 1827, he gently breathed his last, and entered into the joy of his Lord.

His mortal remains were interred on the following Friday in the churchyard of Millbrook, a quiet spot remote from the din of cities and near to the sea. He was buried according to the forms of the Church of England, the Rev. Mr. Molesworth reading the burial-service by the side of his grave. An elegant obelisk of granite, reared by those admirers of his genius who had sought to prolong his life, marks the last earthly resting-

place of this highly-gifted man, and bears, with the dates
of his birth and death, the following simple inscription :—

THF GRAVE OF

ROBERT POLLOK, A.M.,

AUTHOR OF "THE COURSE OF TIME."

HIS IMMORTAL POEM

IS HIS

MONUMENT.

Thus ended, at the early age of twenty-nine, the
earthly course of Robert Pollok — a course too short
for hope, but not too short for immortality. There have
been small critics who, since his death, have sought,
with captious arrogance, to depreciate his poem by petty
and nibbling fault-finding ; and even one great man, in
an hour of conversational ease, let fall a remark which,
when taken at its real value, was more fitted to injure
his own fame than Pollok's. But that poem is not to
be lightly estimated which, in the rapidity and extent of
its circulation, has found no equal in modern times ;
parts of which, such men as John Wilson declared, would
compare to advantage with any thing in British literature,
and which the venerable James Montgomery, with the
generous admiration of a kindred spirit, has pronounced
to be one of the most extraordinary productions of the
age.

Had we any fears, indeed, for the permanent popularity
of *The Course of Time* they would be occasioned rather
by the exuberant and undistinguishing admiration of
that somewhat numerous class who, not content with
obtaining a high place for it in British literature, would
claim for it the first, and would encircle the name of
Robert Pollok with the unapproachable splendour of
him who sang—

    " Of man's first disobedience, and the fruit
      Of that forbidden tree, whose mortal taste
      Brought death into the world, and all our woe."

But that Robert Pollok should sit on equal throne
with John Milton, is a demand whose rash presumption
is apt to provoke a vindictive dethroning of him, even
from his proper eminence. Far wiser was the estimate
which Pollok himself was wont to form of Milton,
when he spoke of him, compared with other bards, as
an "archangel in poetry, standing aloft like the star-
neighbouring Teneriffe among the little islands that
float on the Atlantic surge."

That there were features of close resemblance in the
genius of the two poets—that there are passages in
The Course of Time which Milton would not have
disdained to own,—and that these passages warrant
the belief that had Pollok lived to hold communion
with those choice spirits, to which the fame of his poem
had obtained him honourable passport, he would have
soared with higher and more sustained flight, hovering
around the very summits of the mount of song, is what
even the most grudging and reluctant criticism may not
shrink from conceding. But our business is with what
Pollok actually achieved; and we conceive that nothing
but the blindest partiality would place him in equal rank
with him whose work was the fruit of ripened powers
sternly disciplined by long years of thought, enriched
by foreign travel, and tuned by foreign song, and who,
when at length he did strike his harp, made all literature and all climes do tribute to his verse, evoked a
new harmony from the English tongue, now vied with
the proudest names of Greek and Roman fame, and
outstripped them, and now sitting on the mount with
Hebrew prophets, seemed to share their inspiration, and
to feel the trembling consciousness that that celestial
hand was upon him which erst had "touched Isaiah's
hallowed lips with fire."

Other points of comparison apart, how much of the
merit of *Paradise Lost* consists in the characters that
move before us, from beginning to end, of that match-
less epic; Adam and Eve while yet unfallen,

> " Godlike erect, with native honour clad
> In native majesty   .   .   .
> For contemplation he, and valour formed ;
> For softness she, and sweet attractive grace ;"—

and, above all, that wondrous conception, without
parallel in epic poetry, and yet so inimitably sustained
throughout the whole poem, of the fallen archangel,
whose

> "form had not yet lost
> All her original brightness, nor appear'd
> Less than Archangel ruin'd, and th' excess
> Of glory obscured."

But there are no characters in *The Course of Time*,
except allegorical ones, and even its narrative resembles
rather the successive pictures of a panorama, slowly
moving before us to music, than the progress of events
leading on to some great result, which angels bend
from their thrones to witness, and on which hang the
fate of worlds.

While we have thus sought to qualify a too exuberant
praise, how much remains to justify the fame which has
already placed upon our poet's brow a crown set with
many gems?

Where, in all poetry, shall we meet with a passage
of more high and varied excellence than the character
of Byron? The almost fiendish pride, the almost angelic
power, the conscious misery retiring within itself in
sullen scorn, the affected contempt of his fellows, yet,
in the very utterance of that contempt, betraying that
he would grieve to be forgotten,—all this is described
with such perfection of moral anatomy, with such well-
chosen imagery, with such regretful sadness, with such
sustained power, that had it alone been preserved, it
would have established a claim for Pollok upon the
homage of all posterity. In the description of the
various tribes and nations of the millennium, he reminds
us of some of the noblest passages in Milton ; while,
in many parts of his Resurrection scene, his own soul

seems stirred by the sound of that trump which is to shake both earth and heaven.

In nothing does he more excel than in stripping man of every outward appendage and ornament, and presenting him "of all but moral character bereaved." His love of nature is great, only excelled by his love for the Bible—

> "that holy book
> On every leaf bedewed with drops of love Divine,"

from which God had taught him the divine secret of extracting the bitterness from the cup of life, and of relishing its innocent joys, without resting in them.

He has been compared to Kirke White, but he soared on a far stronger pinion, his eye took in a far wider range, and he could look far longer with unsealed vision on the sun.

He has been likened to Young; but what is there in common between the two, save that they have both written large poems, and both on religious subjects? There is often a false taste and a littleness in Young, of which Pollok is incapable. Witness his description of the last day, which he cannot introduce without two courtly lines to "great Anna," when his whole soul should have been trembling at the final conflagration in which all human thrones and gorgeous palaces are to be dissolved, leaving not a rack behind. The one excels in epigrammatic point and abruptness; the other loves to play with his subject, and to dilate on it; besides, there is, not unfrequently, a gloom about the *Night Thoughts* that brings the churchyard before us, rather than the church, while the light of the full-orbed gospel which has fallen upon Pollok's own soul, pervades his poem, and sheds its radiance upon the grave.

Throughout his work he appears before us as one dealing with realities. There is an intense love of truth, a profound sympathy with man's miseries, a faith and hope awakened by drinking at the pure fount of revelation, and which make him anticipate, with eye undimmed by present mystery and sorrow, the ultimate return of that

> "little orb
> Attended by one moon, her lamp by night,"

to the fair sisterhood of unfallen worlds.

He seems to feel throughout, not merely the fine frenzy of the poet's fire, but the awful burden of the prophet's mission, and in the profound devotion of many parts we feel as if holding converse with a spirit on which has fallen

> "The sanctifying dew
> Coming unseen, unseen departing thence ;
> Anew creating all, and yet not heard ;
> Compelling, yet not felt !"

His work was not "raised by the heat of youth or the vapours of wine, like that which flows at waste from the pen of some vulgar amourist, or the trencher fury of a rhyming parasite, nor to be obtained by the invocation of Dame Memory and her seven sisters, but by devout prayers to that Eternal Spirit, who can enrich with all utterance and knowledge, and sends out his seraphim with the hallowed fire of his altar, to touch and purify the lips of whom He pleases."

Helen of the Glen

Helen of the Glen

Chapter I

" One there is above all others,
Well deserves the name of Friend!
His is love beyond a brother's,
Costly, free, and knows no end:
They who once His kindness prove,
Find it everlasting love!"
— DODDRIDGE.

IT is pleasant, young reader, to contemplate in our day the peace of the Redeemer's kingdom in Scotland. The Lord is indeed the glory in the midst of His Church, and a wall of fire round about her. The still small voice of the gospel is unrestrained by the menaces of power, and its light unobscured by the clouds of bigotry and superstition. Our assemblies meet, and worship, and part in peace. In our land the promise is fast accomplishing, "All thy children shall be taught of the Lord: and great shall be the peace of thy children." The Church in our land, like a well-watered garden, and like a spring of waters, now sends forth her streams into the dry and parched wilderness, and sheds her light on the people that sit in darkness. Her voice, harmonising with the invitations of infinite mercy, is now addressed to all nations, inviting them to share in the same heavenly blessings.

But it is right for us to remember, young reader, that it was not always so in our beloved land. Only two hundred years ago, persecution, and nakedness, and

cold, and hunger, were the lot of those who followed
the Lamb whithersoever He went. The sheep of the
Great Shepherd wandered upon the mountains, and the
hands of the men of power were defiled with their blood.

Such were the perilous and bloody days in which
Helen and William, the subjects of this story, were
ushered into life. Their father, James Thomson, although
born in the moorish districts of Ayrshire, removed early
in life to Glasgow, with Agnes Craig, his beloved wife.
Mr. Thomson was for some years prosperous enough in
business ; but the unsuspicious sincerity of his character
often met with duplicity, and his generous kindness with
ingratitude. Reduced by various losses to bankruptcy,
he was compelled to leave Scotland. To support himself, and send something, if possible, for the assistance
of his family, he entered the service of King Charles II.,
followed the army to the Continent, and in a short time
after died in Holland, fighting bravely for his sovereign.

His farewell with his wife had been short and hurried.
He advised her to return with her little ones, Helen
and William, the former of whom was then four, and
the latter two years old, to her native place ; recommended them to their Father in heaven ; and the last
words which Mrs. Thomson's ear caught from that voice,
which she was to hear no more, were these : Oh, my dear
Agnes, teach these little ones to know and remember
their Creator in the days of their youth, that if I see
you and them no more in this valley of tears, I may
meet you and them at last by the river of life, in the
paradise of God ! "

Immediately after this painful parting, Mrs. Thomson
returned to the place of her birth, in the neighbourhood
of Loudon Hill. I need not tell the young reader with
what feelings she crossed the little moor-streams, by
which she was wont to walk with her James. Now she
looked up the winding glen, where her ear had often
turned to his affectionate voice, or listened with still
more solid delight while he read a chapter from the

book of God to dissipate their fears, and strengthen
their hopes of eternal life,—now, her eyes streaming at
once with joy and sorrow, fell back on her little William,
the dear miniature of his father. A steady habit of
industry ; the remembrance of a youth spent in religion ;
her two infants, and an unwavering trust in the kindness
of her Maker and Redeemer, were all the riches which
Mrs. Thomson brought home to the place of her nativity.
Her near relations, weeded away by the hand of disease,
or cut off by the sword of persecution, had left her
father's house desolate. George Paton, a man who had
been her father's shepherd, now possessed the farm.
He received the daughter of his former master kindly ;
assigned her a snug hut, in which, while a servant, he
had himself lived, and gave her a cow, that her infants
might not be without milk, which the old shepherd very
properly observed was the best liquid Scotland produced,
except water.

Cleughhead, the name of this little habitation, was
situated at the head of one of those solitary glens so
common in the wilder districts of Scotland. The walls
were built with rough granite ; the roof thatched with
the heath of the mountain, and the rushes of the brook ;
—and the interior, where the peat burned on the hearth,
and the smoke rose up unconfined by any chimney, till
it escaped by a little hole in the roof, although very
unlike the abode Mrs. Thomson had left in Glasgow,
was soon rendered, by her own industry and native
cleanliness, and the ready assistance of the old farmer,
neat and comfortable.

Past the door of this humble dwelling feebly murmured a mountain rill : as it rambled in frolicsome
meanders down the slope, now kissing the blooming
heath, now rippling among the green rushes, and again
playing with the shadow of the grey willow, its channel
deepened as the sides of the glen drew nearer one
another ;—here the projecting rock and crooked hazel
on the one side, and the tall fern and stunted sloethorn

on the other, mingled their dancing shadows on the torrent, which, loud and impetuous, forced its headlong way, like the youth impatient for full manhood. Again the glen gradually opened ; the spreading stream, giving back the image of the sober ox and sportive lamb that cropt the verdant herb and wild daisy by its side ; and at length smoothing its surface, laying asleep every turbulent wave, purifying its waters on the gravelly sand of its course, and reflecting the heaven only from its clear bosom, fell, like the dying Christian, without a murmur into the current of the Irvine. The general features of the surrounding scenery were impressed with an air of solemn melancholy. To the north and east extended level tracts of gloomy moorland, relieved here and there by the smoke curling from the shepherd's lonely hut, a straggling dwarf tree or two which grew about his dwelling, and a little verdant meadow plot redeemed from the dark waste which lay before his door. At intervals, too, were to be seen a shepherd boy with his dog ; and spreading around him, in little groups, here and there scattered and solitary, the white-fleeced sheep wandering on the brown heath. To the south and south-west rose the unambitious hills of Dumfries and Galloway ; and conspicuous among them, with its round summit, the _Twelve-hour_ hill, over whose head, the shepherds of that country well know, the sun walks at midday. Spread 'out to the west were the fertile, but monotonous, districts of Ayrshire, watered by those streams, delightfully romantic when you approach them, Ayr, Irvine, and Doon, which carried the eye down their course till it reposed on the glassy bosom of the Atlantic, oftener in those days visited by the dreadful warship than enlivened by the cheerful sail of the merchantman. Terminating the view in this direction were the bold elevations of Arran, on whose castle peaks the cloud delights to sit, and from whose tops the sun of autumn casts his last look of glory on the western districts of Scotland.

In this humble dwelling, surrounded thus by the chaste and solemn countenance of nature, did Mrs. Thomson set herself diligently to educate her children ; to imbue their minds early with habits of industry ; and above all, to bring them up in the fear of the Lord, to teach them to know and remember their Creator in the days of their youth. Every morning and evening she went, leading Helen in the one hand and William in the other, to the farmhouse, and joined with the old shepherd in worshipping the God of salvation. Early on the dawn of every Sabbath was Agnes up, and prepared—not with the anointed hair and tinkling ornaments which employ so much the thoughts of many females on the morning of the Lord's day, but by communing with her own heart, and by expostulating with her God in private—for setting out, often five, sometimes six, seven, or eight miles, to hear preached the glad tidings of eternal life. And in those days, surely you know, young reader, it was no smooth road, no pleasure walk to the house of God. Every one sat not then as we do now, "under his own vine and fig-tree, having none to make him afraid" ; but the solitary moor-hut, the glen of the mountain, or the cave of the rock, were often the only places in which the voice of the true servants of God, the shepherds that shall never need to be ashamed, could be heard. Even here the bloody fiend of persecution pursued them with fire and sword. The meetings, or conventicles, as they were called, of these poor artless Christians were often dispersed by the insolent and merciless soldiers ; many were taken and sent, some to the gibbet, some to dungeons, and many to the British plantations abroad. And all this because they assembled themselves to seek the Lord God of their fathers, in the way which their consciences approved.

But with her daily attention to family worship at the farmhouse, and meeting on as many Sabbaths as possible with the pious peasants around, Mrs. Thomson's religious duties by no means terminated. Often would she kneel down, with her son and daughter at her side, by the streamlet that purled down her secluded glen, and seek, with the fervency of a mother's heart which trusts in God, that her Father in heaven would shed down upon them that blessing which maketh rich and bringeth no sorrow. And never did she unbend her knee, or turn her eye from the heaven on which it gazed, without watering her cheek with one drop in behalf of her dear husband. "If," would she plead aloud, as she kneeled by the heathy knoll or ferny glen, and seen only by God and angels,—"If, O gracious Father, Thou should'st never give him to these arms, nor bless these eyes with another sight of his countenance in this world, oh, give him that faith in Christ which shall open to him the gates of heaven! If Thou should'st lay his bones to rest in a foreign land, oh, may I meet him at last without spot or wrinkle, or any such thing, in that happy place where friends part no more." Every day, too, she read a portion of the Bible, and taught her children to read it—taught them to understand much of it; and, above all, taught them, and chiefly by her own example, to reverence and obey it.

Thus would she converse with Helen, for William was yet too young to profit much by her instructions— "How great, my dear, is the love of God in Christ Jesus? You read in the Bible that we are all sinners; that is, we all naturally hate God, and God hates us because we are not holy, nor willing to be made holy. You read in the Bible, that in Adam all died, and became liable to the wrath and curse of God; and you know that we sin every day against God ourselves. The thoughts of our hearts are evil continually. This is our condition, my dear Helen; this is our sad condition by nature. Do you feel it to be sad? Would you like to be out of it? I love you, my dear, and I can do much for you; but I cannot take away your sins, I cannot make your peace with God. None of your friends—no man in the world—no angel in heaven can pardon your sins. What then are you to do? How great, as I said, is the mercy of God in Christ? In your low and lost estate He remembers you with love. When there was no other eye to pity—no other hand to help, God said, 'Deliver from going down to the pit, from going down to hell, for I have found a ransom.' This ransom is Jesus Christ, who came into the world, and suffered and died that we might live. You remember that He says, 'Suffer little children to come unto me, and forbid them not.' If you come unto Him—if you believe that He died for your sins, God will pardon you, and be for ever at peace with you.

"But you will ask me, my dear, how you can believe in Christ? You must pray to God that you may have this belief. You remember what our Saviour says Himself—'Ask, and it shall be given you; seek, and ye shall find; knock, and it shall be opened to you.' The Holy Spirit will help you to pray. Paul tells us that 'the Holy Ghost maketh intercession for us, with groanings that cannot be uttered.' 'Whatever ye ask in my name,' says the kind Redeemer, 'it shall be given you.'

"So great, my dear, is the lovingkindness of our gracious and Heavenly Father! And surely you will love and obey so merciful a God. You love me, and do all I wish you, because I love you, and am, as you often tell me, good to you; but you see that God loves you far more, and has done far more good for you; you should love Him therefore more than me, or any of your friends, or anything in the world—and you are to show your love to Him by living in His fear, by keeping His commandments, and by doing all the good you can, wherever you may be placed.

"Remember these things, my dear Helen," would the pious and affectionate mother say in conclusion—"Remember these things. You know not how soon you may die, or how soon you may lose your mother. You hear of people dying every day in their beds, or of their lives being taken away by the cruel persecutors. If I should be removed from you, your best instructor will be your Bible. Read it, dear Helen, and read it often."

I repeat to you, young reader, Mrs. Thomson's injunctions to her daughter — "Read the Bible, and read it often."

It is surprising to notice how this sacred book is neglected by sinful men. The votaries of taste and fashion will spend their days and nights poring over the morbid pages of sensual and fictitious narrative; yet if their God was to ask them if they had read the book which He sent them from heaven, where would they look? How could they say that they had never read the precious gift throughout? Wherever you go, learn not of those. Take your Bible in your hand; make it the companion of your way. In the thirsty desert of this world, it will supply you with the water of life; in the darkness of doubt and apprehension, it will cast a gleam of heaven over your path; in the struggle of temptation, and in the hour of affliction, it will lift up the voice of warning, encouragement, and comfort. Never let the Bible lie by you unperused. It is the only helm that can guide you through the ocean of life, and bring you safely to the immortal shores. It is the only star which leads the wandering sinner by the rocks, and breakers, and fiery tempests of utter destruction, and points him away to the heights of everlasting blessedness. The Bible contains the only food that can satisfy the hungerings of the soul; it presents us with the only laver in which we can wash ourselves white and clean; it alone tells us of the garments that are worn in the courts of heaven; it is from the Bible alone that we learn to prepare a torch to conduct our footsteps through the valley of the shadow of death; and it is the Bible alone which can introduce us at last to the glories of immortality!

While Mrs. Thomson was thus teaching her children habits of industry, and disclosing to their young minds

the hopes of a better life, she received the account of
her husband's death, mentioned above. The tears of
love and desolateness and religion mingled on her
cheek. Although Helen and William remembered little
of their father, yet so often had their mother told them
of all his kindness to her, and love to them ; so often
had she repeated to them his last advice and prayer ;
and so often had she told them that he would perhaps
come some day to their little hut, that they sobbed by
their mother's side in the same bitterness of grief as if
their father had died among them. But the good widow
sorrowed not as those who have no hope. The letter
which brought the painful account informed her that
her husband died a good soldier of Jesus Christ. He
was heard, on the bloody field of battle, recommending,
with his last breath, his widowed wife and fatherless
children to the God of the widow and the fatherless.
"And God will hear the sincere request," said the tender
mother, as she wiped her tears, and threw a gleam of
celestial hope and patient resignation on her weeping
children : "God is the widow's stay ; He is the Father
of the fatherless : He forsakes none who put their trust
in Him. To wean us from our sins and earthly attachments, He may afflict us for a moment ; but with an
everlasting love hath He loved us. Be comforted, my
dear children ; remember your Creator as your father
ever wished you to do, and you will meet him at last
in heaven, to be fatherless no more, to weep no more,
and to part no more for ever."

In Mrs. Thomson's outward circumstances, her
husband's death produced no difference. She often
assisted in the old farmer's dairy, and received in
return food, and home-made clothing for herself and
her children. Nor was her mind much altered. The
violence of her grief subsided into a firmer trust in
God, more fervent religion, and more heavenly-minded-
ness. Indeed, this event threw a thoughtfulness and
an unrepining melancholy over all her character, which

expanded every sympathy of her nature, deepened every
feeling of her soul, and warmed every act of her
devotion, as the lingering looks of day cast a
mellower softening and a richer grandeur over the
widely variegated landscape.

Chapter II

——"In solitudes like these
Thy persecuted children, Scotia, foiled
A tyrant's and a bigot's bloody laws ;
There, leaning on his spear,

    .   .   .   .

The lyart veteran heard the word of God
By Cameron thundered, or by Renwick poured
In gentle stream : then rose the song, the loud
Acclaim of praise ; the wheeling plover ceased
Her plaint ; the solitary place was glad,
And on the distant cairns, the watcher's ear
Caught doubtfully at times the breeze-borne note."
                                    —GRAHAME.

MEANWHILE, the rage and cruelty of persecution grew
every day more inveterate. Claverhouse, whose merciless sword widowed many a tender mother and orphaned
many a helpless infant, about this time was routed at
Loudon Hill by a party of the Covenanters, whose
sufferings had driven them to arms. This event stung
to the heart the proud, bold, and cruel Claverhouse.
Backed by soldiers imbued with his own spirit, he
neglected no opportunity, and spared no exertions, to
pursue, torture, and kill all who would not renounce
the service of their Father in heaven for the vassalage
of an earthly tyrant. Some time before this, military
trial was instituted in Scotland ; and all who refused
the wicked test were instantly shot by the soldiers.
The brutal dragoons plundered, tortured, murdered, and
committed every species of outrage at pleasure. At no
hour, in no place, whether in the house, the glen, or

the cave of the mountain, were the scattered sheep of
the Great Shepherd safe from the persevering search
and unrelenting cruelty of their persecutors.

> ——"Every hour
> They stood prepared to die, a people doom'd
> To death ;—old men, and youths, and simple maids."

It was thus in the western districts of Scotland, when,
on a fine Sabbath morning a little after midsummer,
Mrs. Thomson was early up, and preparing, as usual,
to hear the word of God, which was to be preached
that day two miles down the glen at the head of which
the widow's hut stood. She left William, yet only in
his sixth year, in the farmhouse, and, with Helen by
her side, took the little sheep-path down the glen. In
her hallowed imagination—the sun coming up the rosy
east unclouded, threw a purer ray over the solitary
moorlands ; a clearer dew sparkled on the red heather-
bell ; the matin hymn of the skylark, the varied music
of the desert fowl, the bleating of the flocks that
answered from knoll to knoll, the minstrelsy of the
brook, and the gentle sigh of the zephyr that played
among the wild mountain flowers—all assumed a chaster,
holier cadence, and seemed to confess the presence of
the blessed day. Here and there was seen over the
brown moor, like vessels scattered on the ocean, the
solitary peasant travelling towards the glen to meet
the servant of God. Little Helen, with a profusion of
fair ringlets already floating on her neck and shoulders,
now plucked the wild thyme, now looked to the playful
chases of the lambs, and anon listened to her mother,
while she admonished her to hear the gospel with
reverence and attention.

Thus engaged, they arrived at the place agreed on for
meeting with the faithful ambassador of Jesus. The
man of God was already there ; and his little congregation mostly gathered around him. The place chosen
for this day's worship of the Most High was hidden

from the distant view by the sides of the glen ; one of which, withdrawing five or six yards from the streamlet, left a small green plain in the shape of a crescent. Here rose a large grey stone, on which the minister rested the holy book. Before him, on the rising ground, trode by the sheep into paths rising one above another, resembling a flight of stairs, sat his rustic audience, thirsting for the water of life. On a knoll, at a small distance, watched one of their friends, to give the alarm in case of the appearance of the persécuting soldiers. The minister, to whose church Mrs. Thomson, in her earlier days, often walked with her father and mother, had been driven from his flock and his family by violence ; and now, concealed by the peasants who loved him, and fed by their kindness, he took every opportunity which offered, in the cave, the moor, or the sheep-cot, to distribute among the poor hunted followers of the cross the bread and the water of life. His figure was graceful, of the ordinary size ; his countenance mild, full of resignation and heavenly zeal. Time had left his forehead bare ; but behind, and on each side, flowed down plentiful locks, woolley, and white as the snow of the mountains.

The venerable man now threw a glance of fatherly compassion on his little flock, lifted the Bible from the grey stone, opened it, and read these verses from that mournful psalm, sung by the Israelitish captives at Babylon—

> " By Babel's streams we sat and wept,
>   When Sion we thought on ;
>   In midst thereof we hanged our harps
>   The willow trees upon.

> " For there a song required they,
>   Who did us captive bring :
>   Our spoilers called for mirth, and said,
>   A song of Sion sing.

> "O how the Lord's song shall we sing,
>   Within a foreign land ?
>   If thee, Jerusalem, I forget,
>   Skill part from my right hand.

> " My tongue to my mouth's roof let cleave,
>   If I do thee forget,
> Jerusalem, and thee above
> My chief joy do not set."

To the wild plaintive notes of Old Martyr's this sweet melody, from hearts full of gratitude and love and calm resignation, ascended to the ear of the Eternal. The psalm being ended, all arose, and the holy man, turning an eye of faith to the heavens, led the congregation in a prayer, humble, fervent, and appropriate. Again he opened the Bible, and read his text from Proverbs ix. 10 and xxix. 25 : " The fear of man bringeth a snare ; but the fear of the Lord is the beginning of wisdom."

The sermon, though perplexed with divisions, and obscured occasionally by length of illustration, was affectionate, impressive, and highly enriched with quotations from the Holy Scriptures. The folly of fearing men rather than God, the everlasting security of those who fear and obey the Almighty, and the eternal confusion of those who put His fear away from them, were clearly proved, and strongly enforced by numberless passages from the volume of inspiration. As he came to the exhortation, generally the most useful part of sermons, his voice elevated, his language glowed with a deeper pathos, and seeming to forget the present suffering of his audience, in the awful idea that there might be some fearless sinner among them in jeopardy of eternal wrath, he expostulated with them thus :

" Oh that I could so speak of the goodness and mercy of God, manifested through the Saviour, as to win the love and obedience of you that fear Him not ! Oh, that I had the tongue of an angel, to tell you how much God hath done for you, and how unwilling He is that you should put His mercy away from you !—Do ye not know that all your enjoyments come from God? That those lips which never praised Him sincerely, and those knees which never bowed before Him reverently, are the work of His hand : and that your memories that forget Him, and your reasons that despise Him, and your imaginations that ever wander from Him, are the gifts of His goodness? Are ye ignorant that the clothes which warm you, and the food which nourishes you, and the houses which shelter you, come all from the God whom you refuse to fear? Do you not know that your sweet and tender endearments of loves, and brotherhoods, and friendships, that all which delights your eye, or soothes your ear, or warms your heart, descend from the Father of lights, whom ye will not honour? And have ye not heard that God hath not yet removed His mercy from you? Will ye believe it, the everlasting Jehovah, whom ye daily offend, is yet beseeching you to accept of His pardon, is yet waiting to be gracious, is yet lifting up the voice of His mercy to win you from your waywardness, and save you from the fierceness of His wrath? Will ye believe it, the God for whom ye have no reverence is yet casting a fatherly eye upon you, offering His own Son for your redemption, and inviting you up to the land of life and glory? Truly, the heart that is not won by this is harder than the nether millstone, and deserves the anguish that shall ring it.

"But if ye will not hear, and if ye will not consider: if ye will harden your hearts, and not be persuaded to the fear of the Lord by His love and His mercy, I dare not leave you unwarned. I must ask you to look on God's wrath, and measure your arms with the weapons of His indignation. Are ye prepared for this, ye that fear not the Almighty? God is your Judge, and will ye not fear Him? Eternity is at His disposal, and will ye have no reverence for Him? Are ye afraid of death? The God whom we counsel you to fear keeps the gates of immortality. Have ye not heard, that there is a place where the fire is not quenched, and where the worm dieth not? Have ye not heard, that in hell the devil believes and trembles? And have ye not known that it is God, even the God whom ye will not fear, whose wrath kindles the everlasting burnings, and whose frown thickens the eternal darkness?

Surely, 'the fear of the Lord is the beginning of wisdom.'

"You that fear God as ye ought—and I trust there are few of another character here," continued the herald of heaven, "are safe from every evil. Your fear is a holy fear ; it is the offspring of love ; it is a filial awe, accompanied by the trust, and the expectation, and the affection of children to a father, who shields your heart from every alarm. You know that all your present afflictions are but the chastisement of a Father who loves you with an everlasting love. 'God so loved the world,' so loved you, my dear friends, 'that He delivered up His Son unto the death, that whosoever believeth in Him may not perish but have everlasting life ;' and if He has given us his Son, His only and well-beloved Son, shall He not with Him freely give us all things? Oh, the breadth, and the length, and the height, and the depth of the love of God ! it 'passeth understanding' ; yea, the response of your hearts is, It passeth understanding. It is this love of God—it is this love in your hearts which rouses you to all duty, cheers you in every distress, and supports you in every trial. Can you look upon the tender mercy of God in Christ Jesus—can you look upon His everlasting love, and hesitate for a moment to prefer His statutes, which are all holy, and just, and good, to the laws of wicked and cruel men? Will you offend the gracious God who hath all power in heaven and in earth, who preserved Daniel in the lions' den, and the three children in the midst of the burning fiery furnace, or your persecutors who pass away as the wind, and are crushed before the moth? Will you fear to offend the God and Father of our Lord Jesus Christ, who loves you as a father loves his children, who rests in His love to you, who will never leave you nor forsake you? or will you fear to offend those who seek your life, and hate you with a perfect hatred? Verily, it is the answer of your hearts, We will fear our God, for He hath loved us : we love Him, and we will obey Him. We will follow Him

4

through good and through bad report. Well done (may
I not say?) good and faithful servants, ye shall enter
into the joy of your Lord. Oh, ye that love and fear the
Lord! here is comfort, and support, and safety to your
souls. God loves you—the God of life and of death.
Why should your hearts be dismayed or disquieted within you? The Captain of your salvation hath overcome
the world: He hath vanquished death and hell, and He
hath gone to the Father to prepare mansions of peace, of
happiness, of immortality for your reception. If God be
for you, who can be against you? He stands on your
right hand, and bids you fear no evil. In this hour of
trial and desolation, He puts His left hand under you, and
His right hand embraces you. When ye walk through
the fire, ye shall not be burned; neither shall the flames
kindle upon you. Persecution and reproach, and death
and hell, are now banded against you; but the God of
all your salvation, and all your desire, stands by your side,
and ye shall be more than conquerors. What shall
separate you that fear God from His everlasting love?
Verily, it shall be neither death, nor life, nor angels, nor
principalities, nor powers, nor things present, nor things
to come. He regards you as the apple of his eye. In
your afflicted pilgrimage through this world He shall
hide you under the shadow of His wings; He shall walk
with you through the dreariness of the valley of death;
and set you down for ever at the banqueting table in the
heavens. This is the promise of God, of Him who is the
Amen, the faithful and the true Witness. As thy days are,
O Christian, so shall thy strength be. With this merciful, this blessed assurance, may we not exclaim in the
midst of all our afflictions, gracious is the Lord and righteous; yea, our God is merciful! Return unto thy rest,
O my soul! for the Lord hath dealt bountifully with thee."

The sermon was just finished, and the minister again
offering up his heart's desire to God, when the sentinel
gave the alarm that a party of cavalry was approaching.
The venerable minister looked to his audience, then to

SHE KNEELED BEFORE THEM.—*See page* 53.

heaven; and, in a tone of assurance and resignation, pronounced these words : "Into Thy hands, O Lord, we commit our immortal spirits." The congregation then dispersed hurriedly. The good old servant of God entreated them all to leave him, knowing that, as a price had been set on his head, the pursuit after him would be most eager. It happened as he thought. The reverend pastor was taken—placed on horseback—his hands tied behind his back—and his ankles twisted with ropes below the belly of the animal. In this position, without refreshment, without being permitted once to alight, he was driven to Edinburgh, a distance of fifty miles, where, after much torture, he was executed at the Grassmarket, praising his God, solacing his friends, and forgiving his murderers, with his last breath. Surely the latter end of the righteous man, whatever be his external condition, is peace.

Mrs. Thomson and her daughter had fled up the glen, and were now within a mile of their hut when two of the troopers discovered them. As they approached with their prancing steeds and gleaming armour, uttering "strange oaths," Helen turned pale, and seized her mother's hand. The soldiers appeared rather intoxicated, and their whole aspect was fierce and cruel. One of them, Duncan Wrathburn, a north countryman, full of the merciless spirit of his master, Claverhouse, commanded Mrs. Thomson to take the test or the shot that was in his carabine. She kneeled before them—pleaded with them not to force her to violate the dictates of her conscience, and to renounce her allegiance to the King of kings. " None of your canting," bawled Wrathburn, and, with a terrible oath, commanded her again to take the test, to abjure conventicles, or else he would blow out her brains on the spot. " I will not abjure my religion and my God," said Mrs. Thomson ; " but, oh, spare a poor widow—spare me for the sake of my husband, who died fighting for his king—spare me for the sake of that child and her little brother—spare me,

as you expect mercy at the judgment of the great day."
The good widow having refused again to violate her
conscience and dishonour her Redeemer, by submitting
to their unlawful demands, Wrathburn, in a tone of
jeering and ridicule, said she had better pray and confess
herself quickly, as she had not a moment to live. It
was vain to entreat these men of Belial more. Mrs.
Thomson looked with a streaming eye on her daughter.
"They will kill your mother," she said ; "you shall be
left helpless orphans,"—remembering William as she
spoke—"you shall be left helpless orphans in the world ;
but God will be your Father—never forsake Him, and He
will never forsake you. And O my dear Helen ! you
know something of the Christian religion ; instruct your
little brother, that I may receive you both at last into
the happy place." "Short, short," cried the cruel
dragoon, taking hold of his carabine. The poor widow
now turned her eyes to heaven, and commended her soul
into the hands of her Redeemer. The soldier who
accompanied Wrathburn, softened by the tears of the
mother and the shrieks of the daughter, urged him to
let the poor widow escape. But Wrathburn, steady in
his unmercifulness, levelled his carabine, and, as Mrs.
Thomson's eyes were turning again from heaven on her
dear child, fired the mortal shot. It took effect in her
left side, touched the heart, and passed fairly through
her body. Her head fell back heavily against the ground
—she threw a dim look on her daughter—seemed to
breathe the blessing she could not pronounce— drew her
arms convulsively over her breast—again they fell back
on the heath—and her soul ascended up on high.

"Her blood be on her own head," cried the brutal
dragoon, as he turned his horse and galloped away,
unmoved by the expiring agonies of the mother, or
her little daughter, that swooned by her bloody corpse.

And, oh ! shall he need no mercy himself? When
disease shall lay its withering hand upon him, and cast
him on his last bed—when every sublunary hold shall

deceive him—and when hope shall take its leave of him —and when his desire shall fail, and the sun and the light withdraw itself—and the silver cord be loosed, and the golden bowl broken—and the wheel broken at the cistern—and the dimness, and dizziness, and terrors of death fasten upon him—shall he have no lack of the smile of God's countenance? Is he sure that he can enter the gates of death alone, and take a fearless view of the grim and ghastly visage of the king of terrors, and find his unguided way through the valley of thick darkness? Shall he be stout-hearted enough to listen unalarmed to the notes of the last trumpet—and see the earth pass' away, and the sun darkened, and the stars falling, and the moon turned into blood, and the heavens rolled up like a scroll, and the Son of Man coming in the clouds to judgment? When he hears the footsteps of the summoning angels, and draws near the tribunal, and sees the books opening, and the face of the Judge frowning, and the sword of eternal justice flaming— shall he have no need of an Almighty Friend? Is he prepared to take a last sight of God's mercy, and all that is good, and all that is happy? Is he prepared to abide the unmitigated wrath of Jehovah, and take into his bosom the worm that dieth not, and make his dwelling in the fire that is not quenched, and converse with utter despair and utter destruction, and hear the gates of hell shut behind him, and the bolts of his fate driven deep for ever and ever? Ah! cruel soldier, thou art not prepared for this.

The old farmer's shepherd having heard the mortal shot, came up to the place where the body of Mrs. Thomson lay. Little Helen, recovered from her swoon, clung to her mother's breast, and, with her arms clasped about her neck, wept, and cried, "My mother, O my mother! will you speak to me no more! will you lead me no more by the hand, and tell me of my father, of Christ, and of heaven?" The shepherd endeavoured to soothe the child—"Your mother is gone," said he, "to meet your father, where Christ dwells. She is happy, and wishes you to be comforted. And if you be a good girl, you shall see her when you go to heaven, more lovely, more kind than ever."

Talking in this way, the shepherd led Helen to the farmhouse, and made known to the inmates the mournful story. The body of Mrs. Thomson was carried into the house; and it was indeed a day of mourning and lamentation in the house of the old farmer. Every one wept, as if they had lost a mother, so much was Mrs. Thomson loved by young and old for her sober cheerfulness, modest piety, and kind instructions in righteousness. Little William wept aloud; and it was an affecting sight to see Helen, while weeping herself, trying to soothe and comfort her brother. It may be supposed that she could not remember the whole of her mother's dying advice, but her ear had caught these words, and they were imprinted on her memory for ever: "Never forsake God, and He will never forsake you. Instruct your little brother, that I may receive you both at last into heaven." "We shall go to our mother in the happy place," said Helen to her little brother; "I have heard her say, and I have read in the Bible, that Christ loves little children like us; and if we be good, He will come and take us to our mother."

While Helen talked thus, William would wipe his eyes, and seem now to believe, now to mistrust her words. Again would they remember the pale lips and motionless eye of their mother, and burst into tears; and again, the hope of meeting her gleamed on their souls, as clasped in one another's arms the two orphans wept themselves fast asleep, while the darkness of night came down on the untenanted hut of Cleughhead.

On the Tuesday following, the old farmer gathered two or three of his friends, and the remains of Mrs. Thomson were committed to the dust, near the spot (as was frequently the case in those days) where she died a martyr to the holy religion of Jesus.

How much ridicule soever, young reader, irreligion, or misguided genius may throw on her memory, or the memories of those like her, it is to her, and to those like her, that we owe much of our civil liberty, and the plentiful streams of the water of life which flow to-day in the midst of our land. And shall the Christian take up the books of those who deliberately laugh at their memories, and laugh along with them? Shall the Christian hear their sufferings jeered at, their motives misconstrued, and their doings misrepresented, and yet give a smile of half approbation? Were our persecuted ancestors robbed of their goods? were they hunted like the wild beasts of the mountains? were they imprisoned? were they tortured? were they banished? were they murdered? Did they eat the bread of affliction, and drink the water of affliction, and watch at cold midnight, in the caves and the dens of the wilderness? Did they set their breasts of heavenly heroism to the floods and the fires of hellish rage, that the manna of life might never be driven from our native land? Did their blood flow on the scaffold, and their groans lament on the desert, that we should drink in abundance the streams of life, and listen unmolested to the glad tidings of salvation? Did they keep unslumbering watch on our hills, when the storms, and the tempests, and the darkness of hell howled and thickened over our beloved land, that we might walk in the clear and peaceful day of the Sun of Righteousness? Were their patience, and fortitude, and faith, and suffering, and death, made a spectacle to men and angels? Did the seraphim sing them a higher note? Did God lean down from the eternal heights, well pleased to behold them? And shall we, their offspring, forget their memories, or remember them with ridicule?

While the pious peasants pressed the heathy turf on the silent house, and mingled their tears with the streamlet that seemed to lament down the glen, Helen and William, holding one another by the hand, stood by the grave and wept. "This shall be my church,". said Helen; here will I read my Bible, here will I pray, here will I repeat to you, William, our mother's last advice."

Chapter III

"Ah! how unwise the busy fluttering race,
 Who, from themselves, to wanton tumults fly;
 Their reason lost in passion's thorny maze,
 No ray divine beams through their troubled sky;
 A while they rave, and in their raving die.
 Ah! there, my son's a waste of human woes!
 There lions prowl, and filthy harpies cry;
 There syrens lull the mind to cursed repose—
 But in this waste serene the soul is far from foes."

—ANON.

AFTER the death of their mother, the old farmer took Helen and William, the one now in her eighth and the other in his sixth year, into his own family. Helen had been taught by her mother to read, to knit, and to sew a little. William could also read, though imperfectly. As there was no school near the place, his sister, and the woman of the house, frequently gave him lessons; and in the course of a twelvemonth he could read the Bible fluently. Here the two orphans had the benefit of a pious example; and the sweetness of their tempers, and ready obedience, procured them the affection of everyone in the house. As they grew up, William was employed in keeping his benefactor's cows, and Helen assisted in the dairy. During their leisure hours they rambled together by the rushy brooks and sunny hills, gathering here the wild thyme and there the silky white down of the cannach; and never did they return home without visiting their mother's grave, covered now, by the pious care of the shepherds, with a smooth granite stone, on which they had cut, in "uncouth letters," the name of the inhabitant below. A grey willow, whose roots were nursed by the passing streamlet, spread its sweet-smelling leaves half-way over the grave, and by the other side bloomed the heath, rustling on the edge of the stone, while the breeze sighed over the moorland. Here would Helen kneel down, and pray with her little brother that God would be their father, their guardian, and their friend, and take them at length to Himself, where they would be orphans no more—and here would she instruct her brother in the fear of the Lord, and tell him all that she remembered of their mother, while they lived in the little hut—and here, especially every Sabbath morning in summer, early, while the dew yet sparkled on the wild flowers, sat the orphan pair. Oh, how often did they sit on this grey stone, unseen by all but heaven! and while the wild bee hummed its little note of gratitude, and sipped its sweet food from the bosom of the heather-bell, did they drink of the streams of life which flow from the pure word of God! On Helen's soul at least, young as she was, the dawn of eternal day had already appeared. She prayed in faith—she trusted in her Saviour—she leaned on the Rock of Ages. She felt that her own heart was ever ready to go astray—she felt that she was naturally polluted; and she kept her eye on the Star of Bethlehem, and went daily to wash in the fountain that is ever open for sin and for uncleanness.

Helen was remarkable for tender-heartedness. The lamb forsaken or bereaved of its mother, the crippled fowl, the dying sheep, received her ardent attention, and often her tear. She would frequently watch the falcon in chase of the lark or the moss-chirper; and as the little bird, now descending, now mounting above its fell pursuer, struggled for life, she would exclaim, "Oh, would it come to me!" and once she enjoyed the luxury of saving the little trembler in her bosom, while the disappointed falcon swam away on the wind in search of some less fortunate songster of the desert. She would often, too, go out of her way, that she might not disturb the nest of the lapwing, the snipe, or the plover. And when she happened in her thoughtful mood to cast her eye down on the wild flower that seemed decaying, while all around was verdant and lively, she would bathe it with a tear, and say, " We must all die like thee, droop- ing flower. The world will laugh and be gay when we are gone, as the herbage that surrounds thy falling head. Oh, that I may answer my end like thee !   Thou hast grown up, spread thy bosom to the morning, shed thy fragrance around thee, looked lovely—very lovely, and thy duty is complete. Oh, that I may so grow up, open- ing my heart to the Sun of Righteousness, casting around me a sweet savour of piety, shining in the white robes of holiness, and falling at last without a murmur into the grave ; secure that my soul shall have an everlasting place by the fount of life."—There was one rather odd employment into which the tenderness of Helen's feelings often led her.

Whoever has travelled over the moorish districts of Scotland must have observed the webs woven by a large grey spider. They are to be seen in thousands, suspended across the gullies and broken mosses, glitter- ing in the morning dew. The insect generally fastens a single thread to a stump of heath, on each side of the gully, from the middle of which it weaves four or five other threads, fixing them also to one side of the gully. On these it spins a circular network, nine inches or a foot in diameter, in the midst of which it crouches, like death, in concealment, till the coming of the heedless fly.

In her idle hours, Helen would often take a bush of heath in her hand, scramble among the broken mosses, and sweep away hundreds of those frail toils, always letting the spider escape, but disabling it for a time for carrying on the work of destruction.

So far, young reader, is religion from destroying the finer feelings of our nature ; so far from contracting our sympathies, or souring our ordinary pleasures. Indeed, how is it possible that the liker we become to our Father in heaven, who cares for all His works,—the solitary

flower of the desert as well as the seraphim in glory,—
our regards for creation can be diminished? Truly, the
more religious we are, whatever the mere sentimentalist
may say, the more kindly will we look on all the works
of God's hand. The flower of the field is pencilled by
Jehovah; and the good man looks on it with an eye
of admiration. The lark is taught her song by the
Almighty; and the Christian listens to it with delight.
The river spreads its bounties, and leads its meanderings
under the guidance of the God of Israel; and the saint
tastes its waters, and gazes on its romantic banks and
devious course, with feelings of poetical rapture and
devotional gratitude. The Christian feels that he is heir
of all things; and he looks to them all, thinks of them
all, and acts towards them all, as a son. There have
been Christians, and perhaps some of them may still be
found, who seem to despise the natural world, with all
its beauty and grandeur. They turn away their ear from
the music of the grove, as if God had not taught the
songster; they tread on the lily of the valley, as if God
had not arrayed it with glory. But this is a spot in their
character—a sin which the blood of Christ must wash
out; and far from being, as they would have us believe,
a denying of themselves. Dispositions such as theirs
have often caused the philosopher and the sentimentalist
to load our holy religion with the charge of extinguishing
the natural charities, and absorbing the finer sympathies
of our soul. Imitate them not, young reader. God
Himself demands your warmest love; His tender mercy
in Christ your primest gratitude. But let all the works
of creation prove a mirror to your mind. Do the saints
in glory—do the holy angels look on the moon and stars,
walking the paths of the midnight sky, without rapture?
Do they hear the ocean lift up the voice of his waves,
and roar to break up his everlasting prison-doors; or
the river roll down the massy wanderings of his
strength; or the mountain forest shake the locks of his
majesty, without exclaiming, "Great and marvellous are

thy works, Lord God Almighty ; just and true are all thy
ways, thou Creator of the ends of the earth !"

Helen had now finished her fourteenth, and William
his twelfth year, when Mr. Hunter, a gentleman who
had been an acquaintance and friend of their father while
in Glasgow, came to pay them a visit.   His manners
were kind and familiar, such as soon gain the confidence
of the youthful mind.   William, who was never so well
contented with his situation as his sister, listened eagerly
while Mr. Hunter talked of Glasgow, the hurry of its
business, and the way of making money.   Mr. Hunter,
pleased with William's natural capacity, and observing
his dispositions, offered to take him along with him to
Glasgow, and initiate him into the principles of the
commercial concern, of which he was himself a partner.
William accepted the proposal with eagerness ; the old
farmer approved the more easily of his choice, as he
knew Mr. Hunter to be a sober, industrious gentleman,
and well in the world ; and the views of future independence and respectability to her brother, and his promises
never to forget religion, gained the consent of Helen.

It was a morning in autumn when William set out
with his new friend.   And as the old shepherd, with
Helen, accompanied them a mile or two on their way
to Glasgow, he addressed William shortly after this
manner—

"You are now going away, my son," for this was the
kind appellation the old farmer always gave him,—"you
are going from the quietness and sobriety of our
sequestered glens.   Vice and temptation will beset you
on every side.   But trust in God, and He will uphold
you.   Read your Bible ; pray for directions to your
Father in heaven ; attend as often as possible the
preaching of the gospel.   Be obedient to your master,
constant at your business, and obliging to all.   And, if
God shall prosper you, beware of pride and vanity : your
prosperity will last the longer.   Observe the heath on
which we tread.   It heeded not the first shower of

spring : it put not forth its buds till the frosty nights
were gone, and the steady heat of summer come in.
And see, it is still green and vigorous—while the gaudy
flower, which rose and spread its painted leaves at the
first sunshine of the year, has already withered away,
and no trace of it is seen on the mountains. Remember
this short advice, my William, and the God of your
fathers be with you."

Helen held her brother by the hand, enforced the old
man's instructions, and repeated to him their mother's
last advice, with much tenderness and affection, " ' Never
forsake God, and He will never forsake you.' And, oh,
come to see us soon." The two orphans now embraced,
and with tears in their eyes bade each other farewell.
William took his way over the heath towards Glasgow ;
and Helen, often looking back on her brother, for she
loved him with the tenderness of a seraph, returned with
the old farmer to her home.

William, on his arrival in Glasgow, was much amused
with the busy scene. The houses, the streets, the
carriages were all new to him. As new were the habits
and manners of the inhabitants. But his natural pliancy
of manner, and aptness to learn, soon assimilated his
general character to his associates. Constant and
vigilant at his business, he gained his master's favour
and kind attention in return. He was taught writing
and accounts, and whatever might tend to accomplish a
young man designed for the activities of business.

During his first year's stay in Glasgow, the kind
advices of his sister and his old benefactor never left
his memory. He read his Bible, prayed in secret, and
went to church on the hallowed day. When he heard
the boy younger than himself utter horrid oaths, and
take the name of the Holy One in vain, or when he
heard the tongue of licentiousness and scandal, his soul
trembled within him. But vice is a dangerous neighbour.
Like the apples of Gomorrah, how rotten soever within,
it puts on a fair outside ; or, like the vampire of America,

while it sucks away the life-blood of piety, it soothes and flatters the repose of its victims. William's associates, who were most careless of religion, and some of them covertly addicted to the grosser vices, seemed cheerful, free, and generous, and often ridiculed his seriousness and scrupulous observance of the Lord's day. In his master, William had no example of genuine religion. Mr. Hunter, as we have observed, was sober, vigilant in business, and knew well how to gain the world. But his creed was of the easy and accommodating kind. In these persecuting times, he shifted it, like too many of his contemporaries, as best suited his personal safety and worldly aggrandisement. His character was fair in the eyes of his neighbours; but the leprosy of sin was at work in the darkness of his heart. In his house, family-worship was neglected; and his instructions to William were oftener how to manage the fluctuations of trade, and distance his fellows in the pursuit of wealth, than how to avoid the snares of wickedness, and gain "the prize of the high calling of God in Christ Jesus."

Thus removed from the kind instructions of his sister and the old farmer, and exposed to the seducements of temptation and vicious example, like the willow, from whose roots the stream turns away its waters, and on whose leaves come the blighting frosts, need we be surprised if the beauty of William's piety began to wither and decay? Now he would think of the gaiety of his companions, who seemed happy in their neglect of religion; now he would question the utility of so much attention to the well-being of his soul, and again, the former admonitions of his friends awakened in his memory, and his conscience trembled. By degrees, however, he forgot his Bible, or read it heedlessly; went to sleep without committing himself to the care of his Heavenly Father; and arose in the morning without thanking the God who had preserved him. The Sabbath, instead of being spent in the house of prayer, or in devotional meditation, was often profaned in pleasure-walks, or in idle or licentious conversation. Still would the parting advice of Helen come like a warning angel to his soul, and stem, for a moment, the current of his misdoings. His heart beat with fear when he thought that his sister might hear of his dishonouring the Sabbath, or neglecting his devotions.

And had he no fear of God? Will you, young reader, stand in awe of your fellow-men? Will you tremble at the rebuke of the world? Yes, you will grieve to wound the heart of your earthly benefactor. You will stand pale before the offended laws of your country. Shame will blush on your face, when you violate the niceness of the rules and customs of fashion. You will bow to the great ones of the earth; and look with alarm when the hand of man's justice lifts the sword against you. The little tyrant, who couches in the gloominess of his barricaded fastnesses, although but a worm of God's footstool, can make you tremble; and will you not fear God, who can cast both soul and body into hell fire? Will you fear to grieve your earthly benefactors, and will you have no reverence to your Father in heaven? Will ye tremble to offend the laws of man, and blush to be seen in an unfashionable suit of apparel; and will ye trample under foot the laws and the statutes of the God of hosts; and will ye not blush when He sees you stript of the white robes of innocence, and refusing to put on the garments that are worn in the courts of heaven? Surely this is folly.

One thing I shall observe here which may be useful to parents, should this little piece happen to fall into any of their hands.

Among the injunctions which the old farmer gave William, you remember one was, that he should attend the preaching of the gospel. But the good old man forgot to specify what minister of religion he should hear. Indeed, in those days, when the faithful servants of God were mostly driven from their flocks by persecution, it was not easy to find, even in such a place as

Glasgow, a minister who ventured to declare the whole counsel of God. Those whom the iniquitous laws of the time permitted to appear in the pulpits were dumb dogs that could not bark : they prophesied lies, and announced to their slumbering congregations, " Peace, peace, when there was no peace."

Such was the priest under whose ministry Mr. Hunter had placed himself, and William attended the same church. Here he heard little of the original depravity of man—of his natural hatred to God, and all that is holy. Little of the inflexibility of God's justice, and of His jealous and immutable regard to the minutest require- ment of His moral law. He was indeed told that he was a sinner, and needed to be made holy, and just, and good, before he could see God. He was enjoined to do good, to love mercy, and to walk humbly with his God ; to be kind and charitable to all, and to keep God's commandments, as far as frail human nature would permit. He was also reminded that, after all his pious endeavours, much would be amiss ; but, that God was a God of mercy, and delighted to forgive the repenting sinner. But, alas ! he heard little of the great atonement —of God's mercy flowing to sinners, only through Him —of the quickening influences of the Holy Spirit—of man putting away from his trust all his own works, and relying for salvation solely on the merits and propitiatory death of the Lord Jesus Christ.

The minister who concealed thus the essence of preach- ing was called a minister of the gospel ; but, oh ! how unlike a minister of the gospel of Christ ! Under him William's conscience was flattered ; he became more pleased with himself, and was glad to hear that he might expect heaven at last with so little expense to his natural desires and propensities. Thus, one who called himself, and whom the world called, a servant of God, joined with William's companions, and the deceit- fulness of his own heart, in endeavouring the ruin of his soul.

How careful should all be, then, who have the
guidance of youth, to place them under a true minister
of the gospel of the grace of God—an able and a faithful
minister of the New Testament ! We are sorry to have
cause to say, that our pulpits are not yet wholly cleared
of false prophets. Let parents and guardians, therefore,
beware. Let them not make the omission of the old
farmer. Who knows how much William's pious resolutions might have been strengthened, and his backsliding
prevented, by the weekly ministrations of a zealous,
heart-searching, faithful minister of the gospel of Christ !
The state of the Church, as we have hinted, formed some
palliation for the conduct of the old farmer. But the
guardians of youth can have now no such excuse. Blessed
be God, faithful ministers of religion may now be found
in every part of the kingdom.

While William was thus, unknown to his friends, putting
away from him the fear of the Lord, Helen, far retired
from these busy scenes, was training her soul to virtue,
and assimilating her nature to those " who walk with
God, high in salvation, and the climes of bliss." The
mercy and holiness of God, as manifested in the sacrifice
of His Son, was the theme of her sweet and daily contemplation—she did good, and loved mercy, and walked
humbly with her God ; but she looked to Jesus Christ
alone as the author and finisher of her faith, as the
great and only means of her justification with God, and
to the Comforter, which is the Holy Ghost, for those
renewing and sanctifying influences which could alone
prepare her soul for an inheritance among the saints in
light. Helen had often fled from the violence of persecution ; and young, inoffensive, and meek as she was,
suffered oftener than once from its cruelty. One time
in particular, a lighted match was placed between her
fingers by a soldier, to extort from her the discovery of
her old guardian. Helen knew, if the old man was taken,
immediate death would be his lot, for he had not only
been intercommuned himself, but his house was a noted

sheltering-place for the scattered flock of Christ. The
match burned between her fingers, but Helen, with a look
that might have softened the heart of the wolf, and a
voice that might have wrung a tear from the eye of the
tiger, said to her tormentor, that she could not discover
the old man, for he was to her as a father. The oaths
and menaces of the soldier made her tremble ; but looking to heaven for strength, she endured the torture ; and
after her hand had been severely burned, the cruel
dragoon struck her tender neck with the flat of his sword,
and went off cursing her obstinacy, as he called her pious
and faithful firmness.

Meanwhile the arm of persecution was beginning to
weary in the slaughter. The instruments of torture, the
iron boot and the thumbkin, were nearly laid aside in
Scotland, and the children of God were less hunted by
the hounds of oppression. Helen neglected not the kind
interference of Providence. Every Sabbath she was
present in the house of God, where she sat with peculiar
delight. Every morning of the hallowed day she visited
the solitary grave of her mother, reading her Bible and
holding communion with the upper world.

To the affairs of the house, Helen was ever attentive ;
and her modesty, sensibility, and piety made her the
favourite of the sequestered few with whom she lived.
The troublous aspect of the times, and the severe bereave-
ments she had suffered, had thrown a seriousness and
sobriety over her character rather disproportioned to her
years. But she knew nothing of moroseness or melancholy. The fear of heaven dwelt in her bosom ; the
smile of content beamed in her face. She always took a
ready part in the simple and innocent amusements of her
rustic companions. Of music she was peculiarly fond.
Often would she sit on the grassy seat, by the house side,
and listen to the evening song of the shepherd boy,
winding down the glen from his laired flock. And often
in the winter evening—the peat burning on the hearth,
and the wheel humming in the corner—would the old

farmer lay the stocking at which he knitted on his knee, and give his ear to Helen while she sung the sweet melodies of Scotland.

Truly, young reader, religion is no dreary thing. Its light casts a ray of cheerfulness over all the character. It is the Christian who possesses the merry heart. He is on his way to his Father's house ; and why should he be fretted or morose? He sees no darkness on the countenance of heaven ; and why should his face gather blackness? He knows that no frown rests on the face of his reconciled Father ; and why should he offer Him monastic sullenness?

Chapter IV

——" Horror and doubt distract
His troubled thoughts ; and from the bottom stir
The hell within him.　　.　　.　　.　　.　　.
—— Now conscience wakes despair,
That slumbered ; wakes the bitter memory
Of what he was, what is, and what must be
Worse ; of worse deeds, worse sufferings must endure."
　　　　　　　　　　　　　　　　—MILTON.

THREE years and some months had now elapsed since William went to business in Glasgow. He had hitherto been prevented from visiting his sister, chiefly by the tumult and danger of the times. But the bright morning of the Revolution had now driven away from our land the dark fiend of persecution. The laws were respected, the country was eased of oppression, and the persons and property of men safe from violence.

It was on a frosty morning in January that William left Glasgow to pay a visit to Helen and the old farmer. As he crossed the Clyde, the sun looked cold and red through the smoky atmosphere of the town. But as he left the city behind him, the fields and the sky brightened in the splendid, though short, glare of the winter day. The bird chirped on the brown and leafless hedgerow,

and the morning maid carried her pail from the well.
Amusing himself with the objects around him, William
crossed the cultivated parts of Renfrewshire, and drew
near to the moorlands. He now passed a small stream
that washed the north border of the parish of Eaglesham. This brook, called the Erne (as the swains on its
banks say, from a species of the eagle of that name
which lodged here while Scotland was yet covered with
woods), where William crossed it, leads its gentle
waters secluded among grassy hills and little green
holms, on which grow, in their seasons, the primrose,
the fern, the wild daisy, and the violet. As he ascended
the south bank, he noticed a small oval excavation,
called from its appearance the "Chamber's Braes." In
this sequestered hollow, during the hot day of persecution, the neighbouring swains, whose offspring still
possess the ground, often met to hear the joyful sound.
Here the psalm often rose on the breeze of the hallowed
morning, here the holy man of God lifted up the desires
of his people to the ear of the Eternal, and hither the
blessing descended from between the cherubim.

Proceeding on his way, he gained, an hour after midday, the summit of Balagich, a hill about eleven miles
south of Glasgow, which in this place forms the boundary
between the heathy sheep grounds to the south and the
cultivated districts that slope gently down to the river
Clyde on the north. Tired with travelling, here he sat
down on some old grey stones, piled together by the
shepherds, and threw his eyes over the romantic
scenery.

To the east rose Tinto, watching the youthful ram-
blings of the Clyde ; and a little to the north, and
farther in the distance, Pentland Hills and Arthur's
Seat, whence the morning sun looks down on the towers
of Edinburgh. Beneath him, passing in his course the
spires of Glasgow dimly seen in the smoke, and leaving
the eye at the rock of Dumbarton Castle, the ancient
strength of Scotland, the Clyde watered his fertile

valley, surmounted on the north by the fells of Campsie
and the wild mountains of the western Highlands.
Ben Ledi, or hill of God, where our pagan forefathers
worshipped their unknown gods, muffled its spiry top in
the clouds. Ben Lomond, from whose shoulders the
unsubdued sons of freedom rushed down on the Roman
invader, was clothed in his saintly robes of snow, and
the garments of the mist leaned on his head. Shooting
up far to the west were the rocky hills of Arran, on
whose rugged tops the spirit of the storm gathers the
rain and nurses the infant tempest. Round the rock of
Ailsa, hovering in the wave like the guardian angel of
the Frith, rolled the wintry billows of the Atlantic, and
straggling along its shores stood Saltcoats, Irvine, and
Ayr, looking up from the setting-sun on the plentiful
districts of Carrick, Coil, and Cunningham, scattered
with villages and farmhouses, and guarded in the
distance by the grassy hills of Galloway, from which the
sun gazes on the shepherd at midday. Rising out of
the brown level waste to the south was the little round
elevation of Loudon Hill, towards which William now
directed his course.

Silence reigned on the desert, save when it was broken
by the brown cock calling his mate, the bleating of
sheep, or the whistle of the shepherd, who seemed in
more than ordinary solicitude to gather his flocks. His
care was not unnecessary. Although William feared no
danger, the shepherds, who knew well the face of the
heavens, saw an approaching tempest. The sun veiled
his face, a heavy grey fog closed over the sky, the breeze
had left the heath, the little waterfalls were heard at a
distance, and a kind of general sighing prevailed over
nature.

William had proceeded through gullies and moor-
streams a few miles only, when the storm overtook
him. It was sudden and furious. The snow descended
so rapidly and closely that he saw not whither he went ;
and the four winds seemed to contend around his head

which of them should drive the snow before it. Young
and vigorous, he struggled a while against the fierceness
of the tempest; but every moment in danger of falling
into some bog or water-runnel, now choked up with the
snow, and not knowing what way to hold for safety, he
at length stood still, leaning on a hillock of heath. The
tempest grew still more violent, and he began to fear
for his life. No hope of assistance, or of outliving the
storm where he was, appeared. Nothing was heard on
the waste but the roaring of the wind; and the driving
snow that beat against him, and blinding his eyes,
threatened to smother him outright.

It was then that William remembered that he had
profaned the Sabbaths, forgotten his Bible, and neglected
prayer. His conscience rose within him as the storm
increased without. The kind instructions of Helen
rushed on his mind. And "Oh, shall I never see her
again!" was the exclamation of his heart. "Deliver
me, O Lord, this time, and I will no more forget Thy
holy day and religion again!" Struggling thus with
the tempest and the fears of death, which, young as
he was, he had already made terrible by his forgetful-
ness of Him who has conquered death, he shrunk down
to the ground benumbed and hopeless. The storm had
now rather abated; but the darkness of night was
spreading over the moor, and William, unable to rise
or stir himself, felt the piercing frost rapidly fastening
on the functions of life. Another hour, and the wheel
at the cistern would have stood still for ever. But his
deliverer was at hand.

A shepherd's dog approached him, looked earnestly
in his face, and immediately ran off. William tried to
speak to it, but his tongue refused to obey. The dog
needed no entreaty. It found its master, and brought
him to where William lay. The shepherd raised him
up; from his bosom took a bottle of sweet milk which
he carried for his own refreshment, and, giving him the
warm milk in small quantities, succeeded in restoring

him to proper animation and to a partial use of his
limbs. The kind peasant threw his own plaid round
William's shoulders, and supported him on his arm to
his master's house, a lonely hut situated in the midst
of the moor, about a mile from the spot where he had
fallen down overcome by the storm. In this humble
dwelling, which was a noted rendezvous of the people
of God in the time of persecution, he received the kindest
attention. The old man of the house, who had often
fled before the cruel and insolent soldiers, like the primitive Christians, washed his feet with his own hands;
one of his daughters wiped the snow from William's
clothes and hair, another prepared him something to
eat, while their mother warmed blankets for him before
the fire. The old man thanked God for making his
servant and his house the means of saving a fellow-
creature, and William went to bed and fell fast asleep,
remembering the shepherd's dog more than the providence of God that had sent it to deliver him.

In the morning William was roused from sleep by
a deep groan which proceeded from a bed in the same
apartment. The old man, who knitted stockings by the
fire, came to William's bedside and told him not to be
alarmed. "It is an old soldier," continued he, "who
lies there. He was brought in hither, feeble and exhausted, two or three days ago. He has been seized
with a violent fever, and I fear he will not hear many
hours told. His name," added the old man, "is
Wrathburn, well known in the time of the late persecution for his inflexible cruelty, and especially for his cold-
blooded murder of the widow of Cleughhead."

At the name of Wrathburn and the widow of
Cleughhead, William started, and his face changed
colour. "What alarms you?" said the old man;
"the soldier can hurt no one now." "The widow of
Cleughhead was my mother," replied William, "and
I never hear the name of her murderer without
trembling. Discover me not to him," continued he,

"it will make his last moments more bitter." "They
are bitter enough even now," said the old man; "he
refuses to be comforted."

Although the reader already knows something of
Wrathburn, it will be necessary here to make a short
pause in the narrative, and explain how he was brought
into his present situation.

The licentiousness and prodigality of the reign of
Charles ii. spread from the Court over almost every
class of men in the kingdom. The soldiers especially,
who were the instruments of persecution in Scotland,
imitated their master in every species of riot and
drunkenness. Accustomed to plunder and massacre
the recusants, or people of God, at pleasure, they totally
lost every habit of temperance and every feeling of
humanity. The consequence was, that when disease
or old age disabled them for service, deprived of the
means but not of the propensities of dissipation, they
were reduced to poverty and wretchedness. And
hundreds of them, forgotten by the masters whose
cruelty they had served, wandered about, especially
after the persecution, begging their bread among those
very peasants whose lives they had pursued, whose
houses they had plundered, and whose relations they
had murdered. Of this sort was Wrathburn; so
intrepid in cruelty, so inflexible to supplication, that
Claverhouse, the bitterest of all the persecutors, used
to send him on all his bloody errands, where his soldiers
were most apt to be turned aside from his orders by
the courage of the peasants, or the tears of the women
and children. We have already seen one act of his
stubborn cruelty in the murder of Mrs. Thomson.
This was certainly the most abominable deed of his
life! but there was scarcely a family in the moorish
districts of the shires of Lanark and Ayr that could
not bear witness against him for some act of torture
or insolent violence. Disabled at last in his sword arm,
by a wound received from the faithful sabre of Hackston

at Bothwell Bridge, and worn out with old age and
disease, he had now begged his bread for several years.
He had been found, overcome with hunger and fatigue,
in the midst of the moors, by the same shepherd who
saved William; and now he lay fevered, and on the
brink of death, as the old man described him.

As the snowstorm had been succeeded by a rapid
thaw, to leave the hut that day was impossible. William
had therefore an opportunity of seeing the end of this
man. He approached his bedside. The aspect of the
old sinner was indeed terrible. Down from his projecting cheek-bones hung the skin in withered foldings,
that had once been filled with flesh—his head was bald
—his beard long, and of a dirty grey—a mouldering
stump or two appeared in his mouth, that gaped widely
for breath—the violence of the distemper raised up his
eyeballs, now and then glaring from their large hollow
sockets the fiery darkness of despair. Hell and everlasting wrath took hold of his imagination, and he would
often cry out furiously, "Cut them down — cut them
down to the last. The widow of Cleughhead — she
pursues me—see her daughter swoons by her corpse
—that groan was her last—it drives me to perdition—
No mercy, no mercy!"

In the short intervals of the fever, he would endeavour
to sit up on the bed. With his left arm he tried to support his head, but it was too heavy—the feeble prop fell
down, and his right arm lay shrunk and withered by his
side. It was then that the good old man placed his
shoulder below the head of the dying wretch, pleaded
with God for him, and laboured to administer comfort.

"God's mercy is infinite," said the old man; "your
sin in disbelieving the all-sufficiency of His grace is
greater than that of your most wicked actions. Remember what the Bible says: 'The Lord is slow to
anger, and abundant in mercy. Come let us reason
together,' says the voice of His infinite goodness;
'though your sins be as scarlet, they shall be as white

as snow ; though they be red like crimson, they shall
be as wool. Jesus Christ came not to call the righteous,
but sinners to repentance. Whosoever believeth in
Him,' however guilty he may have been, 'shall not
perish, but have everlasting life. The blood of the
Redeemer cleanseth from all sin.' Oh, turn yourself
to prayer, ere it be too late. God hath ever an open
ear to those who call on Him in distress."

"No, no," with a voice of fury and despair, cried the
hopeless sinner ; "I never prayed, and God will not
hear me now. I read not that Bible of which you speak
—I despised that book, and them who read it. I will
not pray—the blood of murder is on my hands—the
gates of heaven are shut against me—the sword of God's
vengeance hath gone into my heart—the eternal fire
burns in my soul—pray not for me—talk not of mercy—
Oh, for utter annihilation ; endless torment is on me—
leave me—leave me—the widow of Cleughhead pursues
me—that was the shriek of her daughter."

Oh ! how dreadful were the agonies of his soul !
Conscience, that had been long disregarded, now put
on the terrors of eternal death ; and truly its voice was
heard. The bed on which he lay shook with the furious
convulsions of his body. The fever again took away his
senses, and nothing but heavy groans were heard. Again
a minute of ease returned, and the old man tried yet again
to administer some spiritual relief.

"Doubt not," said he, "of God's mercy ; He wishes not
that you should perish. Remember the thief who was saved
on the cross, and went to paradise. Remember Paul,
who was the most inveterate of persecutors, and yet he
found mercy. Try, oh, try to pray ! God may hear you."

"Away with mercy," cried the frantic wretch ; "it is
perdition to my soul. Hell calls for me—the devil drags
me away—the wrath of God is on me—the widow of
Cleughhead pursues me—that was the shriek of her
orphan daughter—that is her blood on my hands—hell
cannot burn it off ! "

Again the strong disease fastened firmer upon him—
the mighty strength of the king of terrors was in the pang.
The withered stump of the right arm made a convulsive
motion, as if to search for the sword ; again it fell back
—another lurid gleam flashed from his hollow eye—no bow
appeared on the cloud of eternal darkness—a deep groan
shook his body—it lay still for ever—and his soul was
summoned away to that bar whence there is no appeal !

Surely, oh man, it is a fearful thing to fall into the
hands of the living God ! This man showed no mercy :
he exceeded even the cruelty of his commission. The
tears and supplications of humble widowhood, the shriek-
ings and swoonings of fatherless childhood, melted not
the cruelty of his heart—and how could he expect to find
mercy in the hour of need ? He hated God, and Christ,
and all that is holy—and where could he find a stay ;
how could he see a guiding star in the valley of thick
darkness ? He despised the great Captain of Salvation
—and how could he meet in battle with the king of
terrors ? Truly "the fear of the wicked it shall come
upon him. Terrors take hold on him, as waters ; a
tempest stealeth him away in the night. The east wind
carrieth him away, and he departeth, and as a storm,
hurleth him out of his place. For God shall cast upon
him and not spare ; he would fain flee out of his hand.
Men shall clap their hands at him, and shall hiss him
out of his place."

———————

Chapter V

————"With countenance as mild
As Mercy looking on Repentance' tear ;
Her eye of purity now darted up
To God's eternal throne, now humbly bent
Upon herself ; and weeping down her cheek
A tear, pure as the dews that fall in heaven."
—Anon.

Night had again shrouded all in darkness ; and it was a

night of sadness and trembling in the family of the moor.
The horrible expressions of the dying wretch were still
in their ears ; they still saw his last looks of despair ;
his last convulsions were still in their memories ; his
lifeless corpse lay on the bed, and the dark blast of
winter moaned over the waste. The old man exhorted
them to put their trust in God, and prayed that the
scene they had witnessed might be blessed for their
improvement.

William now went to bed, but sleep refused to visit
him. He thought still of the last looks and words of
Wrathburn. He resolved, and resolved again, never to
forget religion. Was it possible that his end might be
like this man's? If he forsake God now, might not God
forsake him in the hour of desolation? " Guide my feet,
O God, in the path of the just, that my end may be like
his," was the whisper of his fears—and only of his fears.

As soon as morning appeared, William, glad to quit
the present scene, set forward for his sister's. Travelling was extremely difficult. The snow had been mostly
dissolved, but the streams were swollen, and the swampy
grounds in many places covered with water. Resting
himself on a gentle height, about three miles from the
house he had left, he observed, coming out from it, five
or six men. They drove a horse with a car, and seemed
to hold towards a hamlet situated at the distance of six
or seven miles.

It was the funeral of Wrathburn. The very men
whom he had often chased with the sword, and whose
relations he had murdered, and whose memories many
now ridicule, were doing him the last office of humanity.
Through fens and bogs and over rills they carried him,
and in a corner of the village churchyard, at a small
distance from the ordinary place of graves, laid him
down in the narrow house, "far from the ashes of his
fathers."

Meanwhile, William, now skipping from hillock to
hillock, and now leaping the moor-runnels, made to-

TELLING HER AND THE OLD MAN WHATEVER HAD HAPPENED TO
HIM IN GLASGOW.—*See page* 81.

wards the habitation of Helen. She had been watching him making his way over the rough broken masses, like a vessel holding for a difficult port; and although his appearance was considerably altered, she recognised him at a short distance from the house, ran out with all her usual tenderness and embraced him, and led him into the dwelling of the honest old farmer. The evening was spent in kind inquiries and kind answers. Helen related, with beautiful simplicity, any curious or entertaining incident that had happened in the neighbourhood since William's departure; and William seemed unreserved in telling her and the old man whatever had happened to him in Glasgow; but not a word dropt from him that could give them the least intimation of his declining piety. The story of Wrathburn made a deep impression on the whole family: and "Oh!" said Helen, the blood leaving her cheek, and the tear starting in her eye, "was there no hope? Did he die uttering these horrid words? Did you not pray for him, William? I am sure my mother forgave him. Why did he not seek the mercy of God? Oh! did he die unforgiven?"

Helen, perceiving no marks of decline in his religion, was extremely pleased with her brother. William was taller; his glossy jet locks curled plentifully on his healthy cheeks, which had now assumed that smoothness and richness of colouring which precedes manhood; his black eye rolled more freely; his dress was neater; he spoke better; and his whole appearance was more graceful.

Nor had Helen grown up in the desert an unlovely flower. Although seeing few but the old shepherd and his servants (for his wife had now been dead for some time, and he had no children), her native sweetness of temper, her contentment, her sobriety of thought, gave an expression and a dignity to her countenance superior to her situation in life. Her form was handsome; the loveliness and vigour of seventeen imparted animation to every feature; a profusion of sunny ringlets shaded her

6

fair neck, and played on her shoulders ; and her soft blue eye beamed with beauty.

Although William was by no means deficient in natural talent and feeling, in all that concerned religion Helen was far his superior. Her understanding illuminated by the divine truths of the Bible, her imagination enlarged by the boldness of its poetry, and her heart warmed by the pathos of its piety,—she felt and spoke of divine things in a style much above her years. Seldom was she drawn into lengthened conversation on these subjects ; but when the taste or interest of her associates required it, having fully before her mind the awful impression of eternal concerns, she entered into religious converse with an eloquence, a warmth, and an energy which surprised and often deeply impressed those with whom she conversed.

Now gazing on one another, now talking of their days of childhood, and now of their future prospects, the two orphans spent that evening and the following day, the wetness of which had kept them within doors, till sunset ; and now they walked out to visit their mother's grave.

" Does the lamb go with us ? " said William, noticing one that skipped at Helen's side. " It is a foster lamb," said Helen ; "it lost its mother, and I have brought it up in the house. It follows me everywhere ; I have to shut it up when I go to church. Poor thing ! I love its white face. It will go along with us : often has it accompanied me to my mother's grave."

The wind was hushed on the mountain ; the stream purled down its glen ; in the water-spots, over the brown waste, glittered the lamps of heaven ; the vesper star looked solitarily from its hermitage in the west ; up the east, rejoicing in the midst of her constellations, rode the moon ; and the light cloud, passing at intervals over her face, threw its wavy shadow on the heath.

The two orphans now approached the grave of their mother. The grey willow dropped on the stone the

tears of evening. William stooped down and read the
name; Helen kneeled on the heath by its side; the
lamb looked up in her face; she pressed one hand to her
breast, lifted the other up to heaven, turned her blue eye
to the skies, and besought the blessing, even life that
shall never end, for her brother and herself. "Father
in heaven! guide our feet in the paths of wisdom; make
us white and clean in the blood of the Lamb, that our
dwelling-place may be in the house of God for ever."

The two orphans now shed the tear of natural affection on their mother's grave. Nor did they forget that
their father's dust mouldered in a distant land. The
sigh that heaved their breasts for the cruel death of
their mother, deepened as they recollected that their
father had gone before her. "Let us follow their
steps," said Helen to her brother, as they returned
home,—"let us follow their steps, and we shall see them
in heaven. Remember, William, our mother's dying
advice, 'Never forsake God, and He will never forsake
you.'"

During William's stay with his sister, they were often
engaged in cheerful talk and innocent amusement. But
we mean to confine the narration here chiefly to their
private religious conversation.

Before the old farmer, William always demeaned
himself with the strictest propriety; but sometimes he
betrayed a levity and a carelessness, when Helen spoke
of religion and its duties, which alarmed her, lest the
contagion of bad example had been sapping the roots of
his piety. Ever mindful of her mother's wish that she
should instruct and warn William, and ever anxious
herself for the welfare of his soul, she urged him to tell
her all that he felt and thought of religious concerns.
However reluctant William might have been to speak
plainly on these subjects to any other, he could not resist
the entreaties of his sister.

One day, while sitting in the house alone, the pious
sister pressing her brother to speak to her just as he

thought, the following conversation ensued—William disclosing the principles which he had learned from his companions in Glasgow, and Helen endeavouring to root them out of his mind, chiefly by the pure words of inspiration.

"Some attention to religion, sister," said William, "is surely very necessary. But I see some of my companions are cheerful and happy as I, who trouble themselves little about it. They attend to their business, and are getting on in the world; and yet they don't seem to be always reading their Bible. I even hear them swear and take the name of God in vain; and yet they are gay and prosperous."

"And is it not God, dear William, who gives them health and prosperity?" said Helen, gazing on William's face. Oh, how did she gaze when she heard these expressions! "It is from God we receive all our blessings. In Him we live, and move, and have our being. All that is beautiful, or grand, or useful in nature; all our intellectual enjoyments; and all that soothes or endears in acquaintance or friendship, come from our God. Is it any but God who giveth us the former and the latter rain, and scatters the dews of heaven on the grassy bosom of the earth? Is it any but our Father in heaven who loads the fields of autumn, and crowns the hopes of the husbandman? He spreads the table of plenty, and bids all that live eat their fill. He giveth seed to the sower, and bread to the eater. He crowneth the year with His goodness, and His paths drop fatness. They drop upon the pastures of the wilderness; and the little hills rejoice on every side. The pastures are clothed with flocks; the valleys also are covered with corn. They shout for joy; they also sing. Does God all this for us, dear William, and shall we not fear Him with a holy fear?

"And," continued she, her eye kindling with gratitude to God, and her voice softening in compassion for William, "and has our gracious Father done no more than this for His children? Yes, He hath done more—

infinitely more. When we, by the transgressions of His law and by our attachment to sin, had made ourselves His enemies, and the enemies of all that is holy, and just, and good—when we had thus exposed ourselves to His wrath and curse, to all manner of suffering in time, and to inconceivable punishment in eternity, the gracious voice of His mercy was heard, saying, "Deliver from going down to the pit, for I have found a ransom." And what was this ransom? His own Son, who is Himself the Almighty God, left the glories of heaven, assumed our nature, and by His obedience in our room, satisfied the law of God which we had violated; and by His death in our stead, delivered us from that eternal death to which we are exposed. And how did we receive this Messenger of peace and love—this Saviour of a self-ruined world? Did we welcome His coming as all our salvation and all our desire? Ah, no! He was received with reviling and reproach; yet He turned not away His love from us. He who was the brightness of His Father's glory made Himself of no reputation, girt Himself like a servant, went about doing good, preaching peace, binding up the broken-hearted, and submitting to every privation, and trying every endearment to win us to Himself, and save us from the consequences of our guilt. Nor was this the end of His love. The Son of God bore our sins in His body on the tree, suffered the wrath of God for our sake; and on the hill of Calvary, bowed His head and gave up the ghost. On the third day He rose again, and ascended up into heaven, where, in the presence of His Father, He pleads our cause; whence He sends the Comforter to purify our hearts, to cheer and support us through the trials of life; and where He is preparing mansions to receive us, that where He is, there we may be also—holding communion with our God for ever and ever. Hath God done all this for us, William, and shall we not love Him? Hath Jesus Christ redeemed us by His own blood, and shall we not fear to offend Him?"

William, although much moved with this address to his feelings of gratitude, continued thus: "Dear sister, we should certainly be grateful to Him of whom we hold so much. But I have heard my companions say, that God is all-merciful, He will not punish us for our frailties."

"O William," resumed Helen, "that is the fairest lure that vice spreads to entice its prey. God is indeed all-merciful to them who believe in His Son. Jesus Christ died for their sins, and rose again for their justification. His justice has, therefore, no claims against them. They are bought with a price. They are dear to Him as the apple of His eye. They are His own children, and every dispensation they meet with is the dispensation of a Father full of mercy. He hath no pleasure in the death even of the wicked. And He is saying to them, 'Let the wicked forsake his way, and the unrighteous man his thoughts, and let him return unto the Lord, for He will have mercy upon him, and to our God, for He will abundantly pardon.' Truly God is long suffering and slow to wrath. But He will forget to be gracious; He will ease Himself of His adversaries; He will by no means clear the guilty; He will at last rise from His place, and scatter His enemies. And oh, it will be a terrible day for the wicked man when God's mercy leaves him for ever."

Again William tried to find refuge from the eloquence which Helen drew from the word of God. "The Almighty," said he, "will perhaps not punish so severely as He has said. He will perhaps relent at last."

"Dear brother," said Helen, weeping, when she heard William speak in this manner—"Dear brother, you cannot think so. Oh! where is your security for so frail a reliance? Hath God ever failed of His word? 'The mountains may depart, and the hills be removed out of their place; but the word of our God abideth for ever. He is the fountain of truth.' The words of the Lord are pure words. He knows the end from the beginning, and hath no need to change His purpose. He will not be more merciful at the end of time than He was when the morning stars first sang together. His justice, and power, and truth, and holiness, stand pledged for the fulfilment of what He hath spoken. He hath sworn by Himself, that every word that proceeds from His mouth shall be fulfilled. Seek in the book of the Lord, and see if any of His purposes hath failed. The sentence of death was pronounced against Adam if he disobeyed his Maker ; and did it not take its effect? The sword of justice turned in between man and the tree of life. Briars and thorns came up on the earth, and death was turned loose on mankind. And is not the curse still cleaving to our rebellious race ? The careworn countenance, the feeble knees, the pale visage of disease, can tell if God be faithful. The grave can tell if it has been defrauded of its prey. Has not death swept away generation after generation, and made the world a burying-place? Will the multitudes of those who perished in the Deluge bear witness against God's faithfulness? Will the ashes of Tyre and Jerusalem, or the lake of Sodom and Gomorrah, speak against his veracity? Or will the apostate spirit, and the departed souls of the wicked, bring us the tidings that His wrath is exhausted, and His decrees revoked ?

"But God has not been faithful to punish only," continued the earnest pleader, her face brightening as she beheld the tender mercies of God present in her mind—" He has been, and is faithful and mighty to save. Since mercy placed the bow in the clouds, hath anyone seen the waters come over the mountains, and smite every living thing with a curse? Or hath anyone observed seed-time and harvest, and cold and heat, and summer and winter, and day and night, cease from the earth? ' Hath He spoken it, and shall He not do it ? Hath He said it, and shall He not bring it to pass?' The Son of God will not say that the Father is not true.

In Eden, the voice of God's truth and mercy was heard
saying, that 'the seed of the woman should bruise the
head of the serpent.' This was the most expressive promise that God ever gave to man. Yet no jot of it hath
failed. The veil of the temple rent in twain—the earth
shook and trembled—the sun shrouded himself in darkness ; but the purpose of God stood fast. The Saviour
laid down His life, cast the serpent into everlasting
chains, and secured the redemption of man. Hath God
done this to accomplish His sayings ; and shall He not
give effect to His threatenings against those who fear
Him not, and trample on the blood of His Son? Trust
not, William,—trust not, my dear brother, to refuges
of lies. Remember the deathbed scene you have
lately witnessed—remember your mother's last advice
—remember the goodness and wrath of God ; and oh,
think of the ingratitude and danger of offending
Him ! "

Chapter VI

" Thrice happy they! that enter now the court
Heaven opens in their bosoms. But how rare!
Ah me! that magnanimity how rare!
What hero like the man who stands himself;
Who dares to meet his naked heart alone ;
Who hears, intrepid, the full charge it brings,
Resolved to silence future murmurs there?
The coward flies, and flying is undone! "
—Young.

By those addresses, recorded in the preceding chapter,
which were more congenial to Helen's habits of thinking,
and better fitted to touch the heart of her brother, than
abstract argumentation, his objections to strict piety
were silenced, at least for the present. William seemed
to admit the claims of religion to his careful observance,
and promised to give his ear no more to such misrepresentations of the immutable character of God. Helen

glanced a look of thankfulness to heaven, embraced her brother, and shed on his breast a tear of joy.

From the good old farmer, William received many kind advices; one only of which I shall record here.

" Be faithful to your Father in heaven," said the pious old man, "so you shall be happy. Be forgetful of His commandments, so you shall be miserable. You have seen a child set off confidently to catch the wild fowl that sat on the neighbouring hillock; you smiled at the simplicity of the little one; much more simple is he who thinks to gather happiness from the frailties of earth. You have heard of a man chasing a shadow, or the fabled phantom of night; you then heard of one pursuing happiness among the frailties of earth. You have read of those false reflected waters to which the thirsty traveller, in the sandy deserts of the East, hastens to drink, but finds them gone; you then heard of one making haste to draw happiness out of the frailties of earth. You have seen the wildfire dancing on the marsh; it was beautiful, but you could not lay hold of it. You have heard the echo of the glen; her voice was sweet, but you could not embrace her. You have observed the evening star; it was exceedingly bright, but you could not reach it where you stood. Neither, my son, shalt thou encompass true happiness, except the peace of God dwell in thy heart. This happiness you may attain, but religion is the only guide that can keep your feet in the upward road, and direct your eye to her habitation. Take hold of her hand, William, and she will conduct you to happiness."

At William's second departure for Glasgow, Helen shortly addressed him: "Your companions, dear William, seek the honour and the preferment of this world; but oh, remember how frail they are! They, fearless of God, may flourish for a while. Their spring may have been green, their summer vigorous, and their autumn peaceful. But the dark winter comes; and all our pride, our vanity, and wealth, and honour, and earthly alliance, like

the withered leaves of the grove, shall be driven away
before its first blast.   But religion shall outlive the
withering breath ; and transplanted at last to a warmer
soil and kinder skies, she shall strike her roots by the
river of life, grow up under the everlasting smile of
God's countenance, bearing on her immortal branches all
our pious friendships and all our hallowed attachments."

For some time after William's return to Glasgow, his
narrow escape from perishing in the moor, the old
soldier's awful death, and the pious advices and instructions of Helen and the old farmer, made a deep impression
on his mind.   He respected the Sabbath, read his Bible,
and remembered the duty of prayer.   He determined to
persevere in duty, and defy the temptations of vice.   But
his trust was too much in an arm of flesh.   A ray from
heaven had not yet discovered to him the deceitfulness
of his own heart.

With the enticements, the ridicule, and the sophistical
reasonings of his vicious companions, he was again
assailed.   He now wanted the natural timidity and
bashfulness which scared him awhile, at his first coming
to town, from the deformity of wickedness.   Vice knew
the passes to his heart : and as the second attack is
almost always more feebly resisted than the first, it soon
brought him into captivity.   Of his character in the eyes
of men, he was now indeed more careful than formerly.
He could now see how necessary a fair name was to his
worldly interest, and he took some means to preserve it.
He mingled not oaths with the language of his ordinary
business ; he laughed not at religion before the serious ;
and he attended church, what is termed regularly, that
is, on the fore or afternoon of every Sabbath.   To his
business he was generally attentive ; and his natural
shrewdness and observation never suffered an opportunity
in trade, as far as he was concerned, to escape un-
improved.   He seemed, indeed, in the eye of the world
(and perhaps its eye saw the truth in this instance), to
be following the very footsteps of his respectable master ;

and Mr. Hunter loved and cherished him as a hopeful and enterprising son of commerce. Thus William stood before the world. But we must bring him to another examination ; we must take a view of him in the privacy of chosen companionship.

It is a fact, that those who have been disciplined in the strictest rules of virtue, if they are once enticed away from its paths, become its bitterest enemies, and the foremost abettors of vice. They have been servants to religion, and they must deny it thrice ere their companions believe them—they know its defences, and where it is most assailable, and they can direct the attack more skilfully and more effectually against it. Their conscience is more severe and more watchful, and it requires a deeper draught of iniquity to silence its reproaches and lay it asleep.

It was so with William. His talents were superior to those of any of his associates ; and, in the seclusion and concealment of selected intimacy, they shone in ridiculing the sobriety of religion, and heightening the luxuriousness of sensuality. Vigorous of constitution, determined to keep the fair word of men and push himself on in the world, he seldom drank to intoxication, or deserted his business for a single hour. But his vigour and steadiness only fitted him the better for putting entirely away from him the fear of the Lord. Under the shadow of night— even sometimes the night of the sacred day, seated by the mantling bowl of conviviality, surrounded by willing and congenial friendship, did William shine, the very foremost in sporting with the pure words of Scripture, and laughing at those religious duties he had been taught to reverence. He heard the name of his father's God taken in vain without trembling, and he took it in vain himself. But God had not yet left him to utter hardness of heart. The prayers of Helen, the former supplications of his parents, were not forgotten. They lay on the mercy-seat, and rose up before God, as a sweet memorial in behalf of this only son, who seemed treading firmly on in the path to ruin. There were moments, amidst all the obscurity of night, the encompassment of gay and cordial friendship, and the mirthfulness of wanton pleasure, when the bitterness of reflection came back on his soul, and the darkness of futurity stood before him. His early education, the instructions especially of his sister, reminded him he was wrong, and the deathbed of Wrathburn threatened him with the dreadful consequences. Remorse, that forlorn hope which heaven often places on the brink of perdition to drive back the hardy sinner from utter destruction, frequently lifted up its voice within him, and made him hesitate in the midst of his profane joviality. Had a minister of religion, or a pious Christian, glanced on him in the chosen sociality of his hidden wickedness, the profane word would have turned back on his tongue, and the licentious look fled from his face.

Think, oh think, young reader, how weak and inconsistent such conduct is. Will the cautious and calculating sinner fear the look of man ; and will he vent his licentiousness, and jeer at the Scriptures, and utter the language of cursing and detraction and malice, in the presence of Jehovah? Will he creep under the shadow of night, to veil his crimes and his wickedness from the sight of his fellow-men ; and has he no fear of Him who slumbers not nor sleeps ? Shall the scorn of the world make him try every means to cover his deceitfulness ; to put a colouring of truth on his lying ; to hide from the search of his fellow-men the false measure and the unjust balance ; to overshadow his extortion and oppression, his robbing of the poor, and the widow, and the fatherless ; to gloss over his knavery by the wresting and misapplication of human laws ? Shall he do all this to present what he calls a fair character to the eyes of men, and will he have no fear of that God who has the decision of his eternal destiny—who destroys them that speak lies, and abhors the bloody and deceitful man—who hates the unjust measure and the false balance—who is the avenger of the widow and the fatherless—who will

uncover all his perjuries, and develop all his crafty
devices, and bring him before that tribunal where his
false witnesses, and his briberies, and his interest, and
his splendid name, shall be of no avail?

William, as we have observed, lacked not that kindness and warmness of heart which forbid us to forget
our friends and relations. Helen was the only relation
he had in the world; and during his cautious career of
irreligion in Glasgow, he sometimes remembered her
pious advices, but oftener her sisterly relationship and
native loveliness. His constant design and ardent desire
was to bring her to Glasgow, to keep house with him, as
soon as his circumstances would admit, persuading
himself that the gaiety of the town and acquaintance
with the world would soften the severity of her piety, or
at least render her more heedless of his own carelessness
about religion. The conveyance of letters to her remote
situation was difficult. Sometimes, however, he wrote,
and his letters generally informed his sister of his health,
Mr. Hunter's kindness, his hopes of success in business,
and his desire of bringing her, as soon as possible, to
live with him. Indeed, all William's plans and hopes of
advancing himself in the world were ever mingled with
the worthy intention, and ever stimulated by the strong
desire, of raising Helen along with him. To see his kind
and lovely sister by his side, decorated in the attire of
fashion, and assimilated to the manners of the town, was
the ardent wish of his brotherly affection, and the constant
promise of his hopes. Two years had now elapsed since
William's return to Glasgow. Although he had only completed his seventeenth year, his steadiness and watchful
attention induced Mr. Hunter to give him a small share in
the business. Ambitious of wealth and the gaudiness of
fortune, he now set himself with renovated activity to the
management of trade, depending for success entirely on
his dexterity and perseverance. Although as forgetful
of religion as ever, and as fond of hidden iniquity, his
character was fair before men; and looking as little as

possible into his own heart, and driving from his mind, by the hurry of business or the gaiety of pleasure, the unwelcome thought of his everlasting interests, he had nearly succeeded in securing to himself, as far as religion was concerned, that listlessness, that slumber of soul, which so often presses its eyelids till awakened by the voice of death, when an event occurred which gave a new colouring to his life.

Chapter VII

"Just knew, and knew no more, her Bible true,
A truth the brilliant Frenchman never knew;
And in that charter read, with sparkling eyes,
Her title to a treasure in the skies.
The light she walked by, kindled from above,
Showed her the shortest way to life and love:
She, never checked by what impedes the wise,
Believed, rushed forward, and possessed the prize."
—COWPER.

ONE afternoon, in the month of May, as William walked the street with a gay companion, he observed a boy, in the homely garb of the country, pacing slowly along the causeway, and gazing eagerly on the sign-boards. William, who was ever ready to assist and befriend countrymen, who are but too often scorned and laughed at in the town, approached him. It was the shepherd-boy of the old farmer. "What brought you hither?" said William, surprised at the unexpected encounter. There was a meaning in the eye of the simple boy which half told the tale. "Helen is ill," said he; "she was seized with a severe cold some months ago: she is now confined to her bed, and the surgeon is doubtful of her recovery." "Is she ill? Is she very ill?" exclaimed William, fearing the worst, and bringing his handkerchief over his eyes. "Let us make haste," continued he; "I will take a surgeon with me from town." But we cannot

reach home to-night," said the boy; "the sun is nearly
set." "True," said William,—"true, we must be off
early in the morning."

William now conducted the boy to his lodgings,
informed Mr. Hunter of his sister's illness, and that he
would set out at daybreak to see her, sent a message to a
skilful surgeon to have himself in readiness at the dawn
of next morning, and then retired to his room.

Again and again he questioned the boy of Helen's
trouble. "Does she sleep much? Has she much pain?
Does she think herself dying?" "She has little hope of
recovery," said the boy, almost weeping aloud, when he
saw the sorrowfulness of William's countenance, and
remembered all Helen's kindness and pious instructions
to himself. "She says she is dying, and wishes for
nothing but to see you. Oh, how she charged me to bring
you quickly!" "Has she heard anything of me lately?"
said William eagerly. The boy looked down. "She
has heard something," said William; "she has heard
that I have neglected some of her kind advices." The
boy wiped his eyes, and gave an assenting look. "Who
carried the information?" resumed William; "did it
hurt her spirits?" "A travelling merchant who knows
you," said the shepherd, "came our way the other day"
—"And what did he say of me? You must tell me
freely." "He said," replied the boy bashfully, "that he
thought you pay more attention to your worldly interests
than your religious concerns." "It is too true; it is too
true," said William, his conscience taking advantage of
the present state of his feelings. "But has the information hurt her? It would hurt her; she is all tenderness;
she loves me like an angel." "It was only yesterday
that she heard of you," answered the boy, "but she has
never rested since. The servant girl heard her name you
last night about twelve, while she waited on her by the
bedside." "She prayed for me,—I know she prayed for
me," said William, all her kindness to him coming over
his soul. "What did the girl hear? Tell me, good

boy." "She heard your sister say," replied the lad,
"Blot not out my dear brother's name, O kind Redeemer,
—blot not my dear brother's name out of the book of
life!" "When shall it be morning?" said William,
weeping abundantly; "this night shall be a long one."

The shepherd was now conducted to bed, and William
went to his own, but not to sleep. He thought not of
wealth—he planned not the trade of to-morrow,—the
gaiety of pleasure had fled from his imagination. Would
the superior skilfulness of a city surgeon not recover his
sister? Had the disease taken hold of the seats of life?
Had the report of his impiety made her worse? Did she
now struggle with disease, and pray for him again at
midnight? Would all his cherished hopes of seeing her
comfortable and accomplished with him in Glasgow be
disappointed? Would he be left without a relation in
the world? All her native loveliness and tenderness,
all her kind warnings and instructions, came over his
mind. He remembered their wanderings by the glen in
the days of childhood—he saw the innocence and fond-
ness of his sister's look—he heard the sweetness of her
voice—he remembered their visits to their mother's
grave—he remembered how often she had repeated to
him their mother's dying advice—he remembered that
they were orphans in the world. All his ambition, all his
connections in Glasgow, broke away from his mind. He
thought of Helen only—his soul was present at her bed.

The first glance of day saw William and the surgeon
mounted on horseback and on their way to the old
farmer's, taking with them whatever medicine the
shepherd's account of Helen induced them to think might
be useful. The country over which they had to travel
was rough and difficult. But the droughtiness of the
May days had dried up the morasses, and rendered all
the streamlets passable by the horses. At ten o'clock in
the forenoon they alighted before the door of Helen's
habitation. How did William's heart beat as he entered!
How would his sister be altered! The surgeon remained

in the kitchen, and William hastened into the room or *spence*, as it was called, where Helen lay. Oh! how did he gaze on her countenance! It was sweeter than ever —her eye was purer—but there was a hollowness in her face that withered every hope of recovery.

Helen raised herself on her bed, threw her arms round William's neck, who now stooped over her, and kissed him without speaking a word. "Are you ill, dear sister?" said William ;—"oh, I see you are ill." "Not ill, my dear brother," said Helen, a gleam of unspeakable kindness issuing from her eyes. "Not ill; but I have had fears for you." "Oh that the Lord would enable me never to forget your kind advices again!" said William. From his future life this aspiration, breathed in the sincerity of his heart, proved to be the prayer of faith. Then were his parent's prayers, that had lain long on the mercy-seat,—then were Helen's supplications in behalf of him answered. Helen saw the sincerity of the look, and kissed her brother again. "I have brought a surgeon with me," said William: "shall I bring him in?" "You are very kind," replied Helen, "but I fear he can do me no good."

The surgeon was now brought into the room. His skilful eye saw that his art would be unavailing. Helen was hastening to the close of a rapid decay. Every morning found her weaker than the preceding night, and every night than the morning before. Helen thanked the surgeon for his kindness in coming so far to see her, and said, "If you can do no good to me, you will comfort my brother." William turned himself away when he saw the surgeon's face, for it was a face of meaning, and wept plentifully.

As Helen complained of no pain, the surgeon could do little but instruct the servant girl how she might best prepare her cordials.

William now led the surgeon out of the room, and they retired together into a small garden behind the house. "I need not ask your opinion of my sister," said

7

William; "there is no hope. Do you think there is no
hope?" "I will not deceive you," replied the surgeon;
"but I shall wait till to-morrow, and endeavour fully to
understand her disease. I will leave you just now, and
make some inquiries of the servant girl; for your sister
is not able to talk much herself."

William was now left alone in the garden. He threw
himself down beneath an old hawthorn that spread its
blossoms over him disregarded. This was the moment
of the bitterness of his soul. A gleam from heaven, we
have said, had lighted up the darkness of his heart. He
was convinced of sin, of righteousness, and of judgment.
The holiness, and justice, and omnipotence of God, broke
in on his soul. He felt the deceitfulness of his heart, he
remembered his pious education, his narrow deliverance
from death in the snowstorm, he thought of the warning scene of the soldier, and his ingratitude for so much
kindness oppressed his spirit. The destruction, out of
whose jaws he scarcely yet felt himself, made him tremble.
But the bow appeared spanning the mount of Calvary;
he saw the everlasting hand of mercy stretched down
over the cross, he heard the everlasting voice of love
inviting him to lay hold of it, and he had now no other
stay. Oh, how did the greatness of God's mercy in Christ
then overwhelm his soul! How, in this moment, did
Helen's kind advices and instructions, and all her loveliness and tenderness, and her pale countenance, dart
across his thoughts! She had been the means, he felt,
the persevering means of saving him.

If any gentle reader should ever happen to come this
way, that has been long in raptures with the gallant hero
of romance, whose honour ever bears him out, whose
heart is always good, and whose conscience never reproaches him, he will perhaps not be likely to esteem
William much here. I cannot help it. This was a time
of superior joy in heaven; the angels had watched
seventeen years for this moment, and a fuller note now
floated from their harps through the mansions of heaven.

While William was thus engaged in the garden, a short conversation happened between his sister and the old farmer, which we shall record here, chiefly to show what sustained Helen's hopes on a bed of languishing, and allayed her fears in the prospect of death—that last enemy which we must all meet.

Immediately after William and the surgeon left Helen's apartment, the old farmer entered, anxious to know the result of the surgeon's visit. From this he could gather little hope; and although the good old man had often asked Helen how she possessed her soul, he now urged the question with more than his wonted earnestness.

"How is it with you, my daughter," said he,—"how is it with you? Do you feel your peace with God as secure as ever?"

"Yes, my dear father," replied the young saint, "I feel that God loves me with an everlasting love. You know I have had moments of fear and doubting in the expression of death; but the nearer I approach the end of my days, it hath pleased my kind Redeemer to give me brighter views of the King in His beauty, and the land that is afar off. My flesh indeed doth faint and fail; but while I am weak, then am I strong. In the Lord Jehovah is everlasting strength. This is my comfort, 'there is now no condemnation to them which are in Christ Jesus.' It is on Him alone that I rely for salvation. Every day have I sinned against Him; and all my righteousnesses are as filthy rags. I have often read in the Bible, and you have told me, that nothing but the blood of Christ could wash away our sins, but I never felt the truth of this so powerfully as now. When I look back on my life, I see little, I see nothing in my own doings, but cause of repentance; when I look to my Saviour, I see nothing but strength, and hope, and salvation. I know He hath satisfied the law, and brought in an everlasting righteousness. I know He hath unstinged death, and vanished the grave, and though I die, yet shall I live; for my Redeemer

liveth, and I shall live to praise Him with the spirits
of the just made perfect. God is all my salvation
and all my desire. I rest on His mercy in Christ.
Oh how great is His goodness! Thanks be unto Him for
the unspeakable gift which hath brought life and immortality to light. 'O death, where now is thy sting?
O grave, where is thy victory? Thanks be unto God
who giveth me the victory through Jesus Christ my
Lord!'"

"Thanks be unto God," exclaimed the old man, "that
He hath given you these hopes of eternal life. I came
to comfort you, but you comfort me. Your comfort is
in God, your hope in the Holy One of Israel. Oh how
sweet this hope on the bed of death! How sweet to you,
my daughter, and how solacing to me and all your
friends!"

William having breathed a prayer of gratitude, and of
fervent supplication for his sister, endeavoured to com-
pose his spirits, and returned to Helen's room. The old
farmer sat by her bedside. The lamb (for it was still
called the lamb, although now three years old) stood
and looked up in her face. "This is my lamb," said
Helen, observing William rather surprised at its presence;
"you recollect of it going with us to our mother's grave;
it takes every opportunity of coming into the room.
Poor thing! it will attend me to the last. Take good
care of it," continued she, addressing the old man,
"take good care of it when I am gone, it is an innocent
little thing."

The old farmer now withdrew, and Helen and her
brother were left together. William related his thoughts
in the garden. While he spake, every look of Helen was
a gleam from heaven—every sigh the essence of prayer.
"You have been the means of saving me," said William,
"Oh how good you have been!" Helen clasped his neck,
kissed him again and again with the warmth of intensest
love, her eye glanced a look of perfect enjoyment, and
she exclaimed, "I am happy now, O kind Redeemer! I

HELEN CLASPED HIS NECK.—*See page* 100.

come to Thee. My dear brother will soon be with me."
It was too much for Helen. Her hands loosed from
William's neck, the quivering hectic forsook her cheek,
she gave a gentle sigh on her brother's bosom, it was the
last of nature, the wheel stood still at the cistern, and her
soul ascended up into heaven.

I shall leave the scene of this evening to the kind
reader. The old farmer, the shepherd boy, the servant
girl, the surgeon, wept with William ; and the lamb
looked up wistfully in their faces. The good old man at
length opened the Bible ; and they sang together these
verses from the 103rd Psalm—

"Such pity as a father hath
    Unto his children dear,
Like pity shows the Lord to such
    As worship Him in fear.

" For He remembers we are dust,
    And He our frame well knows,
Frail man, his days are like the grass
    As flower in field he grows ;

" For over it the wind doth pass,
    And it away is gone
And of the place where once it was
    It shall no more be known.

" But unto them that do Him fear
    God's mercy never ends ;
And to their children's children still
    His righteousness extends."

The second morning after Helen's death saw her
funeral moving slowly over the heath. The day was
bright and lovely, but no one heeded its looks. The
lamb followed after the mournful procession. "Shall I
turn it back ? " said the shepherd boy to the old farmer.
" No, poor thing," answered George, " it loved Helen,
and it will see her laid in her grave." About five miles
distant was the village churchyard. The sexton waited
at the gate, and conducted them to the newly-opened

grave, the pall was removed, William let down his
sister's head, the cold clay fell from the sexton's shovel
sadly on the coffin, the shepherd boy wept aloud, a tear
ran down the wrinkled cheek of the old farmer, the
lamb bleated mournfully by his side, William heard the
clods of dust fall on the coffin, he looked into the grave,
turned away and wiped his eyes ; again the clay fell, he
looked back into the tomb, and wept bitterly.—" I shall
go to her, but she shall not return unto me !" was the
sigh of his heart.

The green turf was now laid on the silent house of
rest, over which William afterwards caused a modest
stone to be placed, on which was engraved his sister's
name, with these words of our Saviour below it : "WEEP
NOT FOR ME, BUT WEEP FOR YOURSELVES."

Farewell, Helen ! ' Perhaps thou dost not hear me ;
but I shall pronounce thy funeral service. Thou hast done
well. Thou didst look with delight and gratitude on the
scenery of creation. Thou rejoiced with that which
rejoiced, and wept with that which wept. Thy face was
the home of the sober smile and the cheerfulness of
content. This was well. But it was merely like the
sentimentalist and the philosopher, to possess a natural
charity, and cherish an affection for the lower works of
the Creator. But thou hast done more. It was thy
belief in Jesus Christ, as the Author and Finisher of thy
Faith, which gave all thy enjoyments a supernal relish.
Thou hadst no hope in thy own works- in the tenderness
of thy heart, or in the general mercy of the Creator. It
was the mercy of God in Christ, reconciling the world
unto Himself, on which rested all thy faith of eternal
life. It was the Spirit of God to which thou trusted for
progress in holiness and complete sanctification. It was
this love of God dwelling in thy heart, this undivided
trust in the atonement, that excited all thy praise, and
sustained, and comforted, and secured thee in the hour
of dissolution. Nor did this love of God—this trust in
the Saviour—this looking for the hallowing influences of

the Spirit, relax thy own endeavours of well-doing. These were wings to thy feet, and a light in thy path of duty. Thou didst remember thy mother's advice—thy Bible was open in thy hand. Thy heart forgave the soldier—thy faithfulness and gratitude would not discover thy old friend to his enemies. Thou wast the means of persuading one soul at least into the straight path. Thy love to thy brother was great; he will talk of it to thy father and mother in the New Jerusalem. Thou wast not much spoken of on earth. Thy tear of sympathy, thy humility and fervour of devotion, were noticed little by the world. This is thy praise: Thou wast well known in heaven. Thy name was familiar among those who stand, with white palms in their hands, before the eternal throne. God loved thee, and took thee to dwell with Him for ever. Farewell!

Young reader, the same dwelling-place is open for thee. If thou hast not secured the entrance, I counsel thee to make no delay, for thou knowest not *what* an hour may bring forth.

Chapter VIII

"Turned from the reed, that breaking disappoints
The fool that takes it for the oak; and leaning
On the arm, by which suspended worlds hang
Innumerous; and eye upturn'd to where
The sun ne'er sets, where flows the font of life,
Beneath the throne of God, unshaken he stood
By all that earth could do."

PERHAPS the reader wishes to know something of the future fortunes of those few friends Helen left behind her. We shall satisfy him in a very few words.

In his ninety-fifth year, the old farmer was peacefully gathered to his fathers. The shepherd boy, who was the old farmer's nephew, and to whom he left the most

of his substance, succeeded him in the farm, and married
the servant girl who attended Helen in her last moments.
And often did they tell their children, as they sat by the
blazing hearth, in the winter evenings, the simple story
that I have now related.

When William returned to Glasgow, his companions
were surprised at the change which they noticed in his
manners and conversation ; and we think it will not be
unuseful to state briefly, both what means they employed
to draw him back to his former habits, and how he set
himself to resist the arguments and temptations by
which he was assailed.

His wit and talents had rendered his company peculiarly acceptable to his irreligious companions. They
had imitated and caressed him, and showed him all those
flattering marks of distinction of which young minds
are peculiarly fond. They regretted the change which
they remarked in his habits, and tried every means to
allure him into his former ways. They pressed him, by
invitation after invitation, to join in their parties of
unhallowed pleasure—they represented to him the un-
fashionableness and joylessness of a retired and religious
life—they asked him if he meant to spend that part of
his days, which nature had evidently designed for pleasure, in hearing sermons, and reading dull books of
piety — they inquired what had become of his ambition, and his love of gaiety and splendour—and they
wondered what had so blinded his reason, as to make
him refrain from those pleasures which fitted his age,
and to practise those gloomy duties which were despised
by all but the weak and visionary, and which he himself
had formerly treated with ridicule and contempt. They
talked of the religious companions, with whom they now
saw him associating, as men of weak and superstitious
minds, and unfit for the company of one of his talents.
It was unmanly in him, they said, to play the hypocrite ;
for they were sure that one of his understanding could
never believe in those absurdities which bigots call re-

ligion. Not satisfied with their own arts of persuasion, they put into his hands books which represented the Bible as full of inconsistencies, and Christianity as an irrational superstition, unbecoming men of enlightened minds ; and the authors of these books they extolled as men of great intellectual reach, who had risen far above the common prejudices of mankind, and nobly shown that those who follow reason and nature live the most happy, and best fulfil the end of their being.

William had now to deny himself all the praise and admiration of his companions ; he had now to resist all their enticements and arguments, and he had now to abide their taunting and ridicule. This was no easy task. To renounce the society and friendship of those by whom he had been treated with such flattering marks of distinction, to become the butt of their profane wit, and to be regarded by them as fallen into a weak and visionary man, whose reason had sustained a shock —this was a hard trial. Nor was it easy to resist these weapons of false dispute, which in fact he himself had taught many of them to wield. But he had an enemy within still more powerful than these — a dreadful and corrupt heart. The sinful habits which he had acquired were strong, and not easily broken away from. While his companions plied him with every sort of persuasion, the vicious inclinations which he had formerly indulged gave greedy ear to any wicked suggestion, and urged him to those pleasures which he had once relished so much.

But William had now seen the exceeding sinfulness of sin, and was determined, through the grace of God, to abstain from all appearance of evil. He did not now, as he had formerly done, think of resisting the enemies of his soul by his own strength. He had tried this when he first came to town, and he saw how he had failed. The weakness of his own resolutions, he had now discovered, was no match for the power of an alluring world, and the deceit of a wicked heart. But if William had thus learned to distrust himself, he had learned also, that in the Lord Jehovah is everlasting strength ; and he went humbly and fervently to the throne of His grace, asking the guidance of that Divine Spirit which renews and invigorates the pious energies of the soul, and pours the lights of heaven on the eyes of the understanding. He had been convinced that the wrath of God shall at last lawfully fall on the finally impenitent. He knew that none of his wicked friends could stand by him in death, and shield him from the fear of its terrors. And above all, his soul had now tasted that God is gracious. His lips had now got a taste of the sweetness of immortality, his eye had seen the purity of heaven, and his heart felt the joy of peace with God, and he had thus learned rightly to estimate the value of his own soul. The unspeakable love of God, which he now saw manifested in the redemption of man by his Son, filled his heart with love and gratitude, and constrained him to run in the way of His commandments. His soul recoiled at the thought of dishonouring that Redeemer, who, he was now convinced, had died to save him from utter ruin. With the love of God thus warming his heart, with the light of His wisdom illuminating his understanding, and with the power of His grace exerted on his will, he now felt the meaning of that saying " When I am weak, then I am strong." He was now indeed to lose the praise of men, but he felt he had got in exchange for it the praise of God. He had withdrawn his dependence from human strength, which is weakness ; lost the honour of wicked men, which is disgrace ; given up those pleasures which never satisfy, and which lead to ruin ; and abandoned those gaudy hopes, whose promises are false, for the equipment of Almighty power, the approbation of the God of truth, those enjoyments which are pure and never end ; and those sure expectations, which, because they are founded on the promises of God, shall be all fulfilled.

It was thus that William was now prepared for entering on the Christian warfare. And he found that he was complete in God. Knowing that to shun evil company is the best way of escaping the influence and contagion of their manners, he avoided, as much as his necessary business would permit, the society of his former irreligious companions; and when he was compelled to associate with them, he maintained a serious deportment amidst the unhallowed sportings of their profanity. He bore the shafts of their wit with patience, and when he was pressed by their reasonings, he was not averse sometimes to give them a reason of the hope that was within him. He asked them to look attentively into their own hearts, and they would most certainly find that their conduct, which they foolishly believed to be sanctioned by reason, was in reality dictated only by wicked passions. He urged them to read the Bible with humility and attention, and to compare their own hearts with it, and they would be convinced that it was indeed a revelation from God. And further, he silenced their reproaches by calling them to remember their own professions of liberality of opinion. If they ridiculed him for maintaining his sentiments, if they treated him as a hypocrite or a visionary, they had all that bigotry, and all those pre-judices, which they so freely ascribed to him. By such conversation as this he gained some; others forsook his company; and as he advanced in life, he attained that high and enviable religious character which all the good love and revere, which men in general respect, and which the most abandoned fear rather than hate. With such happy results were the early instruc-tions of an affectionate mother, and the kind and watchful care of a tender-hearted and pious sister, rewarded. "Verily the righteous shall not labour in vain."

In business, William was prosperous, shedding, in all his intercourse with the world, the holy influence of a pious example around him. And during the whole of his life he was peculiarly careful of the morals of young men from the country, whom Providence threw in his way. He never married. Every summer, as long as he lived, he visited the graves of his mother and sister—stayed a week or two with the shepherd boy, now become farmer—and it was from this place that he was at last carried to his grave, like a shock of corn fully ripe.

Ralph Gemmell

Ralph Gemmell

Chapter I

"Trust in the Lord with all thine heart, and lean not to thine own understanding. In all thy ways acknowledge Him, and He shall direct thy steps."—SOLOMON.

THERE is no truth in the Bible better confirmed, or more fully illustrated by the experience of the saints whose lives it records, or by the plain declarations of the Holy Spirit, than that God will never leave nor forsake those who put their trust in Him. Yet there is no truth in that sacred book which the young Christian is oftener tempted to doubt. The veteran soldier of Jesus Christ, who had fought long under the banners of the Most High, sees in his own history so many dangers escaped, so many temptations resisted, so many trials endured, and so many battles with the devil, the world, and the flesh, fought and won, that he feels little dismay in the most trying and threatening circumstances. Although, like the children of Jacob of old, the sea be before him, and pathless mountains on the right hand and on the left, and the shout of his enemy behind him, he can exclaim, in the language of faith, "Verily, the Lord sendeth none a warfare on his own charges. He hath delivered me out of six troubles, and in seven He will not forsake me." But when the young Christian is left to experience poverty, and contempt, and shame : when he is tried by temptations, which he feels too persuasive ; and when he meets with enemies too formidable for his single arm ; little acquainted with the

8

experience of others, and little assisted by his own; he is ready to take up the unbelieving complaint, "Hath God forgotten to be gracious? Is His mercy clean gone for ever? Doth His promise fail for evermore?"

It is a pity, young reader, that a child of grace should ever thus complain, and charge God foolishly. And that you may be cautioned against thus dishonouring the veracity of the God of truth, I request your attention to the following story :—

Ralph Gemmell, the subject of the following narrative, was born in the year of our Lord 1669, a period when persecution for religious opinions raged in our country. His father, George Gemmell, possessed, from a long line of ancestors, the small but fertile estate of Craigfoot, situated on the banks of the Irvine, near to where that river pours itself into the Atlantic. From time immemorial, the younger sons of this family had generally devoted their lives to the service of their sovereign, while the eldest son farmed the estate, related the gallant actions of his kinsmen, and boasted the steady loyalty of his house to the reigning prince. And to Craigfoot, in the evening of their lives, had their warlike relations often returned, bringing with them many a story of deeds done in the field of battle, of dangers braved, and honours received. From generation to generation, the castle of Craigfoot had thus been like a garrison of disabled soldiers, where the ever loyal toast, the fearless attack, the hair-breadth escape, the profane jest, the unchaste song, and the daring oath, make their constant rounds. Within its walls was heard neither the humble voice of prayer nor the sweet melody of sacred praise.

But of all the masters of this house, none ever proved himself so careless of religion, or so blindly devoted to his prince, as the father of Ralph. In those troublous and cruel times, when the Church of our land was driven to the wilderness, and when its scattered members hung

their harps on the willows of Scotland's wildest streams,
zealously did he embrace every measure of Lauderdale's
wicked administration to overthrow and destroy the
Presbyterians. Every Sabbath he attended the curate's
church, not to worship God, but to evince his loyal
attachment to the Crown, and his hearty approbation
of all the iniquitous and tyrannical measures its ministers
were then carrying on in Scotland. Sharpe himself was
not more eager to detect and suppress conventicles than
George Gemmell. And in his rancour against the persecuted party, he had been often heard to say, that he
would rather see the waters of the ocean come up over
his lands than one of those fanatic rebels (for so the
Covenanters were called) set a foot on it.

Such was the character of Ralph's father. But his
mother, Isabella Mitchell, of a respectable family of
that name in Ayrshire, was of a very different temper.
She had read her Bible with attention and humility,
before the commencement of the persecution under
which the Church was then suffering ; she had listened
to the pulpit ministrations of a faithful servant of God ;
and she had held communion with her heavenly Father,
through the peace-making blood of His Son. She sighed
for the desolation of Zion, and would willingly have
gone to the mountains in search of that heavenly manna
which no longer dropped from the lips of those who
ministered in the pulpits ; but she feared her husband,
with whom she had been unequally yoked, and chose
rather to weep and pray in secret, than provoke his
anger and resentment by an open avowal of attachment to the interests of the Covenanters. Indeed,
although she had often violated her own conscience to
please him, and thus sinfully regarded him more than
her Maker, her serious cast of mind had frequently been
the subject of his ridicule ; and her sympathy with the
suffering Church, which she could not conceal, had many
a time provoked his anger, and drawn upon her his
severe reproach. But although Mrs. Gemmell had thus

yielded too much for the sake of domestic peace, she
had seen, as we have intimated, the vanity of time and
its honours, the importance of eternity and its glories ;
and she wished to impress on the minds of her children,
Ralph and Edward, the importance of religious duty.
Ralph, the elder of the two, listened to her instructions
with attention, and seemed peculiarly interested when
she told him of the nature of sin and its punishment,—
of the love and mercy of God in Christ Jesus, and of
faith and its everlasting reward. But Edward was
happier when mounted on his little pony and riding
by his father's side, along with the soldiers, in quest
of our persecuted ancestors, whose torture and martyr-
dom he was taught to deride. Nothing could prevail
on Ralph, however, even at the early age at which we
are speaking of him, to mock at the sufferings of his
fellow - creatures ; and often when he saw men and
women tortured by the merciless servants of despotism,
he incurred his father's displeasure by entreating him
to interfere and relieve them.

"He will be like his mother," his father would say,
"ever weeping for those seditious wretches ; but Edward
is a true scion of the old stock of Craigfoot ; I see loyalty
and soldier-like bravery in his face."

Their tutor, a young man recommended to Mr.
Gemmell by the curate of the parish, was entirely
devoted to the wicked government, as on his interest
with men in power rested all his hopes of preferment.
What Mr. Gemmell approved, therefore, he approved ;
what the former condemned, so did the latter ; what
the one practised, the other imitated. From a man
whose creed was ever ready thus to be adjusted to the
suggestions of worldly interest, and whose practice
was ever formed to the humour of those on whom he
depended, Ralph and Edward could imbibe little that
was valuable, either of morality or of religion. Although
Ralph was far superior to his brother, both in the
strength of his understanding and in the kinder feelings

RALPH LISTENED TO HER INSTRUCTIONS WITH ATTENTION.
—*See page* 116.

of his heart, Edward, because he was the father's favourite, was represented by the tutor as possessing a vigorous understanding, a sound and clear judgment, and a ready and tenacious memory; while it was hinted, that, indeed, Ralph might have sometimes more perseverance at his tasks, and more gentleness in his manners, but that his mental endowments were rather inferior, and seemed capable of little reach of improvement. Neglected by his father, Ralph was despised by the tutor and his brother. When Edward was invited forth to the sports of the field, or to attend the savage military in search of conventicles, he was left at home to pass the day with his mother and the servants. Happy it was for him that he was thus despised and left at home; it was then that his mother had an opportunity of freely setting before him the importance of a religious life, and it was then that first dawned on his soul the hopes and the glories of immortality.

"Dear Ralph," said his mother to him, one day when they were left alone, "you are now arrived at your thirteenth year. I have already often endeavoured to explain to you the Christian religion. Do you understand it? have you felt its influence on your heart? are you cheered by its hopes? do you thirst after its glorious rewards? At all times, my son, the Christian has need to be well acquainted with the revealed truths on which he founds his hopes for eternity. At all times he has need to have the proofs of the divine origin of his religion so felt on his heart, as to enable him to gainsay the adversary, and hold fast the profession of his faith without wavering. But in these troublous and trying days, when the followers of the Lamb are hunted like the wild beasts of the field, persecuted, and everywhere spoken against, you have tenfold more need to acquaint yourself with religion, with its doctrines, its comforts, its hopes, and its rewards. Dear Ralph, have you considered these things?"

"I have often thought of them, dear mother," answerd Ralph, "but I like to hear you speak of them. I am never happier than when you speak to me about religion."

"And I am never happier," replied his mother, "than when I see you attentive to my instructions, and storing your mind with those truths which the Bible reveals. Listen, then, my son; and may the Spirit of grace and of wisdom be present in our hearts while I speak.

"We learn, dear Ralph, from the works of nature, that there is a God of infinite power, wisdom, and goodness; but we cannot discern, by all that is around us, our relation to Him. Our own hearts, as well as the unjust actions we commit every day, inform us that we are sinners, and that we have need of a Saviour. But of this Saviour the works of nature give us no intimation. It is the Bible that reveals God to man, as a God of mercy, willing to be reconciled to us through His own Son. It is the Bible that teaches us our duty to our God and to our fellow-creatures—what we ought to do in time, and what we ought to expect in eternity. There we learn that God is not only all-powerful and all-wise, but also infinite, holy, and just; hating all manner of sin, and bound, by His own word, to punish every transgression of His holy law. There we learn, too, that we are great sinners, have broken His law and have exposed ourselves to everlasting punishment; that we are dead in trespasses and sins, totally unable either to keep His law or to ransom ourselves from its curse. But the Bible does not, you know, leave us in this hopeless state. It tells us, that our God is merciful; that He so loved the world as to send Jesus Christ, His well-beloved Son, into it, to fulfil the law for us, to suffer and die for us. Jesus, you know, had no sin of His own: He was holy, harmless, undefiled, and separate from sinners. But He died for our sins, and rose again, and ascended up into heaven to plead for us in the presence of His Father—to plead, that through His merits our sins may be forgiven, and that we may be received, in due time, into those mansions of happiness which He is preparing for us.

"Do you, then, dear Ralph, know and feel yourself to be a sinner, guilty in the sight of God's law, and utterly undone for ever, unless Jesus Christ clothe you in His righteousness, and plead with His Father that your sins may be forgiven through His own blood? Do you believe on this Saviour? Do you think He is able and willing to save you? Have you placed all your hope for time and eternity on Him alone? Alas! kind as our Saviour is, able and willing as He is to save to the uttermost all who believe on Him, many will not listen to the invitations of His mercy, nor accept of His offered pardon! So much hath sin darkened the human mind to its own best interests, that none can believe on Him until the understanding is enlightened by the Spirit of God, and the heart made willing in the day of His power. Pray, then, my son, pray that this Holy Spirit may come into your heart, and abide in it for ever. This is the promise of God to all His children: 'Ask, and it shall be given you; seek, and ye shall find; knock, and all the treasures of free grace shall be opened up to you.' Place at all times your faith and your hope on the Saviour, this Rock of Ages, and you have no need to fear the troubles of life. These troubles you must not expect to escape. It is through many tribulations that the Christian is taken to heaven. It is through fire and water that he is brought into the wealthy place. But your Saviour will be present with you in every trial; and He will never suffer you to be overcome. In the darkest night of trouble and affliction, your hopes shall have rest in heaven; and in your bosom shall dwell that peace which passeth understanding. In death, too, He shall be your friend and deliverer; and after death He shall receive you into that happy place, where you shall be for ever rewarded with the smiles of His countenance."

"I wish to be religious," said Ralph; "but when

Edward laughs at my seriousness, and my father encourages him to do it, I am ashamed, and sometimes
determine to be like them."

"Your situation, my dear," continued his mother,
"is certainly difficult. It is hard to resist the bad
example, and bear the mockery of those who are ever
about you. But, my son, remember this; put your
trust in God, and He will never leave nor forsake you.
He will make you strong to resist all evil, and to set at
nought all the revilings of the wicked. Persevere in
religion, for it is happiness. Edward heeds none of my
advice, and his father commends him for his foolishness,
and teaches him to despise religious instruction. I fear
he will go far astray; but I hope that you, through the
grace of God, will resist bad example, and, by persevering in the service of your God, secure not only your own
peace and happiness, but perhaps yet be the means of
saving your brother."

Young reader, I repeat to you what this excellent lady
said to her son : Persevere in religion, for it is happiness.
Is not religion just a trusting in God who cannot lie, a
renouncing of the vain speculations and opinions and
surmises of erring men, and a placing of our faith on
the words, promises, and appointments of an all-wise
and all-ordering God? Is it not just a withdrawing of
our confidence from the frailty and weakness of human
power, and a leaning on the Lord Jehovah, in whom is
everlasting strength? Is it not just a coming forth from
a land of darkness, ignorance, and slavery, and an entering into the fair regions of light, knowledge, and liberty?
What is it but a leaving of those pleasures which debase
and cannot satisfy, of those hopes which promise but to
deceive, and of those schemings and reasonings which
perplex but give no certainty ; and a taking of ourselves
up with those enjoyments which dignify and exalt us,
while they never satiate—with those hopes which promise
all that is really valuable, and give us all they promise
—with those truths which are sanctioned by God, and

which, therefore, are immutable—and with those plans
which took their origin in eternal wisdom, and which,
therefore, can never miscarry? Religion is a coming
forth from all that is impure and abominable in the
world, from the prison of guilt and anxiety and hopelessness, and forming an alliance with all that is pure,
and holy, and happy. It is a putting away from us that
which is empty and fleeting and perishing, and a laying
fast hold of that which is substantial, satisfying, and
eternal. It is an escape from the terrors of death, and
the wrath of the Great Judge of all, into the bosom of
our God—into the dwellings of peace, and love, and
immortality. This is religion. These are the trust and
the doings, the hopes and rewards, of the Christian.

Sometimes exposed to the taunts of his relations, and
the unholy influence of the unrestrained dissipation and
hardened wickedness of the times, but oftener employed
in listening to his mother's instructions, in reading his
Bible, or in storing his mind from other books of useful
knowledge, Ralph reached his fifteenth year. About
this time he lost his mother. A lingering illness, occasioned by her grief for the distressed state of the
persecuted Church, and by the hard-hearted severity and
wickedness of her husband, deprived him of that loving
parent and kind monitor. Her dying advice to Ralph
was short and simple—

"I have often violated my conscience, dear Ralph,"
said she, as he stood by her bedside only a few hours
before her death,—"I have often violated my conscience
for the sake of domestic peace. I should have been
more resolute and more public in serving my God and
Redeemer. But I know He will be merciful to my
unrighteousness ; and my sins and iniquities He will
remember no more. I shall see Him, because He loved
me. I shall enter into His presence, because Christ
died for me. But I wish not you to follow that part of
my example which I now lament. You will have the
same difficulties to encounter, the same reproach to

bear ; and if you take a more decided part than I have
done in the interests of the suffering Church, and a more
open and avowed path in the service of God, which I
earnestly wish you may, you will have more trials to
endure, and more obloquy to withstand. But, dear
Ralph, that which the word of God and your own conscience testify to be your duty, choose and do. Regard
not the consequences—the reproach of relations, the
malignity of enemies, the sneers of careless dissipation :
these, under the guidance of a kind Providence, will
work together for your good. Remember what the
Bible says, and what I have often repeated to you : Put
your trust in God, and He will never leave nor forsake
you. Protected by His power, you shall be safe, for it
is almighty ; led by His wisdom, you shall not go astray,
for it never errs ; hoping in His Son, you shall not be
deceived, for He shall appear at last in His Father's
presence, bringing with Him all who have put their
trust in Him. And while you walk thus in the strength
of your God, ever seek to be useful to your fellow-
creatures ; and oh, seek especially the spiritual welfare
of your father and brother. I have often prayed for
them. It hath not yet pleased God to answer my
prayers ; but you may live to see them answered, and
your own piety rewarded, by the happy conversion of
your father and brother. Now, my son, remember, when
I am gone, that this was the soundest advice and the
sweetest comfort that your dying mother could give
you: ' Put your trust in God, and He will never leave
nor forsake you.' "

Chapter II

" My son, if sinners entice thee, consent thou not ; walk not thou
in the way with them ; refrain thy foot from their path, that thou
mayest walk in the way of good men, and keep the path of the
righteous."—Solomon.

RALPH, after the death of his mother, experienced little

comfort in his father's house.   Edward, as we have observed, was taught to ridicule his seriousness ; his father was daily telling him that he would be a disgrace to his name ; and the servants, following the example of their master, regarded him as a kind of outcast, and took every opportunity to insult and deride him.

From the curate, whom he still attended on Sabbath, he could gather little either to enlighten his mind or strengthen his piety.   His sermons chiefly inculcated submission to the unjust measures of government, activity in suppressing those whose opinions differed from that of the then existing ecclesiastical establishment, and zeal in supporting the heirarchy to which he belonged.   These were the chief doctrines which Ralph heard at church, and he was not satisfied.   He wished to hear more of Christ, the great Head of the Church ; more of belief in Him who is the way, the truth, and the life ; and more of holiness, without which none can see God.   He had diligently contemplated the features of the times ; he had examined the creed, opinions, and life of the persecuted party ; he had likewise examined the principles, as well as the conduct, of those who persecuted them ; and, young as he was, he could easily see that the former were suffering for holding opinions founded on the word of God, and sanctioned by their own consciences, for their highest privileges as men and their dearest rights as Christians ; and the latter oppressing, torturing, and murdering, for nonsubmission to institutions which their own selfishness had suggested, and which they were ever ready to change for any other that might promise more gain to their avarice or more indulgence to their vicious dispositions.

Impressed by these opinions, it was little wonder that Ralph, alive as he was to the dictates of conscience and the calls of religion, had a strong inclination to join the Covenanters.   But in doing this, he must submit to persecution and reproach, forsake his father's house, lay down all hopes of honour and preferment, abide the contempt and the hate of his nearest kinsmen, and experience the rigorous discipline of cold, and hunger, and cheerless wandering. Surely, young reader, this was no very agreeable reflection. It was enough to make a more experienced Christian than Ralph halt between two opinions.

More than three months after his mother's death he passed in this uneasy state of mind ; now resolving to leave all and follow Christ, now looking forward to the dreariness of a life of suffering, and again, back on that old paternal castle and those fertile fields which might one day be all his own. And verily, were it in man that walketh to direct his steps—were it not God that chooseth his way, it is very probable that Ralph would have turned away from the sufferings he saw before him, and taken up with the ease, and the plenty, and the honour which the world promised him. But God knoweth His own, and it is as certain that He will provide the means of enlightening them in the knowledge of Himself, and of confirming them in His service, as that He will for ever protect and uphold them.

One Sabbath, after returning home as usual from the unprofitable discourse of the curate, Ralph went out at the evening-tide to meditate. It was in the end of autumn. And as he walked along the banks of the Irvine towards the sea, the wild flower, with scarcely its withered stalk remaining, which he had seen in the early year painted with all the colours of beauty—the shrub naked and blasted, which was lately vested in a thick foliage of healthy green—the aged leaf, which fell rustling from its fellows—the stream, which was ever running on to be lost in the ocean—and the light, which faded dimly away on the indistinct summits of Arran ; all had a tendency to draw him into serious musing, and especially to remind him of the short duration and sure decay of all earthly things.

"As for man," said he to himself, "his days are as grass ; as a flower of the field, so he flourisheth ; for the

wind passeth over it and it is gone ; and the place thereof shall know it no more. As the waters of this river run
for a little, and then fall into the ocean, so shall time be
with me ; so suddenly shall I pass into eternity. As the
light dieth away on yonder mountains, so speedily shall
the sun of my days set for ever. What, then, should I
do ? Should I fear the reproach and persecution of man,
which cannot long annoy me ? Should I take the honours
and the pleasures which he can give me, which, short as
life is, may wither and die long before me, and will, at any
rate, slip from my grasp when I go down into the other
grave ? or should I serve my God, whose almighty power
can protect me from every thing that would really hurt
me in time, and whose lovingkindness and tender mercy
will provide for me after death an inheritance incor-
ruptible, undefiled, and that fadeth not away ? Surely
the wisdom of man is foolishness. Why should I listen
to it ? Oh that God would direct my steps, and enable me
to put my trust in Him alone ! "

Thus did the merciful Creator make the contemplation
of His works subservient to strengthen the piety of the
young Christian. Musing on such thoughts as these,
Ralph wandered on to the seashore. Agreeably to those
sudden changes which happen so often in our climate
towards the end of autumn, night, which at its coming
on had been calm and serene, was now wrapt in the
clouds of his thick darkness—the winds came in the
swiftness of their fury—the ocean lifted up his voice, and
roared in the pride of his strength—and athwart the
gloom at intervals gleamed the lightnings of God,
awfully displaying the features of the storm. As it did
not yet rain, however, Ralph walked on. The awful
majesty of nature had something in it which pleased him,
and sanctioned the reflections he had just made—something which reminded him of the littleness of man and
the greatness of the Creator. " How dreadful," thought
he, " to have that God our enemy, who walketh on the
wings of the wind, and biddeth the storm do His pleasure !

who setteth His foot on the sea, and holdeth the waters in the hollow of His hands, who sendeth the lightning, and they say unto Him, Here we are!"

Thus contemplating, he was walking along the coast, when his ear was attracted by the following words:

"How long, O Lord, holy and true, dost Thou not avenge the blood of thy servants! Thy holy city is a wilderness: Zion is a wilderness; Jerusalem a desolation. Be not wroth very sore, neither remember iniquity for ever. Behold, we beseech Thee; we are Thy people. Oh, visit Zion in Thy mercy! Let not the weapon that is formed against her prosper; and the tongue that is raised against her in judgment do Thou condemn. We know that Thy Church is graven on the palms of Thy hands, and Thou wilt bring her out of the deep waters. But, gracious Father! give us, poor helpless sinners, patience and resignation to wait till Thy time come. Give us that abiding faith in our Saviour, and that inextinguishable love, which, in all our trials, will make us more than conquerors. Yea, our eyes are unto Thee, O God, the Lord; in Thee is our trust: leave not our souls destitute: keep us from the snares which are laid for us, and the gins of the workers of iniquity."

After these breathings of holy fervour had ascended up into the throne of God, Ralph heard proceeding from the same place the sweet melody of praise; and now it was lost in the loud voice of the storm, and again, in the intervals of partial calm, it came forth on the ear like the music of heaven. Ralph walked up to the place whence the sounds proceeded; and among the rugged cliffs, by the very side of the sea, did he find ten or twelve of those Christian heroes whom persecution had compelled to choose that secluded place, and that hour, to them of favourable darkness, to hear the word of life, and adore and praise the God and Redeemer of mankind.

At Ralph's approach, they seemed somewhat alarmed, for they knew well, though in so retired a place and under the wing of night, they were not safe from the

vigilant persecution of their enemies. They feared,
therefore, that Ralph might be a guide to a party of
dragoons. But as some of those present had been but
lately tenants of his father, he was soon recognised.
They had heard it reported that he favoured their party,
and that he had for several years suffered little less from
his wicked relations at home than they had endured in
their flights and wanderings. He was, therefore, gladly
received amongst them. The reverend old minister,
part of whose prayer he had just heard, and who had
once been his mother's spiritual guide and dear friend,
was especially interested at his appearance. Ever
zealous in his Master's work, and remembering how
desirous Mrs. Gemmell had been that her sons might be
true fearers of God, he invited Ralph to sit down by his
side on the shelvy rock, and entered into conversation
with him. With fatherly tenderness the venerable
pastor encouraged the youth to describe the circumstances in which he was placed, and lay open the state
of his mind. This was the first time that Ralph had had
an opportunity of conversing with a faithful servant of
the Most High. And truly his heart burned within him,
as the good old man thus concluded a long and tender
advice to him.

"Now, my son," for so tenderly did he address him,—
"now I know the difficulty of your circumstances. I
know how hard it is to leave father, and brother, and
houses, and lands, and goods, and plenty, and honour ;
and to be hated of those of whose love you are most desirous, and to be despised of those in whose eyes you most
wish to appear honourable. We can promise you little
but trial and suffering. We have been driven from our
houses and possessions. Our families are left to wander
and weep in poverty, exposed to contempt, and subjected
to the insults of a brutal soldiery. Torture, imprisonment, and banishment are prepared for us. A price is
set on our heads, and our lives are every day sought
for. We are cut off from all the comforts of life, and

are exposed to almost all the ills which this world can muster up against the people of God. Now, my son, if you will take up your cross and follow Christ, you must be prepared to meet similar trials. But remember that you have His promise, that if you forsake father and mother, and houses and lands, for His sake, He will give you an hundredfold of spiritual blessings in this world, and eternal life in that which is to come. Remember what Christ has suffered for you. All that the wickedness of men could invent, and all that the offended justice of His Father required, He endured for you;—so ardent was His love for you; so inexhaustible His mercy!

"If you are resolved to put your trust in Christ, and follow Him through good and through bad report, although we can promise you none of this world's comforts or honours, we can promise you, that, although you be perplexed, you shall never be in despair; although you are persecuted, you shall never be forsaken; although you are cast down, you shall never be destroyed.

"Are you afraid to put your whole trust in God? Look around you and see. Is there anything on earth or in hell that can snatch you out of the hand of His omnipotence? Is there any power that can effectually hurt you, if ye abide under the shadow of the Almighty? He walketh on the sea, and His path is in the great waters; and He can say to the raging of that vast ocean, Peace, be still! He walketh on the wings of the winds, and He can bid them, when He will, away to their place. He sitteth on the circuit of the earth, and the inhabitants thereof are as grasshoppers. These lightnings which you see gleaming through the darkness of the night, go abroad at His word, and would, if He commanded, in the twinkling of an eye, lay the boasting of human strength and the pride of human greatness in a heap of burning desolation. Are you afraid to put your trust in this God? Are you afraid to meet the fury of man's battle, if He be on your side? Only put your trust in Him, and you are safe. His love and His mercy will never forsake you. Love your Saviour and serve Him, and you may say, in the darkest night of human calamity, I will both lay me down in peace, and sleep; for Thou, O Lord, only makest me dwell in safety."

As the minister concluded these instructions, the gloom began to disperse, and the moon and stars, looking through the clouds, cast their silvery light on the majestic scenery around. Then did Ralph observe the countenances of those about him. Twenty years had the old pastor wandered among the mountains of Scotland, subjected to every hardship, and separated from every earthly comfort. Often had he made the narrowest escapes from his persecutors; and often, exposed as he was this night to the fierceness of the storm, had he met, in the wildest glens and most forlorn caves of our country, with the few who had forsaken all to follow Christ, to instruct, comfort, and animate them; and yet, when Ralph looked on his face, he could see nothing in it but the composure of peace and the sweetness of contentment. The few that were around him, although some of them bore the marks of suffering, their clothes being worn to tatters and their bodies emaciated by fatigue, had all of them in their countenances the meekness of resignation and the fortitude of Christian faith;—so powerful is the grace of God—so sure the comforts of religion.

After appointing where to meet with the minister next Sabbath, Ralph left him and returned home. It was late when he arrived; but as it was customary for him to retire every Sabbath evening from the idle and profane conversation of his relations, his late return excited no surprise. During the week he reflected much on what he had heard. The instructions, arguments, and advice of the old minister had a powerful influence in determining him to keep his appointment next Sabbath. But especially when he considered how many trials the aged pastor and his friends had gone through, and yet how little they regarded them; how many privations they were enduring, and yet how constant they were; how many calamities were threatening them, and yet how calmly they looked forward, resting their confidence and their hope in the all-sufficiency of their Saviour—he determined to hesitate no longer, but to meet with them on the coming Sabbath, and to cast in his lot with theirs.

Chapter III

"He shall lean upon his house, but it shall not stand; he shall hold it fast, but it shall not endure."

EARLY on the Sabbath morning Ralph left home, and in the barn of a farmhouse, about three miles distant, met, according to appointment, with the old minister, and twelve or fifteen people who had assembled to hear the gospel. Scarcely were the psalm and prayer concluded, however, when an alarm was given by one who watched at a little distance, that a party of dragoons were riding towards the house. One of those wicked men, who in those days were well paid by the abettors of tyranny and persecution for bringing information against the Covenanters, during the preceding week had found means of discovering the place and hour of the present meeting; and now, like Judas of old, he came the leader of that savage soldiery who took delight in shedding the blood of the saints.

When the old minister heard that the dragoons were at hand, he recommended all present to God, the preserver of men, and earnestly begged that they would leave him, and take every possible measure for their own safety. But this they would by no means do. He had been the spiritual father, the comforter, and friend of most of those present, from their earliest youth. He had grown grey in the service of his heavenly Master;

and his little flock seemed more anxious to save him than themselves.

" Can you not hide him," said a boy, a son of the farmer to whom the house belonged—" can you not hide him in the hole below the kitchen floor, where Mr. M'Coll once hid himself when the dragoons were here before?"

" Thank you, my good boy," said his father; "the alarm and danger had driven that place from my recollection. He may be safe there. It has sheltered many a worthy Christian from the bloodhounds of persecution."

Under the kitchen floor had been dug a cavity sufficiently large to hold two or three persons. The entrance to it was covered by a thin flag, so light that a single person could remove it, which, when closed, had such a complete likeness to the rest of the floor that it could create no suspicion of any retreat below.

Into this place the old minister was persuaded to descend ; and both because he was afraid that Ralph had too little experience in the Christian warfare, and because he had been the immediate instrument of bringing him into the present danger, he invited the youth to conceal himself in the same place. This, however, Ralph refused. He was young, he said, and able to endure hardships ; but there were those present, with hoary heads, who could ill bear the insolent and cruel treatment to which they should be exposed if they fell into the hands of their persecutors. There was no time for dispute. The owner of the house, and another old man, went into the cave along with the minister, and the flag was instantly returned to its place. Thus, young reader, had our Christian ancestors to hide themselves for their attachment to religion and to their God.

Scarcely were these three old men concealed, when the dragoons, about twenty in number, arrived. They consisted mostly of Highlanders from the wildest districts of the North. Their countenances were fierce and cruel ; and they seemed in general only to understand so much

English as to be able, in that language, to curse their fellow-men and blaspheme their Maker.

The Covenanters, aware that escape by flight was impossible, and knowing that, unarmed as they were, resistance would be vain, peaceably allowed themselves to be made prisoners. Their arms were pinioned to their bodies with cords, which the soldiers had brought with them for that purpose ; and while they were thus bound as the vilest traitors, they were upbraided with the worst of names, and insulted with the most insolent and most contemptuous mockery. After some of them had been tortured in vain, to make them discover the owner of the house and the old minister, they were all conducted to Irvine. As persecution was then in the heat of its rage, I need not tell you what their fate was. Ralph was saved from that death to which the rest were doomed, only by the influence of his father.

Mr. Gemmell was just passing to the curate's church when the prisoners were guarded through the town to gaol. We have already mentioned his violent hatred to the persecuted party, and his displeasure at Ralph's serious and religious cast of mind ; but paternal feelings, which cannot be easily overcome, compelled him to interfere for the safety of his son. To a man whose house had been long friendly to the governing party, and who had attested his own attachment to the present despotism, by the most diligent suppression, so far as it was in his power, of every movement against it, this was no difficult task. It was necessary, however, before Ralph's pardon and liberty could be granted, that his father should promise that his son's future conduct would be agreeable to government ; and further, that Ralph himself should take what was called the test—a kind of oath by which the parties swearing engaged to renounce all communications with the Covenanters, to abjure all opinions not consonant with the institutions then established, and to defend every measure of government, however wicked or tyrannical.

WENT INTO THE CAVE ALONG WITH THE MINISTER.—*See page* 133.

And did Ralph swear this oath? Did he forget so
soon the lessons of the old minister? Did he forget so
soon his mother's last injunctions?—injunctions supported
by the word of God, to abide by his duty, regardless of
the consequences ; to put his trust in God, and to despise
the threatening of men? He forgot none of these ; but
he had leaned too much to the strength of his own arm.
He had not yet rested his unhesitating confidence on the
Rock of Ages. His impressions of religious duty had
been strong ; and he had not yet fully recognised his own
weakness, and his ever-present need of Almighty grace.
And now, when he was threatened with imprisonment
and death ; when he was reproached by a father with
dishonouring his family, and assailed on every side by
entreaties or ridicule ; although his tongue faltered, and
every limb of his body trembled while he took the oath—
he did take it. He engaged to assist in extirpating that
form of religious worship which he thought most agreeable to the word of God, and which his own conscience
therefore approved.

Let us pause here, young reader, and ask ourselves
how we are prepared for meeting the threatenings of
power and the solicitations of sinful pleasure? True,
you are not menaced with the instruments of torture,
with dungeons, and exile. You see not the sword of
persecution laid to your neck, nor the heads and hands of
the people of God nailed to the gates of the towns of our
country. You have no occasion to fly from your dwelling at cold midnight, and seek refuge in the solitudes of
nature. You can go forward in the track of Christian
duty, certain that nothing in the shape of external force
will meet you to force you out of it. You may put on the
uniform of a soldier of Jesus, and march forth to the
Christian warfare secure that no band of warriors, with
sword and buckler, will set the battle in array against
you, with the determined purpose of dragging you away
from under the banners of the Most High. But are you
safer on this account? Have you less need of leaning on

an Almighty arm? Pause and consider! Are there not waiting you, at every footstep of your journey, unlawful pleasures, inviting you, with tongues of sweetest persuasion, to turn aside from the upright path, and promising to entertain you in the gay and flowery fields of unwithering delight? And have you not in your own bosom a set of treacherous inclinations which have an ever-greedy ear to every delusive voice, and which are ever willing to wander from the steep ascent of virtue, and to take themselves up with the indulgent offers of present enjoyment? Are not the reasonings of a sophistical philosophy and the misrepresentations of a false religion ever casting their doubts in your way, to turn you out of it, and draw you into a labyrinth of inextricable difficulties? Will you not meet avarice tempting you with his gold, and ambition directing you away to the gaudy heights of human glory? Will you not, at every step of your Christian progress, have to set your face against the mockery of wanton dissipation, and the studied and pointed ridicule of veteran wickedness? Will you not be solicited by the flattering words and decoying speeches of polished libertinism, which will introduce themselves to your ear with all the warmth of disinterested friendship, and all the gentleness of practised courtesy? Truly, you will find these more dangerous foes, more frequent in their inroads, and more varied and persevering in their attacks, than the most violent of open and avowed enemies.

When the sword of persecution is unsheathed, and when it is plainly seen that something serious is determined against us, we put ourselves on our guard, advance with caution, examine every step we take, canvas every intelligence, and suspect every fair pretender of wishing to decoy us into the snares of the enemy. Besides, when we are beset by external violence, we are assisted in repelling it by that principle of our nature which rejects compulsion, and which will not comply with those who will have us their own way, whether we will or not, however agreeable to us their paths might otherwise be.

But when vice comes in the guise of seeming zeal for our good, which infidel philosophy often assumes—or with the wanton jest and immoral illusion, which polished licentiousness is ever dropping from his tongue ; or with the witty sarcasm and grave ridicule, which flow so profusely from the lips of irreligious genius ; or when it tells us of riches, and honours, and preferments, and whispers in our ears, that if we stubbornly abide by the dictates of honesty, we shall probably die poor ; then, young reader, it is that your enemy is the strongest, and that you have most need to call into service all the energies of your religion. Instead of any natural principle coming to your assistance against foes like these, you have many of their friends in your own breast, wishing every moment to betray you, and labouring with all their might to hasten your defeat and complete your ruin.

Beware, then, young reader, of trusting to yourself ; for if you do so but for a single step, at that step you will fall. Christ hath overcome the world ; put your trust in Him, and you shall overcome it too.

——————

Chapter IV

"The Lord is with you, while you be with Him : and if ye seek Him, He will be found of you : if ye forsake Him, He will forsake you."—CHRONICLES.

"In a little wrath I hid my face from thee for a moment ; but with everlasting kindness will I have mercy on thee, saith the Lord, thy Redeemer."—ISAIAH.

ON Ralph's return -home, after thus renouncing his religion, his father at first assailed him with the most severe and indignant reproof. He reproached him not only for disgracing a family which had long boasted of its honour, but, as he was answerable for the conduct of his family, for exposing him, if government should exact it, to heavy penalties. And besides, he was told he had thrown an indelible stigma on his character by associating with fanatics and traitors; for such was the light in which Mr. Gemmell viewed the Covenanters. And further, he was assured, if ever he ventured again to attend their meetings, or at any future period should show them the least countenance, the paternal estate would be given to his brother, and he disinherited and disowned for ever.

But, as Mr. Gemmell was really concerned for the honour, as he thought it, of his son, he did not leave him with reproach and censure. He assumed a gentler mood, and represented to him how much his disobedience and folly had grieved his heart; promised, if his future conduct were agreeable to his wishes, to pay him the most fatherly attention; to make him his companion in all his visitings and amusements, and to introduce him to the notice of men of the first rank and highest honour in the country—assuring him, at the same time, that by pursuing the course which he himself had done, he would live in ease and happiness, would be respected and honoured by the nobles of the nation, and would add another worthy name to the dignity of his family.

These last arguments had a powerful effect on Ralph's mind. He had seldom heard his father speak kindly to him, and he was entirely overcome by the present tenderness. His conscience, no doubt, still told him he was wrong; but he had the sanction of a father, and he tried to silence its complaining. He rode out with his relations in quest of conventicles; he laughed at his own adventure with the Covenanters; he endeavoured to appear unconcerned about their sufferings; he took a share in whatever licentious conversation offered itself, and imitated the profane scoff and wicked ribaldry of his companions. His father rejoiced in the change, and every day showed him more kindness and respect; and all his relations caressed and complimented him as a worthy heir of so respectable a house. So much more were his circumstances easy and agreeable than formerly

—and so much were his pride and vanity flattered by the attentions and commendation he met with on all hands, that, to the eye of mortal penetration, he seemed to have made final shipwreck of his religion, and to have allied himself, by a league that could never be broken, with the world which lieth in wickedness. But God seeth not as man seeth. As the heavens are higher than the earth, so are his thoughts than man's thoughts.

Ralph, as we have hinted, although pleased and dazzled with his present condition, was not satisfied. His conscience often condemned him ; and as it corresponded to the word of God, he knew its condemnations were just. Oft, in the merriment of light-hearted excursion and the mirthfulness of wanton conversation, did its reproaches sting his soul and suddenly sadden his mind with the bitterness of remorse. But especially when he withdrew to repose, in the darkness and loneliness of midnight, did this censor within, directed by the Spirit of Grace, set his sins in order before him, and point to the awful consequences.

One night, after having taken more than a usual share in the unholy mirth and licentious revelry which were so common in those times, and nowhere more so than in his father's house, he retired to bed, and had almost dropt asleep, when he was quickly alarmed by one of those sudden starts which are caused by a momentary cessation of the pulsation of the heart. Thousands have been thus alarmed at the beginnings of their first slumbers, have felt a moment's uneasiness, laid their head again on the pillow, and slept soundly. But it was not so with Ralph. He thought he felt something like the visitation of death about him ; a cold sweat suffused his body, and he durst scarcely lay his head down on the pillow. Quick as the lightning's flash did his mind traverse the field of his past doings. The many instructions, advices, and warnings he had received from an affectionate mother ; the knowledge he had acquired of the will of God in the Bible ; the conversation that had passed between him and the

old minister ; the resolutions which he had so often
formed to be religious ; the promises which he had made
to God never to forsake his duty ; all stood up as a strong
witness against him. And his renouncing his religion
when he knew he was doing wrong ; his seeking the
praise of men rather than the praise of God ; his coun-
tenancing the endeavour to extirpate that faith which his
own conscience approved of ; his mingling in profane
conversation when the voice within had bidden him withdraw ; his love to the indulgences of wickedness when he
was aware that he should have hated them ; these, like
so many spirits of darkness, gathered around his soul,
and for a moment involved him in the gloom of despair.
The anguish of his mind affected his body ; he shivered,
trembled, and still imagined he felt death laying his hand
upon him. He thought God had forsaken him, and had
left him to try what support or comfort the friendship of
wicked men could give him in the moment of dissolution.
And truly then did he feel how helpless, how insignificant
a thing he was ! how unequal to tread the darkness of
death alone ! how weak, how deceitful, and how despic-
able the pride of human strength and the flattering of
human honours ! He felt that all things below the sun
are indeed vanity of vanities ; that the soul cannot lean
on any of them when shaken by the hand of death ; and
that man is really dependent on his Maker. For a
moment did the terrors of despair convulse his spirit.
He saw no smile from heaven ; and in that moment he
felt a bitterness of anguish which he would have willingly exchanged for a whole lifetime of poverty, and
shame, and bodily suffering. So will you feel, young
reader, if ever you be threatened with death when as ill
prepared for meeting it as Ralph was.

But this was only the hiding of his Heavenly Father's
countenance—only one of those kind chastisements by
which He convinces His children of their own helplessness
—of the weakness of human strength—and of the meanness of this world's glory ; and by which He teaches

them repentance and humility, and the necessity of putting their trust in Him alone, for time and eternity. Ralph was not long left in this state of utter hopelessness : that holy, that watchful, that comforting Spirit, which never loses sight of any whom the Lord hath chosen for His own, came into his soul. Then was his mind turned to the contemplation of that blood which cleanseth from all sin. He wept the tear of true repentance, and prayed in the language of faith, " Lord be merciful to me a sinner ! " He now saw himself more guilty in the sight of God than ever ; but he saw, also, God willing to be reconciled to him through Jesus Christ, and he felt a holy peace and confidence in his Redeemer, to which he had been formerly an utter stranger. So much weakness had he discovered in his own strength, that he durst no longer put the least trust in it ; and so much deceit in his own heart, that he durst not promise future obedience. But humbly did he wish to be enabled by the Holy Spirit to make the will of God and His glory the aim of all his future actions. And humbly did he pray that the same Divine Spirit would ever keep present on his mind the impressions which it had received of its own frailty and the world's deceitfulness ; that He would ever give him to put an undivided trust in his Saviour, and that He would, by His counsel, ever guide his feet in the way of everlasting life. Such are the feelings of the true child of God, to whom He saith, " I will never leave thee nor forsake thee."

Solaced by these thoughts, and committing himself to the protection of his God, Ralph soon sunk into sweet repose.

———

Chapter V

"Blessed are ye when men shall revile you, and persecute you, and say all manner of evil falsely against you for my sake. Rejoice, and be exceeding glad, for great is your reward in heaven."—ST. MATTHEW.

NEXT morning Ralph arose, and resolved, since he could not stay at home without sharing in the wickedness of the house, or exposing himself anew to reproach and ridicule, to spend the day in a solitary walk, and to engage himself in serious thought how to conduct his future life.

He took his favourite walk down the banks of the Irvine. It was the last month of spring. The beams of the morning sun threw an air of sprightliness and gaiety over nature, that smiled around him in the loveliness and vigour of youth. The fields had clothed themselves in their mantle of green, and the singing of birds was heard in the woods. And although he knew how many of Scotland's best friends and most faithful servants of God were that morning wandering in poverty, immured in dungeons, or appointed to immediate death; and although he looked forward to all these evils as embattled against himself, yet, so entire was his resignation to the will of God—so confiding his trust in the all-sufficiency of divine grace, that his heart took in the joy of nature; and the breathings of its love and thankfulness ascended up to heaven with the universal anthem of nature's gratitude.

"Why should I be sad?" thought the young Christian, "or why should my soul be cast down? The flocks that sport on yonder hills, and the herds that browse on yonder meadow, seem grateful for their day of short enjoyment that will soon end for ever. The songsters of the wood warble their song of praise, although they must soon perish utterly; and why should not I be glad? Why should not I, too, join the happy melody? What

are this world's sufferings to me? What is all that the
wickedness of man can do? Is not my soul immortal?
When this body decays, have I not a tabernacle, not
made with hands, eternal in the heavens? Are there not
rivers of pleasure at the right hand of God, secured to
me by my Saviour's death? And when the loveliness of
this world's scenery and the mirthfulness of its irrational
inhabitants shall not be seen nor heard any more, shall
not I, if I trust in my Redeemer and keep His commandments, stand in the presence of God and the Lamb, and
sing the song of the Lamb in eternity?"

Employed with such thoughts as these, Ralph had
nearly reached the seashore, when he was suddenly
roused from his meditations by the sound of the military
drum and the tumult of a mixed multitude of soldiers,
king's officers, magistrates, and others, leading, from the
town of Irvine to the side of the sea, a female, who, by
her looks, appeared to be in her eighteenth or nineteenth
year. This young woman, when an infant, had lost her
mother, and she had seen her father, only a few weeks
before the time of which we speak, torn from her arms
and dragged to the gibbet. But the cruelty of persecution is as insatiable as the grave. The poor orphan girl
had been apprehended on the preceding Sabbath at one
of those field-meetings, whither she had resorted to
worship God as her conscience directed her ; and because
neither entreaties nor threatenings could prevail on her
to take the test which we formerly explained, she had
been sentenced to be put to death by drowning—a kind
of death to which several females were condemned in
those days.

In the channel of the sea, from which the waves retired
at low water, was fixed a stake, whither, between two
ruffian soldiers, the helpless girl was led, and her arms
bound to her body with ropes. In the meantime, she
was again promised her life and freedom if she would
take the test. But with a holy indignation she replied,
"Seek ye the life of my soul by promising me a few

10

years more of earthly existence?   Begone, ye that would
tempt me to violate my conscience and deny my Saviour.
I trust in my God.   I know in whom I have believed.
And I know that He will not forsake me."

SHE WAS SOON SURROUNDED WITH THE WAVES.

[Copyright by Oliphant Anderson & Ferrier, 1895.]

The tide now began to flow, and she was soon surrounded with the waves, before which the crowd retired.
As the water gradually deepened about her she seemed
engaged in prayer; and, when it reached her waist, as
the day was calm, she was heard to say, " Farewell, my

friends—farewell, my enemies—thou sun, and thou earth,
farewell!   Come, ye waters ; why come ye so slowly ?—
come and waft my soul to the bosom of my God ! "   Here
her voice was lost in the sound of the drums that were
beat to prevent her from being heard.   Her eyes looked
up to heaven, and a calm tranquillity settled on her face,
while every succeeding wave advanced farther up her
body, till at last the waters rolled over her head and hid
her from the eyes of the spectators.

You will perhaps ask me, young reader, why I
introduce you to a scene like this ? why I shock your
feelings by the relation of such cruelties, and oppress
your sympathies by the recital of such sufferings ?   Truly,
I am not fond of the tale of distress ; nor would I
willingly sadden your countenance, did I not hope to
make your heart better by it.   And I think your best
interests may be much promoted by thus reviewing the
cruelties and sufferings of our ancestors.   Thus we learn
to what horrible transactions sin leads those who abandon
themselves to its tyrannical guidance.   How avarice,
and ambition, and pride, if harboured and nourished in
our bosoms, eradicate all that is amiable in man, and
carry him forward into barbarity and wickedness, which
place him far beneath the beasts that perish.   And hence
we gather the strongest proofs of the divine origin of our
religion, and how well adapted it is to bear the Christian
out through the darkest night of the world's distresses.
We hear evil spoken of him ; we see him hunted from
place to place, and tortured, and murdered ; but still
we see the grace of God sufficient for him.   We see him
placed on the Rock of Ages, putting away from him, as
things of nought, the waves, and storms, and fierceness
of this earth's most angry assault ; and, calmly reclining
his hope on the promise of his God, looking with a
grateful heart and an eye of brightening gladness to the
land beyond the grave—the land of his Father, and his
everlasting home.   Hence, too, we learn how much we
are indebted to the heaven-supported stand which our

forefathers made against the inroads of civic despotism, and the domination of a secular priesthood ; and thus we are led to revere their memory, which has, especially in late years, been loaded with contempt. And, above all, in reviewing such scenes as these, we cannot help being filled with gratitude to God that He hath now brought his Church back from the wilderness, and permitted us to worship within her walls in peace and safety.

Some of these reflections Ralph made while this work of wickedness was going on before him. For, although he had already resolved, through the help of divine grace, to give no countenance to the persecutors, and to ally himself to that scattered few whom he thought sincere in serving their Heavenly Master ; and the murder of this helpless female—this outrage done both to humanity and religion, excited within him a greater hatred to sin, and a firmer reliance on the grace of God, which he had seen so fully manifested, in supporting, consoling, and cheering this young woman in the last and severest trial to which the Christian can be exposed.

" If these be your doings," thought he, as he wandered slowly along the coast after witnessing this horrible spectacle,—" if these be your doings, ye men of power and this world's honour, let not my soul come into your secret ; unto your assembly, mine honour, be not thou united. Surely the Lord will visit you for these things ; and then He will laugh at your calamity, and mock when your fear cometh : when your fear cometh as desolation, and your destruction cometh as a whirlwind. Oh, my Father in heaven ! Thou knowest my heart. It is sinful, it is deceitful, ever deceiving me, taken up with lying vanities, ever leading me astray ; but in Thy great mercy, for the sake of Him who died that I might live, do Thou deliver me from its vain imaginations—from the snares of an alluring world—from the fear of its threatenings—and from the flattery of its promises. And, oh give me, for Thou hast all power in heaven and in earth, give me strength and resolution to forsake all that is sinful, and follow all that is holy ; to forsake those friends who would ruin my soul, and those possessions which, in a few years at any rate, must be left for ever ; and to follow my Saviour, that friend who sticketh closer than a brother —that friend who will never forsake me—who will stand by me in death, and secure me from the fear of its terrors, who, by His own blood, hath won for me an inheritance valuable as the riches of divine grace— durable as the ages of eternity."

After uttering these pious ejaculations, Ralph began to consider whither to betake himself. To return home was to put himself in the way of all that reproach, ridicule, and alluring temptation, which he had already found himself unable to resist ; and to throw himself into the society of the Covenanters was to deprive himself of every comfort of life, and to expose himself to the severest sufferings. For the present, however, he thought the last his duty. Trusting, therefore, to God, the all-powerful and the all-wise, he took his way to the farmhouse where he was formerly apprehended. When he arrived, the old farmer, whom we formerly mentioned, took him by the hand and said,' "You were once our friend, will you tell us if the soldiers are coming hither ; for we have heard that you are now taking part with our enemies?"

"I did take part with your enemies and mine," replied Ralph, "but I have now left them ; and I hope that my Saviour will never leave me to go so far astray again. I come to seek a night's shelter under your roof, and to be instructed by your experience."

"I cannot promise you an hour's safety in my house," said the old man, "but to what shelter it affords, you are welcome ; and what of meat and drink our oppressors have left, my children shall divide with you. Come in ; there is, at this moment, a minister in my house whom you formerly saw here. He will be glad to see you ; for often have I heard him speak of your mother, and often has he lamented over you since you saw him last."

After a conversation with the old minister, in which
Ralph related what had happened to him since their
last interview, the venerable pastor asked him if he had
ever joined in the celebration of the Lord's Supper. He
replied in the negative; and added, that it was his intention to take the first opportunity of publicly com-
memorating his Redeemer's death.

"You may soon have an opportunity," said the
minister. "I am to dispense the sacrament of the
Lord's Supper to-morrow, if it so please God, in a
retired place about five miles up the country, and you
may go along with me."

"I would most willingly go," replied Ralph, "but
I fear I am not prepared for an ordinance so solemn.
It was but yesterday that I was giving myself up to
profane conversation, and taking part with those who
know not God."

"There are none of us well enough prepared," said
the minister, "but that is no reason why we should
neglect this ordinance. Indeed, if we thought ourselves
fully prepared, it would be a sign that we saw ourselves
not as God sees us; that we flattered our own hearts,
and were really ill fitted for approaching the holy table
of God. If you were lately putting the fear of God
away from you, and breaking His commandments, you
have more need to approach the throne of grace in
the sacrament of the Supper, that there you may manifest your return to His service, and receive a large
supply of His grace, that you may not again fall into
temptation and sin against Him. We do not eat
and drink the Lord's Supper unworthily because we are
sinners, but because we refuse to put on the wedding
garment of Christ's righteousness. Arrayed in this
righteousness, the guiltiest sinner shall then be welcomed
and honoured by the God of holiness. If you see yourself to be naturally poor, and naked, and blind, and
miserable, exposed to the curse of God's law, and
unable of yourself to fulfil any of its demands; if you

put all your hope of salvation in the mercy of God through His Son, sincerely desirous to love, honour, and obey your Saviour, to trust in Him—to be humbly taught by His word to hate sin—to avoid every appearance of it—to love holiness—and to be for ever holy; if you have a sincere desire thus to love and thus to hate what God loves and hates; if you can fall down on your knees before that God whose eye searcheth the heart, and pray to Him that you may so love and so hate, however guilty you may have been, however sinful you still are, you are called by your Redeemer to sit down at His table, and you are assured that He will meet you there in the kindness of His love. Examine yourself, my young friend, by these marks; and may the great High Priest of the upper sanctuary give you that preparation which we all need."

Thus instructed, Ralph spent the remainder of the evening in prayer and self-examination; and after a short repose, set out early on the Sabbath morning, with his reverend friend and the old farmer, to the place agreed on for worshipping God and celebrating the death of His Son. When they reached the spot, which, that it might not be easily discovered, they had been induced to choose in the bosom of a thick wood, there were a considerable number assembled. The bread and wine to be used in his holy festival had been brought by some peasants from the nearest town. And as soon as the little flock was fully gathered around him, the worthy old minister proceeded with the solemnities of the day. After sermon, and an address to those who were to be engaged in the celebration of the Supper, the communicants, among whom was Ralph, arranged themselves together on the grassy turf, and prepared themselves for receiving the bread and wine.

Let us pause here, young reader, and think for a moment on this scene. The celebration of the Lord's Supper is so common among us — we have so often seen it from our earliest years, that, whether we are engaged in it or are merely spectators it makes but too little impression on our minds. But let us reflect upon it for a little; and is it not the most solemn, the most interesting, and the most honourable work in which man engages in this world? It is not obedience to the call of some noble friend, who hath raised us from poverty to some place of ease and distinction: it is a compliance with the invitations of our Saviour, who hath delivered us from the wrath to come, and secured to us an everlasting place in the presence of God. It is not the anniversary of a mortal's birthday or death, who will in time be forgotten: it is a calling to lively remembrance the death of our Redeemer, whose praise will constitute the anthem of eternity. It is not sitting down at the table of a prince: it is sitting down at a table spread by God, at the expense of Messiah's blood; and it is our Saviour Himself who welcomes the guests. It is not a token of some king's favour: it is a pledge of the love of God, of His wonderful love to man. It is not a banquet to regale our bodies: it is a feast that fills the hungry soul with eternal life. And should you then, young reader, be backward or ashamed to sit down at this table, because the men of this world will laugh at you? Should you be afraid to tell, in the presence of the universe, that God is your friend, and that you are His friend? Truly, none will be ashamed to have this to tell on that great and terrible day when this world shall be judged. But, alas! those who are ashamed of Christ now, those who deny Him before men, will He deny before His Father and the holy angels.

After an address to the communicants, the old minister, who, as we formerly observed, amidst all his sufferings, had a look of peculiar peacefulness and contentment, dispensed the elements; and, resuming his discourse, thus concluded—

"Now, my friends, if you have eaten of this bread and drunk of this cup worthily, as I hope you have done, you are the honourable ones of the earth, the wisest, the best, the happiest. God is your friend, and He is the fountain of all honour. He delights to honour you. Your garments shall be ever white: your crowns are sure: He will Himself place them on your heads; and no being can ever wrest them from you. You are the wisest; for God is your instructor, and He is the source of all wisdom. His word is a light to your feet, and a lamp to your path. He hath led your minds into all necessary truth. He hath made you wise unto salvation. You are the best; for you are likest God, who is holy, and just, and good. You are vested in His righteousness. His spirit is in your souls, assimilating them to His own image, warming them with love to God and man, to all that is pure in heaven and on earth. You are the happiest; for all your desires shall be satisfied. With God as your friend, there is enough and to spare. You need but to ask, and ye shall receive—to seek, and ye shall find—to knock, and all His fulness shall be opened unto you. And, in the treasures of His grace, how much more is laid up than you can exhaust in time or eternity!

"It is true, my friends, that we are now hunted from mountain to mountain, and from solitude to solitude; now reviled and persecuted; now in want, in danger, in affliction; now menaced with bonds, with torture, with death. But is it not enough to make you patiently endure present calamity, and boldly face the future, that you this moment sit at the table of an Almighty Saviour, who, to replenish it for you, laid down His life? Will He who loved you so much, suffer aught really to hurt you? Verily, no. I believe, my friends, and I trust you believe also, that we shall be more than conquerors through Him that loved us. He will never leave us, nor forsake us. These are His own words, the words of Him who cannot lie. What, then, have we to fear? Our Saviour is with us. The God of love, the God of all worlds, the God of time and eternity, hath

taken us under His care ; let us then go through this
world, unmindful of its honours and careless of its
revilings. Let us go, singing songs of praise to Him
who goeth with us—to Him who will go with us
through the darkness of death—to Him who will lead
us to Mount Zion, to the city and temple of our God,
where we shall sigh and weep no more ; where we shall
be entirely holy, as we shall be completely happy."

After the services of the day were over the little
congregation dispersed, with more true gladness in
their hearts than the wicked have when their corn
and their wine are increased.

Chapter VI

"Why art thou cast down, O my soul, and why art thou disquieted in me? Hope thou in God; for I shall yet praise him for
the help of his countenance. In the night his song shall be with
me, and my prayer to the God of my life."—PSALMS.

I SHOULD have mentioned in the last chapter, that, as
soon as Ralph resolved to leave home, he wrote the
following letter to his father :—

"DEAR FATHER,—I know what I am now to com-
municate to you will subject me to your displeasure. I
wish I could both please you and obey my God. I tried
that kind of life which you approve of. You then
caressed and indulged me, and showed me all the kindness I could expect from a tender father. But still in
every moment of reflection, I was miserable. I cannot
be an enemy to God's people ; I cannot live with
those who persecute them ; I dare not deny my
Saviour before men, lest He deny me also before His
Father at the day of judgment. Pardon, therefore, dear
father, my disobedience. Since I have determined to
associate with the persecuted party, and as I cannot at
the same time make your house my home without ex-

posing you to the visitations of Government, I have resolved to leave you for some time. I may have to labour for my bread—I may have to beg it—I may have to encounter many a hardship ; but I put myself under the protection of a kind and watchful Providence, and I fear not the frowning of the world. Perhaps the time may soon come when the party with whom I am now to associate will no longer be counted traitors, and when I might live at home without exposing you to any penalties. If that time come, and if my present conduct do not so much offend you as to induce you to abandon me alto-gether, I will be glad to return and live with you. Do not be offended with me, dear father, for obeying the dictates of my own conscience. Forgive me for what I have done ; and be assured that I am still your affectionate son.—RALPH GEMMELL."

You may imagine, young reader, how a man like Mr. Gemmell would receive Ralph's letter. He stamped the ground with his foot, and gnashed his teeth with indigna-tion. He regarded his son as a mad irreclaimable fanatic—a dishonour to his family—unworthy to be any longer remembered by him—and, without a moment's deliberation, sat down and wrote the following letter :—

"RALPH,—Return home and live with me ! No, never ; my door shall be forever shut against you; I will even tear your remembrance from my heart. You have not only disregarded my injunctions ; you have not only rejected my kindness and disappointed my hopes ; you have allied yourself to the vilest and guiltiest traitors ; you have disgraced my name and my house. I blush to think that you are my son. But you shall no longer be recognised as such by me. I shall leave all that I have to Edward. And I hereby charge you never to let me again see your face—never to presume to write to me, or to say that I am your father.—GEORGE GEMMELL."

When Mr. Gemmell had finished this letter he gave it

to Edward, and said, "Go early to-morrow morning," for it was on the Sabbath evening he received Ralph's letter,—"go and deliver that letter to Ralph, who is no longer worthy to be called your brother. You will find him perhaps at the house where he was formerly apprehended. If not, you will probably learn there where you will find him. Go ; put that letter into his hand, and stop not to hear a word from him."

Ralph had just walked out from the old farmer's (for he had returned thither on the Sabbath evening), to enjoy the freshness of the morning, when he observed his brother riding towards the house. Edward came up to him, put the letter into his hand, and turned his horse and rode off—happy that he had now got fairly quit of a brother he never loved, and had the clear prospect of inheriting all the possessions and honours of his father.

Ralph read the letter. He expected something of the kind, yet he was not prepared for so much. All the feelings which a lost home and a lost father could excite rushed bitterly upon his soul. It was hard to be forever forbidden a home where he had spent his childhood with the tenderest of mothers ;—it was hard to be disowned and hated by a father whom he had often endeavoured to please, even against his own conscience. He felt all this ; and, to use the language of Scriptures, " he fell down on his face, and wept bitterly." For a moment he almost wished that, like Edward, he had been content to live as his father wished him. But this was only the passing thought of a moment. He remembered the stings of conscience, the anguish of remorse, and the fears of death, which he had so lately felt. He remembered the love of his Heavenly Father, the love of his Saviour ; and although he continued still to weep, it was not for what he himself had done—it was not for what he had lost ; it was, that he had a father and a brother of whose eternal welfare he had every reason to doubt. But soon he betook himself to the never-failing comfort of the Christian. He addressed himself to a throne of

grace, and besought his God that He would yet have
mercy on his relations, and turn them from the evil of
their ways, and yet magnify His grace by saving them
from the wrath to come. After this fervent prayer to
God for the salvation of those whom he still loved, however much they hated and despised him, peace returned
to his mind. He knew, that although he was disowned
of an earthly father, he had a Father in heaven who would
never disown him ; although he was despised of his
brother, he had an Elder Brother who loved him and
would love him to the end ; and although he had lost an
earthly inheritance, he had treasures secured for him in
heaven infinitely more valuable. These are the reflections, young reader, which fill the Christian's mind with
that peace which the world can neither give nor take
away.

We have seen, in this passage of Ralph's history, how
well adapted the promises of the gospel are to the wants
of the Christian—how securely he leans on the arm of his
Saviour, and reposes his hope on those fair and un-
troubled regions beyond the grave, when the deceitful
rod of this world's strength breaks under him, and the
clouds of adversity darken his earthly prospects. But
where, in the day of sore trouble—where, at the hour of
death, shall the sinner look? who shall comfort him at
that awful crisis, when no earthly friends shall be of any
avail? Who shall guide his steps through the valley of
thick darkness, and where shall his spirit find rest, when
it shall be driven away for ever from the presence of its
God? The latter reflections have been suggested by a
scene which Ralph witnessed soon after his banishment
from his father's house.

Naturally of a thoughtful and contemplative turn of
mind, and rendered still more so by the adverse circumstances of his life, Ralph loved to withdraw himself from
the eye of human observation, and to soothe his feelings
and nourish his virtues in solitary meditation.

One evening, following this propensity, he left a

shepherd's hut, in which he had spent a few days, and wandered forth amidst the peaceful scenery which surrounded it.

"These sheep," said Ralph, as he passed a flock that lay on the heath,—"these sheep rest in peace; they have spent the day in gathering their food, and now their slumbers are sweet. And why is it that man eateth the bread and drinketh the water of affliction, and lieth down in sorrow? Why does rest depart from his eyes, and slumber from his eyelids? Why does he so often say, when it is night, 'When shall it be morning?' and when it is morning, 'When shall it be night?' Must he alone, of all earthly beings, waste the day in sadness, and water his nightly couch with the tears of bitterness? Is God more merciful to the beasts of the field than to man, on whose soul He once impressed His own image? No, Holy Father!" the young man exclaimed, "Thou art not more merciful to the beasts of the field than Thou art to man. Thou hast made him only a little lower than the angels, and hast crowned him with glory and honour. Thou madest him to have dominion over the works of Thy hands, and hast put all things under his feet. But he hath rebelled against Thee, and therefore he wandereth without a guide; he refuses to be reconciled to Thee, and therefore he hath no comforter; he hath himself planted his couch with thorns, and therefore rest fleeth far away. Gracious God! let it not be so with me; teach me to submit myself to Thy government—to accept of the offered Saviour as the great atonement for my sin. Then shall I spend the day in cheerfulness, for Thou shalt teach me to do my duty; and the night in peaceful repose, for I shall rest under the shadow of Thy wings.

"Just and Holy One! I know that thou afflictest not willingly the children of men. It is sin, that abominable thing which Thou hatest, which infuses into the cup of life every drop of its gall. It is sin which embitters reflection and darkens the prospects of hope. It is sin which makes this world a valley of tears and the next,

to him who hath not been redeemed from its consequences, a place of weeping, and wailing, and gnashing
of teeth. All the holy are happy. As that moon, which
clothes the earth in silvery radiance, walks for ever
peacefully and serenely amidst her attendant stars, un-
troubled by the noise of the tempest, while it carries
desolation over the face of this lower world; so, O
Father! if I trust in my Saviour, and keep His commandments, shalt Thou enable me to possess my soul in peace,
amidst all the troubles of life and all the terrors of death."

Ralph was thus engaged in holy communion with his
God, when his attention was attracted by a loud shriek,
which seemed to be uttered by some person in great
distress. He turned towards the direction whence he
imagined the cry proceeded, and, by the light of the
moon, observed two men carrying or dragging a third
along with them. As they approached him, he discovered that they were soldiers, and that one of them,
who was an officer, had received a wound that same day
in an affray with a party of Covenanters. A few of those
dauntless and intrepid sons of civil and religious liberty
had assembled in the desert moorlands, to hear a sermon
from one of those ministers who were then driven to
the wilderness. Sermon had no sooner commenced,
however, than the little congregation was surprised and
attacked by a party of soldiers. As they were mostly
unarmed, they at first made no resistance, and would
certainly have suffered themselves to have been led
quietly to the nearest gaol, had not the following occurrence roused their indignation, and impelled them to set
the arms of the soldiers at defiance.

The officer whom we have noticed, having used some
unbecoming liberties with a young woman who was
among the prisoners, was reprehended by her father, who
was also present. Instead of desisting from his im-
proper conduct, however, he struck the father on the left
shoulder with his sword, and became still more insolent
towards his daughter.

"Thou shalt not be misused in my presence," said the indignant father to his daughter, while he drew from under a loose greatcoat the short and rusty, but tried and faithful, sword of his forefathers, and bringing a sudden and unexpected stroke, disabled the sword-arm of the officer, and wounded him mortally in the left side. In a moment the engagement became general. Some of the peasants with clubs, others with swords, which they had concealed about their clothes, fell violently on the soldiers. And as they were imflamed with rage, and greatly superior in number, they soon put the soldiers to flight. Two of them, however, leaving the rest to fight as they could with the Covenanters, supported their wounded officer, and, after the dispersion of their fellows, were suffered to carry him away without molestation.

This was the man whose shriek had attracted Ralph's attention, and who, as the exhausted soldiers laid him down on the heath, asking if there were any hut near in which they might be sheltered for the night, exclaimed, in the faltering accents of one near dissolution,—

"You shall carry me no farther. I will die here. But, oh! where am I going? What shall become of my soul?"

"You shall go to heaven," said one of the soldiers, wishing to comfort the poor wretch.

"My life has made God my enemy," replied the officer. "I have no hope! I have no hope!"

"If you must die, die like a man," said the other soldier; "you have done your duty to your king, and you have nothing to fear."

"The blood of innocence is on my hands," replied the dying sinner; "I have no hope!—no hope!"

Ralph, although struck with horror at the despairing and ghastly visage of the man, stood near, and tried to comfort him.

"You ought not," said the young Christian, "to despair, because you have been a great sinner. Jesus Christ came not to call the righteous, but sinners to repentance. His blood cleanseth from all sin — the greatest as well as the least. Persecutors have been saved, thieves and robbers have been saved, murderers have been saved. Repent, and seek the pardon of your sins through Jesus Christ. God will hear you for His sake, and save your soul from death."

These words fell on the ear of the poor dying sinner without yielding him any comfort. They were, indeed, like savoury meat placed in the sight of a hungry person who is unable to stretch out his hand and partake of it. They made him feel with double anguish the wrath of God, which now lay heavy upon him ; and he exclaimed, in the fearful tone of despair, "I cannot repent—God hath left me no hope !—no hope ! "

While he uttered these words of despair, his face grew pale as the moonbeams that fell upon it—the shadows of death closed over his eyes—the last agonies of nature shook his body—it lay still on the heath—and his soul was summoned away to the tribunal of its God.

Let us pause for a moment and reflect on this scene. The man whose hopeless death we have just recorded was born of Christian parents, baptized in the name of the Father, the Son, and the Holy Ghost ; and thus, at his entrance into life, dedicated to the service of God. But early in youth he gave signs of aversion to religion, by swearing, breaking the Sabbath, neglecting to read his Bible, and eagerly joining himself with the company of the profane. Conscience at first told him he was wrong, and for some time rendered him miserable by its upbraidings. But the farther we advance over the line that forms the limit of virtue, the voice of conscience becomes weaker and weaker, till it is at last almost lost amidst the noise and revelry of unhallowed pleasures.

So it was with the poor wretch whose lifeless body now lay on the heath. After treading for a while in the dark and ruinous paths of vice, his ear became deaf to the calls of religion, his heart hard as the nether mill-stone, and his conscience seared as with a hot iron.

11

And when the voice of death, that speaks in the ear of conscience like the thunders of God, awoke him with the awful tidings that he must instantly appear before his God, he could not pray, he could not repent, because God, in His righteous displeasure, had left him to the hardness of his wicked heart. All his life he despised the Bible, and, at the hour of need, his own wicked heart rendered him incapable of drawing comfort from its promises. The Holy Spirit, long resisted, at last ceased to make intercession for him. The Saviour, long despised and rejected, withdrew from between him and offended justice. And God the Father, the entreaties of whose love and whose mercy he had long disregarded, took away from him the light of His countenance, and left him to the consequences of that sin from which he refused to be separated.

Thus it is the very nature of sin to harden the heart, and bring upon its miserable victims that punishment which is denounced against it. Every sin we commit stamps another stain on the soul, and renders it less capable than it was the moment before of relishing the beauties of holiness. Every step we take in the path of vice carries us not only farther away from virtue, but weakens our desire of returning to it. Every draught we take of the cup of iniquity, not only increases our unhallowed thirst, but quenches some spark of heavenly fire in the soul. And when the soul is completely defiled, and every desire of returning to holiness entirely rooted out, and every spark of the Spirit's kindling utterly quenched in the heart, what is there to stand any longer between the sinner and the punishment of his sins? What is there that will turn aside from his soul the sword of vindictive justice? What is there that will snatch the wretched victim out of the grasp of eternal death? And who can tell what his sufferings shall be in that place where the worm dieth not, and where the fire is not quenched?

Think on the danger of sin. You do not know how

soon your heart may become hard, and your conscience
deaf, and God may leave you to the fearful consequences
of your iniquity.

Although the two succeeding years of Ralph's life
might afford many interesting and useful incidents, the
bounds which we have prescribed for this narrative oblige
us to pass over them with a very short and general
account. We shall only say, that his sufferings during
this time were great. He often laboured in the fields
with the peasants who sheltered him. Unaccustomed as
he had been to poverty, want, or toil, they were now
almost his constant companions. With clothes that
could ill protect him from the severity of the cold, he had
frequently, in the depth of winter and the darkness of
night, to seek a hiding-place in the dens and caves of the
mountains; and sometimes he was compelled by hunger
to beg a morsel of bread. His life, like that of all his
associates, was every day sought, and he often made the
narrowest escapes from those who sought it. Yet,
instead of repining at his lot, instead of imagining that
God had forsaken him, he had the Christian's peace in
his mind, the Christian's hope ever brightening before
him, and the truth of the promises of God every day
ratified in his bosom. Through all his tribulations he
pressed forward with joy for the prize of the high calling of
God in Christ Jesus. And truly he felt that his Saviour's
words are true, that " Whosoever put their trust in Him,
He will never leave nor forsake."

He had often, as we have observed, escaped the search
and pursuit of his persecutors. The time was now
arrived, however, when they were to be permitted to take
him.

On a Sabbath afternoon, about midsummer, as Ralph
was hearing sermon in one of the moorish glens in the
upper part of Renfrewshire, he and the little congregation
with whom he was worshipping were suddenly surrounded by a troop of dragoons, and apprehended.
Some of the soldiers, as they had then that power given

them by Government, were for putting them instantly to death, others were for sending them to Edinburgh, there to be sentenced and executed. This last proposal was adopted; and the prisoners were accordingly conducted to Edinburgh. On their arrival there, they were loaded with irons, and thrown into the gloomiest cells of the old prison. After two days' confinement they were brought to trial, and all, excepting one or two who took the test, condemned to be executed next day, and their heads and hands affixed to the city gates. As soon as this sentence was read to them, they were remitted to prison, and shut up in separate cells.

You can often talk about death, young reader, with little alarm. You are not sure when it shall come, and your youth, your health, and your attachment to the world, when you begin to fear it, whisper in your ear that it is yet far distant. But to be assured that you were to die to-morrow would indeed bring the terrors of death near to your mind. Could you look on them without trembling? Are you sure that you would have a friend to stand by you, stronger than death?—a friend who could effectually support you in the conflict with your last enemy? To be assured that we should die to-morrow would really be a serious thing, a trying situation; and, in this situation, was Ralph placed.

Once before, you remember, he thought he was dying; now he was sentenced to be executed on the morrow. Let us reflect on his external circumstances and inward feelings in the former instance, and let us observe these also in the present. When formerly he imagined he was instantly to die, and appear at the tribunal of God, he was in his father's house, surrounded with this world's wealth and flattered with its honours; adjudged to no ignominious death, but in his own bed, called, as every one must sooner or later be, to pay the last debt of nature and assured of a tender remembrance in the bosom of his friends, and of his name being ever mentioned with the highest respect. Thus was he then situated, and yet

how did he feel? He had not then put his whole trust
in God. He had been living in sin, and trying to banish
every good impression from his heart. He thought, as
he well might, that God was his enemy : and he saw no
man that was able to protect him from the terrors of
death, or from the wrath of the Judge before whom he
was to appear. How did he then feel? The anguish of
that moment was so insufferable, that he would have
willingly exchanged it for a whole lifetime of the severest
trials. Now the young man was cast out from his
father's house, become the curse and the hissing of all
his relations, forgotten by his acquaintances who once
honoured him, or if remembered, only remembered as a
silly headstrong fanatic, whose sufferings deserved nothing but ridicule ; oppressed with irons like a murderer ;
locked up in the darkness of a dungeon, without a friend
to solace him ; sentenced by the law to die as a traitor,
and to have his head and hands nailed up before the
public gaze, as an attestation to the vileness of his
character. What were his thoughts now in this situation? Still death was awful to him. To be cut off in the
midst of his days, in the vigour and healthfulness of youth
—to break away from every earthly association ; to leave
the light of day for the darkness of the grave, and the
voice of men for the silence of death ; to have his body,
now so pleasant to him, made a meal for worms, and a
prey to foul corruption. These were unwelcome thoughts.
And he felt that death had still power to accomplish
these things against him. But he now beheld the
gloomy king shorn of his substantial terrors ; a guilty
conscience, the wrath of God, eternal punishment, these
are the real terrors of death, the weapons with which he
wounds the soul and destroys it. But Ralph knew that
his Saviour had taken these weapons from his enemy ;
and he could look him in the face, and say, " O death !
where is thy sting? O grave ! where is thy victory?
Thanks be unto God who giveth me the victory through
Jesus Christ my Lord. Though I walk through the

valley of the shadow of death, I will fear no evil, for Thou art with me; and Thy rod and Thy staff, they shall comfort me." Thus did God give the young Christian a song in the night, in the darkest and stormiest night which the wickedness of this world could gather about him. So true it is that God is a present help in the time of need; that He will never leave nor forsake any who put their trust in Him.

Young reader, think on death. It will come; and you know not how soon. Are you prepared to meet it? Are you sure you have a friend secured who will not desert you at that hour? Pause and consider. There is no friend but one who can then effectually help you. This is your God—your Saviour. Be prepared, as Ralph was, by putting all your trust in Him. And come your last moment when it may, you are safe. Your Saviour will deliver you also from the terrors of death.

When morning came, Ralph awoke from a refreshing sleep in which he had spent part of the night, and had just kneeled down in prayer to God, when he heard some person turning the lock of his cell door; and he now expected to be instantly led forth to execution. The door opened, and the gaoler ushered into the cell an uncle of Ralph.

"Young man," said the soldier, "I have come a long way this morning to save your life. I have already got your sentence turned into banishment; and I have even the promise of your liberty, if you will promise that your future conduct shall be agreeable to the wishes of Government."

"A thousand thanks to you, my dear uncle," said Ralph, "for your kindness to me. But how did you know that I was here?"

"That will I soon explain, nephew. One of the soldiers who was at your apprehension had frequently seen you when you lived with your father. He recognised you; and, because he had served under me when I was a captain in the army, had a kindness for the family,

and sent us word immediately that you were taken.
Your father, although he seemed somewhat concerned,
said he would by no means meddle in the affair ; and I
could not bear the thought that any one of my family
should be beheaded, or hanged like a dog. So off I
came, old as I am, pleaded the loyalty of our house, and
my own services, in your favour ; and you see how I
have succeeded. Now, I am sure you have had enough
of these madmen, the Covenanters ; you will now take the
test. What is it ? I could swear a dozen such oaths in
the hour, and be an honest man too. Come, I will introduce you to the minister. You shall be set at liberty ;
and I will do all that I can to make matters up between
you and your father. Come, my boy, fling away that
foolishness, and learn to be a man." Thus did the old
soldier talk ; and certainly Ralph found it no easy task to
reject any of the kindness of a man who had taken so
much interest in him? but he had not so learned Christ
as to be drawn from His service by the promises and
kindnesses of sinful men. After a moment's deliberation,
he made the following reply to his uncle :

"Dear uncle, be assured that I shall ever feel myself
your debtor for the interest you have taken in me. You
have already saved my life. This is enough of kindness ;
more than I can ever repay. Do not concern yourself
further about me. Banishment and slavery are by no
means pleasant ; but I dare not try to escape them by
violating my conscience, and breaking the commandments of my Saviour. I know you will think me foolish
thus to choose exile and captivity, when I might, by
your influence, be set at liberty, and perhaps restored to
my father. But you will not be offended with me for
persevering firmly in what I consider to be my duty to
God. I have never found Him a hard master. He has
supported, and will support me, in every time of need.
I have always found His yoke easy and His burden
light. On the contrary, when I have forsaken His love,
and given myself up to the guidance of this world's

wisdom, and the sinful desires of my own heart, I could see no one that could sufficiently befriend me in the hour of affliction and death. Advise me not then, dear uncle, to do anything against my own conscience; but accept my gratitude and love for the great instance of your kindness I have already received."

"Well, well," said his uncle, when he saw Ralph thus resolved, "you may do as you please for me. You will not find it very agreeable to labour under the heat of a burning sun. But I wish you a good voyage; and I hope you will have learned more sense when you return." With this short reply, the old soldier quitted the cell, and Ralph was left to his own meditations.

Gratitude to God was now his master feeling; for He had stirred up this old man, who in fact cared nothing for religion, to be the instrument of saving his life. He had thus given him a new token of His lovingkindness, and a new pledge that He would never leave nor forsake him. He had given him a new prospect of serving Him in the land of the living; of further storing his mind with new proofs of his Saviour's love, and faithfulness, and all-sufficiency; and thus of being better prepared when the hour of death should certainly come.

Chapter VII

"Many are the afflictions of the righteous: but the Lord delivered him out of them all."—PSALMS.

HAVING remained two or three weeks in prison, Ralph, with a number more, was put on board a vessel at Leith, to be transported to the English plantations in Jamaica. It is almost needless to relate the severe treatment they met with during the passage. The captain, to whose charge the captives were committed, was a man who had never thought of religion, and who had little sympathy with human suffering. The prisoners, crowded

together, were shut up in the hold of the vessel, under
an iron grating. Their food was bread and water, and
even that was but sparingly given them. Thus situated,
with nothing to cheer them but the hopes of a better life,
where their sins, being finally forsaken, would no more
subject them to calamity, they sailed from their native
land in the month of July. The weather was favourable,
and their passage prosperous enough, till they came in
sight of the island of Jamaica. It was near night, in the
month of September, a very stormy time in these
latitudes, when the ship drew towards the land. The
wind, at this time, however, was fair, the sky serene,
and every one expected to be ashore in the course of a
few hours, when suddenly a dead calm ensued—the
heavens grew dark—the sea was troubled—and in less
than half an hour the fury of the tempest came. The
winds blew so violently, and the tumult of the waves
was so great, that to manage the ship became impossible. The rocky shore was before them, and the
mighty strength of a stormy sea was driving them
quickly towards it. In the midst of this danger, the
prisoners entreated the captain to relieve them from their
confinement, that they might have a chance of saving
themselves if the vessel foundered. This request, however, he refused; declaring that he would rather see
them all drowned than give them an opportunity of
escaping from his hands. In the meantime the vessel
ran aground, a very little off the land, and was so
damaged by the shock that she made water rapidly,
while the waves were every moment breaking over
deck. Still, however, the captain refused to release the
prisoners. But he did not forget to provide for his own
safety. Expecting that the vessel would be instantly
wrecked, he ordered the long boat to be manned, into
which he threw himself, with all the hands on board,
except the mate and two or three sailors, who refused to
leave the vessel. Thus he thought to save himself, careless of the fate of Ralph and his companions. But God,

who holdeth the waters in the hollow of His hand, and
bringeth to nought the counsel of men, had not so
determined it. The boat had not proceeded many yards
from the ship when it was upset by the force of two
mighty billows, and the cruel captain, and all who were
with him, instantly perished in the waters.

When the mate observed this he immediately released
the prisoners; and they, with the few seamen who
remained on board, laboured incessantly at the pumps to
keep the vessel from filling with water. But, notwithstanding all they could do, the water still increased on
them; the storm was as violent as ever; and they
thought every moment would be their last.

And how did Ralph behave himself then? Where did
he turn for help? He trusted, as he had done before,
in that Saviour who walks upon the sea, and who can
say to the raging of its billows, "Peace, be still!"
And he cried to Him that He would yet spare him. All
his companions also lifted up their voices to God; and it
pleased Him to hear and answer their cry. He made the
storm a calm by His command; and every man that
remained on board safely reached the shore in the small
boats. The mate now took charge of the prisoners, and
conducted them to the governor of the island, who
afterwards disposed of them to the planters.

For a free-born and enlightened man to submit to
slavery, as Ralph now did, is the hardest task which
can be proposed to a human being. In some respects
it is worse than death itself. To die is the lot of
all. The rich man, as well as the poor, must go the
way appointed for all living; and, therefore, no one can
think himself peculiarly degraded by being subject to
what every other person is. But to be in vassalage to a
fellow-creature; to be bought and sold like the beasts of
the field or the produce of the ground; to be subjected
to toil without even the hope of a recompense; and to
be exposed to the lash of a capricious and tyrannical
master, without daring to defend ourselves, and without

any opportunity of having our injuries redressed—is a descent so far below the common rights of our nature, so far below the common condition of mankind, and therefore so peculiarly degrading, that to stoop to it for the sake of conscience, requires the greatest devotedness to religion, the strongest trust in the promises and grace of God, and the liveliest hope of a sure reward in the mansions of eternal freedom. In this state of servitude, however, severe as it was, Ralph was now doomed to live for a time. The master under whom he and two or three of his fellow-sufferers were placed, treated them with nearly the same severity as the negroes with whom they laboured. To Ralph, this treatment was peculiarly galling. His infancy had been tenderly nursed : he had been brought up, to the age of fifteen, as the expectant of a considerable estate. But now he was compelled to labour daily, from morning till night, under the scourge of a cruel taskmaster, breathing a sultry air, and exposed to the heat of a burning sun.

This, young reader, was a hard and painful condition, peculiarly degrading and revolting to human nature. But if you are doing what Ralph, to save himself from this state, might have done ; if you are disobeying the commandments of God, and giving yourself up to the guidance of sinful passions, you are the willing victim of a slavery infinitely more debasing and severe. Ralph was compelled to his bondage by the wickedness of his fellow-men : you willingly subject yourself to the dominion of your passions, and the vassalage of the devil. He had the approbation of his own conscience, and the smile of his Saviour's countenance : you are providing for yourself remorse and the anger of your Maker. He submitted to slavery for love to God and holiness : you are selling yourself for what is unclean and abominable. He was degraded in the sight of sinful men only : you are rendering yourself vile in the pure eyes of God and every holy being. He was sustained by the hope of eternal life : your wages are eternal death.

His servitude was that of the body only: yours is the bondage of the soul. His could endure for only a few years: yours, if you break not from it, will continue with increasing severity through eternity. In this dreadful slavery, you and all men are by nature. You cannot ransom yourself from it. No man can redeem his brother from this captivity. Christ only can make you free. Examine yourselves, then, and see that you are His freemen—that you have obtained the glorious liberty of the sons of God. If you have, you will not be surprised that Ralph submitted to slavery for love to his Saviour.

In this land of bondage the young man had no minister to counsel and comfort him. On the Sabbath, however, he was not required to labour, and he hailed its dawn with a rapture of holy delight. The former part of the day he spent alone reading his Bible,—the only book he had taken with him from Scotland,—enriching and solacing his mind with its precious truths, examining himself, lamenting his past transgressions, weeping over the sins that still remained in his heart, and lifting up his soul in prayer to God, for a heart to serve Him better and love Him more. In the afternoon he met regularly with his companions who were under the same master. Their place of meeting (for they generally met in the same place) was under a large plantain tree, whose foliage screened them from the scorching rays of the sun. Here they prayed together—read a portion of the Scriptures—sang a song of praise to their God and Saviour; here they conversed of the great love of God' displayed through Christ Jesus; cheered and comforted one another with the promises of the gospel and the hopes of eternal life; and here, too, did they find the truth of the saying, that wherever two or three are met together in God's name, there will He be in the midst of them to bless them; and here did they often experience, in near communion with God, in the joy of the Holy Ghost, in ardent anticipation of heaven, the strongest proofs of that truth which we are so desirous to set before you, that whosoever putteth his trust in God, He will never-leave nor forsake.

That this truth may be the better rooted in the mind of the young reader, I shall relate here a conversation which happened one Sabbath evening between Ralph and one of his companions.

"You seem," said Ralph to him, "very melancholy to-day. May I be permitted to ask the cause of your sadness?"

"I have been troubled for some time," replied his friend, "with the thought that we are deceiving ourselves. In our own country we were persecuted and condemned by the law to banishment; here we are in slavery, degraded from the rank of human beings, and without the hope of liberty: surely the Lord hath forsaken us, else He would never permit so many evils to come upon us."

"Beware of such thoughts," said Ralph; "it is the adversary of God and man who suggests them. He tries to make you weary in the service of God, by persuading you that it is unprofitable. And if Satan or your own heart once persuade you of this, your obedience to God will be no longer sincere, and therefore you will have no right to expect the joy of His presence. But we have no reason to suppose that God hath forgotten to be gracious to us, because we are left to prove our sincerity by severe and long-continued suffering, even slavery itself. Whom the Lord loveth He chasteneth, and He scourgeth every son whom He receiveth. It is through much tribulation that we are to enter the kingdom of heaven. But the wicked, you know, the Bible says, prosper every day; they grow up and flourish like the green bay-tree, and are not troubled as other men. Prosperity in this world, therefore, is no proof of God's favour, nor is adversity any token of His displeasure. It is the feeling in our own bosom that makes us happy or miserable. The poor slave may have a peace of mind, and a hope in the life to come, which will be an ever-present reward for all his sufferings ; while his rich master may have within him the gnawings of remorse, and those fearful forebodings which shall hinder him from enjoying his wealth, and embitter his very existence. You know, my friend, that I tried the pleasures of sin myself. I had then all that I wanted. I was surrounded by friends who respected and loved me, and I was flattered by the hopes of future honours ; but whenever I thought of death and a world to come, I was miserable. Then I was prosperous, and deemed happy by men ; but then I had forsaken God, and was indeed forsaken by Him. Now I am as poor and degraded in the eyes of the world as a human being can be ; but I believe in my Saviour—I trust in God—and I am happy. It is only when I indulge sin in my heart that God leaves me a moment to mourn. Doubt not, my friend, the truth of God's promises. Our sufferings are indeed long and severe ; but if we are rightly exercised under them they will all work together for our good ; and if we are faithful to the death, we shall receive a crown of life."

"You speak truth, my friend," replied his companion. "I am convinced. I am comforted. Let us fall down on our knees, and pray to God that we may have grace given us to resist every suggestion of evil, to believe more and more in the promises of the gospel, knowing that He is faithful who hath promised, and will bring to pass the desire of our hearts."

Ralph had now endured this bondage nearly two years. His body, although naturally robust, subjected to severe toil in a climate noxious to Europeans, was beginning to decay ; and he hoped that death would soon deliver him from his thraldom. But God had yet in reserve for him many days of peace and happiness in the land of the living.

———

Chapter VIII

"Everyone that hath forsaken houses, or brethren, or sisters, or
father, or mother, or wife or children, or lands for My name's sake
shall receive an hundredfold, and shall inherit everlasting life."—
ST. MATTHEW.

ONE day as Ralph and his companions were labouring in
the fields, their master approached them, and saluting
them pleasantly said: "The year of jubilee is come.
You are no longer my servants. A revolution has happened in Britain. A new king is placed on the throne;
and he has sent orders hither, that all who were banished
and enslaved for their religious opinions under the preceding Government, are to be immediately set at liberty.
Vessels await you on the coast to convey you to your
native land."

"Our native land!" they all cried, with one voice.
"Praised be God! hath He at last delivered it from
oppression! O Scotland! Scotland! shall we yet see
thee!" And they embraced one another, and shouted
for gladness of heart.

In a few days after the announcement of these glad
tidings, Ralph, with many more exiles, embarked in a
vessel for Greenock. The wind was favourable; the
passage quick and prosperous. And how did his heart
leap for joy when the white rocks and blue mountains of
his native country rose on his view! With the flow of
spirits which his releasement produced, and the change
of air, his health was completely restored; and he forgot
for a while that he was disinherited and forbidden his
father's house. And now the well-known cliffs of Arran,
the rock of Ailsa, and the shores of Carrick, welcomed
his eye; and now he could see Irvine, and the old castle of
Craigfoot; and the joy of his childhood beat at his heart.

As Ralph and two or three other passengers wished to
land at Irvine, the vessel drew near the harbour, and
they were put ashore in the small boat. But who would

attempt to tell the joy of Ralph's soul when he set foot on the land of his birth? It was a feeling of delight sufficient to repay years of toil. He fell down on his knees and thanked God, who had preserved him through so many trials, and restored him in health and strength to his beloved country. "So may God bring me," said the young man, "when the trials of life have passed away, to the land beyond death and the grave."

It was in the beginning of summer, on a Sabbath, about midday, that he landed. The inhabitants of Irvine were just gathering to the afternoon's sermon. It was a pleasant sight to Ralph. He could observe many, of whose sufferings he had shared in the time of persecution, this day peacefully walking to the house of God, having none to make them afraid. He entered the church, and was both surprised and delighted when he saw the pulpit filled with the venerable old pastor who, after his mother's death, had first instructed him in the ways of righteousness. This worthy minister, having been ejected from his pastoral charge in Irvine at the commencement of the persecution, had, for twenty-eight years, wandered up and down his native country, doing what he could to instruct and comfort the suffering Church; and now, after having undergone innumerable hardships, after having often made the narrowest escapes from his enemies, and after having seen them entirely overthrown, he was restored to the arms of his flock, to his home and his family. Age had rendered him so infirm, that he was compelled to address his people sitting in the pulpit. When he began his sermon, Ralph listened to every word, as it had come from the tongue of an angel And it is no wonder that he listened with delight; for the whole discourse was an offering of thanks to God for the deliverance of His Church. No wonder that the tear of holy joy flowed down his cheek, while the good old man prayed that all those who had been banished from their native land for conscience' sake might be safely conducted home, to glorify and praise their God.

After sermon, Ralph, who had not been observed in church by the minister, called at his house. Although he was much altered, the old man instantly recognised him, and, to use the language of Scripture, " fell on his neck and kissed him."

As soon as this happy salutation was past, Ralph asked the minister if he had heard anything of his father lately.

"You shall lodge with me to-night," said the minister, "and I will introduce you to your father to-morrow."

"And is he indeed reconciled to me?" said Ralph. "And is he well? Is Edward well?"

"Edward is well," said the minister, "but your father has been complaining for some time. Yesterday he sent for me. I had not been in his house for nearly thirty years, and I was surprised at the invitation."

"You might be well surprised," said Ralph; "surely he is greatly changed!"

"Yes, he is greatly changed," said the old man; "for he thinks he has wronged both you and me, and his own soul too. He says he is dying, but knows not what is to become of his immortal spirit."

"I will go to him this moment," said Ralph, "it may be that God will comfort him through me."

"Nay, but I will go too," said the affectionate old minister; "I like to see meetings of forgiveness and love. Your father wished me also to visit him to-day; but, being fatigued with the duties of the Sabbath, I meant to defer my visit till to-morrow. Since you will go, however, we will go together. By the time we have taken some refreshment the cart will be ready, for I cannot walk now."

On their arrival at Craigfoot, Ralph, although he had not been there for nearly six years, was recognised by some of the old servants.

"Here is Ralph!" they shouted; "here is Ralph! his father will now die in peace." And they ran and told his father that Ralph was come home.

"Bring him hither!" exclaimed his father,—"bring him hither quickly!"

The old minister now approached Mr. Gemmell's bedside, leading Ralph in his hand. "I have wronged thee, my son! I have deeply wronged thee!" exclaimed Mr. Gemmell, as he reached his hand over his bed, and drew his son forward to his embrace. "Canst thou forgive me? Will God forgive me for my iniquities to thee?"

"I have forgiven you already," said Ralph, while he wept over his father's breast, "and God is willing to forgive you too."

Here the good old servant of God gave one hand to the son and another to the father, and offered up his heart's desire unto God. After this he exhorted Mr. Gemmell to put his trust in God; entreated him to believe in the promises of the gospel, which, he assured him, were given to the chief of sinners; and then took his leave and returned home.

"You look very ill," said Ralph to his father, when they were left alone. "I am fast dying," replied his father; "I caught a cold last winter, it has never left me; and I am now so weak, I cannot stir from my bed. But where have you been wandering all this while, my son? I need not ask; I know what you have suffered. I have been a cruel father to you. I wished you to live like myself, careless of religion; and because you could not do this, I drove you from my house. Your grievances, however, I can in some measure redress. I have destroyed the former will which I rashly made, and restored you to your proper rights; and thrice happy am I that you have returned to heir that estate you so well deserve."

Here Mr. Gemmell was interrupted by Edward coming into the room. "Here is your brother," said his father to him. "You know how much I have wronged him—how much I have taught you to wrong him."

"But Ralph will forgive me," said Edward; for he

APPROACHED MR. GEMMELL'S BEDSIDE LEADING RALPH IN
HIS HAND.—*See page* 178.

knew the tenderness of his brother's heart,—"Ralph will
forgive me. You have often seen me weep, father,
when we talked about him since you turned ill."

"My dear brother," said Ralph, "you are indeed
forgiven." And the two brothers warmly embraced one
another.

"Now," said Mr. Gemmell, raising himself up on
his bed, when he saw his sons weep for gladness in
each other's arms,—"now I am happy as far as this
world is concerned. You are both well provided for;
and you will be kind to one another. But, oh, Ralph!
I am not yet prepared for death. I have sinned griev-
ously—I have been a curse to my own family—I have
persecuted the people of God—I am the vilest of sinners
—and I fear that God in His anger may cast me off for
ever. Yesterday I sent for the good old minister (so
kindly did Mr. Gemmell now speak of those men whom
he had once scorned as the offscourings of the earth),
and he gave me some comfort. He displayed the way
of salvation through Jesus Christ, and encouraged me
to believe in Him. I do wish to believe in Him. I see
no other way of escaping the wrath to come. But I
fear my heinous sins have provoked Him to leave me
for ever."

Can you imagine, young reader, with what feelings
Ralph heard his father talk thus, or with what eagerness and anxious love he began to comfort him?

"Dear father," he said, "Christ loves us the better,
the more we hate ourselves; and we do Him wrong,
when we think that the greatness of our sins will
hinder us from being accepted of God through Him.
It is not because we are sinners that God will not
accept of us; for if this were true, no man could be
saved. It is because we will not believe in Christ, nor
repent, nor forsake our sins that He will not save us.
This is the saying of God to every man, even to the
chief of sinners: 'Believe in the Lord Jesus Christ,
and thou shalt be saved.' He died for our sins, and

rose again for our justification. His grace is sufficient for us: He perfects His strength in our weakness. Is not the blood of Jesus Christ, the Son of God, sufficient to wash out the vilest sin from our souls? The blood of Christ cleanseth from all sin. God is well pleased with us, that is, with all who believe in Christ, for His righteousness' sake. If, then, we are willing to believe in Christ, if we are willing to forsake our sins, and to be made holy, we have the word of God witnessing to us that Christ is willing to plead His suffering and death in our behalf, to sanctify us by His Spirit, and to present us at last to His Father, without spot, or wrinkle, or any such thing."

"Lord, I believe; help my unbelief!" exclaimed his father, when Ralph had done speaking. And again he cried, "Lord, I believe; help my unbelief!" Ralph saw by his look and difficulty of breathing that death was at hand. He fell down on his knees, with Edward by the bedside, and prayed for his father. It was a fervent, effectual prayer, and it was heard.

Ralph now asked his father if he felt his trust any stronger in his Saviour. "He hath come to me at the eleventh hour," said his father. "I hope all is well. Oh, the love of God in Christ Jesus!" He could utter no more, but casting a look of ineffable affection on his son, he fell back on his bed and expired.

To have been the means of saving a soul from death, will be to every one who has been so honoured a thought of sweetest delight throughout eternity; but what infinite joy of heart must it be to have the conscious feeling that we have been instrumental in accomplishing the salvation of a father or a mother, a brother or a sister! This feeling was now Ralph's reward. It was his zealous perseverance in obedience to God, against so much opposition, that first led his father to think seriously of his own conduct. He was, as we have seen, the means of enlightening and comforting him in his last moments; and he received from him a look of affection and gratitude which recompensed him more than a hundredfold for all his past afflictions. By his example and instruction, Edward, too, forsook the error of his ways; and he had the satisfaction of seeing him, after having devoted himself several years to study, become a faithful and zealous minister of the gospel of Christ.

At his father's death, Ralph succeeded to the paternal inheritance; and we deem it unnecessary to say more of his future life, than that in prosperity, as he had done in adversity, he put his whole trust in his Saviour, walked in the way of His commandments, and to the end of his days experienced it to be a true saying—that God will never leave nor forsake those who put their trust in Him.

Young reader, before I take my leave of you, let us reflect a little on the history of Ralph. You have seen him in childhood reading his Bible, and listening to the instructions of his mother. You have seen him, after her death, trusting too much to himself—breaking his pious resolutions—renouncing his religion—and walking in that way in which sinners go. Then, you remember, he had all that his heart could desire of this world's bounties. He was beloved and caressed by his friends, honoured by his acquaintances, and filled with the hope of a life of ease and prosperity. And what was then the sum of his happiness? His conscience condemned him; remorse embittered all his pleasure; and when he thought he was dying, he shook with the terrors of despair; for he had secured no Almighty Friend to stand by him at that last hour when the help of man is vain. So shall you be overcome by the threatenings and allurements of the world, if you seek not continually the guidance of the Holy Spirit—if you rely not wholly on the grace of your Saviour. And if you continue to live in sin, so shall the bitterness of remorse come upon you, and so shall you find yourself friendless and in

despair at the approach of death. Again, you have
seen him awakened to his duty by the grace of God,
while at the same time he was forbidden his father's
house—despised by his friends—wandering in poverty
—labouring in the field or begging his bread—now with
the immediate prospect of an ignominious and untimely
death before him—and now in banishment and slavery;
and what was then the sum of his happiness? In the
severest moment of his sufferings, he had that peace of
mind which passeth all understanding—he had the hope
of eternal life—he had the smile of God's countenance,
and the assurance that He would never forsake him.
This was his happiness. It will be yours too, young
reader, if you so serve God, so resist the world, and
so take up your cross and follow Christ. We cannot
promise you the same wealth in the world as that which
fell to the share of Ralph; but if you persevere, like
him, in well-doing, you may be the means of saving
some near relation or dear friend; and we can promise
you, on the authority of God, that in poverty He will
enrich you—in suffering He will solace you—in temptation He will strengthen you—in sickness He will be
your health—in death your rod and your staff—and after
death your everlasting reward. Persevere, then, my
young friend, in well-doing; put thy trust in God, and
thou shalt find Him, in life and death, in time and
eternity, thy ever-present and all-sufficient friend.

The Persecuted Family

The Persecuted Family

Introductory Note

THE lives and memories of our Christian ancestors, who suffered so much for the blessings of that civil and religious liberty which the inhabitants of Britain now enjoy, ought, one would think, to be peculiarly interesting and sacred to us, their posterity. Yet it so happens that while the warrior, who has drained his own country of its wealth, and emptied it of its bravest people, to carry devastation and ruin over other nations, attracts the historic pen minutely to record his deeds, and the genius of poetry, in lofty verse, to sing his praise,—those glorious sufferers who exposed themselves to the fury of persecution, and, like the true soldiers of Jesus Christ, patient, persevering, and zealous, fought in behalf of all that is dear to man, are wholly forgotten by many—their characters ridiculed, and their actions misrepresented by others, and the courage with which they suffered for our good too little admired by all. The patriot, who takes the sword in his hand and, at the head of his countrymen, makes extraordinary efforts to repel the invasion of an enemy, or to shake the guilty despot from the strongholds of his tyranny, becomes, as he deserves, the subject of warmest eulogy; and there is not a passage in his history which the young and old of his country cannot relate. But if the patriot, who has saved his country from an enemy or rid it of oppression, is worthy of his laurels, is he less worthy who abandons the comforts of plenty, submits to every privation, and offers himself to every trial, that he may do his duty to

God while he lives and hand down religion in its purity
to after generations ? With more pomp, indeed, are the
steps of the patriot soldier attended ; but the sufferings
of the persecuted Christian bring more glory to God and
more good to man. The one fights, that he may secure
our possessions from plunder and our bodies from
slavery : the other suffers, that he may preserve for us an
inheritance which fadeth not away—a peace which
passeth understanding—a liberty which is spiritual—and
a life which is eternal. The one fights for the reputation
of his country, and our rights as men : the other suffers
for the glory of God, and our privileges as immortal
beings. Every sigh, we know, of our persecuted
ancestors is recorded in heaven ; every tear which they
shed is preserved in the bottle of God. Why, then,
should their memories not be dear to us, for whom they
bled and for whom they died ?

But it is not only that we may pay them our debt of
gratitude that we ought to acquaint ourselves with their
lives ; it is that we may gather humility from their
lowliness, faith from their trust in God, courage from
their heaven-sustained fortitude, warmth from the flame
of their devotion, and hope from their glorious success.
In this age of peace to the Church, the love of many hath
waxed cold. Because God requires less hard service of
us than He did of our forefathers, we seem to grudge the
performance of it. To rekindle the dying embers of zeal
and warm the heart of coldness, we know nothing better
than to peruse the lives of those who suffered so much,
and with such willingness of heart, for those religious
privileges which we now enjoy in peace and security.
Youth, especially, have need to make themselves well
acquainted with their lives ; for they can scarcely fail to
meet with books in which heedless genius has held them
forth to laughter ; and if they are not taught to revere
them, they will soon be taught to hold them in ridicule.
Many of their lives, however, are either written in so
antiquated and ungainly a phraseology as to be noways

inviting to the youthful mind, or are blended with circumstances so extraordinary as to discredit and destroy the effect of what is true. It is a belief of this which has induced me to lay before the public the following narrative, the different parts of which, although I do not pretend to say they happened in the very same relation which I have given them, are all severally true, and such as require no credence in those miracles which have so hurt and discredited the character and actions of our persecuted ancestors.

Chapter I

"There stands the messenger of truth ; there stands
The legate of the skies ! His theme divine,
His office sacred, his credentials clear.
In doctrine uncorrupt : in language plain,
And plain in manner : decent, solemn, chaste,
And natural in gesture ; much impressed
Himself, as conscious of his awful charge,
And anxious mainly that the flock he feeds
May feel it too. Affectionate in look,
And tender in address, as well becomes
A messenger of grace to guilty men."

—COWPER.

THE REVEREND Mr. JAMES BRUCE, the head of that family whose lives we are briefly to record, was the youngest son of a very respectable gentleman in the upper district of Lanarkshire. In his boyhood he gave such indications of superior talent and love of piety and learning as induced his father to educate him for the ministry. During the course of his studies in the University of Glasgow, James applied himself to the various branches of education which were then taught, with an assiduity and success which proved that his father was noways wrong in the profession he had chosen for his son. In divine literature, to which the pious bent of his mind, as well as his future views, directed him chiefly, his progress was

extremely rapid, and his acquirements solid and extensive.
Of controversial theology he was by no means ignorant ;
although his mild and peaceful mind delighted itself
especially in contemplating the plain truths of the Bible,
and how they might be impressed with the happiest
effects on the souls of men.   The New Testament he read
continually ; and his heart was warmed with its love,
and his soul fashioned to its precepts.   As his judgment
was sound, so his feelings were strong.   The history
of our Saviour's life, and sufferings, and death, made
a most extraordinary impression on his mind ; and
while he read, and loved, and adored, his soul took
on the likeness of the great Testator, in the holy simplicity of his character, in resignation to the will of God,
in devotion to the duties of religion, and in love to
mankind.   To those acquirements, without which a minister is ill fitted for his office, he added a pretty extensive knowledge of philosophy and books of taste ; and
withal he was not an unsuccessful student of the human
heart.

The romantic scenery amidst which his childhood had
been nursed had strongly imaged on his mind the pure
objects of nature ; and following his own propensity, as
well as imitating the writers of the Bible, he made ample
use of them, in summoning them forth to bear witness to
God's power, and wisdom, and goodness, and in illustrat-
ing by them the doctrines of the gospel.

With a mind thus prepared, in his twenty-sixth year,
Mr. Bruce received a call from the inhabitants of S——
(a small village on the water of Ayr) and its neighbourhood to be their minister.   The call, as every minister
of sincere heart would wish, was cordial and unanimous.
The situation of the village, although this was only a
secondary consideration with Mr. Bruce, was such as
peculiarly concorded with his feelings and desires.
Placed in a sequestered hollow, through which the Ayr
led its stream, winding pleasantly, covered with hills
which rose abruptly on every side, giving root to the

beech, the oak, and the birch, which interwove their varied robes in Nature's taste, the little village seemed to be the very home of pensive goodness and holy meditation. These things urged him to accept the call. Above all, that he might be like his Saviour, continually engaged in his Heavenly Father's work, instructing the ignorant and training immortal spirits for heaven, he gladly complied with the invitation, and was accordingly settled among them.

Soon after this settlement he married Miss Eliza Inglis, the daughter of a gentleman who lived in the neighbourhood of Mr. Bruce's father. This marriage was the result of a long-nourished affection, founded on like tastes and like desires. As they had spent their childhood and youth near one another, they became early acquainted, and early attached to each other. Miss Inglis, as she grew up, added to a handsome person and an engaging countenance, the prudence and industry of domestic management, as well as some of those more liberal acquirements fitted to render her a proper companion for a person of learning and taste. But what had attached Mr. Bruce to her, and what was still the charm that bound his heart closer and closer to hers, was the natural tenderness of her soul, and the meek loveliness of her piety. It was this holy kind-heartedness, this simplicity of nature, added to the humility of the Christian, that threw enchantment into her look, and made her the more beloved the more she was known.

Such was the young lady whom, in her twenty-fourth year, Mr. Bruce made the partner of his life. Her good report had reached the village before her, and she was received with joy. The meekness and innocence of her countenance was a passport to the hearts of all with whom she conversed ; and the young as well as the old, the rich as well as the poor, applauded Mr. Bruce's prudent choice ; and, no doubt, conscious as he was of this world's vanity, he pictured to himself a long perspective of the purest and sweetest of earthly felicity. And, indeed, if youth and health, the comforts of plenty, wedded affection, mutually and fondly cherished, founded on the best of motives, and strengthened and tempered by the influences of religion together with the esteem and love of neighbours, and peace with ourself and our Maker, could warrant any man to hope for much and long-lasting happiness under the sun, surely Mr. Bruce might well entertain this hope.

In the pulpit, Mr. Bruce was truly the messenger of God. He knew the dignity of his office and its awful responsibility ; and, regardless of the face of man, with an earnestness which was of the heart, and with a voice, and look, and gesture, which suited themselves at all times to his subject, he made known the momentous commandments with which his Master had entrusted him, and enforced the practise of them. Although he was by no means remiss in setting before his flock the terrors of God's wrath, which shall awfully fall on the finally impenitent, his natural mildness of disposition rather led him to enlarge on the eternal love of God, manifested in the scheme of redemption ; and to allure his people from the evil of their ways, by painting the beauties of holiness, bringing home to their minds the joy of peace with God, and pointing their eye away to the rewards of immortality. He rather drew his flock after him, as with the suasive of irresistible melody, than drove them into the straight path by the frownings of offended justice and the threatenings of coming vengeance.

The abstract doctrines of Christianity he did not leave untaught ; but he urged incessantly the practise of heartfelt godliness, faith in Jesus Christ, love to God, and charity to man. He never thought of wasting time, and defrauding his hearers, by heaping together numberless meanings for one passage of Scripture, or proving what no one ever doubted, or in endeavouring to bring to the level of human capacity those truths of revelation which Infinity alone can fully understand, and which we are rather commanded to believe than comprehend. He did not so much give reason after reason to prove why God had a right to enjoin this or that duty, because he knew that few doubted this right, as he set himself to persuade his flock to the doing of it. What is practical in Christianity, he exhorted his people to practise; what is subject of credence merely, he believed, and taught others the reasonableness of believing it, and its influence on the heart and life; and instead of bewildering himself, and producing doubt and darkness in the minds of his auditors, by entering boldly, like many divines, on the explanation of what is in itself incomprehensible, he stood still, and believed, and adored, and took from it a lesson of humility.

But what, in his public ministrations, drew every ear into attention, and, through the blessing of God, produced such effects on the heart, was not more the soundness of his doctrines than the earnestness of his persuasions. His was not the cold-hearted address of formality, which suits so ill a servant of the ever-earnest Jesus. He seemed to know the worth of an immortal soul, and the value of eternal happiness; and he pleaded for God and truth—for man's welfare here and hereafter, as one would plead for the life of an only son. He taught, he warned, he rebuked, he comforted, with his whole heart; and was not ashamed that, like his great Master, the tears of love and holy sorrow should be sometimes seen weeping down his cheek.

His daily manners suited his character in the pulpit. He was grave, decorous, and affable; dignified without loftiness, and familiar without meanness. He disgusted not the old by levity, nor terrified the young by austerity. Regarding himself as the spiritual father of his flock, and naturally kind, he made the interest of all his own. The child, as well as the man of grey hairs, found in him a cheerful friend and a pleasant instructor. Mr. Bruce spent much of his time in visiting from house to

13

house ; a duty enjoined by the Bible, which the ministers
of the seventeenth century seem to have recognised, or
at least practised, better than those of the nineteenth.
Although his learning and cultivated manners made him
noways disagreeable to the higher circles, and his duty
sometimes called him to mingle with them, yet you
would not always have seen him in the train of the
wealthy, or seated by the table of luxury. He went
about comforting the broken-hearted, infusing the balm
of heavenly comfort into the wounded soul, and ad-
ministering here and there, out of his little income, to
the wants of the needy. He entered into the hut of
widowed loneliness, and took his station by the bed of
poverty in distress. The dying saint saw him enter his
chamber, and caught brighter views of the land beyond
the grave from his conversation, and felt his faith
increase in the earnestness of his prayers. Nor did he
pass by the house where the wicked man lay on the bed
of death ; but drew near his couch, and laboured, with
admonition, with prayer, with entreaty, to turn the
sinner's eye to the cross of Christ, and save his soul
from death. His character was indeed a model which
his parishioners might have imitated with as much safety
as they obeyed the doctrines which he taught. He
never thought of preaching humility, and yet walking in
the stately steps of pride ; of recommending purity of
heart, and yet indulging in the pleasures of sense ; of
eulogising and enforcing charity, and yet shutting his
own ear to the cry of want.

While Mr. Bruce was thus engaged, feeding his flock
and endearing himself to them by his constant vigilance
for their welfare, he enjoyed the utmost domestic peace
and happiness. Mrs. Bruce's prudent management
saved him from all trouble with household affairs. His
stipend was small, but she regulated her expenses
accordingly. His manse, like many of the clergymen's
houses in those days, was, when he came to it, a very
inconvenient and dull-looking building ; and had been

suffered, besides, to fall into sad disrepair by the former
incumbent, who had lived a single life, and, although
peculiarly careful of his charge, had minded little about
the comforts of his own house. The rain found its way
plentifully through the ragged roof; the windows had,
in many instances, exchanged their glass panes for
boards, or something still less befitting, and were nearly
darkened by the honeysuckle and rose-trees, which had
been left to spread at will. Up the walls, too, clambered
the dock and the nettle ; and the little plot, which gently
sloped from the door to the river, was so overgrown
with brushwood and weeds of every description, that the
passage to the stream in that direction was almost
shut up. The inside of the house was in no better state.
The cornice and plaster, in many places, had fallen from
the walls ; the floor was so decayed as to endanger the
fall of those who walked on it ; and in the closets and
bedrooms, spiders and other vermin had long taken up
their abode.

As Mr. Bruce was generally beloved, the heritors, of
their own accord, agreed to repair his house ; and, under
Mrs. Bruce's care, everything about the manse soon
assumed a livelier and more handsome appearance.
The vermin were driven from their settlements, the
windows filled with glass, and everything within assorted
with taste and elegance. The improvement was not less
conspicuous without. The little plot before the house
was cleared of its brambles and weeds, and assumed the
smoothness of a bowling-green ; the dock and nettle
were uprooted ; and the rose and honeysuckle, although
preserved with care, were now taught to bend their
branches in subordination to taste and usefulness. The
broad stone which lay immediately before the front door,
and which had been hid under a thick coat of dirt, was
cleaned and washed ; and, indeed, all without looked so
cheerful, orderly, and comfortable, as well bespoke the
peace, and concord, and happiness that dwelt within.
So inviting the old dwelling looked, that the traveller

would not have passed it without wishing to see its inhabitants ; and the weary wanderer would have approached the door in confidence of a kind welcome to nourishment and repose.

Mr. Bruce, as we have observed, as he had no need, gave himself no trouble about household affairs. His hours of leisure, which were indeed but few, were therefore spent in some innocent amusement. At these times Mrs. Bruce was always ready to attend him. Her conversation, cheerful and varied, never failed to refresh his mind when it had been exhausted by study, and to restore it to tranquillity when it had been disturbed by any unpleasing occurrence. Mr. Bruce was very fond of the simple songs of his country ; and although his wife's voice was not surprisingly fine, or her management of it very tasteful, her singing would have pleased any one who admired simplicity and feeling. But her husband was delighted ; for he gazed on her with eyes of the tenderest affection while she sung to him the sweet melodies of Scotland. Sometimes they read together in some useful and entertaining book—sometimes they walked by the banks of the Ayr, enjoying the loveliness of nature, and giving audience to the song of the thrush and the blackbird, which from the birch or hawthorn joined their minstrelsy to the mellow pipe of the wind and the purling voice of the stream.

To all these enjoyments were added, first a son and afterwards a daughter : the one, Andrew, as everybody said, the very image of his father ; the other, Mary, no less the likeness of her mother. Eager to instruct all, Mr. Bruce was doubly so with regard to his own children. He observed, with a father's and Christian's eye, the opening of their infant faculties, and at an early hour shed upon them the light of truth, and spared no pains to warm their young and tender hearts with love to God and religion. He taught them betimes the way to heaven, setting their faces thitherward : and it pleased God to bless his teaching, and render it effectual. He taught

them love to one another and to their fellow-creatures ;
and he turned the attention of their minds to those pleas-
ing and sublime ideas which the objects of nature are
fitted to produce.

Andrew, who seemed to resemble his father in his
mental as well as corporeal parts, was early designed for
the ministry. His education was, therefore, conducted
chiefly under his father's eye ; while Mary learned the
more gentle and delicate accomplishments, befitting her
character, from her mother ; and never had parents more
comfort in instructing and watching over their offspring.
They loved their parents, and did everything to please
them : they loved each other, feared God, and delighted
in obeying His will. They increased daily in knowledge
and stature, growing up like well-watered plants which
the Lord hath blessed. The rose of health bloomed on
their cheeks, and the sacred spirit of religion looked
already from their eyes.

Religion ! thou art happiness. Thou infusest the
calm of heaven into the bosom of man, and pourest into
his heart the sweetness of celestial enjoyment. Thou hast,
indeed, special rewards to give in the land of glory.
There thou openest the arms of everlasting felicity to
receive all thy followers at last, into the fulness of its
embrace—there thou securest them a place by the font
of original life. But thou art even here infinitely superior
to every other thing in the purity and sweetness of thy
enjoyments. Thou art thyself fair as the light of God ;
and thou stampest on all the pleasures of thy sons the
imagery of heaven, and minglest them with the relishes
of immortality. Woe unto him that seeketh his happiness apart from thee ! He shall be miserably disappointed.

Chapter II

" Unpractised he to fawn or seek for power
By doctrines fashioned to the varying hour ;
Far other aims his heart had learned to prize,
More skilled to raise the wretched than to rise.
To them his heart, his love, his griefs were given,
But all his serious thoughts had vent in heaven.
As some tall cliff that lifts its awful form,
Swells from the vale, and midway leaves the storm,
Though round its breast the rolling clouds are spread,
Eternal sunshine settles on its head."

FOURTEEN years had passed over this happy family, when the Restoration threatened the overthrow of the Scottish Church. Charles, advised by his English and Irish ministers, Clarendon and Ormond, and latterly by Lauderdale, Secretary for Scotland, introduced the episcopal form of worship into Scotland. Patronage was renewed, and the clergy required to procure a presentation from their patrons, and collation from their bishops, to acknowledge their authority and the spiritual supremacy of the king. The clergy in the northern districts complied without hesitation ; but their more pious and zealous brethren in the west, however willing they might be to submit to and support the civil authority of the king, rejected his spiritual supremacy, refused submission to the Episcopalian judicatories, and preferred rather to suffer the extremity of persecution than to sacrifice what they deemed the truth and their duty to God. The people were no less averse to this encroachment on their religious privileges, and resolved to imitate their pastors, whose engaging familiarity and sanctity of manners had gained them the esteem and love of their flocks.

But if they had determined to suffer rather than renounce the Covenant and their beloved presbytery, the bishops, who had now got all power in Scotland into their hands, determined no less than the destruction of both. Burnet, Archbishop of Glasgow, and the apostate

Sharp, Primate of St. Andrews, with a cruelty little be-coming mitred heads, prepared to carry this into effect. Ambulatory courts were established, on the principles of the Inquisition, in which the bishops were the judges of those whom they wished to destroy. No regard was had to remonstrance or entreaty, or even to evidence. To these courts the military were subordinate, and instructed to carry their resolutions, which were often formed in the midst of riot and drunkenness, into execution. By this procedure three hundred and fifty clergymen were ejected from their livings in the severity of winter, and driven, with their families, to seek shelter among the peasants. The most ignorant and vicious of their northern brethren, who scrupled at no compliance, were thrust, by the strong hand of power, into their places. The ignorance and shameful lives of these apostates from the covenant, who were now metamorphosed into curates, disgusted the people on whom they had been forced. Their doc-trines had none of that heavenly relish which suited the taste of those who had been formerly taught by the best and most affectionate of men. Their churches were deserted ; and the people went into the mountains in search of that water of life which no longer flowed from the pulpits.

But this was only the beginning of their trials. Their pastors were soon forbidden to preach even in the fields, or to approach within twenty miles of their former charges ; and all the people, as well as their pastors, who were not prepared to abjure their dearest rights, and to submit to the most galling and iniquitous civil and religious des-potism, were denounced as traitors, and doomed to capital punishment. To admit any one who refused com-pliance into shelter—to favour his escape, or not to assist in apprehending him—subjected the person so con-victed to the same punishment. To this, military per-secution succeeded. The soldiers were both the judges and the executioners. The very forms of justice were now wholly abandoned. Gentlemen, and peasants, and

ministers were driven out to wander among the morasses
and mountains of the country—were crowded into gaols
—sent into exile and slavery, and multitudes were daily
writhing in the torture, or perishing on the gibbet.
Rapes, robberies, and every species of outrage were
committed by the soldiers with impunity. The west of
Scotland was red with the blood of its own inhabitants,
shed by their own countrymen. The spirits of darkness
seemed to have entered into the bosoms of the persecutors, and to actuate all their doings. They appeared to
delight in cruelty, and in shedding the blood of the
innocent. But the glorious sufferers, relying on the
goodness of their cause, and hoping in the promises of
God, opposed sanctity of life to licentiousness and riot ;
the spiritual weapons of truth, to the swords of their
enemies ; patient endurance, to fatigue, and want, and
torture ; and calm resignation, to the most ignominious
deaths. And truly they suffered not nor bled in vain.
God at last gave them the victory over all their enemies,
and, through them, secured to us the religious privileges
we this day enjoy. From this short sketch of the times,
which we thought necessary to explain what shall afterwards occur, we return to that family which we left so
happy.

Among those clergymen who bravely refused compliance with the iniquitous orders of Government was
Mr. Bruce. Although naturally mild, an ardent lover of
good order, and ready at all times to impress on his flock
the duty of submission to all the lawful commands of the
civil authorities, he could not think for a moment of
violating his conscience, and of teaching his people to
violate theirs, by forsaking what he deemed his duty to
his Heavenly Master. But there was only one alternative.
Either he must comply with the sinful and tyrannical
requirements of the bishops, in whose hands the civil
power was, or relinquish his pastoral charge, and quit
his house and his living. Mr. Bruce was not a man to
hesitate whether to seek the praise of men or the praise

of God. On the last Sabbath on which it was permitted him to enter his pulpit, he thus took farewell of his beloved flock :

" You know, my dear friends," said he, " what orders I have received from the bishops, who possess, for the time, the civil as well as the ecclesiastical authority. I am required to acknowledge the king as supreme head of the Church ; to submit to the diocesan jurisdiction of the bishops ; to be reordained, and converted into a curate ; and to introduce the episcopal mode of worship into this church. In a word, I am to renounce presbytery ; preach, not as the Bible and my own conscience direct me, but according to the wishes of a drunken and licentious court, and the dictates of a self-interested and domineering priesthood. And all this I am enjoined to do, or leave you, my house, and my living.

" You cannot but know that I have determined on this last. I have not so learned my duty, as not to be able to sacrifice a little of this world's comfort for conscience' sake ; and I would rather that my tongue should be for ever dumb, than that it should utter one word from this sacred place merely to please men in power, and secure my own worldly gratification. I can part with the comforts of a home, but how can I part with you, my dear friends ? We have lived together in the bonds of love. Every one of you is endeared to me by some particular kindness given or received. I have watched over the childhood of many of you, and now see you advancing in the knowledge of religion as you grow up to manhood. Others of you I have seen growing grey with years ; and I have endeavoured to smooth your way, and stay your steps down the slope of time. All of you I have cared for—all of you I have set my heart upon— all of you have been to me as fathers or sons, as brothers or sisters. How can I part with you, my beloved flock ? How can I leave you like sheep without a shepherd, and like sheep in the midst of ravening wolves ? O God !" he exclaimed, and the people rose up as if by enchantment—" O God! who seest my heart, Thou knowest what love I bear to this people; Thou knowest how dear their souls are to me. Oh, hear my cry! keep them from the evil of the world, from the snares which are laid for their feet; and if they should never hear the word of life from my lips again; if Thou hast, in Thy wise providence, wandering and weeping prepared for them, O Father, so watch over their souls, that I may meet them all at last by the right hand of their Saviour and my Saviour, of their God and my God. Father in heaven, into Thy hands we commit our immortal spirits!"

When he had thus spoken, he sat down in the pulpit and wept bitterly. Nor did he weep alone. The man of grey hairs wept, and the child sobbed by his side. And when they looked to the holy man, whose sorrow was all for them—and when they turned their eyes to the seat where his wife sat, bathed in tears, and her children, Andrew and Mary, weeping aloud, and looking up to their father; and when they thought that they were to be driven out from their happy home, to wander in poverty, again their tears flowed, and again they looked and wept.

Mr. Bruce was the first to recover some degree of composure. He begged his sorrowing audience not to give themselves up to vain lamentations; but rather to be thankful for the comfortable days they had spent together; to be putting their hope and their confidence in God; and to be preparing for the sufferings to which it was likely they would soon be exposed. In surveying the aspect of the times, he said, he had no doubt that the entire destruction of the Presbyterian Church was meditated; and a severe persecution, he had every reason to believe, was about to commence, in which their faith and their patience would be put to a severe trial. He advised them to be as inoffensive as possible to the civil powers, and to give prompt and cordial obedience to all their lawful commands; but exhorted them rather to suffer than renounce the Covenant, or make the smallest compliance in violation of their own consciences; assuring them, at the same time, if they suffered now they would rejoice hereafter. God would remember every sigh, and treasure up all their tears in His bottle. Their patient endurance would tire out the arm of persecution. They would thus leave the blessings of religious liberty to their posterity; and if they themselves suffered to the death, they would be rewarded in heaven with a crown of life.

After this valedictory admonition and encouragement, having recommended his flock again to the care of Heaven, he descended from the pulpit, amidst the weepings of his congregation; and when he had, with difficulty, withdrawn himself from them, he retired with his wife and children to his house.

In the pulpit, Mr. Bruce had carefully avoided making any allusion to his own family. His feelings of sorrow, on their account, were of that deep and sacred kind which we rather wish to shut up in the sanctuary of our own bosoms, than trust to the sympathy of the most confiding friendship. How could he see her, who had been long the companion of his life, endeared to him by every tie that can draw kindred souls into the closest fellowship,—her who had been ever used to the comforts of plenty,—driven from a home which she had made so comfortable, exposed to fatigue, to homeless wandering, and perhaps, to want itself? How could he see his dear children, whom she had nursed so tenderly, and in whom resided his dearest earthly hopes, turned out, unable as they were to provide for themselves, on the sympathies of the world? He knew, indeed, that as long as he and his family were permitted to wander among his flock, they would be in no danger of want; but it was easy to read, from the face of the times, that even this would soon be denied them; and he already saw his family, in the forward eye of imagination, suffering under all the evils of insult and beggary.

On this subject he had not dared hitherto to enter,

even to Mrs. Bruce. She observed it, and was well aware of the cause; and anxious to relieve his feelings, on the Sabbath evening, while they sat in their snug parlour, gazing in silent dejection on their children, she thus began the conversation—

"Do not be so sorrowful on our account, dear James," she said. "I have shared in all your enjoyments, and I can suffer with you too; and so can these children. We may have many hardships to encounter, but we will have the approbation of our own minds—we will have the protection of that God in whom we have always trusted, and we know that He will not suffer anything effectually to hurt us. We will have your love, my dear James; and we shall still be happy in sharing your trials and soothing your cares."

"Dearest Eliza," said Mr. Bruce, "you are indeed right. God will be our protector. Why should we hesitate to cast ourselves upon His care? I could have easily made up my mind to this trial, but for you and these children. But why should I cast one lingering look on these comforts, which my Master bids me leave? He can protect you as well as me. Under His guidance we are safe. To-morrow we quit this house, which is to be occupied by another; and let us quit it without a murmur. What is the threatening or indulgence of this world to us? What are its joys or its pains? To do our duty to God, our Creator and Redeemer,—to love, to honour, and to obey Him,—this is sufficient for us. He will see that no evil befall us."

Here Mr. Bruce paused for a little, and then proceeded thus:—

"But let us act with prudence, my dear Eliza. Might it not be proper for you and the children to go and live with your friends at Lanark for the present? You will then have a settled home; and I am sure you will be kindly treated. For my own part, I am resolved to continue among my flock, and to take every opportunity of serving their spiritual interests."

"No, no," said Mrs. Bruce; "we will not leave you.
I am determined to suffer with you. Nothing but death
shall part me from you."

"But these children," said Mr. Bruce; "think of
them, dear Eliza."

CLASPED THEIR HANDS ABOUT THEIR FATHER'S NECK.—*See page* 206.

"They are stout and healthy," replied Mrs. Bruce;
"and you shall see how cheerfully they will submit to
everything, rather than part with you. Will you leave
your father, Andrew? Will you, Mary?"

"No, no," they both exclaimed ; and weeping, clasped their hands about their father's neck, alarmed to hear their mother speak of their leaving him.

Andrew was at this time in his thirteenth year, a fine smart-looking boy ; stout at his age, his hair black and bushy, and his eye, full, dark, and penetrating. Of his talents we have already spoken. They were of a high order ; and, under his father's assiduous culture, he had already made considerable progress in learning. Indeed, his acquirements of every kind were beyond his years. His father was his only companion as well as instructor, and his attention had thus been turned at all times to something useful. His susceptible mind had rapidly imbibed his father's ideas, and, in fact, had already stored up most of his knowledge. In piety, in the love of learning, in the amiableness of his disposition, Andrew resembled his father ; but his mind gave indications of more boldness and originality. Indeed, there already appeared in him a decision of character, a steady adherance to his resolutions, and a firm perseverance in the pursuit of whatever caught his attention, which, in union with his religious spirit, promised a life of the highest usefulness.

Mary, who was now in her eleventh year, with cheeks fair and rosy, a fine soft blue eye, and a profusion of golden ringlets flowing on her shoulders, had all the light-hearted gaiety and innocent loveliness which girls, properly educated, generally have at that age. Impressed thus early with the sacredness of religion, its purity seemed to beam from her eye. Her love to her relations was in proportion to her tenderness of heart. To please her mother, her father, and her brother, to hear them say she had done well, made her happy. A fairer and a sweeter plant hath nature nowhere ; and, in the retirement of the secluded manse, she looked like one of those flowers which the traveller may sometimes meet in the desert, so lovely that he cannot feel in his heart to pull it, and yet knows not how to leave it behind.

Mr. Bruce, perceiving it was needless to say anything

more about his family leaving him, turned their attention for a considerable time to those truths of the Christian religion which are best fitted to prepare us for bearing changes and trials with fortitude and resignation. And then the family, after joining as usual in the worship of God, withdrew to repose.

Chapter III

" He establishes the strong, restores the weak,
Reclaims the wanderer, binds the broken heart,
And, armed himself in panoply complete
Of heavenly temper, furnishes with arms
Bright as his own, and trains, by every rule
Of holy discipline, to glorious war,
The sacramental host of God's elect ! "

—Cowper.

Early on the Monday morning, Mr. Bruce and his family arose ; and having committed their way to God, prepared to leave their house. The furniture was dispersed among the neighbours, except a few articles necessary for their comfort, which were sent to Braeside, a farmhouse, situated in a romantic glen about four miles from the village, whither Mr. Bruce had chosen to retire. Everything was soon put in order for their departure.

And now the venerable pastor, with Andrew and Mary, holding each other by the hand, before him, and his wife by his side, slowly and silently left the manse. The two youngsters tript on cheerfully, happy enough that they were going with their parents. Mrs. Bruce could not be very sad when her husband was by her side ; and the minister had prepared himself too well for this event to show much uneasiness. Yet neither he nor his wife could help dropping a tear as they passed the church, and entered the street of the little village through which their road lay. But the grief of the villagers was excessive. They saw their spiritual guide, their comforter,

their adviser, their friend, in the coldness and severity of
a winter morning, with his wife and children, driven from
his comfortable dwelling and about to leave them.
Would he assemble them no more on the Sabbath, to
refresh their souls with the water of life? Would they
see him no more going from door to door through the
village, relieving the poor, comforting the sick, and instructing all? What hardships would these children, and
that amiable woman, who, although by no means un-
healthy, appeared to them so delicate, have probably to
endure? And was his pulpit to be filled, and his house and
living seized, by some time-serving, cold-hearted stranger?

Full of these sorrowful thoughts, every inhabitant of
the village, both old and young, crowded about Mr.
Bruce and his family. So anxious was everyone to be
near their beloved minister, that they eagerly pressed
forward, and often compelled him to stop. He conjured
them to leave him: but it was not till they had accompanied him more than a mile out of the village that he
could prevail on them to think of parting with him.
Here he shook hands with each of them: exhorted them
to avoid all evil; and lifted up his voice and blessed them,
while they stood drowned in tears.

Now Mr. Bruce and his family, with a few who had
determined to accompany him, set forward to Braeside,
while the villagers and peasants returned to their homes,
sorrowing in heart, and determined rather to suffer all
than make any compliance to an ecclesiastical government which had begun so harshly. Such were many of
of the people, and such many of their pastors, whom the
unwise politicians of those times thought to force into
their measures by the violence of persecution.

Mr. Hill, the farmer of Braeside, a worthy old bachelor,
had rendered his house as comfortable as he possibly
could for the reception of the new-comers; and with what
articles they brought along with them, and with Mrs.
Bruce's ready hand, under which everything about the
house seemed at once to take its proper place, they found

themselves, although not very well lodged, yet as well
as they had expected. The house, however, like most of
the farmhouses in those days, had only two apartments,
a kitchen and a spence, as the room was called. The
room, Mr. Hill 'gave them up entirely, and the kitchen
was common to him and them. Mr. Bruce had been
deprived of his stipend due for the preceding year. It
had been always small. He was by nature, as well as
principle, generous and charitable, and had therefore
saved no money. It was evident that he must now
depend for his subsistence on the freewill offerings of
his people; and in these they were not backward.
Although Mr. Hill was able and willing enough to support the family for some time, this he was not permitted
to do. Scarcely a day passed but some of Mr. Bruce's
flock arrived at Braeside, with what they could spare for
their pastor (for such they still considered him) and his
family. They had thus a plentiful supply of all the
necessaries of life. The education of Andrew and Mary
went on as usual. Mr. Bruce preached in the houses of
the peasants, or in the open fields, on Sundays. Mrs.
Bruce was kinder than ever to her husband, and almost
as cheerful. Andrew and Mary were healthy and contented; and indeed, while they were permitted to remain
at Braeside, they had nothing to complain of.

Meantime the violence' of persecution every day increased. The ejected clergy were forbidden to preach
even in the fields: the people, under the severest penalties,
were forbidden to shelter them, or even to give them a
morsel of bread. People of all ranks and conditions in
life, who would not comply with the tyranny of the
times, were driven from their houses, and were every
day perishing by the hand of the executioner.

The curates, who had been thrust into the livings of
the west, were the most active in informing against the
Covenanters. The zeal and austere morals of the former
pastors were a continual reproach on the vicious habits
and indolent dispositions of many of those prophets of

Baal, as they were not unfitly called; and they wished to have that example, which they were unwilling to imitate, out of their sight.

Mr. Macduff, the curate who had been put into Mr. Bruce's place, was a Highlander, and really spoke the English language, as well as the Scottish, so ill, that the peasants among whom he was settled, had they been willing to hear him, could have understood little of what he said. He was a robust, huntsman-looking young fellow, as ignorant of books and all sorts of learning as he was indecorus in character. He hunted, fowled, drank with the officers who were stationed in the village, and, in fact, did almost everything but what was becoming the character of a clergyman. The parishioners regarded him with horror, and fled from his presence as they would have done from a beast of prey. In no place in Scotland were the curates well attended, but Macduff's church was entirely deserted. Neither threats nor entreaties could induce as many to collect on a Sabbath as to give the appearance of an audience. And what has been perhaps seldom attempted in any other place, soldiers went every Sabbath morning through the village and, with their bayonets on their guns, compelled a half-score or dozen of the inhabitants into the church, where they sat, with countenances of disgust and horror, while the unsacerdotal curate went most indecorously through the cold and formal service of the day. Mr. Macduff had, however, abundance of that pride which is founded on ignorance; was naturally cruel; devoted to the wicked Government, because he could expect only to be countenanced by such; obsequious to every mandate of the bishops, because from them he held his living; and, withal, possessed of an unbounded hatred to the Covenanters, because he knew, if they prevailed, he should soon be displaced. These qualifications rendered him fit enough for the purposes for which his superiors had chiefly designed him. These were, to harass and destroy the Presbyterians.

To assist the curates in gathering information of the resorts and conventicles of the Covenanters, spies were numerously employed. Sometimes they mingled with the people, professing themselves to be their zealous friends; sometimes they went through in the character

COMPELLED A HALF-SCORE OR DOZEN OF THE INHABITANTS INTO THE CHURCH.—*See page* 210.

of travelling merchants; and sometimes they assumed the garb of shepherds, that they might thus conceal their true character, and therefore be admitted more freely into the designs of the Covenanters. Sharpe had multitudes of these in his pay, scattered over the country. And it is not surprising that they brought in abundance of information, when we consider that many of them— and those the vilest and most worthless of men—were paid in proportion to the number of accusations they preferred. These spies, as long as the Covenanters were brought to anything like a trial, were always witnesses at hand, ready to swear anything against them.

Two of these wretches, in the pay of Sharpe, were entertained by Mr. Macduff. Every day they traversed, in one character or other, the surrounding country, and always returned with abundance of information. All was believed, or, at least, pretended to be believed, that they reported; and the soldiers, with them for guides, were sent forth to plunder, to apprehend, to torture, or to kill, all whom those scoundrels accused of Presby-terianism, which in those days was termed sedition.

Mr. Bruce and his family shared in the increasing calamities of the times. After residing for a year at Braeside, they were compelled to take themselves to a wandering life—now sheltered in some barn, now in some shepherd's hut, but now exposed without cover to all sorts of weather. The minister especially, and his son, who always accompanied him, were often com-pelled to hide themselves in the caves and wild glens of the country. The place whither they most frequently resorted was a cave on the banks of the Ayr, about five miles above the village. It had been formed in the precipitous banks by the hands of men, as a hiding-place in the former troublous times of Scotland, and was roomy enough for admitting five or six persons. The entrance to this retreat was by rude and difficult steps cut out of the stone; and over its mouth, concealing it from the view, hung the straggling branches of the birch and hazel, that had struck their roots into the freestone rock. Two or three rude seats, some straw and blankets, made up the furniture of the cave. Here Mr. Bruce and Andrew, and, indeed, Mrs. Bruce and Mary too, often concealed themselves ; and hither, in the darkness of the night, did the peasants of the surrounding country come with food for their worthy pastor and his family, and to receive in return, instruction, advice, and comfort.

This, Mr. Bruce gave them with all the prudence of a wise man, and all the earnestness of a serious Christian. He exhorted them to place all their trust in God ; to bear up with becoming cheerfulness against the severe trials to which they were exposed. He called them to remember how much Christ had suffered when He was in the world, and with what calmness and resignation He endured it all. He warned them to beware of attempting anything against the Government ; well knowing, however much he might despise the exploded doctrine of non-resistance, that the Covenanters, deprived as they were of the gentlemen of their party, who were mostly in prison, could make no head against their oppressors, supported by a strong military force. He counselled them to oppose patience and hope to the swords of their persecutors, assuring them that God would at length interfere in their behalf. And above all, he comforted and sustained the minds of the poor, hunted, houseless peasantry, by often directing their hopes to the rewards of immortality. Nor did he destroy the effect of his teaching by his own example. The following conversation, which happened one night in the forlorn cave, will show how bravely the Persecuted Family bore their lot.

The night to which we have alluded was in the end of autumn. The minister, with his wife and children, were seated in the cave. A few embers burned on the floor, and half lighted the rude habitation—the Ayr was heard murmuring down his pebbled bed—the wind whistled in the mouth of the cave, blowing in the fallen leaf that rustled about the floor—and the lightning flashed, at intervals, its momentary gleam into the solitary abode.

"Do you remember," said Mary to her brother, " how fresh and beautiful these leaves were in summer ? "

lifting one that the wind rustled through the dwelling. "You remember how we watched them as they spread, and shaded the mouth of the cave?" "They were very beautiful," said Andrew, "and kept the wind out of the cave. But their season is past, and we will see them green no more.

"And what should that remind you of?" said Mrs. Bruce. "Should it not remind you of the transitory nature of all earthly things? We all do fade as the leaf; we are cut down, and wither as the grass. But the leaf hangs on the twig till autumn, and falls not till it is dried and withered with age. We, my dear children, may be cut off in the midst of our days. From disease we are never secure. But we may have soon to die by the hand of violence. Are you prepared, my dear children, to suffer all for Christ? Do you repine that you have been driven from your home to seek shelter in such a place as this for His sake?"

"I am as happy here," said Andrew, "as when we lived at the village. My father and you have taught me to regard my duty to God as the end of my being; and I am resolved, trusting in His grace, to suffer the utmost, rather than violate it. I know He will give me strength to do what He may have appointed me."

"Yes," said Mary, who was no stranger to the Bible, "His grace shall be sufficient for us. I know what He says: 'The Lord is nigh to all them that call upon Him, to all that call upon Him in truth. He also will hear their cry, and save them.'"

"Yes," said Mrs. Bruce, while her husband shed a tear of joy to hear his children talk thus—"yes, if you put no trust in yourselves, if you believe on the Lord Jesus Christ, He will give you resolution and strength to suffer all for His sake. 'Whatsoever ye ask in My name,' says that Redeemer, who hath all power in heaven and in earth—'Whatsoever ye ask in My name, you shall receive it.'"

"Happy are all those who trust in God," said Mr.

Bruce, taking up the conversation, while he threw a glance of unspeakable satisfaction on his family. "Happy are all they, whatever be their external circumstances, whose God is the Lord. We have, it is true, been driven from the comforts of this world's property; but we have, therefore, less to seduce us from the path of holiness. We are exposed to trials; but, through His blessing, they will prepare us the sooner for the enjoyment of His immediate presence. We are exposed to the winds of night; but our souls take shelter under the wings of the Most High. Our enemies are strong, and exceedingly mad against us; but He who is for us is stronger than they who are against us. Those lightnings that flash athwart the night are the lightnings of God: they say unto Him, Here we are; and at His bidding, can lay the pride of the wicked in the dust. As His power is omnipotent to protect you, my dear ones, so is His love infinite. It passeth all knowledge. We are lost in the contemplation of His astonishing love, manifested in our redemption through His Son. He hath given His well-beloved Son for us, vile and miserable sinners; and surely He will allow nothing really to hurt us. What, then, should we not rather do than forsake our duty to Him? Severer sufferings may be yet awaiting us, my dear ones. But let us always lay the grasp of our dependence on God; let us have our eye on the promised land, the dwelling of life and immortality, and let us suffer without a murmur. O my dear ones! in this trying time may we all so believe, and so do, that we may find ourselves approved when men shall be finally judged. If anything should occur which may separate us, let us direct our steps to heaven, where we shall meet to part no more. Our Church is now driven to the wilderness. The blood of her people flows on the scaffold; their groanings are heard in the desert. But God hath not forsaken her; she shall yet shout for joy, and clap her hands for gladness of heart. We may

be gone, my dear ones, ere the day of her mourning
end ; but by suffering cheerfully, we shall have done
our part—we shall have our reward ; and when our
Church takes her sorrowful harp from the willow, and
tunes it to the melody of joy in the peaceful temple,
our memories shall not be forgotten."

When Mr. Bruce had thus spoken, he kneeled down
with his family in the cave, and besought for them
the blessing, even life that shall never end. And then
you might have heard the psalm of praise, mingling
its holy melody with the blast of night.

Still, religion, thou art happiness ! Thou hast,
indeed, trials appointed for thy followers — but thou
comest in the strength of God, and leadest them out
through them all. As the darkness of the world
thickens around them, thou sheddest a brighter light
on the cloudless clime whither they are travelling.
As the cup, of which the wickedness of man forces
them to drink, comes nearer the bitterness of its dregs,
thou pourest more copiously into their souls the sweetness of eternal life. As they have days of severe fatigue
and wandering, and nights more wearisome and watchful, thou layest the repose of their souls nearer the
bosom of their God. Woe unto him who seeketh his
happiness apart from Thee ! He shall be miserably
disappointed.

Chapter IV

" Their blood is shed
In confirmation of the noblest claim—
Our claim to feed upon immortal truth,
To walk with God, to be divinely free.
Yet few remember them. They lived unknown,
Till persecution dragged them into fame,
And chased them up to heaven. Their ashes flew
—No marble tells us whither."
—COWPER.

FOUR years of suffering had now passed since Mr.

Bruce and his family were driven from their comfortable home. But although many of his flock had been
thrown into prison and sent into banishment — had
endured the cruelties of torture, or died on the scaffold,
and although they had themselves often made the
narrowest escapes from the vigilance of their fell
pursuers, none of them had yet fallen into their hands.
The time was not far off, however, when they were to
feel more severely the cruelties of persecution.

On a Sabbath evening in the month of September,
Mr. Bruce, with his wife and children, left the cave
to meet some of his flock in a wild glen in the neighbourhood, where he was to deliver a sermon. When
they arrived at the appointed place, there were about
a score assembled—some of them stood, some seated
themselves on the cold turf, while Mr. Bruce took his
station by a large stone, on which he rested the Bible,
and read, or rather repeated, for the night was dark,
the following verses from the twenty-third Psalm :—

> " The Lord's my shepherd, I'll not want ;
>   He makes me down to lie
>   In pastures green : He leadeth me
>   The quiet waters by.
>
> " My soul He doth restore again,
>   And me to walk doth make
>   Within the paths of righteousness,
>   Even for His own name's sake.
>
> " Yea, though I walk in death's dark vale,
>   Yet will I fear none ill :
>   For Thou art with me ; and Thy rod
>   And staff, me comfort still."

Then, as it is beautifully expressed by Grahame,—

> ———" rose the song, the loud
> Acclaim of praise. The wheeling plover ceased
> Her plaint ; the solitary place was glad ;
> And, on the distant cairn, the watcher's ear
> Caught doubtfully at times the breeze-borne note.

After this, Mr. Bruce lifted up their fervent prayer to the throne of grace ; and then repeated his text from the same Psalm which had been sung, "Though I walk through the valley of the shadow of death, yet will I fear no evil : for Thou art with me ; Thy rod and Thy staff, they comfort me."

This consolatory passage he illustrated, by showing how they who had the rod and staff of the Almighty to support them needed fear no evil. This rod and staff, he showed, were no less than the infinite love, and wisdom, and power of God, engaged in the preservation of the righteous. This truth he illustrated at considerable length, and with more of elegance than was common to the preachers of the time. We shall content ourselves, however, by giving the concluding part of the discourse.

"If, then," said the fervent preacher, "we have the love, and wisdom, and the power of God engaged in our protection, what have we to fear from the cruelties of men, the malignity of evil spirits, or the terrors of death itself? His love fills our heart with unspeakable delight, and secures us the guidance of His wisdom, and the all-shielding covert of His almighty power. If we had to set our faces to the machinations of this world, under the direction of our own wisdom, we would soon be entangled in its snares, and decoyed into the pit which is dug for our destruction. But to guide us through every footstep of this earthly journey, to guide us through every footstep of the dark pass of death, we have the infinite wisdom of God, which hath all things present to its eye in the natural and moral world, in heaven and in earth, in time and in eternity. The most sagacious spirit that contrives our ruin in the darkest gloom of the bottomless pit is noticed by our God, and those means taken which can never err in their operation to defeat its purposes against us. He observes all the plottings of man's wisdom against us, and turns the best laid schemes of their wickedness to the profit of His people. The kings of the earth set themselves, and the rulers take counsel together, against the Lord and against His anointed. But He that sitteth in the heavens laughs: the Lord hath them in derision. He casteth the glance of His all-comprehending intelligence through all the varied workings of natural and moral being, the most intricate, the most profound, the most secret; and the wisdom of the wisest agency, that acts not by His guidance, seemeth to Him the folly of fools.

" But, however ardent the love of God might be to His children, however provident His wisdom, if there was any being that could resist His power, still we should not be safe. But our Father hath in Himself all the resources of infinite might. In the Lord Jehovah is everlasting strength. He hath created all things. The arm of His omnipotence sustains them all. Turn your eyes to the stars that look through the breaking of the clouds; the multitude of their host are suspended to the girdle of His strength, and guide all their revolutions to the bidding of His will. He bringeth forth Mazzaroth in his season, and guideth Arcturus with his sons. He stilleth the raging of the waves; and the fierceness of the storm lays itself to rest at the whisper of His word. And shall any other of the beings He hath made—the spirits of darkness or the worms of His footstool—stand up in proud rebellion against Him, and try to wrest the people whom He loves—the people for whom He hath given His own Son—out of His hand? Did Pharaoh's or Sennacherib's host accomplish aught victoriously against His children? Did the powerful and malignant dealings of Satan touch the life of Job? No, my friends. In the estimation of our God, the strength of man is less than weakness; and the most stout-hearted of the spirits of perdition trembles at the uttering of His voice, and is held fast in the chains of His power. It is this God, my friends, who is our God. It is this all-wise, all-mighty being, who hath sworn by the eternal

Godhead, that he who perseveres in well-doing who fights the good fight of faith and turns not back, shall sing victory over all his enemies, and shall inherit glory, and honour, and immortality.

"We are persecuted, my friends ; we may soon have to lay down our lives. But let us lean on the rod and the staff of our Redeemer ; and whatever be the cunning of man's contrivance against us, it shall be turned to our account ; and whatever be the shape that death may assume, we shall behold him shorn of his terrors. O my friends ! let us do what the Bible hath taught us to be our duty : let us keep our conscience inviolate ; and whatever may be appointed for us here, we shall have the welcome to our Father and Redeemer at last into the dwellings of immortality."

When Mr. Bruce had finished his sermon, so well calculated to encourage the minds of his suffering audience, he took occasion to speak shortly of the times, the substance of which we shall record.

It was easy to see, he said, that the Presbyterians would yet be persecuted with still greater severity ; that the persecutors wished to gratify their ambition and avarice with the spoils of the Covenanters, and it was hard to say how far these passions would carry them. It had been the labour, he observed, of the Stuarts, for several reigns, to get into their hands the ecclesiastical supremacy in Scotland. They had hitherto been disappointed, and would, he had no doubt, be so still. "That infatuated race," continued he, "seems to be hastening its own ruin." And the venerable pastor dropped a tear as he thought of the incurable folly of that house. The nation, he could see, would tire of oppression, and would most certainly assert its liberties. Oppression would, as usual, destroy itself by its own cruelties. But, for the time, that patience and hope must be their support ; that anything attempted against their oppressors, when they were in no state for it, would only render their condition more intolerable ; that ready submission, for the time, to every thing that violated not conscience, and patient endurance of those evils which were measured out to them, were the means which, under the blessing of God, would at length most certainly restore to them and their children the blessings of civil and religious liberty.

Such were this man's sentiments, on whose head the infatuated administration of the time had set a price as a rebel and sower of sedition; and such were the sentiments of many of those heroes of the covenant, whom some historians represent as the visionary and fanatic leaders of a visionary and fanatic sect. We do not pretend to say that the sentiments of all the Covenanters were as moderate and just as those of Mr. Bruce. Among a great number there will always be weak and turbulent minds; and, under severe sufferings, they will be driven to extravagence. The calumniators of the Covenanters ought to remember, that none of them became bad subjects till oppression had rendered them desperate; and that, if some of them latterly adopted not very rational sentiments about civil government, the great body of the Presbyterians who suffered at that time approved as little of their notions as their persecutors did.

The little congregation had again joined in a song of praise, and the old minister was just about to dismiss them with the blessing, when suddenly they heard the trampling of horses, and in a moment saw advancing rapidly towards them, with lighted torches in their hands, a number of dragoons. Not expecting any alarm at such an hour and place, they had neglected to appoint a watch. A little eminence, which the soldiers had been taught by the spies, who acted as their guides, to keep between them and the conventicle, had concealed from them the light of the torches until the dragoons were almost upon the little assembly. Short as the time was before the soldiers could reach them, they fled into a morass, near to which they fortunately were; and the softness of the ground prevented the pursuit of the horsemen. But when the commanding officer saw that they were likely to escape, naturally cruel and blood-thirsty, and chagrined at the loss of his prey, he ordered his men instantly to discharge their carabines after the flight of the poor people ; and, without waiting to examine the result of his orders, wheeled and rode off.

Several of the people were hurt, but Mrs. Bruce received a mortal wound. "I am gone," she said, while her husband caught her in his arms to keep her from falling. "I am killed. I must leave you. O my dear husband ! I leave these children to your care. I leave you all to the care of my God !" She tried to say more ; but death was too near. She threw one look on her son and daughter, clasped her hands convulsively about her husband, and expired in his arms.

Mr. Bruce for some time held her fondly in his embrace, and stood speechless and motionless. Andrew wept not, but threw himself on the ground in the depth of silent grief. Mary shrieked, and took hold of the bloody corpse of her mother, while the peasants gathered round and wept in silence.

It was some time before any one could find self-command enough to speak. Andrew, whose vigorous mind would not permit him to give himself long up to unavailing sorrow, was the first to break the mournful silence.

"Father," he said, "let us now consider what is best to be done. We cannot stay here."

Mr. Bruce, at these words of his son, recovering himself a little, stretched the bloody corpse on the heath, and, lifting up his hands to heaven, in a tone of resignation said, "The Lord giveth, and the Lord taketh away : blessed be the name of the Lord !"

After a short consultation, it was determined to carry the dead body to a neighbouring hut. Assisting in turn to carry the corpse, they took their way over the broken mosses to the place agreed on. On their arrival, the first thing was to settle where the body should be interred. Mr. Bruce wished to be present at the interment ; but this he could not be, if they buried the remains of his wife in the village churchyard, for he was sure to be apprehended if he appeared so publicly. And yet he thought it was somewhat disrespectful to bury her on the moor.

"It matters not," said Andrew, when he saw his father's hesitation,—"it matters not where our bodies rest. There is no distinction of place in the grave. Is it any difference to my mother where we lay her ashes? God will have His eye upon them, and angels will hold the place in honour. For my part, had I my choice, I would rather be laid at last in the solitary glen of the moor, than be entombed amidst the mockery of funeral pomp, and have the marble monument to record my praise."

"You are right my son," replied his father. "The grave is a bed of rest to the just. Their bodies rest in hope ; and it matters not where they lie."

It was now resolved that the remains of Mrs. Bruce should be buried next evening ; and the place appointed for laying them to rest was near to where she had been shot.

When they had thus settled, and after joining in prayer with the sorrowing few who had accompanied him to the hut, Mr. Bruce, sad in heart, withdrew to the cave ; for the search after him was so vigilant that he durst not remain a night even in this remote and lonely hut. Mary refused to leave her mother's corpse, and Andrew stayed to watch over and comfort his sister.

Next evening Mr. Bruce returned to the hut. About twenty peasants had assembled. A rude coffin had been prepared, and under the covert of night the mournful procession moved slowly towards the place of interment. The clouds, clothed in the sombre garments of mourning, stood still in the heavens ; and here and there, from out their rifted sides, peeped a solitary star, with an eye that seemed to weep as it looked on the wasteful heath, and glimmered on the sorrowful countenances of the mourners. Sadly down their glens murmured the streams of the wilderness; and the woful voice of the snipe traversing the wide air, the forlorn whistle of the plover, and the melancholy sound of the wind, that now and then rose on the heath, fell on the ear of Mr. Bruce like the accents of some doleful prophecy, presaging to him and his family the coming of a still more wasteful desolation.

When the procession arrived at the place of interment, which had been chosen near to where Mrs. Bruce had been murdered, a grave was dug, into which the coffin was let down, and the attendants covered it up; while Mr. Bruce and his two children watered with their tears the cold earth, that now hid from their eyes the one who was dearest to their souls. "But there is a joy in grief, when peace dwells in the bosom of the sad." They sorrowed not as those who have no hope. Mr. Bruce wiped the tear of affection from his eye, and thus addressed the peasants, who could not refrain their tears as they stood around and looked on the grave.

"Weep not, my dear friends," said the resigned man, "she hath done her part well. She loved her God and served Him; and He hath now taken her to Himself. Happy they who are thus taken from the evils of this world! Although we have been compelled to do our last office to her under the darkness of night—although we have erected no marble to record her memory—she shall be held among the honourable in heaven. Let us, too, be prepared to lie down in the grave. If we be fitly prepared for this, it matters not when or in what manner we die. The sooner we reach our Father's house the better. But we must fight out our day, like the true soldiers of Jesus Christ. We must not repine that He keeps us long from our home. He knows best when to call us home to rest. Let us, in His strength, fight the good fight of faith. Let us abstain more carefully than ever even from the appearance of evil. Let us devote ourselves wholly to God. Let us, my friends, be prepared to die well, that when the earthly house of this tabernacle shall be destroyed we may like all the righteous have a building with God, a house not made with hands eternal in the heavens."

When the minister had thus said, he bade the peasants farewell; and, with Andrew and Mary, returned to the cave.

Chapter V

" The clouds of winter gather: fast the leaves,
  One after one, fall from the storm-beat tree;
  And o'er the humbled face of nature flap
  The wings of desolation. 'Tis the hour
  And power of darkness. Men of evil life,
  Of horrid cruelty, now compass round
  The just man's bed, with chains, and swords, and death."
                                        —ANON.

IN the meantime an incident took place in the south of Scotland which rendered the condition of the Covenanters more intolerable. The persecutors in that quarter had laid a heavy fine on a poor old man, who being unable to pay it, the soldiers bound him, and, regardless of his prayers and tears, were dragging him to prison, when a handful of peasants, who had gathered around, pitying the poor man, and indignant at the cruelty of such a proceeding, set violently upon the soldiers and rescued the prisoner. Aware that no pardon could be expected for this action, they took arms to defend themselves. Their number, small at first, soon increased to nearly two thousand; and in the heat of their zeal they determined to march to Edinburgh, to compel the Government to redress their grievances. The wise and the prudent among them saw the impolicy of this attempt, and tried every means

15

to dissuade their friends from their rash purpose. They represented the strength and discipline of the king's forces, and their own want of arms and discipline, and the impossibility of procuring skilful commanders, as the gentlemen of their party in the west were either in confinement or had fled out of the country. They exhorted them rather to disperse and seek shelter from the cruelty of their oppressors in flight and hiding, than thus, unprepared as they were, to rush on certain destruction. Moreover, they affirmed that it would be more consistent with the spirit of Christianity, yet to try to procure a mitigation of their sufferings by petition and entreaty.

Nevertheless, the multitude, afraid to lay down those arms they had once taken up, their minds rendered desperate by suffering, and encouraged by some of the less prudent of their pastors, directed their march towards the capital. This was the very point which the persecuting Government aimed at. They wished to have some better pretext than they yet had to plunder and ruin the Presbyterians. They had often attempted, by their emissaries, to excite some insurrection. This their own cruelty had now produced. And a band which at the most was never more than two thousand, and which had taken arms without any previous concertment, was magnified by the reports of the oppressors into a general and preconcerted rebellion of all the west.

The result of this insurrection is well known. Having reached the neighbourhood of Edinburgh, reduced by fatigue or fear to less than half of their number, and having effected nothing to better their condition, they were returning peaceably home by the Pentland Hills, when they were pursued and set upon by Dalziel, at that time commander of the king's forces in Scotland. They fought for some time with more spirit than could have been expected from men in their forlorn situation; but a party of soldiers from another quarter coming behind them, they were thrown into disorder, and put to flight. Fifty were killed on the spot (where a very handsome monument has since been erected to their memory), some fell in the pursuit, and a considerable number were taken prisoners. These were treated without mercy. Ten of them were executed on the same scaffold, and their heads and hands sent to Lanark, where, in passing, they had renewed the covenant. Besides these, many were sent into the west country, and executed before their own doors.

The persecutors had now got, as we have already mentioned, the pretext they wanted, and they hesitated not to proceed to the most wanton and most inhuman cruelties. Dalziel and Drummond, who were now the commanders of the military in the west, added the ferocity of the Muscovites (in which service they had for some time been) to the cruel and inflexible cruelty which characterised the persecutors in general. Dragoons were stationed in every village; and even the private men had power to shoot, without any form of trial, all who refused to take the test to Government. In no place were the poor scattered members of Scotland's Church safe from the vigilant search of their enemies. The ejected clergymen especially were pursued with unremitting diligence, and among these none were hunted with greater eagerness than Mr. Bruce.

The curate, Mr. Macduff, who had succeeded to his place, as he disliked all the Covenanters, so he hated Mr. Bruce with the most bitter hatred. He considered this worthy man, whom he knew to be still lurking about the parish, as the chief cause of preventing the people in that quarter from complying with the established form of worship. The villagers, too, were sometimes bold enough to contrast, even to his face, his character with that of their former minister. These things were sufficient to irritate an ignorant and cruel being, such as Mr. Macduff was, to implacable resentment against Mr. Bruce; and he determined to have him cut off. Night and day the two spies whom the curate still entertained were in search of him, and their search was the more diligent as Government had not only offered a considerable reward for his apprehension, but Mr. Macduff had promised them a handsome sum if they would bring him certain intelligence how this good man might be taken.

Mr. Bruce, although he seldom left the bounds of his former charge, had still, however, eluded their search. He was so esteemed and beloved by the peasants among whom he wandered, that they would have cheerfully risked their own lives to procure the escape or conceal-ment of their pastor. And what was very surprising, such was the faithful secrecy of the inhabitants of the place, to whom alone it was known, that although Mr. Bruce had for several years made the cave the place of his frequent resort, it had never been discovered by his enemies. An occurrence at length took place through which the persecutors hoped to secure the apprehension of Mr. Bruce.

Andrew had one afternoon left his father and Mary in the cave to amuse himself, as he frequently did, with the conversation of a shepherd who kept his flocks hard by. Scarcely, however, was he half a mile away from the cave when a party of soldiers, with Macduff, came suddenly upon him. They had been out, we believe, that day chiefly for the purpose of killing wild-fowl, but at the same time they required every one they met to take the test—an oath by which the party swearing renounced the covenant, owned the king as supreme head of the Church, and tendered submission to the then existing ecclesiastical establishment. Andrew, without hesitation, refused to comply. According to the laws, or rather to the lawlessness of the times, this refusal authorised the soldiers to shoot the young man on the spot. But although his dress was that of a peasant, they remarked something so superior and striking in his countenance, as well as in the manner in which he spoke,

which immediately led them to the suspicion that he
might be the son of some gentleman of rank in disguise,
from whom useful discoveries might be elicited, or on
whose account a handsome sum of money might be
extorted.

Induced by those considerations, they spared his life for
the present, and conducted him a prisoner to the village.
On their way thither they repeatedly endeavoured to
learn his name ; but Andrew, knowing well that if they
once knew whose son he was he should have no chance
of escape without discovering his father, was careful to
conceal it. ·· When they reached the village, however,
the inhabitants gathered round to see the prisoner ; and
perceiving the son of their beloved minister, they assailed
the soldiers with the most bitter execrations, exclaiming
that the judgment of heaven would fall upon them,
and crying at the same time, "Will ye murder the son
of our dear minister? Ye have already murdered his
wife, and is your cruelty not yet glutted?"

When Mr. Macduff heard these words, "The son of
our minister," he looked to Dalziel, who was himself of
the party, and said with a smile of grim satisfaction,
"We have made good sport to day. We shall now get
on the scent of the old fox."[1]

Dalziel now asked Andrew if he was the son of the
rebel Mr. Bruce? for so he termed this meek and peaceable servant of Jesus. Andrew replied boldly, "I am
the son of Mr. Bruce." This short answer, and the tone
and expression of countenance with which it was uttered,
convinced Dalziel that they had got a youth to deal with
from whom severity would not be likely to elicit much.

They now shut up Andrew in the church, which for
some time had been more used as a prison than a place
of worship and having placed a guard, retired to
consult how they might best draw the desired intelligence of Mr. Bruce from his son.

[1] The curate's language, which would be ridiculous if introduced
as he used it, is here translated into English.

The brutal Macduff was for proceeding immediately to torture, but Dalziel, who had better observed Andrew's spirit, resolved to try him first by gentle means. Accordingly he returned to the young man, and addressed him in the following manner :

"Your refusing to take the test, young man," said Dalziel, "you know, according to the laws of your country, forfeits your life ; and you might be led, without further delay, to execution. But we have no desire to proceed to such an extremity with you. Your appearance has gained you our respect, and we have a strong wish to mitigate the rigour of the law in your case. But this we are not authorised to do without some little submission on your part. We shall not require of you, however, to take the test, since it seems to be so unacceptable to you. If you will only tell us how we may find your father, you may have your liberty, and you need not be afraid of your father's life. He has, indeed, rendered himself obnoxious to Government, but we promise that his life shall be safe. We shall be careful that nothing worse happen to him than a short imprisonment."

To these arguments he added, that if the young man could find it agreeable to make the necessary compliances, and if he liked the military life, he would endeavour to procure him some honourable post. Or, if he rather wished to prepare himself for the Church, he would recommend him to those from whom he might expect preferment.

Andrew, distrusting the promises Dalziel had made concerning his father as much as he despised the offers proposed to himself, looking firmly in the soldier's face, absolutely refused to make any discovery of his father.

"Torture," exclaimed Macduff, who stood by, "will make you reveal what our mercy has failed to do."

"Yes," said Dalziel, "we still promise that your father's life shall not be touched. But if you will not make the discovery we want, we have torture prepared that will make you speak out. And if you still persist in your refusal, your own life shall pay for your obstinacy. We leave you till to-morrow morning to consider whether you will accept your own liberty, with no serious danger to your father, or expose yourself to torture and death, which may, perhaps, not preserve him long from our hands." So saying, the inquisitors withdrew to spend the night in mirth and revelry.

Andrew, who had no doubt that the promises made concerning his father would be broken the moment his persecutors had him in their power, determined, without hesitation, not to say a single word that might lead to his apprehension. Aware, also, that what had been threatened against himself would be most certainly executed, he prepared for meeting it like a man and a Christian.

As it chanced that night, there was no prisoner in the church except Andrew. In and around the church, as it stood at a little distance from the village, all was stillness, save when it was broken by the guard chanting a verse of a song, or cursing the times which kept them on foot at midnight. The interior of the building was faintly lighted by the moonbeams that glimmered through the old Gothic windows. From the windows Andrew could see the manse, half concealed amidst aged trees. He saw, too, the pulpit where from his father's lips had often dropt the word of life. He looked to the seat where he used to sit with Mary and his mother; he cast his eye on the manse, where they had lived so happily. But his mind soon hurried from these objects to what the family had suffered since persecution had driven them from their home. They had wandered on the mountains; they had endured cold, and fatigue, and fasting; at midnight, in the depth of winter, they had been often unsheltered from the severity of the weather. His mother, so tender, so affectionate, had already fallen by the hands of their persecutors, and her ashes lay cold in the loneliness of the moor. His father and sister were at this moment lurking in a forlorn cave, and in bitterness of soul on his account. He himself was a lonely prisoner, to-morrow to feel the agonies of torture, and to be cut down like a tree in the verdure of spring. These were the sorrowful and oppressive thoughts which forced themselves on the mind of the young man.

Andrew, as we have already said, had by nature sufficient of that boldness and fortitude of spirit which bends not easily beneath misfortune, and the many sufferings and hardships he had endured had only served to call forth and strengthen the natural firmness of his mind ; for although trying circumstances may depress and overwhelm the weak and the timid, they never fail to summon forth the energies and heighten the courage of a vigorous spirit.

But Andrew trusted not to the bravery of human strength. He set himself not, like the distressed hero of romance, to call up the natural fortitude of his soul, and to prepare to meet all the evils that were gathering around him in the strength of man-created might. He had been taught that the strength of man is weakness, his wisdom folly, and all the resolutions of his natural bravery, fear and trembling at the approach of death ; and he turned himself to the throne of that God whom he had always served, knowing He had sufficient help to give in every time of need ; and, in the fervour of confiding prayer, sought the protection of His power, which no being can resist ; the guidance of His wisdom, which never errs ; and the comforts of His free grace, which can never be exhausted. He had seen the wickedness and deceitfulness of his own heart ; he had been made acquainted with the strictness and purity of God's law, and he thought not of preparing to meet his God in the uprightness of his own character. But he looked with a humble and believing eye to the cross of Christ ; and on the atonement which He has made, he placed all his hopes of justification and acceptance with God. Verily, he put no trust in an arm of flesh ; but he took unto him the whole armour of God ; his loins girt about with truth ; having on the breast-plate of righteousness, the shield of faith, the helmet of salvation, and the sword of the Spirit. While the afflictions of this world were thickening around him, and the terrors of death before his face, he had the peace of God dwelling in his heart, the hope of eternal life brightening in heavenly vision ; and he could sing in prison and in the loneliness of midnight, ' The Lord is on my side ; I will not fear what man can do unto me. Yea, though I walk through the valley of the shadow of death, I will fear no evil ; for Thou art with me ; Thy rod and Thy staff they comfort me." He felt that, strong in the all-sufficiency of God, nothing could seduce him from his duty ; none of the powers of wickedness could wound his soul. Verily, the Christian's weapons,

> ——"from the armoury of God,
> Are given him tempered so."

While Andrew was engaged with such thoughts as these, his father and sister, in the solitude of their cave, were deeply afflicted on his account. The shepherd, to meet whom Andrew had left them, observed him apprehended, and carried the tidings to his father. Mary wept for her brother, as if he had been already dead, and Mr. Bruce feared the worst. He knew, and he was proud at the thought, that Andrew would not renounce his religion. He was well aware, also, that no mercy from the persecutors was to be expected for his son. Those into whose hands he had fallen, he could easily foresee, would leave no cruelty unexercised against the son of one who was so hated by them, and whose life they had so eagerly sought. The distressed father thus looked upon the death of his son as almost certain. And if ever a father had reason to love a son, or be grieved at the intimation of his untimely death, that father was Mr. Bruce.

Andrew was an only son. From his childhood till the

present time, when he was in his nineteenth year, he had been his constant companion. He had watched with the tenderest care the development of his faculties, turned their energies into the proper channel, and he had seen his care rewarded by the rapid progress his son had made in the acquirement of knowledge. His talents, the acquisitions he had already made, his love of learning and his devotedness to religion, warranted the highest hopes of his future usefulness and respectability in the world.

This was enough to render Andrew peculiarly dear to his father. But he had more than this to draw his son nearer to his heart. Andrew had been his companion in his suffering, and the calm and unmurmuring manner in which he had endured the severest hardships had not only taught his mother and sister to bear their afflictions with patience, but even Mr. Bruce had frequently learnt courage and constancy from his son. Those who have suffered much together have had opportunities of remarking one another's qualities, and of endearing themselves to each other by numberless offices of kindness which can never have occurred to those who have passed all their days in prosperity. These opportunities had been too often afforded to the minister and his family. Andrew had gradually become the second hope on which they relied. In all his wanderings he had scarcely ever left his father's side. He had watched with him at cold midnight, on the side of the mountains and in the glen of the desert; he had fled with him from the fell pursuit of the enemy, exposed to the storms and darkness of winter; he had hungered with him, he had mourned with him, he had endured every hardship with him, and in all he had been his father's comforter, and had showed him the most ardent filial affection. It was this son whom Mr. Bruce was now in all likelihood to see taken from him by the merciless hand of persecution, in the very spring of his days. And we need not wonder if he found it hard, in this instance, to submit with resignation to the unsearchable appointment of heaven.

But, if the trial was severe, he had the best comfort which a parent can have when he sees a beloved child about to be wrested from him by the hand of death. He had every reason to believe that whatever his enemies might accomplish against the life of his son, his soul would be received into the bosom of his God.

Now, consoling himself and his daughter with those sure and certain consolations, derived from that trust and confidence in God which the Holy Scriptures point out as the duty of every Christian, under the most severe afflictions—now turning to the throne of grace in prayer for his son, and again giving way to all the depth and bitterness of paternal sorrow—he spent the night in the gloomy cave, hoping sometimes that the morrow's light would bring him an account of his son's escape, and yet fearing oftener it would announce his death.

Chapter VI

"Suffering for Truth's sake,
Is fortitude to highest victory,
And, to the faithful, death the gate of life."
—MILTON.

NEXT morning Dalziel and Macduff entered the church, and the former instantly asked Andrew if he had come to a resolution about what had been proposed last night.

"My duty was so plain," said Andrew, "that it required no deliberation. I am prepared to die."

"But you are perhaps not prepared for torture," said Macduff, with a grin of fiend-like malignity, pointing to a thumbkin which one of the spies, whom we formerly mentioned, held in his hand by the curate's side. "That will make you speak out."

Andrew glanced an eye of scorn on the curate, looked without emotion at the instrument of torture, and remained silent.

Dalziel then asked him if he would not send someone to his father, to persuade him to deliver himself up to them, again repeating the promise of safety to his father's life.

"Thrust your sword through my body" said Andrew, "but think not to extract from my lips one word, by all the tortures which you can inflict, that may lead to the discovery of my father. My only fear is, that he may hear of my danger and deliver up himself."

"Try that on your thumb, then," said Dalziel, ordering the spy at the same time to apply the instrument of torture, while the dragoons that kept guard held the young man, to prevent resistance.

The thumbkin was an instrument of exquisite torture, and on this occasion it was applied without mercy. For some time Andrew bore the pain it occasioned with a firm and unchanging countenance; but, as the instrument was screwed closer and closer to his thumb, the colour in his face came and went rapidly, and he writhed himself with the agonising pain.

Dalziel, seeing it was in vain to expect any discovery, was just about to order the tormentor to desist, when Macduff prevented him by saying, "Another twist yet! it may have more virtue in it." The obedient spirit of wickedness turned the screw, and the thumb of the young man was heard crashing within the instrument. Nature could bear no more. The blood entirely forsook his face, and he fell down in a swoon.

Fearing that their hopes of yet eliciting something might be disappointed by the immediate death of the sufferer, they hastened to relax the instrument. And, as soon as Andrew had recovered a little, he was again asked whether he would endure the same again or discover his father.

"You may torture me to death," said he, in a firm and resolute tone, "but I trust in God, in the Rock of my salvation, and you cannot touch my soul. It is covered by the shield of the Almighty. You shall not wring one word from me to endanger my father. The Lord comfort him ! "

Having tried the torture again with the same effect, Dalziel, by nature and habit cruel, and enraged that his

CLASPED HER ARMS AROUND ANDREW'S NECK.—*See page 238.*

cruelty had entirely failed in the purposes for which it had been exercised in this instance, ordered the young man to be immediately led forth to execution, alleging

Andrew's refusal to take the test as a ground for this proceeding, although the true reason was his refusal to discover his father. Hanging, as being the most ignominious of deaths, was that appointed for Andrew; and the gibbet on this occasion was an old elm-tree near the manse, under which he and Mary had often frolicked in the days of their childhood. He had just been led to the foot of the tree, and the spy, who was the only one to be found who would undertake the task, was fixing the fatal rope to one of its branches, when the attention of all present was suddenly arrested by the appearance of a young woman, who, screaming wildly, rushed through the soldiers, and clasped her arms around Andrew's neck.

This was his sister. One of the villagers, who on the preceding night had learned the determination of Dalziel with regard to Andrew, before the day went to the cave, and informed Mr. Bruce.

"I will go and put myself into their hands," exclaimed Mr. Bruce, as soon as he heard the tidings. "Better that I die than lose my son." And he was hastening to leave the cave for this purpose when Mary laid hold of him, and besought him not to go.

"They will murder you both," said she, weeping, "and what will become of me? Rather let me go. I will plead for my brother's life, and surely I will move their compassion."

"No," said her father, "you know them not. The tiger of the desert hath more of compassion than they. I know with what violence they hate me and my family. No, no; nothing but my death will save my son. But why do I thus tarry here? Perhaps they lead him out even now to execution."

"Go not, my father, I beseech you," said Mary. "Do you think that your death will save Andrew? "Oh no, my dear father; they will murder you both. I shall be left alone in the world Be persuaded, my dearest father. Let me go. I am sure they will have pity on us."

Mr. Bruce, considering that it was indeed likely that his delivering himself up would not procure the liberty of his son, a spirited young man deeply imbued with principles at enmity with the existing establishments— and imagining that the tears and entreaties of Mary, which appeared to him so eloquent, might excite some compassion in the hearts of those into whose hands Andrew had fallen ; and taking pity on his daughter, who he saw, would be left in a state of distraction if he went to give himself up, looked sorrowfully upon her, and wiping a tear from his eye, said—

"Go, then, my daughter. But, stop—I may lose you, too ! Who knows where their cruelty may end ? But no, no ! They will have pity on your youth and your tears. Surely there is not in the form of man aught so cruel that will murder my children. God will protect you. Haste, you, my daughter. It is your brother's life that calls you. Haste to the village ; and the Lord be with you and my son." The distressed father then knelt to wrestle at the throne of grace, while Mary flew with the speed of lightning to the village.

She arrived, as we have seen, just soon enough to have an opportunity of trying what her entreaties could do. The apparatus of death, which she noticed at her approach, and her brother standing bound between two soldiers, had so terrified her, that it was some time before she could so recover herself as to be able to speak.

"You have come," said Andrew to her, when she had recovered a little—"you have come to afflict yourself in vain. My death is determined."

"No, they will not kill you," replied his sister ; "these men will not kill you." And then falling on her knees before Dalziel, whom she knew by his dress to be of highest authority, and, with tears fast flowing down her face, more lovely in grief, thus addressed him :

"Have pity on my brother. If you knew how my father and I love him, you would not kill him. I am sure he has never hurt you. Ever since we were driven from the manse, he has lived peaceably in the moors. He has lived with me; and I never saw him do injury to anyone. Have pity, sir, on our family. You have already taken our dear mother from us, and will you now take from me an only brother, and from my father an only son? Oh, sir, have you no son, that you may know what my father will feel? Have you no brother, dear to you as mine is to me? My dear, dear brother! Oh, let him go, and I will die in his place!"

These words, when uttered by Mary, were eloquent, and Dalziel felt some movements of humanity within him.

"If your father will put himself into our hands," said he, "we will save the life of your brother."

"Wicked and unfeeling wretch!" exclaimed Andrew, interposing here, — "wicked and inhuman wretch! wouldst thou have her save her brother's life at the expense of her father's? Nor would you set me at liberty though my father were in your hands. Entreat them no more, my dear sister. Weep not for me. I suffer with joy for the glory that is before me. Leave me, dear Mary. Go; and if ever you see our father, tell him I died with joy for the liberties and religion of Scotland. Tell him not to regret that he did not deliver himself up. It would have been certain death to him, and would not have saved me. Tell him that I am prouder to lay down my life for him, and for the righteous cause in which Scotland suffers, than if I had been lifted up to the loftiest pinnacle of human distinction. Dear sister, be you comforted. I go to our mother. I go to the enjoyments of heaven. You and my father will soon follow; and there we shall again dwell together in peace, far beyond the change and turbulence of time."

Dalziel had been, as we have already observed, rather moved by Mary's entreaties; and still, as he saw her turning from her brother's embrace, and again casting herself down before him in the agonies of unspeakable grief, he felt something like the kindling of compassion hovering about his heart, and he looked to Macduff with an eye that said, " Might we not have some mercy on this girl? "

The curate, with a look of horrible ferocity, and in a tone of reproach, replied, "Will you be drawn from your duty by the snivelling of girls? If you pardon rebels for their tears, you surely will be accounted a very merciful man, and the Government will certainly sustain the grounds of pardon."

Dalziel, as if ashamed that he had shown he yet possessed some little human feeling, without waiting a moment, ordered the executioner to proceed. At this word Mary shrieked wildly, fainted, and was immediately carried towards the village by some women who had gathered around her on her arrival.

Andrew now mounted the scaffold, which had been erected beside the old elm. Here he was again asked if he would not save his life by complying with the terms formerly offered. The young Christian, strong in the might of God, regarding his tempters with a look of indignation, remained silent. "Prepare, then, instantly to die," said Dalziel.

Andrew kneeled down, and having recommended his soul to the care of his God he arose and exclaimed, "Farewell, my father," as if he could have heard him. "Farewell, my sister. The light of the sun, the hopes of earth, farewell! And, O holy Father, ere I depart, hear my cry. In Thy mercy haste to deliver the suffering people of Scotland. Now, welcome death; and welcome eternity!" When he had thus said, the executioner did as he had been ordered, and the soul of this Christian hero fled away to receive the crown of life.

What suffering was here! What did a father and a sister feel! And how might they have escaped it all?

16

If they had deserted the cause of liberty and religion; if they had submitted tamely to those chains which a licentious and tyrannical Government had forged for them, and which, but for their noble resistance, and that of their fellow-sufferers, might have this day been fastened around our necks, this persecuted family might have lived in peace in their manse, undisturbed and uninjured by the troubles of the times. But their souls despised the thought. They had the glory of God in their view—they had the liberty of their country at their heart—they had the welfare of us, their posterity, before their eyes, and, without a murmur, they laid down their lives in a righteous cause.

Is there no one that loves to wander about Zion, "and the flowing brooks beneath, that wash her hallowed feet," and to sing on sacred harps the achievements of the saints? Is there no one warmed with the flame of their devotion, and touched near the heart with their patriotic sufferings, that will twine laurels to their sacred memory into the sweet numbers of immortal melody? Is the theme not soft enough for the refined ear of modern taste, or is it too sacred for the song of the bard? But why should we call for the poet's lyre? Even now their praises sound from harps angelic. "What are these which are arrayed in white robes? and whence come they?" "These are they," respond the choirs of heaven— "these are they which came out of great tribulation, and have washed their robes, and made them white in the blood of the Lamb. Therefore are they before the throne of God, and serve Him day and night in His temple: and He that sitteth on the throne shall dwell among them. They shall hunger no more, neither thirst any more, neither shall the sun light on them, nor any heat. For the Lamb, which is in the midst of the throne, shall feed them, and shall lead them unto living fountains of waters: and God shall wipe away all tears from their eyes."

After the execution, Dalziel and Macduff having stood for a little, glutting their eyes with the effects of their cruelty, or rather of the Government under which they served, Macduff, sadly disappointed at the failure of this attempt to draw Mr. Bruce into his hands, said to Dalziel, "Might we not try what torture would elicit from the daughter? She might be less obstinate; or the father, moved by her sufferings, might deliver himself up to us."

"Inhuman man," replied Dalziel, touched with some compunctious visitings of nature, "would'st thou lay thy hand on the distracted girl? No. I will not permit it. Let us find the father as we may, but the daughter shall not be touched."

Macduff, being thus reproved by one who was noted for his inflexible rigour towards the Covenanters, ignorant, savage, crocodile-like as he was, seemed to feel a slight movement of shame; and, without resuming the subject, said to Dalziel, "Let us go and despatch the prisoners whom the soldiers brought in this morning."

The corpse of the murdered youth was left hanging upon the tree till evening, when some of the villagers ventured to take it down; and, having dug a grave beneath the shade of the elm, laid the remains of the son of their minister in the narrow house.

Chapter VII

"It matters little at what hour o' the day
   The righteous falls asleep, death cannot come
To him untimely who is fit to die;
   The less of this cold world, the more of heaven.
   The briefer life, the earlier immortality."
                                        —MILMAN.

ONE grand and peculiarly excellent characteristic of the Christian religion is, that its resources are always in pro-

portion to the wants of its true professors. If the
wickedness and cruelty of men gather about them with a
more frowning aspect, their Redeemer looks upon them
with a kinder countenance. If the calamities and sufferings of life embattle themselves thicker and thicker
around them, the objects on which they have fixed their
hopes beyond the grave come into a better light, and
fill their souls more abundantly with their heavenly
relishes.

The truth of this remark was well illustrated in the
conduct of Mr. Bruce. When he received the tidings of
his son's death, with the account of the unmurmuring
and triumphant manner in which he had closed his short
life, the resigned father, looking to heaven, said, " My
son, thou hast died in a good cause. The name of the
Lord be magnified."

Having uttered these words, he turned suddenly to the
peasant who had brought the sad intelligence, and said,
" My son is now safe ; but where is my daughter? Have
they murdered her too ? "

" Your daughter," replied the peasant, "is in the
village, with the old woman whom she used to be so fond
of. She was so overcome by her brother's cruel death,
that she remained for some time in a state of insen-
sibility ; but she is now recovered somewhat, although
they are afraid she is still in a dangerous condition."

" I knew it," said Mr. Bruce ; " I knew she would
never survive her brother's death. Her heart was too
tender. It is broken ! it is broken ! O my dear
daughter ! must I lose thee too? My two children in
one day ! O Father in heaven !" he then exclaimed,
" Thou knowest what is best for me, and all that is mine.
Do with us as seemeth good unto Thee." And then addressing himself to the peasant, said, " Can I not see her
once ere she depart? I must see her. I will venture
into the village under the shadow of night. If I should
fall into my enemies' hands, the Lord will deliver my
soul."

"You must not venture," said the peasant. "If you fall into their hands, we will all lose a father, who is our instructor and comforter in all our sufferings. Your daughter may soon be able to meet you in a place where you shall be in no danger."

"Nay," said the affectionate father, "but I must see her to-night. She hath need of comfort. Perhaps she will not see another day."

"Well, well, reverend sir," said the peasant; "we will all do what we can to get you into the village safely. We will let you know when the soldiers have gone to rest. Then will be the safest time for you."

"Do accordingly," replied the minister. "I will approach the village after nightfall, and wait in the hazel glen till you or some of your friends come to me. Go, and be mindful of your appointment."

When Mr. Bruce was left alone, he ventured out to the top of a hill hard by, whence he could espy the grave of his wife, and the smoke rising from the village, where his son had that day been put to death, and where his dear daughter, his only remaining earthly hope, lay on a bed of distress. And, truly, it needed something more than the mere firmness of natural fortitude to sustain his spirit while he waited in anxious expectation the coming darkness.

Mary, to whom we now return, when she lived at the manse in peace, as we formerly remarked, was cheerful as the lark of the morning, and lovely as the flower on which hath never breathed aught but the purest and gentlest breezes from the chambers of the south. And, till her mother's death, she bore all the sufferings to which the family were subjected with little change of spirit, and often did she cheer their wanderings by the sallies of her innocent mirth. Ever after her mother's death, however, although her father watched over her with the eye of a guardian angel, and her brother tended her with the most vigilant affection, she had lost much of her cheerfulness, and her health had been rather declining. The circumstances in which the family had been placed had rendered her mother peculiarly dear to her, and her tender feelings never fully recovered from the shock they received by the sudden and cruel death of her mother. And now the still more untimely and cruel death of her brother, together with all the affecting circumstances with which it was connected, had entirely overcome her. After she had been carried into the old woman's house, and had recovered from the swoon into which she had fallen when she heard that her brother's death was sure, she exclaimed, for some minutes, "My brother! my dear brother! what will my father do?" and then relapsed into the swoon. During the whole course of the day, although she had resorted to the treasures of comfort that are laid up for all afflicted Christians, and although the peace which is from above had stilled the tumult of her soul, she fell at intervals into fainting fits; and, as the evening and night approached, they came on oftener, and continued longer. She felt that she was dying, and she had only one wish, she said, unfulfilled—that was, to see her father. "But he cannot come here without endangering his life," she would say; "and why should I wish him? I shall soon see him in heaven. He will not take care of himself when we are gone, and the persecutors will soon get him; but my father is prepared to die."

At the approach of night, Mr. Bruce, anxious to see his daughter, drew near the village. He stayed in the hazel glen, as agreed on, till about midnight, when the peasant, faithful to his appointment, met him. As it happened, most of the soldiers who were quartered in the village and its neighbourhood had been sent the preceding day on a distant excursion, and had not yet returned, and the few who remained, the peasant assured Mr. Bruce, had all retired to rest.

Mr. Bruce, in coming to the house where his daughter lay, passed the place where his son was buried, and the church which he had so often entered with holy joy; and he saw the manse where he had lived so happily with his family. But these times were past. His Master had called him to severer service. And the worthy pastor, without giving way to the sad reflections which every object about him tended to suggest, hurried on to the hut where his daughter lay.

When he entered the house, he beheld Mary stretched on a humble bed to all appearance lifeless. "I am too late," he said to the old woman and some of the neighbours who stood by. "My daughter is gone." "We hope not, sir," replied the old woman. "She has fallen into a swoon, but she will recover yet."

Mr. Bruce examined his daughter narrowly, and he could discover that life had not entirely left its seat. Sometimes, however, he could discern nothing but the paleness and stillness of death about his dear child; sometimes a slight quiver moved her lips, and her eye half opened; and he leaned over her and wept, praying that he might yet hear his daughter's voice ere she departed.

After continuing nearly half an hour in this state, she gave a deep sigh, and looked up in her father's face. "Are you there, father?" she said. "I am now ready to die. They will tell you," continued she, looking to those who stood by—"they will tell you what my brother said to me when I saw him last. Haste you, dear father, from this place. They will torture you if they get you. Is it not night? Leave me before the day come. Dear father, I go to my Redeemer: He is all my salvation, and all my desire."

"Dear daughter," he said, grasping her hand, and half embracing her—"dear daughter, what can I wish more? The Lord our God take you to Himself!"

"Farewell, father," Mary said. "We shall soon meet again."

Oh, how lovely in that moment did she seem in her father's sight! Her eye, always beautiful, shed at its setting the purity of heaven, and no earthly commotion stirred the composure of her cheek. For a moment she looked on her father, not like the solitary star, which looks by the skirts of the gathering clouds which are soon to wrap it in darkness, but like the last star of the morning, about to fade away into the light of day. And now her eye closed ; she grasped her father's hand convulsively ; it loosened its hold ; the last quiver forsook her lips, and her gentle soul fled far away beyond the sufferings of time.

"It is done," said Mr. Bruce, still gazing on his daughter—"it is done ; persecution hath accomplished its worst against me. But why should I repine ? My dear family hath now escaped from the evils to come. This world was not their home. It was the country of their enemies ; and blessed be the name of God, that He hath so early taken them away from suffering to that place which His everlasting love hath prepared for them. I have now less to care for in this vale of tears. Let me now, Holy Father," said he, lifting up his hands to heaven—"let me henceforth have nought but Thy glory before me. In Thy name and strength let me fight out the Christian warfare. Make me more and more the comforter and helper of Thy scattered people ; and if Thou shouldst deliver me up to my enemies, give me to die without a murmur in the cause of my country's liberty !"

After uttering these words, Mr. Bruce desired the corpse of his daughter should be interred as privately as possible ; and, taking leave of the sorrowful few who had gathered around him, immediately left the village, and returned toward the place of his concealment.

The objects of nature had early made a deep impression on the mind of Mr. Bruce ; and his manner of life, spent for the last six years amidst its wildest scenery, had still deepened this impression. Night, as it was the only time when he could venture safely abroad, had especially engaged his contemplation, and often in his nocturnal discourses did he turn the attention of his audience to the grandeur of that magnificent temple in which they met to worship God.

Notwithstanding the losses he had sustained that day, Mr. Bruce, resigned to the will of God, and having the Christian's peace in his bosom as he walked towards the cave, could look with his usual relish to the magnificence of the starred canopy and the shadowy grandeur of nature around him. And as he ascended, with a peasant who accompanied him, an eminence near his cave, he made the following reflections,—standing lonely on the hill—with no wife, no child remaining ; but standing firm and dignified, like the oak of the mountains after its leaves have been torn away by the violence of the tempest :

"Turn your eye to those stars," said he to the peasant, "that look forth like angels' eyes from heaven. How pure and tranquil they seem ! None of the storms which agitate this lower world disturb them. They shone on the beings that trode this waste a thousand years ago, and still they shine on us. Do not their serenity and duration seem to write a satire on the tumult and brevity of the life of man ? How much of his folly have they seen !—how little of his wisdom ! How much of his cruelty to his fellow-creatures !—how little of his brotherly affection ! How many have they seen going forth, under their holy light, with the dagger of vengeance, to carry into execution the dark plots of wickedness !—how few have they noticed crossing the valleys of earth on errands of mercy ! How many deluded human beings have they observed bowing down to stocks and stones !—how few bending the knee sincerely to the living and true God ! Yes, they have seen hundreds of generations bustle away the little hour of their vanity, and they have seen their everlasting destiny sealed. And yet man is still as foolish as if none had ever proved to him that he must die. He grasps at the shadow of earth's happiness, more fleeting than that which the passing cloud casts yonder on the heath. And so eagerly does he run after the spectre, that neither the tears nor the execrations of thousands dying under his feet, nor the sword of eternal wrath which gleams over his head, can stop him in his frenzied pursuit. Sure there is something miserably wrong in the human heart. Surely the true eyes of the human understanding have been, indeed, put out. The shadow that falls from yonder mountain, and hides the vale in gloom, is itself brightness, compared with that cloud that broods on the human mind, and benights all its faculties. So dreadfully dim is mortal vision, that it cannot discern the glory of God Himself, even when He comes to redeem, to forgive, and to save. Oh, when shall that star arise which led the wise men of old to the manger of Bethlehem, and guides the way of every man to the feet of Jesus, who, although He created the heavens, and heard the harps of angels sing His glory divine, died to make us wise unto salvation? Surely the time will come, for the Lord hath sworn it, yea, He hath sworn it by Himself, when the earth shall return to its allegiance, and be cured of its folly."

Here the holy man looked to his companion, whom he had forgotten in his contemplations, and, casting his eye of faith far into days yet to come, and filled with the blessedness which the promises of God have pledged to the world, exclaimed, "Yes, my friend, we have the God that made all these worlds to support us. We have His promise, that truth shall ultimately prevail. Let us boldly do our duty, that we may be partakers of that joy unspeakable, which shall fill the hearts of the just when all shall be complete in Christ, and when these stars shall melt away at His second coming."

When Mr. Bruce had withdrawn his mind from these contemplations, he parted from the peasant and returned to the cave—by wife or child no longer made cheerful.

———

Chapter VIII

> " Servant of God well done !
>   Rest from thy loved employ ;
> The battle fought, the victory won,
>   Enter thy Master's joy.
> The pains of death are past,
>   Labour and sorrow cease ;
> And life's long warfare closed at last,
>   His soul is found in peace.
> Soldier of Christ, well done !
>   Praise be thy new employ ;
> And while eternal ages run,
>   Rest in thy Saviour's joy."
>
> —MONTGOMERY.

AFTER the loss of his family, Mr. Bruce continued to instruct and comfort his scattered flock with more assiduity and zeal than ever. The sufferings he had endured had given a bolder and firmer tone to his character. The more he saw the devastations of cruelty and tyranny spreading around him, the warmer his heart glowed with the love of liberty and the blessings which accompany it. The lovely flowers which, that he might guard and cherish them, had hitherto rendered him more careful of himself, were now gathered into a place of safety. With nought to bind him to earth but an ardent desire to instruct and counsel the Presbyterians, so as they might best attain the glorious purposes they had in view, he now ventured forth boldly, and seized with eagerness every opportunity of strenthening and consoling them. Thus employed for a considerable time, he wandered from place to place, always visiting, as often as he durst, the people of his former charge.

But, in proportion as Mr. Bruce became more conspicuous among the persecuted party, the malignity of his enemies, and their exertions to cut him off, increased ; and what they had so long and so eagerly sought was now drawing near.

One Sabbath evening, in the depth of winter, he met,

according to a previous appointment, a few of his own flock in a remote house not very far from the place where he had so often concealed himself. There he preached a sermon ; and as if he had felt some presentiment that this sermon would be his last, he exhorted his hearers, towards the close of his discourse, with extraordinary warmth and energy, to be faithful to the death, to live peaceably, to bear all with patience, assuring them that God would most certainly plead His own cause and deliver His servants from oppression. He represented how much Christ had suffered for them, and with what meekness and resignation,—what blessings they could secure to posterity, and what rewards they would themselves receive, by bearing nobly up against the storm that beat on them so severely. On leaving the little audience, whose hearts had burned, whose eyes had wept, whose faith had increased, and whose purpose to bear all, for the cause in which they had engaged, had been more firmly established while listening to his discourse, he said to them in a cheerful manner, " My friends, when we part in these times, we have very little certainty of meeting again. But our best friend, Jesus Christ, goes with us all. He is company enough ; and should anything happen to any of us, when we have no one to give us assistance, He will take care of us."

When he had thus said, he left the house, fearing that he had been already too long there, as it was not improbable that same notice of the meeting might have reached the persecutors. Both because it was the safest place, and because he meant to spend the remaining part of the Sabbath night in private prayer and supplication to God in behalf of the suffering people, he withdrew unaccompanied to the cave, never suspecting that any of his enemies observed him. But there had been a Judas among those who embraced him at parting.

One of those spies, whom we have had occasion to mention before, eager to gain the reward offered to any one who should bring information which might lead to the apprehension of Mr. Bruce, took the following method to compass his design.

With the consent and privacy of Macduff he entirely forsook his house, lived among the peasants, and, as he was one who had formerly sworn the covenant, he manifested the deepest contrition for the aid he had given to those who sought the ruin of the Covenanters. He gave proof of the greatest zeal in everything which had for its end their safety—revealed to them many schemes which were contrived for their destruction—and showed always the most sensible alarm lest he should fall into the hands of those he had last deserted. By these artifices he gained the confidence of those with whom he now associated ; and had continued with them more than a month, supporting always the same character, before Mr. Bruce happened to visit his people. The night of which we have spoken was the first time he had ever got into his presence. Mr. Bruce noticed him, but, both from the manner in which he behaved during the meeting, and from the account he had received of him, he entertained no suspicion of his real designs. This man, if he deserve the name, dogged Mr. Bruce, through the darkness of night, to the cave ; and, as soon as he saw him enter, hastened to the village to give information.

It was midnight when he reached the curate's house. And, although this monster would not have risen from his bed at that hour to save a soul from death, he instantly got up, and, with the malignant satisfaction of an evil spirit when it hath compassed some infernal aim, hastened to inform the few soldiers who were in the village. No time was lost. It was at first resolved to bring Mr. Bruce to the village, and send him thence to be executed in Edinburgh. But, as the appearance of a Dutch fleet on the north coast of Scotland had, at that time, occasioned the withdrawing of most of the troops from the west, they were afraid that the handful they could collect would not be sufficient to repel the peasants, whose ardent attachment to Mr. Bruce, they had every reason to suspect, would excite them to attempt a rescue. Urged by this reason, and determined, at any rate, to make sure of Mr. Bruce's death, Macduff said to the commanding officer, "Go and shoot the rebel wherever you find him. The king will reward you for it."

The soldiers, about ten in number, set out from the village, conducted by the spy, and led by an officer well fitted to execute a bloody command. As the ground was covered with snow, and the way extremely rugged, they could make no use of their horses, and were therefore obliged to leave them behind. But, although the storm of winter howled around their heads, and the darkness of night brooded on the rough and wayless moors, keeping, by the direction of the spy, not far from the stream up which the cave lay, they urged on, as if they had been going on a message of extraordinary mercy.

About three in the morning they reached the vicinity of the cave. Two or three soldiers were posted on a crag above it, one or two on the opposite side of the stream, to prevent the possibility of Mr. Bruce escaping, while the others scambled up the difficult ascent which led to the mouth of the cave. The spirit of the blast of night moaned dolefully among the forlorn cliffs ; the Ayr, half fettered in ice, grumbled at their feet ; and the leafless trees by which they supported themselves as they ascended the rock, waving to the wind, seemed to utter curses on the ruffians' heads. Hardened as they were in ruthless deeds, their guilty hearts interpreted every sound they heard as an indication of coming wrath. They trembled like the leaf which the wind passeth over ; and, as they stood still involuntarily before the abode of the holy man, they heard, issuing from the mouth of the cave, the following words: " Yea, for Zion's sake will I not hold my peace, Holy Father, and for Jerusalem's sake I will not rest, until the day of her mercy come. Hast thou forsaken Zion, O Lord ! hast Thou forgotten the people of Thy love? Our temples are desolate ; the courts of Thy holiness are defiled ; Thy children are scattered on the mountains ; they weep and cry in the desert. The harp of their sorrow hangs on the willow, and mourns to the blast of the wilderness ; the wastes of nature are watered with their tears ; their blood is poured forth, and there is none to pity them ! Surely we are a sinful nation—a people laden with iniquity. We have forsaken Thee ! we have provoked the Holy One of Israel to anger. But, O Merciful and Holy One ! God of salvation ! look down from heaven, and behold from the habitation of Thy holiness ; and let the bow of Thy mercy be seen in the wilderness. Thou wilt not forsake us. I know Thy Church is graven on the palms of Thy hands ; her walls are continually before Thee : and the point of every weapon that is lifted against her wilt Thou at length turn into the soul of him that lifted it. Haste, O God and Father, to deliver us ! Turn the hand of oppression from our country, that Thy people may dwell in freedom and peace. And while Thou seest meet that they should wander on the mountains and suffer in the cause of their country, oh, give them patience, and fortitude, and strength. Let them take comfort, that in all their afflictions the Captain of their salvation is afflicted, and that the Angel of Thy presence shall save them. Stretch over them the shield of Thine omnipotence ; guide the path of their trials by thine all-comprehending wisdom ; fill their hearts with thine inexhaustible love ; save them, O Lord—save and support them in death ! And, O Father ! when the day of Thy vengeance arriveth, and the year of restitution to the spoilers of our land doth come, have mercy on those who have had not mercy on us. Soften the hardness of their hearts ; open the blindness of their eyes. Oh, cast them not away from Thy presence for ever ! For who among them shall dwell with the devouring fire? who among them shall dwell with everlasting burnings ? "

Thus did the holy man, in the darkness of night, in the cave of the cold rock, plead with his God for our Church and our country.

The fell assassins still stood before the cave, trembling at the words they had heard, and the holy confidence with which they were uttered. And the most fearless and stout-hearted among them wished the task of murdering this servant of Jesus had fallen to other hands. After a short pause, however, the officer, ashamed to have felt something like humanity moving within him, which he considered as cowardice, suddenly entered the cave, ordering two of his men to follow.

Mr. Bruce, who was kneeling when he entered, arose. A few embers that burned on the floor of the place helped to show his appearance. His forehead was bald, and his few remaining locks were grey. His figure, although nothing improved by his half-worn and little-befitting clothes, was elegant; and the serene and peaceful dignity of his countenance, which changed not at the entrance of the soldiers, was such as might impress the beholder with respect and awe.

"You are come," said he mildly, addressing the officer—"you are come to apprehend me. I am prepared to go with you. You, perhaps, have a better lodging for me than this; although, as it is, I have been often glad to get to it."

"My orders are," said the officer, "to offer you the test, and if you refuse it, to put you to death on the spot."

"Nay, then," said Mr. Bruce, smiling, "is heaven so near? You are going to send me to better lodgings indeed."

"But will you take the test," said the officer, "and save us the expense of a shot?"

"God be my witness," said Mr. Bruce, the true fortitude of the Christian strongly marking his countenance as he spoke,—"God be my witness, I will never swear away my allegiance from the King of kings, who is my Saviour and Master. I will not submit to that which my conscience condemns. I will not connive at the enslaving of my country."

"Have done," said the officer ; "have done."

"I have done," replied Mr. Bruce, with unfaltering voice. And, lifting up his hands, he prayed, and said, "Lord Jesus, forgive my enemies. Lord Jesus, be with the poor people I leave in this wilderness. Father, Son, and Holy Ghost, receive my spirit !"

When he had thus spoken, the officer commanded his men to discharge their carabines on Mr. Bruce.

THEY REFUSED TO OBEY.

The reverend minister glanced a look upon them, and they refused to obey. "Faint-hearted slaves," exclaimed the enraged officer ; and, snatching a carabine from the hand of one of the soldiers, discharged its contents into the breast of Mr. Bruce. The martyred saint instantly fell down, and expired while the report of the fatal shot yet echoed among the wild cliffs

17

around. Farewell, good and faithful servant! Thou hast entered into the joy of thy Lord!

Still, religion, thou art happiness! The joys which thou pourest into the heart lie not within the reach of any weapon that the hand of man can form. The calm which thou settlest on the soul, the wing of no earthly blast can disturb. The light by which thy children walk is the candle of the Lord, which can never be quenched. Thou plantest a torch for them in the gloom of death's darkness, and supportest their goings on the rod and the staff of the Almighty. Thou conductest their spirits to the feast of immortality, and layest their bodies down to sleep in peace till the morning of the resurrection. Woe unto him that seeketh his happiness apart from Thee! He shall be miserably disappointed.

———

READER, I have now finished this short account of the Persecuted Family. In it I have had occasion to introduce thee to some of the sufferings that were endured, and some of the cruelties that were exercised, by our ancestors of the seventeenth century—the former for the sake of religion, and all the dearest rights of men; the latter to extirpate liberty, and leave to posterity the chains of servitude. The sufferings of the family, to which I confined myself, did not lead me to bring into view the most exalted Christian heroism which was in these times manifested; and, unwilling to shock the tender feelings of the heart, I have studiously avoided some of those monstrous cruelties which were then exercised, and which, without going out of my way, I might have introduced. Thou hast seen enough, however, kind reader, of the latter to abhor it, and of the former to admire it. I know thou hast praised their patience, and their resignation, and their hope, and their faith, and their fortitude in death. Thou hast marked their staunch adherence to the dictates of conscience, the ardour of their devotion, and their love of liberty and their country. And, while thou sittest in peace, conscious that thou mayest worship thy God as thou thinkest the Bible orders thee, thou perhaps givest them, who suffered so much to secure thee this liberty, the sacred applause due to their exertions. It is right that it should be so.

But I wish thee not to stop here. I wish thee to trust in and to adore the grace of God, which supported them and gave them victory; to admire the wonderful resources of that religion which they professed—how sufficient they are to instruct and advise the Christian in the devious and difficult paths—to keep his heart warm in the coldest winter of adversity—to invigorate him as he climbs the steepest ascents of virtue—and to uphold and sustain his soul in the face of the most violent of deaths.

Nor hath the Christian of the present day need only to admire the marvellous sources from which his suffering ancestors drew. He hath not less need than they to draw for himself. His enemies are more concealed, more mannerly, more deceitful, and therefore less apt to excite his suspicion and put him on his guard. Persecution labours to force the Christian out of his way, whether he will or not; and therefore the spirit of liberty within him encourages him to make a bold resistance. In the days of peace and prosperity he is assailed by pleasures, which, endeavouring to draw him out of his path by the sweetness of their song and the fairness of their promises, excite little suspicion of their design, and are therefore often little resisted.

If the persecuted Christian needs more of comfort, of steadiness in peril, of patience, resignation, and fortitude —he who lives in peace requires more of watchfulness, of self-denial, and of resistance to temptation. If our wants are, therefore, as numerous, so should our applications be to that inexhaustible source which supplied all theirs, and which will supply all ours if we approach it with our whole heart.

General View of the Covenanters

General View of the Covenanters

General View of the Character, Literature, Aims and Attained Objects of the Covenanters

To pass from a living story to an analysis may seem a cold and deep descent : still it is necessary to make it, and perhaps it may be so managed that whatever true sympathy has been excited by the memorial of the covenanting deeds and sufferings, shall not be lost in an attempt to seek more minutely to contemplate the moral and intellectual qualities of the men.

The first and most prominent feature in their character was *earnestness*. That they possessed this is beyond all question. Earnestness is not, as some seem to imagine, a quality recently discovered, like Californian or Australian gold,—it is as old as the heart of man, or the purposes and plans of Almighty God ; and in the heroes of the Covenant we find it in all its strength, if not in all its purity. They were terribly in earnest. The passion which was in them, like all great passions, refused to be divided. Their idea possessed them with a force and a fulness to which we find few parallels in history. It haunted their sleep—it awoke with them in the morning —it walked, like their shadow, with them to business or to pleasure—it became the breath of their nostrils and the soul of their soul. Ever does such possession give consistency to character, elevation to feeling, nobility to endurance—shall we say ?—sanctity to error. At least, the errors of earnest ecstacy are not to be weighed in the balance with the deliberate mistakes and voluntary madnesses of a false system. What a contrast between the Covenanters in their rugged devotedness, their almost insane sincerity, and the occasional excesses into which they were hurried, and the society of the Jesuits, with their cold colossal faults, their systematic falsehood, the low arts which mingled with all their stupendous exertions, the dark veil which has hung around them in all their manifold and tortuous movements. The history of the Covenanters was a current of rapid volcanic fire ; that of the Jesuits has been the course of a glacier, cold, creeping, and carrying destruction with it wherever it has gone. The earnestness of our fathers was that of deep attachment to a cause, and that of the Jesuits, of devotion to a defeated and exposed sham. As they have sown, they have reaped. The Covenanters have passed away, but the liberties and religion of Scotland form their everlasting monument. The Jesuits remain, but they walk in darkness ; they are tracked by suspicion, hatred, and terror, and now for a long time "their judgment lingereth not, and their damnation," as a party, "doth not slumber."

Much of the covenanting spirit of devout earnestness is gone from the Scottish character, but it is not yet too late to behold at least the skirts of its departing glory. The practice of tent-preaching, which till lately prevailed, was one of the most striking of these remains. That this was sometimes abused we know from Burns' Holy Fair, as well as from other sources, to be an unquestionable fact ; but the abuse was almost entirely confined to the neighbourhood of great cities. At all events, amid the peaceful solitudes of Perthshire we never witnessed aught but what was reverent, interesting, and even imposing. The use of the tent was latterly confined to the summer sacrament.

It is a bright Sabbath morning in the end of June, or the beginning of July—a little before eleven ; crowds are seen approaching from all directions to a tent made of wood, painted blue, and set in a field hard by the murmuring Earn, which a little below is joined by another mountain stream. The scene around is magnificent. To the west stand up a chain of bold precipitous mountains, black in winter, but now in this summer day clothed with the freshest green which ferns and Alpine grasses can supply. On the south, beyond the river, a fertile plain expands till bounded at the distance of two miles by a lower ridge of hills, which close the valley and confine the prospect. Eastward, the river pursues its course towards some low wooded fells, through which it finds a narrow passage into that broader strath which extends to the Tay. On the north is the village, and behind it a glorious glen covered with woods and surmounted by a monumental pillar, which stands on a bare rock above them. The sun is warm, but a tree or two are near, under which some of the multitude find a shelter, and a cool breeze from the stream passes ever and anon across their countenances, and bedews them with delicious refreshment. The crowd is scarcely less interesting than the scenery. It is composed partly of the villagers and partly of farmers and country-folks. You see here the keen, hard-featured faces of weavers and shoemakers, and there the bluff and ruddy countenances of ploughmen. Not a few aged men are there, wearing broad blue bonnets over their silver hairs. Some shepherds' plaids are to be seen ; and, here and there, you see a mountaineer wearing the kilt of his fathers. Old women are there, with round linen-caps instead of bonnets. Blooming virgins, too, abound, with modesty and beauty meeting together under the shadow of their simple headgear. Children people the outskirts of the assembly, or sit on the dyke dividing the field from the river ; and lo ! there is one boy who is sitting apart from all the rest, and is musing with half-shut dreamy eye—with the shadow of a whole tree screening him from the summer-heat. Many of the multitude have come from distant parts of the country, over " muirs and mosses many," to join in the solemnities

of the day ; *that* little company of men and women have
risen early from the banks of Loch Earn, have been first
at the tent, and shall remain till the stars appear trembling over the Abruchill Hills.   The service at last begins.
The preacher mounts the tent.   He is a man apparently
of sixty and upwards—his hair is a sable, thickly silvered
—his brow is lofty, his face has once been almost handsome, and is still manly and bold ; in stature he
approaches six feet, and age has not yet prevailed to
bend his erect figure.   His eye is quick, eager, and
restless ; earnest simplicity pervades his whole aspect.
He gives out the psalm in a clear, strong voice, which
rings afar "like a trumpet with a silver sound."   The
voice of the multitude then arises, swells, sinks, dies
away ; but how melodiously has it peopled the solitude
and awakened the echoes of the hills !   He prays, and
his prayer is fervid and powerful.   He announces as his
text, "They spake of the decease that he was to
accomplish at Jerusalem ;" and straightway the minds
of the large throng are transported to the top of Tabor
—a loftier hill than any in sight—and their hearts begin
to burn within them as they see their Lord talking to
the celestial messengers on that memorable transfigura-
tion morn,

" When in the sad days of his flesh, o'er Christ a glory came,
   And light o'erflowed him like a sea, and raised his shining brow,
   And the voice came forth which bade all worlds the Son of God
     avow,"

and talking not of heaven's splendours but of Calvary's
death !   The preacher is not imaginative in thought, or
refined in language ; but he is in earnest : he is possessed,
moreover, of true natural eloquence ; and as his voice
rises with his subject, and his eye kindles, every heart in
the audience is hushed, and not a few tears are seen
stealing down the cheeks of both young and old.   Now
he quotes a few lines of poetry ; and now he tells some
interesting or plaintive anecdote, and their attention is

still faster riveted. By and by his earnestness becomes overwhelming in its intensity, he has seized the two-edged sword of appeal, and is wielding it with a giant's arm. He alludes to their privileges : he contrasts that peaceful field-meeting with those of their forefathers in the days of the Covenant. "You have no arms in your hands—there are no watchmen posted on these silent hills. How great should be your gratitude!" Ere finishing, as if from an irresistible impulse, he takes occasion to enumerate the years of his own ministry ; to allude to the tent-preachings of the past on that same spot ; to speak of those who once worshipped there, but who were now in a better world ; and to talk of death as impending over his auditors and himself. He closes, and a thousand loosened breasts return him the truest applause. His word has been prophetic. Never more shall he preach at that tent. Never more shall he there see the June sun, hear the murmur of that silver Earn on the sacramental Sabbath day, or behold the thick daisies of that green sward where

"You scarce can see the grass for flowers."

Long ere summer has revolved his manly form is to be consigned to yonder graveyard on the west, which surrounds the parish church, with its spire. The sunshine of October is to look in upon his deathbed—his dying eye is to rest upon the autumn stubble—the fallen leaves are to play upon his grave—and that dreamy-eyed boy under the tree is to awake one awful morning, and to encounter almost the bitterness of death as he feels himself *Fatherless!*

The services of the day go on. Part of the multitude now repair to the church where the communion is being celebrated, others remain at the tent, where a succession of ministers appear, and, with various degrees of power, unction, and eloquence, perpetuate the impression made by the opening sermon. We notice with peculiar interest

one remarkable man, preaching to the smallest audience
that has been collected on that green to-day. Fit though
few is his audience. Yet, note well his aspect. His
stature is tall—his brow not broad but lofty—anxiety and
suffering have anticipated the work of age, instamping
premature wrinkles on his forehead, and shedding
premature specks of snow upon his head. His eye is
small, sunk, self-involved—his face has retired into a
dream, but on his lips there is carved a perpetual smile.
He reads for his text, "Thy righteousness, also, O Lord,
is very high." His manner at first is slow and embar-
rassed—his gesture is uncouth, and at times furious—
his voice sometimes sinks into an inarticulate murmur,
and is at times exaggerated to a yell. But, as he con-
tinues to preach, a strange fascination seems to exhale
out of him—a fine train of thought is found to underlie
the woof of his words, and you cry, "Is not this
genius?" And when he speaks of the lofty righteousness of the Lord, and compares it to the inaccessible
grandeur of the blue summer heaven, and points his
finger up toward that "terrible crystal" in which the
afternoon sun is now glowing, the climax is perfect—
and you bow down melted and thrilled beneath the
sublimity of his thought.

The evening service is the most solemn of all. But
here let us shift the scene six miles to the east, and look
at another tent-service there. It is taking place in a
field, near the town of Crieff, and commands a more
striking distant amphitheatre of view than even the
"green" of Comrie. The dark mountains on the west
are seen relieved and softened in outline against the far-
off sky. Another chain, invisible from the banks of the
Earn, appear in the north-west, resting against the
horizon like leaning Titans. Two of the loftiest of
Scotland's mountains are here also seen—Ben Voirlich and
Stincknachroan—looking in, as from another world,
over the tops of the inferior hills, and with sprinklings of
snow on their brows, unmelted amid the blaze of June.

Evening is casting its divine hues over this noble expanse
of prospect. A large star or two has come out, and,
like a quiet, thoughtful, happy eye, is watching the
scene. The broad, pale, spectral moon

> " Has climbed the blue steep of the eastern sky,
> And sits and tarries for the coming night."

The sun meanwhile is dying, like a king on a couch
of gold, supported by the blue ethereal mountains, and
with curtains of purple and crimson waving around the
gorgeous bed. In such a scene the last preacher of the
sacramental day begins its closing service, not uncon-
scious of the interest of the circumstances and the
romance of the scene. Perhaps he selects the subject
of the judgment-day—and, to a silent and awestruck
throng, describes the gathering of the clouds of doom
—the tolling of the funereal bell of the universe—the
going out of "that moon, that sun, and those stars—
the appearance of the Saviour in the sky—the rising of
the dead—the commencement of the great trial—the
judgment-seat—the books opened—the heavens and the
earth fleeing away—and that final rolling in sunder from
each other of the two streams of mortal being—those of
the evil and of the good—which at this tremendous
point are to dispart and to meet no more for ever.
Words would fail in describing the impression made by
such a subject, treated amid such a scene. There was
no outbreak of emotion, few tears, and no cries; but the
soul of the whole assembly was touched to the quick;
the faces of all, as they left the meeting, carried a soft
deep shadow upon them—and, as they wound their way
under the night canopy towards their homes, their hearts
were softened and solemnised, and often their minds and
language exalted to a pitch which now it is difficult to
realise.

Such scenes enable one to realise the covenanting
period—to believe implicitly in the existence of an

earnestness of which this which was daily witnessed was only a faint, though true, relic ; and to feel, moreover, how much the presence of natural beauty and grandeur can serve to increase the power of spiritual truth. Not that these plain masses of men were all fully aware of the impression made by external scenery on their minds. Indeed, one of them was somewhat scandalised when spoken to of the fine view from the tent of Crieff. But it told on them not the less really that they were not conscious of the cause—

> " Like some sweet beguiling melody—
> So sweet we *know not* we are listening to it."

Thus did the natural beauties of the scene incarnate the profounder religious emotion so softly and thoroughly that they were not felt in the process. Perhaps even some of the hearers thought the glances which they could not but cast around at Nature's loveliness, and the emotions which sprung from them, rather "carnal" than otherwise. But no matter ; they *had* combined with the sublimer "powers of the world to come" to produce a complex emotion of love and fear, of delight and of solemnity, never on earth or in eternity to be forgotten.

This serves to suggest as the next general remark, that, along with this pervading earnestness in the Covenanters, there were mingled many elements of blindness and bigotry. These stern justice forbids us to overlook. Every allowance should, indeed, be made for the age in which they lived—and for the popish scales which still hovered before their eyes. But, after all these deductions are made, there remain about them a form and shape of character, as well as modes of feeling and of thought, which constitute most undesirable models, and which indicate a sad declension from the days of primitive Christianity. It were an easy task to "rake up the ashes of our fathers," and to prove them guilty, not merely of occasional outrages which humanity condemns, but of extreme narrowness and illiberality of view ; of profound misconceptions, in many respects, alike of God's character and Christ's faith ; of ignorance of natural laws, and of greater ignorance still of much that is implied in the important word so often in their mouths, God-spell, or Gospel.　But why throw out a current of invective against the noble dead who were cut off in the morning-twilight, when we find, even in the comparative noonday of our time, most of their mistakes not only extant but far more offensively protruded.　The hard dogmatic edge given to the flexible and ever-flowing form of Christianity —the clinging to creeds and confessions, as if they were the essence, and not the poor abridgment, of divine truth —the bibliolatry, the trust in external schemes of propagation—the belief in a modified civil tyranny as the grand method of spreading the gospel—the crushing contempt for differences of opinion and varieties of spiritual insight—the dream of uniformity as possible, *without a theocracy*, on earth—the sidelong and suspicious attitude held toward science, philosophy, even nature—as if the God of the dead and of the living were not the same. All these, and more than these, we might pardon and pass by in the Polyphemi of the past, but not in their unhappy imitators in many churches and lands of the present, who, like owls half-awakened at noon, have come out, screaming their midnight inspiration into the ears of a new age—and whose voice is only able to recall the darkness, to re-suggest the horrors and falsehoods, but not to bring round the worship, or the love, or the zeal, or the faith, of a bygone day.

There is, however, in every day's experience, much to demonstrate that, in the worst sense,

> " The ancient spirit is not dead ;
> Old times, methinks, are breathing still.'

Honour to the men of the past ! but none to their dregs, their mimics, their caricatures.　None to those who would, in the earnest or affected pursuit of their steps, reproduce

most of their errors without the vantage-ground of their
darkness, and commit many of their mistakes without
that fine madness which alone can atone for them. A
sincere, somewhat bigoted, enthusiast in the seventeenth
century may be compared to one of the vast creatures
of the bygone chaos—the magnificent miscreations of
geology, interesting and most instructive as a fossil
remain; but should some stray relic of the mastodon or
ichthyosaurus come out now from a distant desert, would
not man unanimously hoot him back or hunt him down,
and say, "Your day is over; your race has served its
purpose and cannot be perpetuated. Besides, you are
but a degenerate specimen. Begone!" Lingering,
nevertheless, with interest and admiration around these
heroes of another age, we notice the deep, disinterested
piety of their natures. Would, indeed, this quality were
to return—and undoubtfully it will, although in a more
liberal guise! Their "life was hid with Christ in God."
They habitually "saw Him who is invisible." They fed
on the "hidden manna"—a heavenly and immortal food.
Like the steeds of Achilles, no pabulum less than celestial
touched their spiritual palates. It was this which supported them in the moors, and gave them in solitudes and
on scaffolds meat to eat of which their enemies knew not.
In a manner we can hardly even now conceive, they seem
to have realised God in all their ways and wanderings.
"His word was nigh them." His awe was a second
shadow along their path. His love was felt like another
mantle around their chilled and cowering frames. They
renewed, in many points, the Hebrew's feeling of his
Maker. No need of demonstrating a God to them, or of
demonstrating Him to others. This process—a process
in itself impossible—they never even attempted to per-
form. They lived, moved, and had their being in God.
Every shadow or sunbeam which fell on them was that of
the Great Whole. *He* watched over their slumber; *He*
was the real guard upon their mountain-tops; *He* delivered them out of the hand of their enemies, and some-

times he delivered their enemies into their hands. It is curious how the religion of the Jews has rooted itself more deeply in Scotland than in any other quarter of the globe ; how this fiery exotic of a torrid clime has flourished best in the land of mist and snow. Many reasons might be assigned for this. Both countries, amid their diversities of climate, are mountain-lands, full of bold, rocky scenery, of ravines and of rivers, and with lakes reposing in the midst of barren mountains, and with rich vales alternating with gloomy desolations. Owing partly to their scenery, and partly to their poverty and insulation, both the Hebrews and the Scotch have been a thoughtful people, inclined to religion, awestruck by the visible phenomena of the universe, and fond of looking at things in their great masses. More of the analytic element has gradually, indeed, been developed from the Scottish mind ; but the fragments of Celtic and border poetry which are extant serve to prove a striking original resemblance between the genius of the two nations, which in both was bold, figurative, lyrical, and fonder of the rude sublime than of the delicate and the beautiful. Hence one reason of the ready and warm reception with which Christianity was welcomed in Scotland, the tenacity with which it has been retained, and the deep and solemn colouring with which it has tinged the popular mind. Hence, too, the reason why the spirit of the Old Testament has met with a profounder response than that of the New ; the cosmopolitan aspect, the loving spirit, the gentle and childlike tone of which were less congenial than the severer purpose, the sterner fire, the more condensed and darker zeal, and the poetic ardours of the prophets, and have been less diligently and successfully transplanted into the Scottish soil. The apostles of the Lamb are less suggested to us by the Camerons, Renwicks, and Rutherfurds, than are the Elijahs, Ezekiels, and Malachis of the old dispensation, in their " deep-furrowed garments of trembling," their metaphorical speech, the hurrying movement of their thought

18

and style, which seems to fling itself, like an impatient eagle, from crag to crag, and the anger which surrounds them as with flames of devouring fire, and renders the place where they stand dreadful and insulated, like the top of Sinai on that morning when it was "all of a smoke," as the feet of Jehovah burned upon it.

The piety of the Covenanters has often been charged with cant. Nor are we disposed altogether to deny the charge. We find much in their spoken and written language calculated to offend our modern taste. We find undue familiarity with divine things, extravagant and absurd expressions of religious feeling, a profusion of such epithets as "Sweet Jesus," "Dear Jesus," and "To sleep in the arms of Christ my Lord," etc., and a use of scripture language in circumstances which render it little else than disgusting. We could easily cull whole pages from Samuel Rutherfurd, Andrew Wellwood, and others of their time, which would excite risible emotions as certainly as the ravings of Mause, or the sermons of Habakkuk Mucklewrath, in *Old Mortality*. But this, while it might make sport to the profane, could not fail to make the judicious and the pious grieve. The laughter produced would be poor and cheap; the sting left behind would be sharp and deadly. 'Twas often a barbarous *patois* which these men spoke, being that of their age and country; but their spirit being that of earnestness, faith, and Christian principle, would have redeemed ten thousand greater faults than slips of taste and errors in language. Piety, like charity and genius, should cover a multitude of sins, and will do so to all manly and ingenious minds. Great excitement seldom picks its words; it deals in blunt and powerful language; and he were a wretched critic who, in hearing a Burke, a Chalmers, or a Wilson, in their hours of "torrent rapture," should pause to mark with malignant accuracy the harsher tones in their voices, the slight blunders in their syntax, or the petty provincialisms in their accent. But such views may be more appropriately developed in the course of an examination of the literature of the Covenanters, which has met with great injustice.

We mark, next, with no little admiration, the courage and constancy of this remarkable people. What courage was theirs, let the records already given of the fights of Pentland, Drumclog, and Airsmoss, not to speak of innumerable smaller skirmishes, attest. Even the battle of Bothwell was lost less from the want of courage than from untoward circumstances and the evil effects of party spirit. The covenanting warriors were often imperfectly armed—many had only scythes, or bludgeons, or pitchforks ; they were for the most part untrained to the use of arms ; they were almost always forced to fight at odds, and yet even their enemies have never denied their bravery. How great the daring required in those little parties who ventured, at Rutherglen and Sanquhar, to burn the acts against the covenanting reformation, and to issue declarations against the ruling powers—in Cargill and Cameron publicly excommunicating the king ; in the manner in which imprisonments, or confinements in damp caves, were borne ; in the unmurmuring silence or holy triumph with which the martyrs mounted their scaffolds, and found themselves "face to face with death ; " and in the patience with which they bore the exquisite tortures, or, worse still, the cruel scoffings which attended their trials. Even the flight to which they were often obliged to betake themselves becomes a new element in our estimate of their courage. There is a difference between even the back of a brave man and the back of a coward. The Covenanter had often to run, but it was before a superior force—often he turned round upon his pursuers—he retired, as well as advanced, like a lion—skill, sagacity, self-possession, distinguished and secured his retreat, and in the last extremity he was more ready to fight and die than to yield. Sometimes, hearing that the dragoons were approaching, he, like Thomas Brown, the cousin of John of Priesthill, went out calmly to cross their

track, passed himself off for a stranger, and when asked
if "the fanatic Brown" was at home, truly answered
that *he was not*, and was permitted to pass on his way.
Sometimes, like John MacClement, pressed hard by his
pursuers, when he turned the corner of a hill, seeing a
sheep lying dead on the heath, he took off his coat,
lifted the sheep on his back, met his enemies—who mis-
took him for a shepherd—entered into conversation with
them, and succeeded in sending them on a false scent in
pursuit of himself. Sometimes, like John Dempster,
when pursued so hotly that the horse of the nearest
dragoon was pressing on his shoulder, he turned round,
plunged a large pair of scissors, his only weapon, into
the horse's forehead, which made him rear, throw his
rider, and enable John to escape into the shadow of an
adjacent wood. Sometimes, like John Fergusson, when
chased to the brink of a dark, deep pool, in a river
surrounded by thick willows, he first threw his bonnet
and a rake, with which he had been working in a hayfield,
down the stream, and then plunged under the water,
screened by the shade of the willows, and keeping his
head above the waves—his pursuers imagining, from the
bonnet and rake, that he had drowned himself and been
swept down by the current. The whole annals of
romance, in short, including the marvellous escapes
described by Le Sage, Godwin, Radcliffe, Scott, and
Bulwer, contain no adventures more striking, no incidents more intensely interesting, no such "hair-
breadth" escapes as those which abound in the history
of the Covenant, and which corroborate the well-known
statement,

> "Truth is strange—stranger than fiction."

The courage, too, of the women of the Covenant must
not be forgotten. Truly, from Lady Hamilton—standing
on Leith shore, with her pistol and gold bullets, ready to
shoot her son if he landed—to Isabel Weir, sitting silent
and with covered face beside her husband's corpse, they

were high-hearted women, those of the covenanting times!—true, full of a noble simplicity, blended with yet a nobler guile—most disinterested in their attachment, most devoted to their principles, and equally brave and sagacious in the use of means in their husbands' or lovers' rescue or defence. Their ornaments were not of gold, or pearls, or costly array—the simple snood, the coif, the plaid were their dress, but there was that within which passed show, and the enthusiasm which pervaded Scotland nowhere beat more powerfully than in the hearts of her daughters. Now they concealed their husbands under beds, or in lumber-rooms, and then went out and firmly met the pursuers, and answered their questions. Now, when their husbands were away with their babes to be baptized at conventicles, and when the dragoons came in search, they filled the empty cradles with rags, and continued to rock them, lest the absence of the infants should awaken suspicions as to the errand of the parents. Now, like the immortal Bessie Maclure, in Scott, they sat at the turning of two ways, at the eventide, and warned the lonely fugitive that there was a lion in the path. Now they assisted their husbands in scooping out hollow spots of refuge among the hills. Many a time and oft did they keep the midnight fire burning in their cots, and have a midnight morsel ready, that their husbands—cold, and wet, and hungry—might steal in and spend an hour or two, in trembling joy, at their own hearth-side. Often, when this was impossible, whenever the darkness fell, and the darker the better—and better still if the wind was loud, and the rain falling thick—did these gallant matrons lift up their small bundles of provisions, draw their plaids closely around them, and set out to visit the dark caverns, or pits, or the sides of the precipices, where their husbands were lurking, and feed and comfort them there. When tried by horrid tortures to reveal the spots of their retreat, they refused. When led out, as was often the case, to die beside them, they took it right joyfully. And many a drink of whey and piece of oat-cake did they, standing at the door of their dwellings, give, at the hazard of their own safety, to haggard wayfaring men who were pursued by the voice of the blood of Magus Muir, or fleeing from the echo of the rout of Bothwell.

Honour to the memory of such noble daughters of Almighty God ! No theatrical airs or meretricious graces about them. Never does any one of them, like Charlotte Corday, step out of woman's sphere and become a sublime assassin—nor, like Madame Roland, mingle a certain affectation and grimace with the grandeurs of a heroic death. They were as simple as they were great. Their characters seem modelled upon that of Scotland's scenery—their hearts were soft as its vales, while their principles were like its hills, high, firm, and unmovable. And Scotland can boast of a similar class of women still, who are worthy of having sprung from the daughters of the Covenant, and in whom superior knowledge and re-finement have not deadened the sense of right, damped the glow of piety, or degraded the fine instincts of virtuous and disinterested womanhood. Female atheists there are even in Scotland—victims of a morbid sensi-bility, or of morbid and false culture ; but in general our female heart beats in the right place—it is not disposed to cast off Christianity as a garment, to change it as a vesture is changed, and to substitute for it a vague pantheism, or a distinctly-defined rationalistic creed. Here, indeed, as well as in England, the men, particu-larly the young men, are passing through that strange burning fiery furnace of doubt which has been kindled from abroad, and many of them have been consumed ; but our women, as a whole, have not had a hair of their head touched by its flames. The good, the active, the benevo-lent, the true-hearted women of Scotland are Christians in faith as well as in practice, and are the real blood and life of all her churches.

Not inferior to the courage was the constancy of this people. The word applied to them by Scott, in *Red-*

gauntlet, describes them in this point admirably. "The whigs," says Wandering Willie, "were as *doure* as the cavaliers were fierce." Yes, *doure* (from the Latin word *durus*,) is the word for their perseverance and intensity of resistance. It was an assault of lightning—flash after flash, bolt after bolt ; they had to encounter here the forked fire of a Claverhouse, and there the dull thunderbolts of a Turner or a Dalziel. But grim was the array of rocks which met and repelled it ; and while the lightning exhausted itself and passed, the rocks were found split, scorched, but REMAINING. This constancy was partly created by the depth with which religion had ploughed itself into the southern Scottish heart—partly by the activity and energy of the ministers, partly by a certain stubbornness which adheres to the national character, and partly by the recoil and reaction generally produced by the very severity of a persecution. The Scotchman driven desperate, may be likened not so much to the stag at bay, as to the wolf, in the *Lays of Ancient Rome*, which

> " Dies in silence, *biting hard*,
> Amidst the DYING hounds."

This "doureness" may be partly, also, owing, at once in its spirit and its success, to our scenery. "Deep calleth unto deep." The contemplation of fixed features in nature—of changeless moors and granite mountains, of rocks on whose faces each wrinkle is the work of a century, of the monotonous surface of the ocean and the unalterable splendours of the stars—is calculated to create a certain rugged determination in the minds of the inhabitants. They become fierce as the tiger, yet patient as the camel when passing over his interminable deserts. The motto of such men is, " I bide my time." Hence the revenge, the love, the fear, the loyalty, the super-stition, the manners and religion of North Britain, have all been distinguished by a slow fire, a long deep fervour, and are well described in one of their ballads re-

ferring to the attachment of the Highlanders to Charles
Edward—

> "And sure that love must be sincere,
> Which still proves true whate'er betide,
> And for his sake leaves a' beside."

In fact, it is only in the sturdy devotion of the clans to
the Stuart family that we find a complete counterpart
in later ages to the determined attachment of the Covenanters to their banner. And it is remarkable that both
these enthusiasms were sheltered, strengthened, and
conserved by the fact that they divided between them
the two great mountain-tracts of the country—the northern and southern Highlands. From these, as from two
peaks, flared up, in contradiction and reply to each other,
for a century and more, the two fierce, tremulous, waving,
yet fixed, flame-pillars of Jacobite and Presbyterian zeal.

There are some remarks of William Howitt which
bear eloquently on this topic: "Thanks be to God for
mountains! When I turn my eyes upon the map of
the world, and behold how wonderfully the countries
where our faith was nurtured, where our liberties were
generated, where our philosophy and literature, the
fountains of our intellectual grace and beauty, sprang
up, were as distinctly walled out by God's hand with
mountain ramparts as if at the especial prayer of the
early fathers of man's destinies, I am lost in an exulting
admiration. Look at the bold barriers of Palestine!
see how the infant liberties of Greece were sheltered from
the vast tribes of the uncivilised north by the heights of
Hæmus and Rhodope! behold how the Alps describe
their magnificent crescent, inclining their opposite
extremities to the Adriatic and Tyrrhene Seas, locking
up Italy from the Gallic and Teutonic hordes till the
power and spirit of Rome had reached their maturity,
and she had opened the wide forest of Europe to the
light, spread far her laws and language, and planted the
seeds of many mighty nations!

"Thanks be to God for mountains! Their colossal

firmness seems almost to break the current of time itself.
While a multitude of changes has remoulded the people
of Europe, while languages and laws, and dynasties and
creeds, have passed over it, like shadow over the landscape, the children of the Celt and of the Goth, who fled
to the mountains a thousand years ago, are found there
now, and show us, in face and figure, in language and
garb, what their fathers were ; show us a fine contrast
with the modern tribes dwelling below and around them ;
and show us, moreover, how adverse is the spirit of the
mountain to mutability, and that there the fiery heart of
freedom is found for ever."

Public spirit, and the presence of impersonal enthusiasm, are qualities often connected with such earnestness
and piety as we have already attributed to the Scottish
Covenanters.   But there have been times in which
piety and earnestness have flowed more in personal and
less in public channels, in which the question has been
more, " What shall I do to be saved ? " than What shall
I do to save the Church at large ?   In the era of Metho-
dism, the former was the question which ran through
the land and created the excitement.   In the days of the
Covenant, although personal piety flourished and revivals
abounded, the great point was the best mode of promot-
ing the extension, the liberty, and the power of the
general Church.   There was then in Scotland little purely
theological controversy.   The shadow of scepticism upon
individual minds, although not unknown, did not lie so
heavily as often now ; doubt was lost in action ; and
every noble mind and heart, instead of tormenting itself
and others with unanswerable questions, rushed eagerly
into public work " as the horse rusheth into the battle."
With this devotedness to a public " testimony-bearing,"
there were indeed many formidable evils connected.   In
the first place, it to a great extent foreclosed the exercise
of free thought and inquiry.   It added a dogmatic stamp
to opinion, and hurried it to an untrue test, that of the
sword.   It hindered progress, and often stereotyped

error. But it had important advantages too. It prevented all half-measures, all halting between two opinions,
all useless scruples, and secured unity, consistency, and
energy in the prosecution of their views. They felt that
their duty was not to think, but to do. We quote a few
remarks on this subject from a deceased Scotch divine
of great eminence in his day.[1] "Our fathers have often
told us how much, in their earlier years, they were embarked in the cause of religion as an object of great
public concern ; and have complained that the good fame
which well belonged to it as a public cause is now abandoned by a generation who feel, or pretend to feel, that
their religious concern is only and properly directed about
their own individual interest or personal salvation. In
contemplating the history of the Church of Scotland in its
earlier days, and comparing it with the appearance of the
religious world in our country at present, we cannot help
being deeply struck with the difference of regard then
and now paid to the public cause, or the welfare of the
Church of Christ, with the far deeper concern they took
in it, compared with the little interest which we feel in
the great sacrifices which they made for its support, in
comparison of the scorn which in many instances we
attach to its name. It was a remarkable feature of the
second reformation, in the year 1638, that the fine spirit
of concern about the public cause, which the enemy during the preceding apostacy had attempted by every
means to eradicate or repress, once more sprung elate,
and, recovering all its former buoyancy, spread its renovated and unabated influence over the Church of Scotland.
The Church proceeded in reformation, and everywhere
the word of God grew and multiplied. In that auspic-
ious period, one of the most sublime enterprises which
the conception of man ever has at any time grasped
began to be put in progress—the Church of Christ, exerting her moral and religious power on the world, and

[1] The late John Jameson, of Methven. The reader may find him
described as the *second* minister of the tent-preaching scene, p. 268.

bringing a whole nation under the practical influence of the word of God. It might have been expected that the public spirit, which in 1638 resumed its elasticity, would, at the revolution, when it made its escape from a more fiery trial, have burst forth with a purer fire and blazed with a brighter flame. What shall we say? The storm, indeed, was laid, the clouds had been dispelled, and the sun again had broken forth; but it was a sun shorn of his beams. That fine spirit which could not, or would not, temporise, which in matters of God, between truth and error, light and darkness, duty and sin, the rights of God, and the pleasure, or the vanity, or the folly of man, could admit of no compromise—that spirit was sadly dissipated. The Church of Scotland came to the revolution a goodly vine withered in the blast. Abashed at the sight, the genius of the reformation hung her head, and wept over her wasted and departing spirit."

We do not entirely coincide with these eloquent remarks; and continue to believe that whatever may be said of the design of the second reformation, the means employed to promote it were unchristian, and therefore abortive. But it may be granted that the prevalence of public spirit in the covenanting age led to noble results on character. These men of the Covenant were in the last degree unselfish. They were swallowed up in their cause. They never thought about themselves at all. Their language was, in effect, that of Danton, " Let my name be blighted—what am I?—the cause alone is great!" Hence we find little egotism in their words, and none in their actions. Never is the most gifted of them found asking the question, " What shall I do to be for ever known? but, what shall I do to make known God's great name, and to bind His Covenant for ever around the loins and heart of my country." Base and self-seeking men there were, doubtless, among them, but nations are never hypocrites *en masse*, and, in general, the covenanting people were as disinterested as they were brave. It is not necessary to decry the love of fame, nor even that inferior shape of it, the love of reputation. There is equal truth and spirit in the words of Milton—

> " Fame is the spur which the clear spirit doth raise,
> The last infirmity of noble minds."

And the love of reputation, even to the degree which made Johnson value the "praise of every human being," is a natural and a noble principle. But there is something higher than both. Echoes are found at the foot of rocks, but above them there is a lofty region whence no response can be returned, because the canopy is the sky ; so are there those who speak at once to heaven, and who, as they do not expect, are not astonished to receive no audible answer. On that eminence, where the future verdict of God is alone appealed to, and where immediate human applause, and even the calm decision of posterity, are not regarded, stood the better and braver of the children of the Covenant.

The eloquence of such men was precisely what might have been expected from their character, their excitation, and their circumstances. Polish or elaboration, *lucidus ordo* or *concinnitas*, were hardly to be expected in the oratory of those who mounted the pulpit at the hazard of their lives, and whose sermons were apt to be interrupted by the shots of the foe. But the elements of astonishing eloquence were found in their extempore harangues. Macbriar's supposed sermon in *Old Mortality*, at the close of the battle of Drumclog, is probably a very fair specimen of the discourses which acted with such trumpet-like effect upon the peopled moorsides of Fife and Galloway. In such sermons a profusion of Scripture was used ; every resemblance that could be found between their circumstances and those of the old Jews and Christians were carefully brought forward ; there was little didactic matter, but there was much stirring practical appeal ; the metaphors were massive and bold— the allusions to the natural objects around them were not so numerous as they would be in similar circumstances now, but they always told, and the general effect was to create in every breast the irresistible cry, " Lead us to battle !" The manner of their preachers was far from graceful : they almost invariably *sang* a gamut of their own ; their voices were more sonorous than sweet, and their gesture was uncouth and uncultured. But some can testify from recollection how powerful *singing*, as it was called, became, particularly on sacramental occasions and in the serving of communion-tables. We have heard at such times wild strains of oratorical melody, no doubt handed down from the days of the Covenant, and which, if at first they rather tended to excite a smile in the young, rarely failed, ere they closed, to melt both young and old, both speaker and audience, into tears. Power there certainly was, however rudely disguised, in those mountain preachings, which drew and detained thousands in the wilderness—which nerved men for the most unequal and bloody contests—which soothed agony, awakened faith, relieved the pangs of hunger, covered the shame of nakedness, and kept hope burning, like a torch in the wind, for twenty-eight terrible years.

The literature of the covenanting age, like its oratory, must not be tried by a severe æsthetic standard. During the persecution, indeed, it was confined chiefly to protests, declarations, and dying testimonies. In these last, as collected in Napthali and elsewhere, there is a certain severe, purged simplicity, a pathos and grandeur which move you to your depths. There are not many individual expressions that will bear quotation ; the power is in the whole, and you cannot help admiring the manly sense, spirit, calmness, dignity, and piety which distinguish the sufferers to a degree so equal that you fancy them a band of brothers. You see, undoubtedly, much of the narrowness of the times, but not a particle of the indiscreet and insane fanaticism usually ascribed to the party. One Thomas Brown, who with four others was executed on Magus Muir, *in terrorem*, although neither he nor any of his fellows was concerned in the death of

Sharpe, speaks out with great boldness. He prays God
to remove the "deluge of wrath which is hanging over
the head of these lands for the breach of Covenant in
them." He says, "I die in the faith, that the seeds
sown at Bothwell Bridge shall have a glorious spring and
harvest, which shall be renowned in the eyes of all the
beholders of it." Elsewhere he identifies the cause of
the Covenant with Christ Himself, and says, that "He is
forced to go to the mountains and dens and caves of the
earth." He expects soon to be "a sharer of the heavenly
mansions, and of the peaceable fruits of righteousness,
which the Lord, the righteous Judge, shall give me." The
rest of his testimony is distinct, weighty, and vigorous.
And yet this man was only a shoemaker !

How far more imposing those fine stammerings of
sincerity, those gasps of great dying hearts, than the
most elaborate efforts of cultivated talent ! They remind
one of the dumb son of Crœsus bursting silence and
speaking out. Or it is "as though the rocks of the sea
should speak, and tell us what they have been thinking
of from immemorial time." We contrast them
favourably with the scaffold speeches of the French
revolutionists. If wanting their lurid sublimity, as of
dying thunder, they have a softness and holy calm, like
the lapse of an autumn sun. Danton cries out, "My
dwelling shall soon be with annihilation?" John King
says, "Welcome everlasting life, everlasting glory, everlasting love, and everlasting praise." Vergniaud and
his doomed Girondists sing, on the last night of their life,
tumultuous songs, and weave ghastly dialogues with
Satan about their enemy, Robespierre. The five at
Magus Muir pass away to glory singing Psalm xxxiv.,
with these, among others, of its words of celestial
cheer—

> "The angel of the Lord encamps
> And round encompasseth
> All those about that do Him fear,
> And them delivereth.

The lions' young may hungry be,
And they may lack their food ;
But they who truly seek the Lord
Shall not lack any good."

But the Covenant, before the persecution, had produced a peculiar and very interesting literature. It is not, indeed, so well known as the contemporaneous works of the Puritan writers. Nor can the writings of either the early or the latter Covenanters be placed upon anything like an equality with those of the English divines of the same periods. It is vain to seek among the Scotch for a John Howe, that gentlest and most symmetrical of the sons of Anak—strong as an earth-born Titan, and yet beautiful as a woman, and with the fiery air of a seraph breathing around his vast form—a Plato added to the eastern sages, and with them bending at the manger, and spreading out treasure of myrrh, frankincense, and gold before the Divine Child ; for a John Owen, the weighty, the minute, the learned—with all the solidity, the wide compass, and the gnarled knots of the broad old oak ; for the "incomparable Culverwell," as one enthusiastically calls him ; for Bates, the " silver-tongued " ; for the massive Manton ; for the ingenious Charnock ; for the richly practical Flavel ; for Bunyan, the inspired dreamer, to whom in sleep, as in that isle of enchantment, the " clouds opened and showed riches," and who when he awoke "cried to dream again ; " and, if we may class HIM with any cluster in any firmament—for a Milton—

" Whose soul was like a star, and dwelt apart."

Still, we find among our rugged lowland men some writers worthy of long memory, and who in sincerity, and perhaps in native force, if not in art and culture, are inferior only to the highest of those English authors just named. Among these, Hugh Binning's works, which fill a thick quarto volume, are distinguished by clear arrangement, evangelical richness of matter, and, for that age, correctness and elegance of style This author died in his twenty-sixth year, but not till he had, besides writing much, acquired great fame as a pulpit orator. One bad but characteristic pun of Cromwell's is recorded in connection with his name. He had once, it is said, held a dispute with the general's divines on the points in contest between the Independents and Presbyterians, and had succeeded in silencing them. Cromwell asked what bold and learned youth this was. He was told it was one Binning (the Scotch for "binding"), and answered, "He hath *bound* well indeed, but," laying his hand on his sword, "*this* will loose all again!" William Guthrie, of Fenwick, in Ayrshire, cousin of James Guthrie, the martyr, and reputed the "greatest preacher in Scotland," has left one little treatise—"The Trial of a Saving Interest in Christ"—which deserves perusal as a most searching and vigorous tractate, and which, if it does not captivate the heart or the fancy by its beauty, casts very strong grappling-irons upon the conscience of its reader. Durham's treatises on Isaiah, on the Song of Solomon, and on the Revelation, were once very popular, although they have outlived their day. He was undoubtedly a man of great industry and attainments, and of eminent talents. He was born in the neighbourhood of Dundee, became a minister in Glasgow, wrote at least ten volumes, and, like many of the covenanting worthies, died young—ere he had completed his thirtysixth year. Robert Blair, Alexander Henderson, and George Gillespie, who were all reputed men of first-rate abilities, have left little to substantiate their reputation, and with that little few are acquainted. Robert Traill's works were written after the revolution, and, although dry and systematic, are able, and their Calvinism is somewhat ultra. The names of Brown, of Wamphray, of Calderwood, and of Woodrow, are familiar. But by far the most remarkable specimens, both of the power and the weakness, the faults and the merits, of the covenanting school, are to be found in the works, and particularly the letters, of Samuel Rutherfurd, and in a

little book breathing a similiar spirit, entitled, *A Glimpse
of Glory*, by Andrew Wellwood.

Samuel Rutherfurd was the son of a gentleman in
Edinburgh. He attended its university, and at an early
age was made professor of philosophy ; predecessor thus
of the many illustrious men who have taught philosophy
in that chair—of Stewart, of Brown, and last and greatest
far, of Wilson, now, alas ! in the sere and yellow leaf of
one of the most glorious minds which ever emanated
from the Creator. From the chair of philosophy
Rutherfurd passed to be minister in 'Anwoth, Galloway,
without being required to bend before the golden calf of
the bishops. Here he published his " Exercitationes de
Gratiâ," a learned and powerful tractate against Armini-
anism, for which he narrowly escaped punishment at the
bar of the High Court of Commission. Neverthless, he
persisted in his nonconformity to the prevailing powers,
and was, on the 27th of July 1636, deprived of his
ministerial functions, and confined in the city of
Aberdeen during the king's pleasure. At the end of a
year and a half he returned to his flock, and renewed his
labours with greater zeal and energy than ever. He
appeared at the famous Glasgow Assembly, where he
gave an account of his proceedings, his confinement and
its causes, and was by it appointed divinity professor at
St. Andrew's, where he created an excitement only second
to that produced by Chalmers two centuries afterwards in
the same place. St. Andrew's has had the fortune to be
twice revived from the deepest lethargy by two extraordinary men — from the lethargy of the prelates by
Samuel Rutherfurd, and from the lethargy of the
professors by Thomas Chalmers. Its grass-grown
streets owned in each the presence of a Man, and the
echoes of its halls and churches awoke in both cases
to the voice of a Christian orator. In the year 1643,
Rutherfurd, as we have seen, went up with three others
to the Westminster Assembly, and played his part there
manfully and ably. Shortly after he published his *Lex*,

19

Rex, an elaborate volume in which he wields a two-edged sword, against what he thought the extremes of Independency on the one hand, and of Erastianism on the other. This book—now totally unread, except by antiquarians or history-writers, and the very name of which is unknown to many who devour daily his Letters —had the honour to be answered at the Cross of Edinburgh, in letters of fire, and by the hand of the common hangman. This was in 1661. What a pity that this same swift and summary method of disposing of unanswerable and "untoward" books does not still exist! Then we might witness, although not assist at, the burning obsequies of many modern works, to which fire, as a type of unreasoning and unsatisfied fury, were the only possible reply. While Rutherfurd's book was thus consuming, his noble body and mind were environed in another furnace—that of death. The parliament, after burning his treatise, were about to indict him at their bar while he was lying quiet and joyful, waiting for a higher summons. His book was burned, indeed, at the very gates of the college wherein he lay dying. The scent of its conflagration seems to have reached him on his deathbed—but he cared for none of these things, his soul had soared already far above *Rex* and *Lex*, far beyond the loftiest reaches of even his Letters, far beyond Beulah and the black River of Death. He had said, "Mine eyes shall see my Redeemer—I know He shall stand at the latter day upon the earth, and I shall be caught up to the clouds to meet Him in the air, and so shall I be ever with Him." "This night shall close the door, and put my anchor within the veil ; and I shall go away in a sleep by five o'clock in the morning." And so it was : at that hour he gave up the ghost, and, in the striking language of one of his biographers, "The renowned eagle took his flight to the mountains of spices."

Samuel Rutherfurd had his faults, which have been blazoned and exaggerated by one or two late writers, who are not worthy of unloosing his shoe-latchets. Let them speak as they please of his "spiritual sensualism," and throw out dark hints that there was another sensualism of a less pardonable kind behind it. But surely every man who has ever candidly studied either his character or his writings, must be persuaded that he was not only essentially a holy man, but an earnest and a "burning one." He breathed and lived and had his being in celestial love! He would undoubtedly have been greater had he been more calm—had, in other words, the insight and the affection, which were both in him, been more thorougly reconciled and attempered to each other—had the cherub looked through the seraph's eyes, and had the seraph added his fiery edge to the cherub's wings; but, as it was, he has in his Letters attained rare heights of a sublime and rapturous devotion.

There are books which seem to have been written, and which should be read, in summer. At other seasons they may appear somewhat over-coloured and exaggerated ; but let

> "Summer be the tide, and sweet the hour"—

let the old deluge of day be pouring from its old source—let every heart and eye be drinking in the unmeasured radiance—let each soul feel that in accepting the sunshine he is receiving it as God's gift, and as the type and emblem of the higher light of the Sun of Righteousness, and then, in the intensity of the commingled emotions of sense free from sensuality, and of faith free from form, let him sit down, with his mind thus in sympathy with his subject, to read carefully and admiringly Rutherfurd's Letters. Whatever he may have been for months before employed in perusing, with an interest however intense and a sympathy however deep, when he comes to read those wild, beautiful, and holy lyrics of Rutherfurd, penned from prisons, and huts, and ocean-sides, he will become conscious, more fully than ever, of a higher something—a far grander sincerity of soul, a nicer and

truer melody of tenderness—more, in short, of heaven
labouring and striving to reproduce itself on earth (like
the sun shooting up in wheat and daisies and roses and
golden corn) than, save in Milton and Bunyan, he has
ever witnessed before. He may see, but will not feel,
the extravagances of his style and manner. These will
be lost in the earnestness of his purpose, and the holy
beauties of his thought and language. Sometimes,
indeed, the mark is overshot—the boundary of good taste
is overleaped, but this is never through affectation or
weakness, or even the wantonness of power, but from
the excess of ecstasy and of high emotion. His soul is
a river of God, not only lip-full, but running over. And
to think of all this as issuing from dungeons and darkness
—written in proscription and in the prospect of death!
As with all true Christians, Rutherfurd's heart was
deeply smitten with a passion for Christ. It was not a
cold, systematic Christianity he believed in, but a living
Saviour. It has been said of Robert Hall, that when
engaged in prayer he seemed actually to *see* Christ—so
personal and absorbing and ardent did his devotion
become. Just so was it with Rutherfurd. No need for
his ascending to heaven or diving into the depths in
search of Christ—"the Word is nigh him, in his mouth,
and in his heart," and in his eye; hence the passionate
peculiarity of his language. It is that of a lover, not
writing to his betrothed, but clasping her in a pure and
warm embrace. Take one out of a thousand expressions
of this passion for Jesus : " I avouch, before God, angels,
and men, that I have not seen nor can imagine a lover
comparable to Jesus. I would not exchange or barter
Him for ten heavens ; if heaven could be without Him,
what could we do there ? " Hear him again on a cognate
subject : "My Lord now hath given me experience
(howbeit weak and small) that our best *fare* is *hunger* ;
we are but at God's by-board in this lower house ; we
have cause to long for supper-time, and the high table
up in the high palace : the world deserveth nothing but

the outer court of our soul. If ye take the storm with
borne-down Christ, your sky will quickly clear and your
morning dawn." To a widow he says: "What missing
can there be of a dying man when *God filleth the chair?*"
Again, "The *parings* and *crumbs* of glory that fall under
Christ's table in heaven—a shower, like a thin May-mist,
of His love would make me green and joyful, till the
summer sun of *eternal glory* break up." What a sentence
is the following!—"Oh, sweet for evermore, to see a
rose of heaven growing in so ill a ground as hell; and to
see Christ's love, His peace, faith, goodness, long-
suffering and patience, growing and springing, like the
flowers of God's garden, out of such stony and cursed
ground as the hatred of the prelates and the malice of
their high commission; and antichrist's bloody hand and
heart is not here art and wisdom—is not here *heaven
indented in hell* (if I may say so), like a jewel set with
skill in a ring with the enamel of Christ's cross." Speaking of a dead lady, he says: "I grant death is to her a
very new thing, but heaven was prepared of old; and
Christ exalted in His highest throne, *loaded with glory*,
incomparably exalted above men and angels, having such
a circle of glorified harpers and musicians above, com-
passing the throne with songs, is to her a new thing—
but new as the first summer rose, or as a new paradise
to a traveller broken and worn, out of breath with the
sad occurrences of a long and dreary way." Or take, in
fine, some extracts from his letter to that noble youth,
George Gillespie, written a little before Gillespie's death.
It is difficult to imagine that any one can ever read them
without a sense of mournful sublimity, melting at last
into tears:

"REVEREND AND DEAR BROTHER,

"I cannot speak to you. The way ye know, the
passage is free and not stopped, the print of the footsteps
of the Forerunner is clear and manifest. Many have gone
before you: ye will not sleep long in the dust before the

day break; it is a far shorter piece of the end of the night to you than to Abraham and Moses; beside all the time of their bodies' resting under corruption, it is as long yet to their day as to your morning-light of awaking to glory; though their spirits, having the advantage of yours, have had now the start of the shore before you. I dare say nothing against his dispensation. I hope to follow quickly. I fear the clay house is taking down and undermining, but it is nigh the dawning; look to the east, the dawning of glory is near — the nearer the morning the darker. Some traveller seeth the city twenty miles off, and yet within the eighth-part of a mile he cannot see it. Some see the goal at once, and never again till the races end—it is coming all in a sum together, when ye are in a more gracious capacity to tell it than now. 'Ye are not come to the mount that might be touched; nor unto blackness, and darkness, and tempest; but ye are come to Mount Zion, unto the city of the living God, the heavenly Jerusalem, and to an innumerable company of angels, to the general assembly and church of the first born, and to God the Judge of all, and to the spirits of the just made perfect, and to Jesus the Mediator of the New Testament, and to the blood of sprinkling.' Ye must leave the wife to a more choice husband, and the children to a better father. If ye leave any testimony to the Lord's work and covenant against both malignants and sectaries, let it be under your hand, and subscribed before faithful witnesses.

"Your loving and afflicted brother,

"SAMUEL RUTHERFURD.

"*St. Andrews, Sept. 27th*, 1648."

Thus, two hundred years ago, wrote one saintly sufferer to another, and there is something still vital in his simple yet noble and touching words. What he says in this letter is not equal to what he says *not*. He seems curbing the boundless consolation he might have poured into the soul of his gifted and prematurely-expiring

friend. We think that even Mackintosh's letter to Hall,
on his coming down from the "thunder-hill" of frenzy,
is not superior to this last pressure of Samuel Rutherfurd's hand upon that of his friend, Gillespie, ere he went
away alone into the valley and the shadow of death.

And yet these letters give no idea of Rutherfurd in his
whole capacity. They show his genius, his piety, and
his heart; but the man who could weep like a babe, and
love like a woman, could also, as some of his other
works prove, act and reason like a man. It is so with
all the really gifted. They are great *all round*; and only
blindness or malignity can deny it. We never hope to
see his genius fully recognised: his subjects, and his
peculiar treatment of them, render that impossible; but
we are certain that he possessed genius of a high order,
and that some, at least, of his fine rhapsodies of thought
and feeling shall long survive. He has been compared
to Bunyan, and there was a resemblance in the lofty
reach, the imagination, the devotion, and the semi-
sensuous tone of their minds; but the difference is, on
the whole, to Bunyan's advantage. He had less learning
and less fancy, but he had much more creative, dramatic,
and imaginative power, and has framed what life is—a
story, and a story so true that every heart on earth
with whom it has ever come into contact has accepted
and rejoiced over it, as if it had been its own work.

Andrew Wellwood was the son of a minister in Annan-
dale, and was himself designed for the church, but died
in his youth of consumption. This event took place in
London, where he had probably fled to escape the heat
of the persecution. This is all his brief history. But he
has left behind him a little volume, *A Glimpse of Glory*,
which may, with a certain class of readers, preserve for
a time his name. It rather palls, as a whole, from the
unflagging rapture of the writer, but contains striking
passages and thoughts. We open the book almost at
random, and find the following passage:—"How oft
have I thought, if the wilderness is so sweet and pleasant,

what must the inland be ! Is there such ravishing
variety of beauty, glory, and sweetness, all along in my
pilgrimage—what can I imagine to behold in my native
country? Is the habitation where devils, wicked men,
and beasts inhabit, so excellent and glorious—what can I
think of the place where Jesus, the Emmanuel, with His
fair company of saints and angels everlastingly abides ?
Is my God's footstool so glorious—what must His throne
be ? Is the under-vault of this base dungeon so majestic
—oh, the higher hall of glory, where the glorious King
and His magnificent court remain ! No veil there drawn
between the lower and the higher habitation—no smoky
fumes betwixt heaven and earth—no winds nor storms,
pinching cold or piercing heat—no vicissitudes of summer
and winter ; nothing but an eternal spring-tide and endless summer—a constant harvest—all are in their blooming estate and fullest perfection ! What wonder ! Is it
not the centre of infinite influences ! The sweet influences
of Pleiades are never bound up—the bands of Orion are
ever loosed !" And, in the same style, for two hundred
and fifty pages, does this dying youth describe the little
of the glory of the place which the dim glass and his own
trembling hand enable him to descry from the summit of
Mount Clear ; and when the long soliloquy is over, his
soul has taken its bound upwards, and his weary body
drops down, dust to dust, in the "sure and certain hope
of a blessed resurrection."

Poor, after all, it may be said, is all this literary spray
you have been able to collect from the ocean of the
Scottish persecution. But let us remember that it is
not during persecutions or revolutions that literature is
either read or written. Then the "nations are angry" ;
and it is not amid the hot passions of angry nations that
the richest dews of genius descend. The true literature
of such periods must be sought for afterwards ; and a
subsequent chapter will describe the influences which the
covenanting day has exerted on some of the best recent
writers. The impression made on the heart and the

imagination of Scotland was too profound either to be
easily or early expressed, or to be soon exhausted.

Much has been said of the persecuting spirit of the
Covenanters. "Why should they complain of persecution, when all they desiderated for being fierce persecutors was power? The other party had the sword; they
had dropped it—that is all." Some truth, of course, there
is in this statement. Almost all the errors of the Covenanters sprung from their ignorance of the spirituality of
Christ's present kingdom, and their absurd notion that
the magistrate's sword was a necessary weapon in the
Christian armoury. But we have no reason to believe
that they ever would have organised such a systematic
and bloody persecution as that which they suffered.
During the time they were in power, they did indeed
commit some unjustifiable acts—such as the massacre of
the prisoners after the battle of Philiphaugh; but their
general administration was mildness itself compared to
the subsequent conduct of their adversaries. They made,
as we have seen, no reprisals upon their enemies after
the revolution. The acts of violence committed by them
were chiefly in self-defence, or [extorted from them by
despair. Above all, they were, with all their faults,
Christians. They did not, like their enemies, stimulate
themselves to outrage, or harden themselves against its
remorse, by habitual drunkenness. What they inflicted
was done in dignity, and with that measured gravity
which attends judicial acts. The cruel deeds of the
cavaliers might be compared to those of beasts of prey or
of cannibals, "torturing, mangling, devouring, drinking
the blood of their victims." Those of the Covenanters
were the solemn sacrifices of mistaken religious men in
honour of an imperfect but profoundly-believed idea.

That idea was unquestionably a bold if not a satisfac-
tory one. So far as it consisted in aversion to Episcopacy,
or in the maintenance of the rights of Presbyterian parity,
or in dislike to the "ill-mumbled mass" in its weary
monotony and vain repetitions, or in its resistance to

the insolent aggressions of the civil power, or in its determined animosity to popery—in all its phases and under all its disguises—multitudes in the present day will fully justify it. Had it confined itself to these, it had been, in every respect, a cause worthy of more than all the blood and suffering expended in its defence. In this case, we could more freely have classed the Covenanters with the Waldensees, or the early Christian martyrs, as objects of unmingled sympathy and respect. But they went further than this. They held not only that the making of public covenants was a part of Christian duty —although there is not the slightest evidence for this in the New Testament—but that the covenant of one age is binding upon all successive ages, a most untenable proposition ; as if thought could thus be chained, or opinion stereotyped ; as if each age had not a right to its own idea ; as if the future should not be painted with face looking forward, and not slavishly reverting for ever to the past. This Covenant of theirs, again, as we have seen, sought an impossible object—that of uniformity of doctrine and of discipline throughout the three kingdoms. That there shall yet be a substantial uniformity of religious sentiment and worship throughout the world may be devoutly believed. But probably this never can or will arrive, save in the train of that " new and most mighty dispensation," without which, as Foster declared his conviction, " Christianity can never reform the world." Least of all could such a clumsy solvent as a solemn league be expected to melt down all differences of opinion. The method, too, followed was not that of the gospel. *That* had no banner and no sword when it first began its immortal journey. It was like Mary Howitt's exquisite Marien—a simple child, going forth shielded only by its own divinity and simplicity, and by " manifestation of the truth, commending itself to every man's conscience in the sight of God." But the Covenant must have its arms, and its blazonry, and its banner, and its warlike lords, and its covenanted king, and its

" Pride, pomp, and circumstance of glorious war."

From that moment its fate was sealed. It left the
regions of the spiritual and the ideal, and became inex-
tricably mixed up with the troublous politics of a troublous time. We do not find fault with the persecuted
employing defensive weapons in the cloudy and dark day
which befel them ; but we do deplore the offensive
attitude they took from the beginning, and the occasion
they thus gave their adversaries to echo the words,
"They that take the sword shall perish with the
sword."

No men ever saw more clearly than the Covenanters
the objective evils springing from the interference of the
State with the Church. But they were absolutely blind
to the subjective cause, the impossible problem of
properly or profitably connecting the two powers in any
formal alliance. They thought that the State was bound
to feed them, but denied it the power of arranging the
meals or fixing the form of the platters. They found
the yoke of the State intolerable, and they threw it off
for a season ; but it never occurred to them that it was
and ever must be a yoke, restraining their liberty, and
liable at any time to be tightened to strangulation. The
ministers did not sufficiently feel how dignified their
position when they were out among the moors, living on
the voluntary principle, though it was on bread and salt,
and water and goats' whey, with clear consciences, and
joys fresh from heaven visiting their hearts every night
and morning, compared to even their return to their
manses and glebes, when again they became subject to a
Government which could, at any hour, begin a new persecution. They abhorred formality and absolutism, but
they did not see that these were just the putrid result of
that very system which was supporting them, and that
in all church establishments there is a strong tendency
toward them, which, sooner or later, must conduct
thitherward, as certainly as a corpse hung up before the
summer sun will rot. They hated bishops, but saw not
that, as long as establishments existed, the compact

slavery of Episcopalianism will be preferred by governments to the republican genius of presbytery or independency. They disliked patronage, but did not foresee how determinedly their paymasters would cling to it, as a strong curb at once to the popular element and to the priestly influence in the Church, and how it was certain at a future day to break up and shatter their entire ecclesiastical system.

The grand aim of the Covenanters was certainly not gained. The moment the persecution ceased, the memory of the Covenant seemed silently to drop out of the minds of men. Loudly, indeed, did the Cameronians continue to bellow words of menace and to wail out notes of woe over "covenants, burned, broken, and buried." But their voice met with no response, save in the echoes of the hills, which seemed to return it now rather in derision than in sympathy. Covenanting continued occasionally, indeed, to be practised by various sects down to a late period. But long ere its occasional use came to an end, it had lost much of its meaning and interest, and seemed rather a caricature of the past than a living expression of the faith of the present. There was no more signing of the Covenant with blood. The people who signed it were in no danger, and it was at last felt to be a belated and unmeaning rite. The Free Church of Scotland, too, has set its face against renewing the Covenants. Still, very important ends appear to us to have been served by the covenanting struggle, and the statement of these shall close the present chapter.

First, the Covenant has added a rose to Scotland's chaplet ; it is the truest moral crown that has yet been bound round the forehead of the land, just as the Puritan struggle is the greatest in which England has ever been engaged. Before it there had been, indeed, the War of Independence and the Reformation ; but the first involved no religious element, and the second was very speedily, and on the whole, easily determined : few battles were fought, and very few martyrs suffered. But the struggle

of the Covenant not only stirred all the religious heart of
the country, but it was waged with most determined
courage for a quarter of a century and more. Besides,
at the Reformation, a large section of the nobles early
connected themselves with the movement ; whereas the
cause of the Covenant was pleaded principally by the
peasantry and small proprietors. Hence, to no passage
in their history do genuine Scotchmen look back with
such pride. You can see the eye of the shepherd sparkle
and his cheek flush as you talk to him on his hill of these
covenanting days. There is, perhaps, no one name
among its heroes of whom you can say, as Burns of
Wallace,—

> " At Wallace' name what Scottish blood
> But boils up in a spring-tide flood ! "

the interest and the enthusiasm are diffused among
many ; but never are Cameron, Renwick, Peden, and
Hackstoun forgotten.

> " And far and near, o'er dale and hill,
> Are faces which attest the same,
> And kindle, like a fire new-stirred,
> At mention of their name."

No enthusiasm has followed equal to that, or which has
had the power of eclipsing it in public regard. The
Scottish people flung themselves into even the Reform
Bill and Chartist agitations with greater spirit that the
field-meetings then held, and the peculiar kind of popular
excitement, and the prayer which was in the last of these
often mixed up with politics and political assemblies,
reminded them of covenanting days. Some most excited
political meetings were held in and near Edinburgh in
the years 1831, 1832, and 1834 ; and truly they were very
furnaces of glowing and seething feeling. They were
generally held in a park under the shadow of Salisbury
Crags, and with Arthur's Seat watching grimly in his
green shaggy coat behind. Many of the scenes interesting in covenanting story were in sight : the Castle rock

the Pentland ridge, the hills of Fife, the ocean linking Dunnottar Castle to the Bass ; the Grassmarket, too, where the martyrs suffered was not far off. Very different, in many points, the objects sought by these fierce and heated throngs from those of their fathers ; very different their own character and bearing, for at that desperate crisis, oaths and curses, both deep and loud, pervaded every multitude ; very different the speakers, for they made no pretensions, in general, to even the appearance of piety. Yet still there was much that reminded you of the open-air meetings of the seventeenth century. The earnestness and terrible animation and daring language of the orators ; the fixed brows, the compressed lips, and the flashing eyes of the hearers, none of whom bore arms, but each of whose hands seemed grasping an invisible sword ; the wild, wave-like, tempestuous motion of the crowd, their thick cheers awakening the echoes of the rocks, the glories of nature adding their inestimable background, from the green pastures around up to the immeasurable calm of the May heaven above —all carried the mind two centuries back. Then there was the purpose visible and audible throughout, and the shadow of prospective rising and blood which lay over the assembly. And when one gifted man (since well known as the author of *Nimrod*) alluded, both in that King's Park and again at a meeting held in the Grassmarket itself, to the days of the Covenant, and spoke of the coming of new Drumclogs and of more fortunate Bothwells, and pointed to the Pentlands and the Bass, the living furnace became heated seven times—now cheers rent the sky, and now a deep silence dissolved in a more terrible murmur, and the sun and the mountain-scenery seemed drawing in around the impassioned multitude, to witness the oath or to hear the amen of their resolute souls ; and it was felt that the manes of the murdered in the cause of liberty would soon be propitiated, and that the injured genius of a former age was already smiling down well pleased.

The success of the great covenanting struggle secured civil and religious liberty to Scotland. The apparent narrowness of the point to which the controversy seemed at last reduced, contributed to this result. Suppose, as Episcopalians maintain, and as Mackie the younger almost admits, in a passage already quoted, that it came, through the various indulgences granted, to little else than this question, "Surplice or no surplice? Liturgy or none?" Still the Covenanter could reply, "If this be a trifle, why urge it on us at such tremendous expenditure of blood and treasure? although it may be a trifle, in itself it represents great questions — the surplice or liturgy is the contraction and symbol of mighty evils; if we admit these, not only other evils of a more formidable kind may be afterwards introduced, but the authority of the magistrate over our consciences is conceded,—and if he once be permitted to be our tyrant in religious matters, what is to hinder him from becoming in civil affairs equally absolute? Therefore, on this little point we take our stand, and find here the narrow Thermopylæ of a wide cause!" Whether this reasoning was perfectly sound or not, mark the consequence that followed. On this little and, if it be so, vexatious point, a great victory was gained. The Government, having failed on such a small matter, felt it for ever impossible, by persecution, to obtain greater. The empire of brute force received its final blow. From that day forward the current set in, slowly but decidedly, toward larger and larger concessions to the rights of conscience. Therefore, if the question be asked, Who broke in twain the yoke of the despotism in Scotland— Who secured the inviolability of conscience in that realm —Who paved the way for the abolition of patronage, aye and for the establishment of voluntary associations? the answer must be, "These noble, hair-splitting men of the Covenant; although verily they knew not what they did." They aroused the land to a spiritual consciousness —to a feeling of the supremacy of scripture and of the moral sense; to an attention to the minutiæ of Christianity—to the very fringes of the tabernacle, which has never since been permitted to die away, and which, while it has been productive of much small and captious evil, has been productive, on the whole, of a vast superabundance of good.

To that strong, unconquerable struggle we owe, also, many of those recent movements in the Church, which, although troubling the waters, have made them vitalising. It was in the remaining night of the covenanting spirit that the fathers of the Secession came out, like Abraham from Haran, not knowing whither they went, though but four in number, strong in the firm negative of their position, full of faith and hate and zeal, doing well to be angry, and destined to create a sensation in Scotland which has not yet entirely subsided, and to found a sect which has acted and prospered for more than a hundred years. From a similar source sprang the Relief body, which has since, like a vigorous tributary, augmented the current of the Secession. To this, too, the Free Church will be proud to acknowledge its filial claims. Whatever may be thought of some of the actions of that body, and especially of its equivocal position in reference to the voluntary question—living on its fruits and yet ignoring its principle; holding, like Arminians, works without faith—none can fail to see in its movements, its energy and zeal, the after-growth of the rich field which the Covenanters cultivated.

The late amiable " Delta," [1] in a note to a poem of his, entitled " The Covenanters' Night Hymn," while condemning the prejudices, errors, and occasional crimes of this peculiar people, takes true and strong ground in their defence. He says that, in the first place, they fought and gained the battle of an entire century; and, secondly, that their victory was the victory of the Protestant cause in Scotland. Both these statements are correct. The

---

[1] An eminent writer in *Blackwood's Magazine* lately deceased.

Covenanters' struggle must not be judged from the duration of its darkest point, any more than the duration of an eclipse from the moment of its deepest obscuration. From the Reformation downwards to the settlement at the revolution, the conflict, in its merits and its blunders, its superabundant good and evil, was strictly *one*; and if the result has not been so absolutely unique, yet, unquestionably, it has been intimately intertwined with the success of the Protestant religion. It was the extreme—at least, the only extreme THEN possible in Scotland — of Protestantism which the Covenanters defended. For this they suffered and died; and although they gained not the full amount of their reiterated and blood-bought demand, the instalment they did obtain, like the sybil's books, was more valuable than the whole, and has become the germ of all the after Protestantism of Scotland. It fared with them as with most reformers. They wittingly or unwittingly sought for more than they were able or entitled to receive; they urged their question too far; they exaggerated the evils under which they were really suffering, and thus they secured a less complete, but a final, victory for the general cause.

Hence, to a great extent, the profound and practical hatred felt in Scotland against popery. There are no Smithfield fires in the Scotch annals, but they record the covenanting persecutions carried on, not indeed in the first place by popery, but by its disguise—its alias—a disguise and an alias which our fathers in a larger degree were able to penetrate. They regarded it as the devil's creed and caricature of Christianity, and its history as briefly this: that the infernal spirit saw that Christianity had come into the world, and was threatening to destroy his empire; that he said, "I must destroy it;" that he tried it first with fire, but in vain—the fire fell on it like rain; it grew the faster for the fire—the blood of the martyrs became the seed of the church; that he then concocted a deeper and a darker scheme, and said, "I'll become a Christian myself—I'll get myself baptized—I'll

20

form and circulate a creed of my own;" and that thus popery arose as the devil's creed, and spread over the face of the Church. To their minds popery presented itself as a monkey making mouths behind the back of a man, and they shrank in disgust and horror from the lame and blasphemous imitation. They saw in it a system at once diametrically opposite to, and ludicrously like, Christianity, which had fastened its polluting grasp upon all the rites and the doctrines of the true religion; which for the real unity of the Church in Christ had substituted the false centre of the pope; which had yoked dead works to living faith in the important matter of justification; which had, for the spiritual presence of Christ in the Lord's Supper, substituted the revolting fiction of transubstantiation; which had degraded that mysterious spot "under the altar," where the souls of the righteous wait for the redemption of their bodies, into a vulgar vault of fire called purgatory; which had created for its own sensuous ends a female god, in the abused form of the Virgin Mary; which had snatched the cup from the lips, and the Bible from the hands, of the laity, and given them a half-supper and no book of God at all; which had corrupted manly chastity into monachism, and temperance into austerity and abstinence; which had given to the clergy unlimited power over ears and hearts and consciences, at the same time that it bound them to their cause by the unnatural bands of celibacy, and which in every form had set itself—to cement despotism, to oppose human progress, to dwarf the intellect of man, to inculcate persecution and breach of faith, and to deluge the earth with blood. What name, in their view, could describe at once the broad malignant antagonism, and the strange and impudent likeness which this system bore to Christianity, except the name Anti-Christ, the often-predicted power who was to hinder the advance of the faith, to defer even the day of the Lord, who was to sit in the temple of God, showing himself that he was God, and for the destruction of whom the

Lord had reserved the breath of His own mouth and the brightness of His own coming? And not only did the Covenanters succeed in rebutting the advances, whether open or concealed, of this anti-Christian power, but they did more; they instilled into the minds of their children a hatred and scorn of it—a determination to do battle against it to the death, which are burning unmingled in most Scottish hearts still, and which ever and anon burst forth and make the crest of the "old red dragon" to tremble. In other countries, popery has been trifled with, opposed, ridiculed, or hated, according to the peculiarities of the national mind, but in Scotland the repugnance to it has assumed the form of a universal and unconquerable loathing.

Another effect springing from the Covenant was to produce a deep respect and warm attachment on the side of the people to their ministers. That this had its evils there can be no doubt. It did engender a certain super-stitious reverence for the persons, the profession, the characters, and the preachings of ministers. Certain lingering traces of this feeling may still be remembered, as, for example, that the parish minister used to be regarded by many as a kind of ghost in black—children fled from him as he walked through the village—a certain fearful stillness pervaded its streets—unspeakable were the depths and angles of declension with which men bowed to him. On Sabbath, his veriest platitudes, and his iteration of sermons for the twentieth time, were received with profound respect; and his faults, if faults he was admitted to have, were treated with wondrous lenity, if they did not, as was often the case, become models of conduct. It was with him as with Hotspur—

> " Speaking thick, which nature made his blemish,
> Became the accents of the valiant."

This was true of ordinary ministers. But if the minister possessed superior powers, or eloquence, or diligence and piety, he became a god to his parishioners, and was regarded now with the warmest love, and now with the most undissembled terror. His word was law, and his very silence assumed an imperative mood. And yet this, although an evil, sprang from a good principle deeper still ; it was the last instalment of the debt which had been accumulated in the days of the Covenant. Then the clergy, by the sacrifices they made, the sufferings they endured, the purity of their lives, the energy of their preaching, and their thorough identification with their flocks, impressed themselves on the affections of Scotland, and gained a glory to their order, the last ray of which has not yet wholly ceased to shine. How much people will forgive to and bear from those who really love them, live among them, and labour for them ! In such a case, faults are regarded with the partial eyes of the brother, the friend, or the lover. Endurance, too, adds a dignity to the sufferer. It was a gleam, accordingly, from the " auld Scottish glory " of the covenanting day, which shed more than common lustre on the grey head of the aged minister as he mounted the pulpit or the tent, which secured attention for the trembling speech of the young orator addressing audiences, some of whose veterans might remember Renwick, and trace a likeness between them in the flushed cheek and ardent gesture ; which surrounded the steps of the minister wherever he went with a peculiar halo of sacredness, and gave a certain grandeur even to his extravagances of language, his undue exercise of authority, or his bursts of passion. This is now to some extent over in all parts of Scotland ; but it did, doubtless, while it lasted, much good. The respect for the clergy secured for the peasantry precisely that kind of stimulus to the intellect, and that information for the memory, which, at the time, they required. In some measure barbarians, they required a rather barbarous exertion of authority to reduce them to spiritual discipline. Thus, too, were religious principles roughly but profoundly riveted upon the minds of the people ; and through this it was that a

system of education, very imperfect, indeed, pregnant
with many evils, and which is now far behind the wants
of the country and the age, was established and worked
out with such success that Scotland for a time was the
best-instructed country in the world.

It were beside the purpose to dwell on the causes
which have led to "the contempt of the Protestant
clergy," as old Eachard called it ;—to the comparatively
low degree in public estimation to which, as a class,
they have sunk—such causes as the prevalence of the
infidel spirit—the spread of extreme political opinions
among the lower orders, and of attachment to popery, or
to a Protestantism that stimulates it in the upper—the
class-feelings which have distinguished the clergy ; their
outrageous *esprit-de-corps* — their obstinate clinging to
exploded forms of speech and thought and worship—
their frequent *hauteur* and bigotry—their no less frequent suppleness and subservience, now to a king, now
to a mob, now to a bishop, and now to a congregation—
the opposition they have so frequently given to the onward movements of society—the fact, in one word, that
they have, unlike their brethren in the seventeenth
century, not taken the lead and directed the genius of the
age, but have rather hung as drags upon it.   But grant-
ing all this, it may yet be maintained, in the first place,
that the clergy are exerting more power, and that of a
more legitimate kind, in Scotland than in any other
country under heaven—except perhaps America, where,
however, their influence in the matter of slavery has
become the curse of the land ; and that, secondly, this is
in a great degree owing to the memory of, and to the
deep impression made by, the ministers of the Covenant,
as well as to the remains of their spirit and conduct, which
are still found extant among their successors.   Here our
ministers practise all the pastoral and many of the public
duties which their fathers voluntarily imposed on themselves.   They preach perpetually, they visit the sick, they
call on their flocks, they teach the young, they super-

intend public and private schools, they engage, on all
proper occasions, in public, political, civic, and pro-
fessional movements, they take a part in the proceedings
of church-courts, they read much, they write much, and
like their fathers, too, they have often much to suffer
from misappreciation, from calumny, from rudeness and
ignorance, from the complication of labours we have
described, and from the *res angusta domi*—an evil which
is now almost equally divided among ALL the different
denominations of Christians in the north.   But these
labours and difficulties form, in part, the chains which
bind the office of the ministry in the present, even as
heavier difficulties did still more strongly bind it in the
past, to the respect, affection, and sympathy of a large
portion of the Scottish people.

The covenanting struggle, again, was a grand testimony to the truth of the Christian religion.   More than
all stereotyped evidences, more than the writings of all
the apologists, from Tertullian down to the most recent
defender of the Christian faith, as a proof of the reality
of Christianity, was this living, blood-stained moorland
page.   To prove Christianity by argument seems an
attempt as contemptible and hopeless as to bottle up
some of the foam-drops of a spring-tide, and show them
as a specimen and proof how high these waters once
ascended.   Or it is like preserving a little of the air of a
hurricane.   The real proofs of Christianity are to be
found in the effects which it has produced, is producing,
and promises to produce ; and, whenever we see a mass
of people moving to the power of religion, as the " trees
of the wood to the wind," we see an evidence, not easily
to be gainsaid, of the influence of Christianity upon the
heart, the conscience, and the character of mankind—to
which elements, indeed, and to which alone it has ever
appealed—the only fields in which it has sown, or expected, or reaped a true crop.   It is this kind of proof
which has made the deepest impression, both upon the
popular and upon the thoughtful mind.   Religion, as an

idea, rather tends to stupefy and overwhelm us—we cannot understand it—it seems at once far from us and near,
like the telescopic moon ; but let it once be *realised*—let
our own hearts feel it, or even hear of others who have
really felt it, and it ceases to be a mystery and becomes
a living fact. Even a single heart, feeling and acting on
Christian principle, is a distinct evidence in favour of the
Christian religion. But how that evidence grows at
more than an arithmetical ratio, when an age, a century,
embraces and to a certain extent incarnates it in life,
action, and suffering! That psalm at Drumclog—that
short terrible struggle at Airsmoss—those death-scenes
at the Grassmarket, intended at first as evidences of
sincere Protestantism, have now sublimated into proofs
of the common "faith as it is in Jesus," and their records
are or should be admitted among the general archives of
the Christian religion. When was there ever, or when
shall there ever be, a great suffering for the sake of the
infidel cause? How Voltaire and Rousseau cringed and
crouched before the dangers to which they were exposed!
How Hume himself would have shuffled had he been
called to answer for his "ideas and impressions of religion!" And suppose our modern sceptics subjected
to a *fiery trial*, we can conceive results rather ludicrous
than calculated to confirm the common notions of their
sincerity and enthusiasm. One would prove himself
innocent by eating up in haste his most daring words ;
another, by "quartering" the favourite child of his
brain ; a third, by swearing an "alibi" for his senses
while he had been engaged in such and such an
obnoxious work ; a fourth, by withdrawing word after
word of his statements, till they were made to turn right
round, and to say at last the contrary of what they had
seemed to say at first (like the famous garment of
Scriblerus, originally of silk, but which by frequent darn-
ings became at last of worsted, and yet remained meta-
physically the same!) ; and a fifth, with "impudent
face" and "brazen forehead, refusing to be ashamed" by

retorting the charge of infidelity upon his accusers, and attempting to show that HE had been nearer the Wondrous Sham,—the "Great Carbuncle,"[1] than any Christian on earth. But would one of them, for their theories of "the everlasting yea and no," or the supremacy of moral law, or the "oversoul," or the "Church of the Saviour," submit to a month's privations? and how much less to long sullen rains of fire, famine, and nakedness, to peril and sword, to banishment, to contumely more intolerable than death, or death itself in its ghastliest and least ideal forms? God forbid that such measures as these should ever be put in force against sceptics! But few can be blind, nevertheless, to the assurance of their own eyes and judgments, that were such measures applied either to infidels or to nominal Christians, there would nowadays be bootikins with no legs within them, empty scaffolds, walls of fire containing nothing, and an infinitely greater number of retractations than of dying protests—many Cranmers signing their recanting deeds, but few burning in the flames the traitor hands which had signed them.

That 'the covenanting contest, in fine, served to promote what is well called *vital* religion in Scotland, appear undoubted. That principle, previously feeble, drowned in formalisms, and too often held in deceit and unrighteousness, was, by a long persecution, driven into the heart of the nation, and has never yet been entirely expelled. We grant, again, most distinctly, that there is a vast difference between the godliness of the seventeenth and that of the nineteenth centuries in our land. That in the first found but one channel—the prosecution of the cause of covenanted reformation; the other has diverged into manifold and sometimes contradictory courses. It would not be well for any

---

[1] See (although the reference in the text is not to *him*) Hawthorne's *Twice-Told Tales*, in which a "Great Carbuncle" seems to represent his notion that Christianity is a beautiful, impossible dream.

enthusiast in the cause of the Covenant, whether from England or from abroad, to repair now to one of our rural districts, even on sacramental occasions, in order to judge of the calibre, or the sincerity, or the intelligence of Scotland's piety. Truly, it is a winter sun that he must be prepared to see. The services of the "preliminary" days, as they are called, of the communion, as well as of all the rest, are now conducted entirely in the church. The tent—once a remaining rag of the covenanting banner—latterly, a mere signal of distress, is extinct. The people flock to the church with perfect punctuality, but with listless looks. They sit before the preacher, not as hearers, not as partaking of the same burning enthusiasm, for there is little on either side, but either as formal worshippers or as meagre and captious *critics*. Some listen, some look, some sleep, some yawn, some note down objectionable and others favourite passages ; the question with some is, at the end, "How long has he been?" and with others, "Has he not said something against the standards of our faith?" In the covenanting days, one watchman on the hills kept the congregation, now a half of the congregation becomes a company of watchmen, to keep itself from imaginary and ridiculous danger. The old rote and routine of sentiment and of language still prevail. It is as if the earth had stood, and opinion been frozen up for two hundred years. Not a word that recognises the new earth now below our feet, and the new heavens which now expand above, is ever heard or would be suffered were it heard. When you look, you see faces like those of the dead staring at you ; and when you listen, you hear tones of the sepulchre reverberating on your ears. The worst of it is, that the men are often clever and conceited persons, imagining that their view of religion is the only one possible among the good at present—that all who do not preach it are heretics, and that all who come not up to the very letter of its requirements are in imminent "danger of hell fire." At the close of the day, and as

the multitudes return them to their homes, it is with
deep sadness that you follow in their progress over hills
and through morasses—some talking of "bullocks,"
others of the weather, others of politics—many comparing preachers with preachers, and giving almost
uniformly the preference to the worst ; and others
indulging in a saturnalia of thought and language,
which grieves you the more that you know that it has
been purchased at the expense of much "tear and wear"
of conscience, habitude, and heart.

Subtracting, however, all this, we see a certain thing
called True Religion subsisting amongst us, and which,
on the whole, may be traced rather to the influence of
covenanting days than to aught later in our land.
There are still noble hearts among the peasantry, in
spite of narrowness and vulgarity of views and feelings,
and among the artisans, although infidelity has laid its
withering grasp upon many of them. In the middle
ranks, again, there is a great amount of manly and
enlightened piety. A sober evening light of devotion
pervades many portions of the country—the relict
radiance of that fervid covenanting noon, and it is remarkable that it is found precisely in those districts which were
most zealous in the covenanting cause—in the south and
west. The great centre of Scottish religion is the city
of Glasgow. This is the mighty heart which supplies all
the veins and supports all the pulsations of our spiritual
life. Edinburgh, with all its intelligence, is a cold,
sceptical, and heartless city. From the influence of
David Hume's atheism it has passed into the shadow of
the modified materialism of Combe. Religion is indeed
able to maintain its ground, but little more, and dwells
too evidently in an enemy's country, sneered at by one
species of philosophies, and ostentatiously patronised by
another, finding many partisans in every quarter of the
city, but not pervading it all like a transforming leaven.
In Glasgow it is very different ; it is, perhaps, the most
Christian city on earth. A vast amount of wickedness, of

course, and infidelity there is in it, but the pulse of the town is true, its heart is sound—evangelical religion free from bigotry abounds, and in it almost all Scottish schemes of Prostestant Christian philanthropy either take their rise or find their most efficient support. The spectacle of Glasgow on a Sabbath morning is one of the most delightful kind; the streets are all in a flood, and are all pouring in the one direction of the house of God: masses of the middle-class, grave parents leading perhaps their children by the hand; active, alert, intelligent young men; graceful and interesting females, mingled with multitudes of well-dressed working men, all apparently seeking "the way to Zion with their faces thitherward;" nor is there the slightest appearance of that starched formalism and grim morosity of which the Scotch were once accused. It is a "cheerful godliness" that their countenances and their conversation discover; and while great is their faith, and great their charity, yet to them the "greatest of these is *Hope.*" It may be fairly admitted that the fashion of the town, use and wont, the influence of Chalmers and other causes, may have combined in producing this state of things, and that with it, as with all outward displays of piety, much hollowness and hypocrisy are mingled. But we attribute more still to the influence of the seventeenth century. Glasgow has been peopled in a great measure from the surrounding counties, all of which were saturated with the covenanting spirit and soaked with the martyrs' blood; and their descendants have not, even amid the crowded thoroughfares of the towns, forgotten the glorious solitudes where their fathers worshipped and died; and, after deducting the necessary amount of pretence and affectation of piety, there seems to remain an ample and a pure residuum. A gentleman of a sceptical turn once inquired of a Scottish minister, "Do you know any now who believe in Christianity?—of course, every body admits it to be the best thing we have got; but do you know any who believe in its peculiar claims as the

one divine religion? I, for my part, meet with none."
The reply was, waiving the personal affront implied in
the question, that not only did he know many individuals
of high intelligence who did believe in the highest
pretensions of the Christian religion, but that there was
Glasgow, a city pervaded and penetrated by living,
moving, and having its being in a profound believe of
evangelical religion.

How long this may continue is an inquiry which suggests fears and gloomy forebodings, in consequence of
that cloud of scepticism which has covered the Continent
with its gross darkness, which has crept like a mist over
large portions of the community both in Scotland and
England, at last folding its fearful mantle round the
country of the Covenant, and changing the character of
Glasgow, till it becomes worse than one of our English
large towns ; but the certainty is not more manifest than
is the temporariness of this eclipse. Whatever may be
the case with other countries, Scotland can never long
part with the blessed faith of Jesus. Were infidelity or
were popery becoming rampant in it, it were enough to
move the ashes of the dead ; the tomb of Knox might
be disturbed ; the bones of Bothwell Moor might come
together, bone to his bone, once more an exceeding great
army ; Cameron might spring from his mossy grave ; the
German ocean might render back Burley and the rest of
the brave dead which were in it ; and on the grim Grassmarket might reappear the array of the men who had
thence ascended, amid execrations and agonies, the
nearest way to the celestial gate. At all events, the
slumbering embers of the spirit and the fire of the
martyrs would be blown up into a blaze ; and, even were
the Church once more driven into the wilderness, she
would keep her post and maintain her quarrel there till
the time came when, on the wings of a great eagle, she
should again emerge, and, endowed with new life and
purified from old error, shine forth " fair as the moon,
clear as the sun, and terrible as an army with banners."

No easy thing, verily, can it be to root out a religion which, apart from its own transcendent claims, has interwoven itself around the heartstrings of a nation, mingled with its earliest and dearest associations, coloured the thought, the feeling, the very blood of the land, become a source of innumerable traditions, brought the national character to its culminating point, and been baptized again and again in holy blood. It is true that a "thing of beauty is a joy for ever," but it is still more so, that a thing once believed on good evidence to be divine, and which has surrounded itself with divine trophies, is independent of time, may be darkened but cannot be destroyed, may even set like the sun, but like the sun can only set to rise again in greater splendour than before, and shall remain a joy, a power, a truth, and a terror for evermore. Honour, again, to those men whose efforts have tended to cement and to strengthen such a system; and in reference to whose sufferings, and to the results which have already and shall yet more richly spring from them, may be applied the poet's line—

"How that red rain has made the harvest grow!"

THE END.

www.ingramcontent.com/pod-product-compliance
Lightning Source LLC
Chambersburg PA
CBHW060547030726

47498CB00005B/1299